UNCHAINED

BOOK THREE

KAY CAMDEN

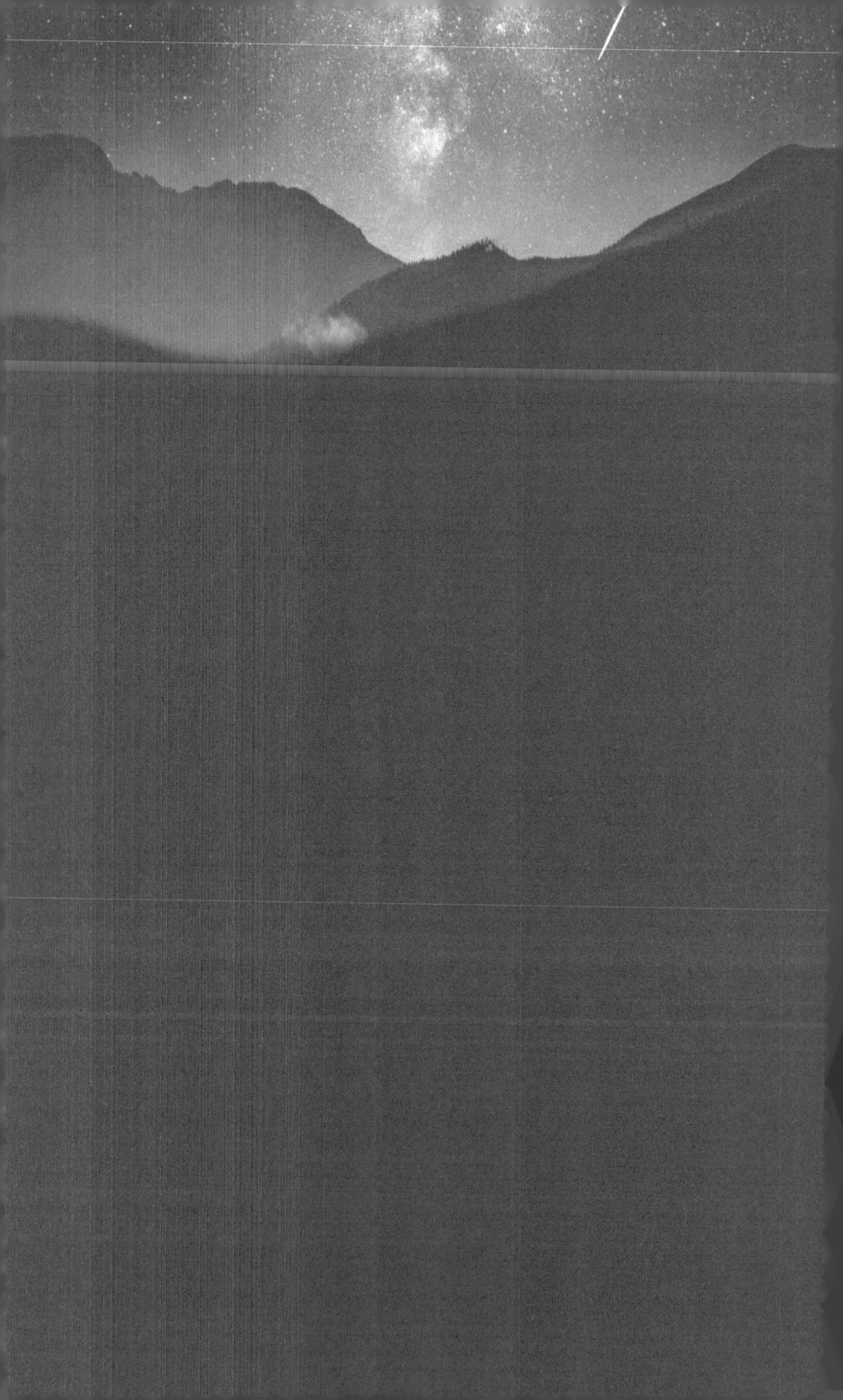

UNCHAINED

Chapter 1

The woman sleeping in Mick's bed showed no sign of life when he set the breakfast tray beside her. Just like she hadn't for weeks. He worried she'd never wake, that she'd crossed into a state between undead and dead that had no link to his living world. That Waapikoona, once risen from the grave into perfect vitality, would now sleep forever.

Mick fought the urge to check for a pulse. He'd done it so often in the first days and had since decided if she was going to die, she'd have done it already. When he'd gotten her home safe and in his bed, he expected her to sleep a day or two. At some point he'd tried to wake her. He scrubbed dirt from under her fingernails and dug rocks from her skin, and still she slept. Her bruises turned every color of the rainbow, and her wounds scabbed over. Proof of her healing gave Mick hope. So did the little girl sitting patiently beside her unconscious sister, holding her hand as if somehow the contact would guide her back.

Now, nestled against the sleeping woman, that little girl opened her eyes, acknowledging Mick with the same reluctant alliance she did each day.

"You make sure she eats some of this if she wakes up, all right?" It was a slight deviation from what he said every morning. And every evening he came home, the tray would be empty, the little girl would be content, and Waapikoona would still be deep asleep.

He prayed for the day Waapikoona woke. He also feared it. It was too easy to imagine finding the bed empty, Waapikoona awake and alive and back in the world of the living and gone from his life again. She'd take the girl, Isabel—too little to be her sister, but such was the result of being raised from the dead decades apart—and she'd leave no trace, no explanation, and no way to contact her just like she had before.

What he ought to do was shackle her to the bed. Board up his apartment, lock it from the outside. Leave his bad luck and the trust he'd earned from her untested. But then she would wake with a rope around each wrist and that trust would turn fragile once again, a strain between them. He'd worked too hard to give up what he'd earned. When he'd put her in his bed and drawn those covers over her, they were two parts of one team. A match so unexpected they'd combined into something unstoppable. He wasn't so sure about that anymore. She wasn't supposed to go to sleep and never wake up again. And to expect her to wake and accept his care, his help—*him*, without argument until she regained her strength ... he had to shut that thought down for the false hope it gave him.

It was a good thing Isabel would never let him shackle Waapikoona because he was definitely tempted. He dribbled some fresh water between her lips with a straw then set the glass on the tray for Isabel to use during the day.

Before walking out the door, he told Isabel, "If she wakes up, make her stay in bed."

Strange how it was the first day he'd thought to say it.

Outside in the gravel driveway, he stopped halfway to the orange Pontiac GTO waiting for its driver. Across the expanse of dry winter grass, shadows in the forest leered. He watched them, hoping they'd see his thought: *soon.* The quality of light around him felt raw, unfiltered, like the earth had changed its path so February was no longer the end of a bitter winter but the midst of a hopeful spring. His eagle felt close by, but not near enough to be layering its vision onto his. Or maybe that was where he was mistaken. Maybe he'd become too accustomed to notice. Maybe the fear he'd been living with—that the border between his human self and his eagle was thinning—had become true. He was seeing undead creatures in spaces a human shouldn't. But was he really seeing them or just remembering they were there?

It didn't matter. He still had to go to work. And he needed another cup of coffee, which was waiting for him at Virgil's shop. He got in the car.

Two crows dove off the top branch of the sycamore in the front yard as he started the engine. They flapped to rest on the overhang above his basement apartment's door. If he was more knowledgeable about the world that had crashed into his reality the day he met Waapikoona, he might understand their purpose, or lack of. They could be everyday birds, doing what everyday birds do: raiding his landlord's bird feeders and crapping on his car. They could be his allies, other soldiers of the upperworld, there to hold the fort while he was away. Or they could just as easily be working for the enemy—for the underworld and The Silent One himself. Spies. Assassins. Shape-shifters who could take the form of something much worse, something he'd never dream up. Working for that side meant they were allies of the woman and girl inside, so he wasn't sure which situation was favorable.

He knew his situation of being stuck between the two worlds was a real pain in the ass.

"Ordinary birds," he said to himself, shifting the GTO into reverse. Sometimes he just had to turn it all off and pretend his life was normal. It was the only way to not drive himself crazy. The only way to claim his human form as his real form and not spend every minute as a golden eagle. The only way to convince himself his day job needed doing and his bills needed paying ... never mind the world was falling apart.

He cracked a window, hoping the cold air would wake him up. All it did was make his nose run and his eyes water enough to wipe against his shoulder. His brain remained fuzzy, his core still too warm from his shower. He down-shifted for a turn, feeling the wind smack him in the face as he blinked the morning blur from his eyes. A good long sleep felt like a luxury he'd never had and would never expe-rience anyway, so how did he even know how to crave it?

Lately, his eagle teemed with power, unfazed by how exhausted he was in human life. It was almost like Waapikoo-na's return had charged his eagle full of strength, almost like her simple presence powered the bird...

As he backed into his usual parking space at Wyona Automotive, he spotted three cars that were likely over-night drop-offs, which meant he already had a good bit of work lined up. Not a huge problem, except that the other morning mechanic was a young guy prone to oversleeping and somehow knew to hit the snooze an extra time for each overnight drop-off. Mick didn't know how the kid was so goddamn psychic.

"Andy called in sick," was Virgil's answer to Mick's *good mornin'* as he entered the office. From the look on Virgil's face, he'd done enough cursing to cover for the both of them, so Mick poured a cup of coffee and plugged his mouth with that instead. Virgil hadn't filled the other Saturday position that had been vacated a month ago, so it was going to be Mick by himself all day long.

"I made some calls and no one can fill in. And we got four drop-offs—"

"Four?"

"Yep, one of 'em was left in the back." Virgil looked up over his glasses at Mick. "You get to 'em, great. If not, no biggie. You want the easy ones first or the least patient customer first?"

Intrusive music blared from the waiting room TV. They both looked at the screen as breaking news interrupted the morning talk show. *Strange disappearances continue across Missouri and Arkansas, the latest being reported by Ellis County sheriff...*

"Gimme the least patient one." Mick was in no mood to hear Virgil getting chewed out by anyone today. Neither was his eagle. And since he couldn't turn a screwdriver with wings or talons, his eagle needed to stay far away. He'd also prefer to not hear another news report about more missing people. It had become too widespread, too inexplicable. The vanished were now being tracked and tallied all across the country. Everyone except the assumed experts had answers for what was happening, and the less people understood, the more they made up. Mick knew the *real* experts. He was one of them. He also knew his answers and explanations would never be accepted. The public would more likely believe rumors and conspiracies than the truth he could give them. His truth didn't fit the world they knew, and they'd call him nuts.

He'd also made a rule weeks ago to keep his mind off eagle duties when he was at the job that paid the bills. Sipping his coffee, he walked to the front window to size up the cars. A blackbird flew across the parking lot, directly over the GTO, dropping a wide white splotch right on the hood.

Ordinary birds, my ass.

All day he watched Virgil turn away business. Some of them would be loyal and return another day, but most would head to the chain shop north of Wyona that had more bays, more employees, and was open on Sunday. And that was where they'd go from then on. Thirty minutes before closing time, Mick saw Virgil lock the front door and flip the sign over to CLOSED. Then the old man was rolling up his sleeves and settling in next to Mick, like he was going to test his arthritis real good that day.

"I don't got a U-Fill shift tonight," Mick said. "I can stick around and finish both—"

"Cool it, Svendsen. You ate your lunch under a car. Least I can do is help you get outta here on time."

Mick had two cars torn apart. Both customers still sat in the waiting room. He'd already figured he'd be leaving two hours late, but now with Virgil's help ...

He mentally walked through both jobs and weighed which one was less wear on arthritic hands. "All right, if you can take over here, I'll finish up that other one."

"You make any new friends that might make a dependable worker, you send them my way."

All afternoon Mick had been thinking about that, probably because he knew Virgil was going to say it. As he'd worked, he thought about what it might be like to have

Waapikoona in there with him working side by side. What a change it would be, fixing cars together instead of crawling through demon-infested caves and killing people. If she stayed with him, even temporarily, the idea of a dual income … He'd never ask her, but if she offered, he'd have a hard time saying no.

"I know someone who's dependable but has got no experience with cars."

"He a quick learner?"

"She. And yeah. But she's … " Hardheaded. Strong-willed. Irritating. Impossible. "… got a real mind of her own. Might not like being bossed around by me. You remember that woman who showed up to see me here a couple months ago?"

"The Indian woman?"

"Yeah. She's—" Now that it was voiced, Mick could more realistically see how it would be. They'd spend more time bickering than working, and she'd probably draw every supernatural creature straight into the shop. He'd be turning wrenches and fighting his eagle more than he did on a normal day. Never mind that she was currently unconscious and had been for weeks. "Ya know, never mind. It ain't gonna work out. She's too much of a pain in my ass."

"More a pain in your ass than Andy?"

Mick laughed. It was a good point. Virgil also needed the help, and if Waapikoona could contribute to the monthly bills he'd damn near cry. "I'll run it by her."

If he ever got the chance to speak to her again.

MUNDANE THOUGHTS CARRIED him home as night sky overtook a boldly painted sunset. The air held a slight warmth that trickled into the car through his cracked window. It smelled of thawing earth, of spring and possibility. The death and gore he'd experienced all winter couldn't be so easily packed away. As much as he felt burdened by that knowledge, his eagle felt powered, so finding common ground with the memories created a battle inside him. A breath of fresh air felt so overdue, so curative to the bleakness and loneliness that he relished the sensation, hitting higher RPMs and taking the tight Ozark mountain turns like they were meant to be taken in a car like his. He'd make up for the gas mileage some other day.

In his driveway he muttered a curse at the sight of Raúl Soto's glossy black Nissan 300ZX ... and a Jeep Wrangler? He drove on the grass around both vehicles and parked, yanking the hand brake with more force than needed. After a workday like he'd had, he didn't need company and certainly didn't need any work for his eagle. A shower, a quiet meal with a quiet little girl, and a couch to crash on. That was all he had the energy for on this night.

Cold settled against him as he climbed out of the GTO, making that earlier hint of spring feel like a con. He hadn't yet shed the body heat from working his ass off all day, and the contrast of outer and inner temperature made him feel even hotter. He had to get out of these coveralls before he caught on fire.

"Hey," he said to Raúl, slamming his door.

"Yo." Raúl didn't look at him. His wide-shouldered bulk stood in the open door of his car, one arm resting on the shiny black roof. He focused on Mick's apartment as if waiting for some cue.

Mick followed Raúl's gaze. The man's hazel-eyed, ever-vigilant, made-of-steel woman who gave no excuses for her distrust of Mick was backing away from the apartment—and from a tall female silhouette in the light-filled open doorway. It couldn't be Waapikoona—but there she was. Awake. Alive. He nearly choked from the rise of emotion, from the mundane colliding with the extraordinary, the unbelievable, the perfect. Seeing her upright propelled him back in time to the moment her broken, lifeless body spoke his name. *Mick, don't leave me.* Pulled from the darkness and muck of her second grave, revived, by him. And a good bit of sheer luck.

"What's goin' on?" It came out angry.

"Teresa and I brought the Jeep."

All Mick knew about anything then was what would happen to someone, even an ally like Raúl, should a person pose any threat to Waapikoona. He and Raúl were brothers in the sky, two thunderbirds with a duty to rid the upperworld of people just like Waapikoona. But to destroy a threat to her, he wouldn't need his eagle form. Watching—and helping—Waapikoona kill all those terrible men had desensitized him to the process. Now he could do it all himself. It occurred to him he was missing something, and he couldn't recall what Raúl had just said. "What?"

"You okay, *amigo?*"

Teresa had made it back to the 300ZX. She slipped behind Raúl and under his arm, stealing the driver's seat, and started the engine.

Mick didn't need any of this. He needed to go to Waapikoona. "I'm fine. What's all this—"

"We figured Sarah might need it. Just a favor. She doesn't seem won over, but we'll keep trying." In a raised voice aimed at Waapikoona, he said, "And I know a guy who can haul that mobile home if you change your mind." He took an elbow in the leg from Teresa, shuffled out of the way to avoid another. "Crazy woman. Thinks these wheels belong to her."

Sarah. Raúl knew her by the name she gave strangers. The name she'd first given Mick. Raúl also knew she was here, in this apartment. Did he know she was awake today, or was this visit a coincidence?

Raúl walked around to the passenger side. "Jeep key is in the ignition. See if you can put in a good word for me." With one pointed nod toward Waapikoona, he got in the car.

Mick watched them leave. It took eons, but he had to see the risk gone. As the taillights turned the corner onto the road, he moved his attention to his apartment door. She was still there, but her silhouette shifted, losing its upright form. He crossed the yard and caught her before she collapsed to the ground.

Her breath ragged, she clutched his coveralls. He swiveled to reposition her arm around his shoulders and take on her weight. Weakness howled through his bad leg. "That's it. I got you. Back to bed—"

Wind rushed against them from inside, and they both ducked as what looked like part of the room took flight and shot past them through the door and into the dusk.

"Isabel!" Mick shouted, but the little girl—now turned falcon—was too fast, and only another set of wings could catch her. But not without some skill. The thunderbird that dwelled inside an undead girl blended into the night, her translucent body like camouflage and nearly invisible to anything but his eagle. "Damn it."

Something dripped off Waapikoona and landed on his coveralls. He checked her face and found her nose bleeding. Her head fell back, her body turning to dead weight. Staggering under the added burden of a now unconscious woman, he dragged her inside and into the bedroom—where she should have stayed.

Her eyelids fluttered as he straightened her neck and limbs against the bed.

"I'm fixin' to tie you down, you hear that?"

She reached and caught his sleeve in a grip too tight for someone who'd just passed out. He tried to pry her loose, but her fingers only tightened until he looked into her eyes, now wide open and glued to his.

"I'm serious," he added.

"Isabel," she whispered.

"She's just spooked. She'll come back." He looked away from her to fix the covers because he knew what she was asking, and he had not one second of stamina remaining in his human self to consider an evening spent in eagle form, searching for that girl. He needed food, sleep, some damn peace and quiet. "She's fine," he added, hearing how it sounded more like a hope than a sure thing.

Of course he had to go look for her. Of course he was going to do it. Head bowed, he let out all his breath. For just one minute he wanted to meditate on this moment of Waapikoona here, with him. Alive, in his world. Not a breathing body with a consciousness in some realm he'd never reach. He looked at her then, to take it all in, make absolute sure that it wasn't a dream.

"How ... " she whispered, straining to see past him.

And he realized Waapikoona didn't know what he knew. Her sister wasn't just a once-dead-now-alive person raised from the grave by a great underworld demon like her. The little girl was also a thunderbird, like him. But unlike his golden eagle that could fly the upperworld and not raise too many suspicions, her falcon appeared ghostlike, with trans-lucent wings that could absorb the night. And one slight imperfection that created a struggle with her flight due to being reborn missing a couple small bones from her hand.

Waapikoona waited, her attention back on him.

"Not sure how. She just shifted one night. Spooked by some ... " He remembered that swarm of flying demons circling Old Mae's house, Doug and Isabel in the apartment below. How his eagle had killed, relishing the hunt and feast until he had gained enough power to pull electricity from the clouds and scorch the whole swarm. Then he'd fallen back into human form and dragged his spent body inside to find Isabel had turned into a thunderbird herself.

"... by some activity. Like she did just now."

"Thunder-Being ... and also raised? How is that ... "

"Possible? You tell me. You're the expert on this stuff."

"She can't be out there." This time her eyes weren't demanding. They'd softened, like she was reading something from him, like she knew he was going to bring Isabel back, like she remembered he would do anything for her. He'd track Waapikoona across the country, walk himself into the heart of danger to find her. He'd use all his power and break every upperworld law to revive her from an early grave. Blood trickled from her nose along her cheek, and Mick got up to grab a rag from the other room. When he dabbed her face, she took the cloth from him and caught his collar in her other hand. Her eyes held his in a silent universe—unity, gratitude, solace—with a solemn longing that tore him to the bone.

This winter he'd been wounded by loneliness; she was both the cause and the salve. With the way she held onto his coveralls and searched his eyes, it was clear she felt the same way but hadn't yet made her peace with it. She was looking for something to dissuade her, some proof of her mistake, of a way out. He looked back openly, offering everything he had—man and eagle—and there was no doubt she could see deeply enough to uncover the thunderbird that had woken inside him because of her.

In allowing her to see all of him, he was able to see into her too. Something new dwelled in her eyes, a haunted look he'd never seen before. He knew enough of her past to understand the torment she carried, but it had never presented itself so boldly. It hollowed her face and deadened her gaze. She wasn't just weakened; she'd given in, and it was dragging her away from him. He'd wondered where her soul had been these weeks that she remained unconscious in his bed, and now he wasn't sure he wanted to know.

She tugged his collar. He leaned toward her as she wrapped her arms around his neck and held on. The scent of blood, earth, and ozone lingered from that nightmarish scene of her second death. With a deeper inhale he found the soap he'd used to clean her face and neck, the tinge of woodsmoke always present in her hair. Through her shirt her skin was cold, her ribs sharp, but he held her and breathed her and couldn't let go as she crushed her face into his collarbone. He suddenly felt lifted up, weightless, free. He turned his head and kissed her temple.

"I'll be right back," he said, before he lost this swell of spirit. After untangling himself from her, he went outside, stripped off his clothes, and burst into the night sky.

CHAPTER

2

The falcon's direction was no secret to the watchful woodland creatures that pointed the golden eagle toward the right path. What a thunderbird asked, they granted. He ruled their skies and patrolled their land. Sometimes the hierarchy came in handy.

The convergence of human roads marked a spot below him, lit by a puddle of light. A familiar place, but more familiar to his human. Now that he'd closed the distance between himself and the underworld falcon, he could see the glowing trails left by her presence. Past the road where his human had once left his wheels to walk on two legs into the woods, the trail disappeared. One of many openings to the great demon's caverns hid among the exposed rock there. The falcon had disappeared inside.

He could not enter as eagle or as human. He banked, pumping wings against a hit of wind, and aimed for home.

As Mick fought to get his stiff bad leg back into his jeans, a shadow bounded from the edge of the woods to the old ramshackle barn at the rear of the yard. Another followed the first. He didn't need eagle vision to know Waapikoona's little demons had returned and wanted back inside her hand. His eagle swelled, outraged at the intrusion so close. He grabbed the rest of his clothes and went inside before his eagle was further tempted.

His heightened senses hadn't yet dulled. For that reason alone, he took no time to worry Waapikoona had left. He sensed her in the bedroom. He could hear her breathing. If she was asleep, he wouldn't wake her. There was no point. With Isabel in The Silent One's cave, there was nothing to do but wait. He dropped his boots beside the couch and laid his shirt and coveralls across the back of a kitchen chair.

The bed creaked, and sheets shuffled. "Mick?"

He went into the bedroom to find Waapikoona awake, waiting for him, her eyes still distant and haunted.

"Your pocket demons are outside."

"My Helpers," she corrected. She worked an elbow underneath her, propping herself unsteadily. "Would you mind opening the door so they can come in?"

Mick shuddered so hard against a thrash of his eagle that he had to brace a hand against the foot of the bed. "Ain't sure that's a good idea right now."

"Did you find my sister?"

He gathered himself. How to give her the news, without her getting out of bed and demanding he drive her to the cave—hell, there was a Jeep outside now that was supposedly for her. She didn't even need to demand anything of him.

"Listen." He sat down, laying a hand on her shin as if that might keep her down. Could he get away with holding her here? How? He ran a rough hand through his hair.

"Mick." His name spoken so expertly, he could hear her say it until the end of his life and he'd never grow tired of it. She couldn't possibly know how much it grounded him.

"Yeah, I found her. She's somewhere I can't get to right now, so we're gonna have to be patient—"

"Is she okay?"

He didn't know. Neither did his eagle. "No way to know that till she comes home."

She took a moment to ponder that. He probably shouldn't have used that word. *Home.* It sounded permanent, a concept he knew Waapikoona wasn't fond of. Finally, her voice quiet, she said, "Where is she?"

There was no use in keeping it from her. "Her trail ended at the opening to your boss' cave. The one where you and I gone in that day lookin' for the healer."

She leaned back against the pillows, her gaze slowly shifting toward the ceiling. He saw her remembering what he knew. He couldn't navigate that cave without her, and he wasn't so sure she'd be welcome in there anyway. Isabel was safe in that cave with The Silent One. She'd been raised by him and hadn't committed any wrongs against him. When Waapikoona didn't speak, Mick said, "So we gotta trust she'll be back. And in the meantime, I need to get you fed."

She scoffed. It was nice to see that kind of fire in her. Maybe that haunted look in her eyes would soon dissolve.

"You ain't had nothin' to eat for weeks. Your sister would want you to eat somethin'—"

"Don't talk about her like she's dead, Mick."

"Never figured she was." Mick had a hunch, brought up by his eagle on the flight home, that made enough sense to stall any panic over Isabel being in any danger. He'd planned not to divulge this, but here he was, about to say it. "What

I figured was, she's goin' to see him on her own. And now I think it's not the first time she's gone there."

"She's not me. She's a little girl. It's dangerous, and she shouldn't be going there alone."

"She's a being from the underworld like you, and like … him."

Her eyes narrowed, and she studied him fiercely. "So what happens to her, she deserves?"

If she was trying to stoke his earlier anger, she'd succeeded. "You know that's bullshit, and … " He paused, not at all wanting this night to go this way. "You know what? I'm gonna fix some supper."

Mick got up and left the bedroom. He took a five-minute shower and yanked on some cotton pants and a T-shirt. In the kitchen he found two baking potatoes and started one in the microwave. In the middle of chopping broccoli, he felt a draft of cold air and turned, finding Waapikoona bent in the doorway, outside air ruffling the papers on his coffee table. He could guess she'd gathered her demons by the jolt that went through him and dispersed as quickly as it had come. She shut the door against the night and limped into the kitchen, one hand pressing against the wall for support, other hand still wrapped in the bandage he'd put on that morning. Her hair was loose and tangled, missing the contrast of gloss on its dark length. She was wearing his Pontiac GTO T-shirt his sister Kari had found at a thrift shop. The long beaded earrings were gone from her lobes, but he could still see the glint of the studs and rings in her upper ear. Her legs and feet were bare. It was too cold in his apartment to be walking around like that.

"I'm dying for a shower," she said.

"I'd say you oughta be in bed, but I know you're just goin' to do what pleases you, never mind all the trouble it took to save your damn life."

"Don't try to hold that over me. We're even now, if you remember."

A sickening tremor ran the length of his bad leg, as if the cold steel blade had just met bone all over again. Even given more time for his shin to heal, he wasn't sure it would ever be right again. "Ain't ever gonna forget."

"There are three more Helpers out there. I can't carry them, so you'll just have to tell your eagle to leave them alone."

"I don't tell my eagle nothin'." He turned back to his chopping but still felt her gaze on him. He didn't know how he could so desperately long for the company of this woman and also want to stab her eyes out.

"Well, you should. If you kill them, I won't be happy."

"God forbid I make you unhappy." He wondered how she'd accumulated more corpse-devouring helper demons and why she couldn't scoop them up like she could her other two. Should he ask? Probably not. "Are you collecting a baseball team of 'em? Gonna play some demon ball in the spring?" He put on the broccoli to steam and turned around to look at her.

At his kitchen table sat a woman so unamused she appeared encased in ice. He'd smile at her to melt her, make her smile herself, but the light above the table had turned her cheekbones sharp, her collarbone skeletal. God, he had to get some food in her before she wasted away. And what was that mark on her neck, crawling around her shoulder ...

He stepped closer, hooking his thumb around her hair to brush it to the side. Jagged purple-black lines scattered down the back of her neck, as intricate as the branches of a tree. He tugged the collar of her shirt down, finding the pattern continue low across her skin. "Take off your shirt."

"Get real."

"I'm dead real. I need to see what this is." When she made no move to help him, he found the bottom of her shirt and yanked it up, hooking it over both shoulders.

The angry jagged lines tattooed her entire back, forking and splitting in all directions.

"You see this?"

"I've been unconscious and lying on my back for a long time, Mick."

"This ain't somethin' from being in bed. It looks almost like—"

It looked like lightning.

"Stand up."

To his surprise she obeyed, swaying a little, one hand gripping the top of the chair. The pattern continued down the back of her legs all the way to the floor. He laid a finger on her shoulder blade where the most severe part appeared to have changed the texture of her skin. She winced. A miniature mountain range of scar tissue followed the darkest lines, like he was running his finger along his nephew's globe of earth with bumps where the mountain ranges stretched across the surface. She straightened against a shiver that traveled visibly up her spine. Against his warm hands, her flesh was icy. Wounded, hurting, freezing cold, and stubborn enough to walk around his chilly basement apartment like she was invincible. Clearly she was not. He let the shirt fall down into position, grabbed a throw blanket from the couch, and wrapped it around her. She sat in her chair under the blanket, scowling, but uncomplaining.

How could he have not noticed those marks before? She had been sleeping on her back in his bed, but he'd wiped her neck, undressed and dressed her. But the room's light he'd purposefully kept dim, and he'd been a bit distracted by her other wounds. Either way, it didn't seem to matter. He wasn't sure what he could have done for it. She was marked by his eagle. Temporarily? Or forever?

"You oughta go in the bathroom and have a look at that in the mirror," he said over his shoulder as he returned to his meal prep. He wasn't sure how she'd feel about it. He wasn't sure how he felt. And he sure didn't want to enable the memory of that hellish night when his eagle's lightning strike tore through her. *Better alive and burned than dead.* Some practical part of him believed it. The rest didn't want to see her ever harmed, especially not by him. Even if the reckless act had saved her life, couldn't he have found a different way? He shook his head at all of it, releasing a tight breath, feeling the weight of her eyes on him. If she wanted to know his thoughts, she'd have to ask. He wasn't reliving it unless he had to.

He served her first, but she waited until he sat down across from her to pick up her fork. It was a bad time to bring up any of the other things he needed to explain to her. All those things had hollered in his head those first few days after he'd brought her home. Since then, they'd had a lot of time to cool down. Except for one. His baby niece was on his mind every minute of the day. His sister had prepared herself to bury a child, until Mick had promised a miracle he wasn't even sure was possible.

Now there was no need to explain Isabel's falcon or Raúl Soto and Teresa. Well, no need to introduce the subjects anyway. He was sure he'd have to explain all she'd missed. Right now, he didn't want to talk about anything. He just wanted to look at her. The bruises on her face had faded, would soon be gone. The crescent-shaped scar around her eye remained but was losing its edges to healthy skin. Her lip had healed, both the tear in the corner and the vertical split. No one would see it but him. He would always see it, long after it was gone.

"I'm not going to eat with you staring at me like that."

He needed her to eat, and he wanted to stare, so he had to come up with something to talk about. Something lighter than missing thunderbird sisters, dying nieces, and a million underworld creatures escaping through a crack in the world.

"That Jeep out there stolen?"

"It was a gift."

Her idea of a gift might be different than his. "The owner gonna want it back?"

"He's dead."

Her definition of dead might also be different. "He comin' back anytime soon?"

"His bones were destroyed." She eyed him. "It's a no, Mick."

"I'm just wonderin' how you'd go about destroyin' someone's bones—" He cut the thought short at the look of breathless, watery-eyed shock that overtook her, as if she'd been pulled into a memory or vision. Such an unfamiliar look on her features propelled him from his chair, worried she was about to pass out again.

She blinked, closing her eyes, tightening her jaw. The pain that had forced its way across her face, now gone. "He killed himself and was cremated against his wishes. There's no way to ever get him back."

There was a story there, but Mick didn't feel it was his place to ask right now. He settled back in his seat. "I'm sorry."

"So am I." The wound in her eyes rattled him so much he had to look away. She took a breath and said, "I can't stay here, Mick."

He expected this, so he wasn't sure why it felt like such a punch in the gut. He wished he'd prepared something to say.

"*We*—Isabel and I—can't stay here."

Also expected. What he didn't predict was his rising outrage of Isabel being uprooted and taken to who knows where. He knew Isabel didn't like him, didn't fully trust him, maybe never would. This fact made no nick in her contentedness in his apartment or her comfort in the daily routine they'd established. She'd befriended his nephew, the only one who could make her laugh. She brightened every time Dougie showed up at the door with a new book or toy to share. Her time with Old Mae upstairs had benefitted them both, and she'd turned one of Old Mae's crankiest cats into the cuddliest purr machine. Sometimes that cat would follow her downstairs and spend the night in bed with her and Waapikoona—but Waapikoona didn't know that. She didn't know any of it.

If he fought Waapikoona on this now, he'd lose. His temper beat hot. The injustice of it all was like wind against flame. She'd rise to the battle, stubbornness blinding her. Through Isabel's entire time here, Waapikoona was either gone or unconscious, and if Mick dared to suggest he knew what was better for the little girl he'd never win. Waapikoona needed to see it for herself.

He kept his gaze carefully away from hers. If he looked as pissed as he felt, she would take the bait and start swinging. "When you're done there, I need to look at that hand."

A long moment passed before she answered, her voice as careful as his averted eyes. "It's fine."

"It ain't. You were cut to the bone. It needed a doctor and never got one. It was blind luck the skin finally closed up, and I'd like it to stay that way." She was going to bristle at that but let her. "And I'm not comfortable with you tryin' to stand up in the shower, so I need to get you upstairs to the tub in Old Mae's spare room." That's when he returned his eyes to hers.

Bristling wasn't the word. She was inflamed, visible anger bubbling atop deep, unguarded awe. If the table wasn't separating them, he'd be bracing for a hard shove—or a murderous kiss she seemed damn near ready to give.

"You're doing a bad job of hiding that eagle."

Mick got up and reached for her plate. "All done?"

She leaned back against the chair, watching him. He cleared the table then went into the bedroom for a change of clothes that might fit her and a clean bandage for her hand. When he returned to the kitchen she was in the same spot at the table, still watchful, the blanket tight around her shoulders. He tucked the clothes under his arm and offered her a hand. One five-second battle of wills later, she laid her good fingers in his and he hauled her up, hooking her arm around his shoulders. Remembering his idea to offer her the job at the shop, he chuckled. He was either batshit crazy or a real sucker for punishment.

"What's funny?"

"How much a pain in my ass you are."

"You sure you don't have that backward?"

"Real damn sure."

He tried to remember the worst of the lightning scar's position on her back. If he was hurting her, she might be too proud to speak up. Not long ago he'd had a similar looking scar branching across his skin around a venomous demon bite. Maybe her scar was more than the path of electricity. It could be the result of his eagle's power as a toxin to her raised-from-the-dead flesh. The upperworld was poison to her as the underworld was poison to him.

They were poisonous to each other.

Heading up the few stairs from his basement apartment into the yard seemed easy enough. Missing so much weight she was a husk against him, feather-light and sharp-boned, shivering against his warmth. The cold stone steps shocked his bare feet, probably hers as well, but they pushed on. The path across the side yard was slow going—Waapikoona's long-legged stride had shrunk by half. Her feet seemed unsteady and unsure, her knees ready to give at any moment. Across the moonlit yard, a dozen wavering upright forms loitered. In the past he might have mistaken them for a patch of fog or a play of the shadow and gone about his night. Not anymore.

"Must be checkin' on you," Mick said.

"They're just restless. Many of your dead are left forgotten."

Mick knew her statement had no personal stab, but he felt it deep into the quick. He'd made an effort to visit his mother's grave more often, but he was failing again. "Remembering ancestors isn't really built in to us … " He heard it as more of an excuse than an answer—and a generalization—and decided to stop talking.

"But it's always the unquiet Native bones, isn't it? The haunt of the Indians, the ones who were wronged. Easy to see us that way and ignore how many of your ancestors wander the earth."

"I think the last few hundred years of this country were unquiet. And still are."

"And your American heroes are the ones sentenced to an unquiet grave, while my people rest."

"It's hard, Waapikoona. What we're taught in school—"

"I know. I was taught the same things."

Mick stood there, holding her up as they watched the spirits wander the grass at the edge of the woods. He imagined what it would have been like for her as a child in her first life, and as a child in this one, asked to stomach a glorified history when she had lived the grim reality.

"Tellin' history with a bias ... I'm not sure that'll ever change. It's human nature."

"Is it? Or is it the nature of the ones we allow to take power? The ones who silence other voices?"

Instead of allowing the generalization to live in his head, he decided to ask, "Were you taught to remember your ancestors?"

"I was. But in this life, I don't know who they are."

Mick watched her face as she gazed across the yard. He could make suggestions, like online DNA testing or research—and he would find time in his day to help her—but he knew this moment didn't call for a fix she likely had already thought of herself. With her arm tight around his neck and her body against his, he allowed the silence to build like a prayer. In that moment he understood there was more to knowing specific names and places. A nudge of chilly wind brushed her hair against his neck. "Let's get inside."

At the steps leading to Old Mae's front porch, Mick stopped to position himself to take more weight off her legs, wondering if this was a bad idea and he should turn around and put her back in bed.

"Don't chicken out now that you've made me go this far," she said.

Months ago he wouldn't have recognized it as a ribbing. The possible catastrophe of two grown-ass people tumbling down a set of steep stairs would be easier to accept with a deadpan rib back. "Shut up before I toss you over my shoulder and do this the right way."

"Wow, is that sexist *and* racist?"

He chuckled, urging her forward. "Ya know, I oughta drop you right here and leave you."

Her foot caught the lip at the first porch step, nearly jerking her from his grasp. The motion unsteadied him. He grabbed the handrail and held Waapikoona tight, losing the bundle of clothes from under his arm. Mick cursed himself for his stupid bare feet and the brittle cold that had settled with night. His purchase on the painted wood held just enough to haul her up them. Any more dew on those steps and they'd be a tangled mess at the base of the porch, and Old Mae would be biting his head off for being so careless.

Finally, up on the porch, he knocked, turned the knob, and nudged the door open with his elbow. "It's Mick," he called down the hall toward the kitchen light. "You mind if we head upstairs to use your spare tub?"

He held onto Waapikoona and looked up the long steep staircase. If it was alive, it would have laughed at him. The shudder that had started in Waapikoona outside turned hostile. Her teeth chattered, and she was crumpling against him.

"Mick—"

"Yeah, hold on, let me—" He scrambled for the switch that would light the front room so he could find a couch to plant her on. Cursing, he gave up and walked her to a shadowed armchair and she slid down into it, hunching against the onslaught of shivers. He tightened the blanket around her, holding it snug under her chin. "Can you hold onto this?"

She nodded, her eyes wide and smudgy in the dim slant of light, her mouth a serious line. Never had he seen this woman afraid. It sunk a weight in him he wasn't sure he'd ever extract. Curled into the blanket, she looked small in that chair. Like a dependent, not an equal. It pinched deep in his heart. He hated it.

"Where have you been?" he whispered. He knew her body had been healing in his bed. Her spirit had been somewhere else.

She looked back at him, defiantly mute.

He went to the hall and ran straight into Old Mae.

"Boy, if you can't hear me comin' on these creaky floors you need to turn up your ears. Now what's this?" She left the bony hand that had stopped him on his arm and leaned around him to examine her unexpected visitor.

He'd already told her Waapikoona was recovering in his place, and Isabel had no doubt brought an update every time she came up to the house. Still, he remembered Old Mae's wariness of Waapikoona months ago when she'd first arrived, and the old woman's insistence that his guest would dismantle her quiet country life. Mick's quiet was long gone. For just tonight, he hoped Old Mae would forgive him for disrupting hers.

"I was hopin' for use of your spare tub. My shower is … well, she can't hardly stand up on her own."

"How 'bout I ready the tub in the bathroom behind the kitchen so she don't have to go up them stairs? And even better, you go on back to your place, let me handle this." With that she turned toward the hall, not waiting for an answer.

Chapter

3

Submerged to the chin in the now cooling bath water, Waapikoona dozed. She thought of her sister, out there alone in the cold night. Of Mick, banished to his apartment by the old woman. Answers for how to proceed dwelled somewhere within her, but they were blocked behind an old enemy she felt too weary to confront: fear.

When the water touched her lips, she knew she'd slid too close to actual sleep. A third death of drowning in this tub felt like real possibility, and Mick—well, he just might break. She'd done many bad things in her life, but inflicting that kind of grief on Mick, she could not do. She opened her eyes. A silky black cat sat on the edge of the tub, watching her with large round pupils that mirrored the flickering candle flames around her.

The old woman had insisted electric lights would ruin the bath's medicine. It was a word that meant something different to the white man. Something both more and less specific. In this case it seemed the old woman used it as Waapikoona's people would. Combined with the rituals she'd used, the runes, the prayer … none of it was Native, but based on what Waapikoona learned from the white people in the Indian school in her first life, it wasn't Christian either.

Four paws hit the tile and the cat slipped out the cracked door. A minute later, the old woman's slippers shuffled down the hall. She pushed the door open and took a towel off the rack. "You come up here every third night for my bath, and I got no problem with you stayin' with Mickey."

Waapikoona accepted Old Mae's offered hand and struggled free of the water. "And what if I don't?"

"Then you find somewhere else to stay."

"And my sister?"

"She's young. I forgive the creatures she lures to my doorstep. I don't forgive yours."

Waapikoona felt her eyebrows rise even though she tried not to react. She wanted to mention that Mick seemed to lure a few himself but decided against it. The comment would include herself as one of those creatures.

"And that little girl's better off here than anywhere else." She steadied Waapikoona as she stepped from the tub to the soft mat and then wrapped the towel around her shoulders. "Don't you forget that."

How was this woman related to Mick? Because she had an identical method of getting straight under Waapikoona's skin.

"Another for your hair," Old Mae said, handing her a second towel. "You can wear them britches Mickey brought in, or you can wear the nightshirt and robe I set out on the couch. That's where you can wait for 'im." She turned to leave. "Unless you want to join me in the kitchen for some tea."

This was a test, Waapikoona was sure of it. And she had no idea if the couch or the kitchen was the correct answer, or which was the safe answer. Or if one was both. Since the thought of obediently waiting for Mick to escort her back downstairs seemed like a coward's choice, she toweled her hair dry, dressed in the nightshirt and robe from the couch, and headed for the kitchen.

The black cat trailed her down the hall. She paused to steady herself against the wall and the creature rushed past her, stopping several paces ahead to turn around and offer a questioning trill.

"I'm coming," she answered, angry with herself and unsure why. She hadn't decided to stay in a coma so long. She didn't purposefully avoid food for weeks. If her loss of strength and weight were to be remedied, she'd have to muster the will to rebuild herself. She wasn't sure if there was a way to recover from the place she'd been while unconscious in Mick's bed. It had sunk hooks in her skin, weighted by memories she'd never escape. Every step forward tore flesh from her bones and fractured her spirit. How did Mick know to ask where she'd been? She could never tell him.

She followed the cat toward the light at the end of the hall, holding the wall for support. Never in this life had she felt so helpless.

The old woman worked at the counter, ignoring her as she entered and took a seat at the table without waiting for welcome. Her knees had not agreed to such a long walk down that hall, and finding somewhere to fall that wasn't the ground seemed more important than manners. In front of her lay two mismatched place settings surrounded by fruit and cheese on well-worn Depression glass.

"You call me Mae. Old Mae, if you want to follow the others. What do I call you?"

Such a strangely belated introduction caused the question to get lost in her foggy brain.

"All right, I'll call you Sarah, since that's what your sister's been callin' you. Here, fix your teacup."

Waapikoona turned her teacup upright on the saucer, and steaming light-bodied tea flowed in. Old Mae waited for Waapikoona to right the other teacup then filled that one as well. Under the table, a sturdy softness knocked against her legs.

"Don't you mind Eros. He's just tryin' to make you his."

She looked down, into the wide yellow eyes of the black cat who'd kept her company while she bathed. He trilled another question before butting his forehead against her legs. She wondered what he would think of the Helpers she carried in her palms. If he could sense them, he was either brave or a fool. She wondered what this woman knew about her, her sister, or the man living in her basement whom she treated like family.

"Is Mick your grandson?"

"Not quite. Now get some food onto your plate. You ain't leavin' this room until you've ate all this in front of you. And while you do that, I'll get some bandages to fix up that hand."

"Mick just fed me dinner."

"And you been in that bath for an hour. You can find room for more."

Old Mae shuffled out of sight. Eros jumped into the opposite chair, peering at her over the table.

A sip of tea sparked a newfound appetite. She smeared cheese on crackers, dipped apple slices in caramel, and refilled her teacup. Old Mae returned and scooted a chair over, gesturing at Waapikoona to keep eating with her good hand while she applied ointment to the drying scab on her palm and then wrapped it with a clean white bandage. As she was tucking and taping the edges, Mick appeared in the doorway with sleepy eyes and ruffled hair, his T-shirt wrinkled and boots untied. In the time she'd been unconscious in his bed, his beard had grown in, a shade darker than his hair that now looked blonder, with a bit of added length that brought out the natural wave and a touch of the sun. She felt drunk on the vision of him.

"Sorry. I fell asleep," he said

Old Mae waved his words away. "You shoulda stayed put. Your woman's in good hands."

Waapikoona's indignation dissolved before she could form a proper scowl and aim it at Mick. Surely he was the one responsible for the idea she belonged to him. And she was glad her face remained neutral because Mick's lazy half smile and slow shake of his head proved it was more of a tease than the truth. It was clear he expected Old Mae's needling.

"How's her hand?"

"Looks like hell, but then I ain't seen it when it was fresh, did I?" Old Mae turned accusing crinkled eyes on Mick. "I expect that'll be the last kind of trouble she'll see."

Mick made a sound somewhere between a laugh and a scoff. "Might want to ask her that."

"I ain't askin' her. I'm tellin' you."

"Well sorry, but I can't speak to that. And considerin' what's goin' on—" Mick caught himself, ran a hand over his face. "I can walk her back down if she's ready."

"I like how you're talking about me like I'm not here," Waapikoona said to him. Apparently, she liked to needle him too.

Mick leaned against the door frame. He looked on the verge of collapsing himself. "I'm just not used to you bein' awake and able to talk back. That's all."

"Then get over here and help me up." She knew attempting it herself would only prove how incapable she was. And ordering him around was a good way to irk him. She might even be rewarded with the steely look she knew so well.

It seemed he was too tired for that. He simply offered a hand and pulled her to standing, sliding her arm around his neck like it was second nature. The solid heat of his body against her felt more comforting than that bath.

"Come lock the door behind us," Mick said over his shoulder.

Old Mae muttered something Waapikoona didn't catch. It occurred to her she should thank the woman for the bath and meal, but the effort of forming words was lost to the act of moving her legs. Those slippery steps from the porch to the yard were ahead, and she didn't want to unbalance Mick as badly as she had on their way up.

"And, thanks." Mick aimed a courteous nod behind them as he said it, looking like a handsome cowboy in an old western. Automatic, yet still sincere. It would have to cover for her own gratitude because she could never hope to be so effortlessly polite. He maneuvered her out the door.

"We ain't leavin' till we hear the lock click," he called into the house.

"Aw, go to bed, boy."

The door closed behind them. The lock scraped then slid home. Mick paused, analyzing the porch steps in front of them. "That look like ice to you?"

Waapikoona's eyes were taking too much time to adjust. There was a sheen to the treads, but she couldn't determine if it was the shine of the paint or the glaze of ice.

"'Cause I can't hardly tell," he said. "My human eyes are shit, now that I got somethin' to compare to. Seems unlikely they'd ice up in the short time I was in there, right?"

"Your call. But if you break anything else on me, you're going to have to answer to that old lady."

"According to her, you're my woman. So, over the shoulder then?"

She stifled a laugh, afraid it would hurt. "Try it."

He got them down the stairs slowly but safely. The treads were cold enough on her feet to be ice, but since the two of them didn't end up in a heap at the bottom she assumed Mick had guessed right. His own boots crunched through stiff grass to his apartment steps. She vaguely felt her feet leave the ground, and then she was on Mick's bed, horizontal, unable to recall the moments between cold stone steps and soft mattress.

Mick's face appeared before her. "You with me?"

She reached out, just to make sure he was real. Everything felt circular and dreamy. Glimmer and shadow danced before her eyes. Her hand found coarse hair across a hard jaw, her thumb brushing warm lips.

"You good?" he asked. There was something very different about his voice this time.

"I'm surprised this town hasn't burned that woman at the stake."

He drew a blanket across her and chuckled under his breath. "Why's that?"

"She painted runes on my skin and made me soak in salt and boiled herbs. Said it was the only way she'd let me stay in your place."

"Is that right." His words seemed indirect, distracted.

"You think I'm making it up?"

"I think you're a bit gone. Get some sleep. I'll see you in the morning."

Her eyelids were closing, and she couldn't stop it. She wanted to argue, but the room had grown dark, the air still.

She wondered if he'd been gone for seconds or minutes. Or even hours. Perhaps that exchange had taken place long ago, and she was waking up from hours of sleep. There wasn't even an outline of light around the bedroom door. He was out there on the couch, probably long asleep. Or was he—

She reached for the other side of the bed and found it empty. Sleep claimed her again before she had a chance to wonder any further.

Seconds or hours later, she felt warmth against her arm and turned, recognizing the slight shape of a little girl snuggled beside her. Isabel had returned. Safe. On her own … or found by Mick? Panic climbed through her. She could be locked in a coma again, a prisoner in that terrible place, and these brief spans of sleep could be days … weeks. Mick could have gone to bed on the couch and woken up twenty times. Trudged back and forth to work, prepared breakfasts, dinners, changed her bandage. She felt for the soft wrap on her hand, trying to determine if it was the same bandage Old Mae had put on after the bath supervised by the black cat. It felt like any other bandage. She rubbed her eyes, squinting into the room, trying to make sense of time. The darkness around her was endless, unfamiliar, the only consolation the sleeping girl beside her. She fell off the cliff again, into a sleeping nothingness.

IT'S OKAY. LISTEN, I know … Don't—no, don't call Pop. I'm comin' right now. Stay where you're at. It's gonna be okay. Just like I told you—remember? It's gonna be okay.

Cold air crossed Waapikoona's shoulders. She lifted her head to see the covers peeled away and Isabel sitting up beside her as the conversation from her sleeping mind turned real. She heard Mick's voice, hushed but hurried, its enforced calm doing little to mask the obvious alarm. In the other room, something clattered against the floor and Mick swore. A light blinked on, highlighting the bedroom doorway.

"Just a few minutes, Kari. Keep talkin' if it helps. I'm on my way now."

The apartment door squealed open and slammed shut.

"Where's he going?" Isabel whispered.

The door of their room swung open, throwing light across the rumpled covers. Waapikoona jolted upright as something large slammed itself onto the top of the bed. Isabel caught her arm—blocking a blow aimed at the creature she now saw was not there to attack.

"It's Spot," Isabel said, confirming what Waapikoona's sleepy mind had caught almost too late.

The last time Waapikoona had seen the dog was months ago, but from the wild flap of his tail and his determination to lick her face, he remembered her well. Once starving and homeless, he'd wriggled his way into her life and didn't appear ready to give up on that. Content with a quick ear scratch, he turned three circles and lay down at their feet.

Isabel snuggled in too. But Waapikoona was wide awake, staring at the triangle of ceiling illuminated by the light coming in from the other room. Mick had left, that was obvious. He'd been talking to his sister on the phone. She tried to remember the earlier part of the conversation she'd heard while half asleep. The frantic notes of it lingered, putting an uneasiness in her heart that kept her awake and staring at the ceiling until the triangle of light mixed with daylight tones from the rising day. Night held its ground in this windowless bedroom. Without the day spilling in through the doorway, she'd never know it was morning.

It was hard to imagine how Mick ever woke in this cave of a room.

She could get up on her own if she did it slowly. She'd done it yesterday before Mick came home—that had ended with her passing out and him carrying her back inside. But she'd done it again later, and made it all the way to his kitchen table on her own. Her skin crawled in odd disconnected places, like an itch that moved every time she tried to scratch it. She found one on her arm and gave it her nails—and winced at the raw skin. She must have been scratching at it all night. Another against her shoulder a quick rub against the sheets did nothing to subdue. If she didn't get out of bed, she'd end up scratching herself bloody.

Lifting to her elbow, she blinked against the shadows that encroached on her vision as a lingering headache settled behind her eyes. Isabel still slept peacefully beside her. She swung her legs off the mattress and located the robe flung on the foot of the bed. As she tugged it from under the stubborn dog, she got a flash of the runes the old woman had painted on her that now appeared embedded into her skin. Clearly a nightmare still hanging on. She needed to get up. Move around. Find some way to convince herself she truly, surely was alive again.

She made it to the bedroom doorway and clung to the frame, catching her breath. Sunlight streamed through the small windows high against the wall of the main room. She aimed for the couch and caught herself on the back of it. Mick's scent wafted against her—clean soap, spicy deodorant, cold crisp night sky that clung to his eagle whether he was bird or man. His pillow bunched against the arm of the couch. A partially wadded fleece blanket spilled over the opposite end. She glanced toward the darkened kitchen and tried her best to ignore the pressure of his absence. Being alone felt too much like another dark, mud-slicked grave she would soon drown in.

Somehow, a worse thought entered: she had no clue how to repay him. He expected nothing, and that made everything worse. She couldn't fathom how she'd leave him. The act itself, the logistics of gathering her things and saying goodbye. Of tearing Isabel from her new home and breaking what felt like a promise to the old woman upstairs. There was an empty trailer in Oklahoma with two friends across the street and her foster parents a short walk away. But Soto had offered—threatened?—to tow that trailer here. He knew where it was, and he could bring the upperworld down upon her, Mick included. Her methods of acquiring spending money required a traceless lifestyle with no permanent address—a lifestyle she'd never drag her sister into. *Nomadic freak,* Mick had called her once. She'd never seen him so angry. He'd threatened to kill her and had meant it. Nothing had ever touched her like that. It had been grafted onto her heart like a new, incompatible living tissue, fighting to assimilate and find a permanent place inside her.

The state of her life could not be solved until she could cross a room without passing out, though, so she gripped furniture and walls as if an obstacle course lay before her. To the light switch then onward to the refrigerator. She set out breakfast for three and cooked hers first, ears tuned to the sounds of Mick returning or Isabel waking. In the end she ate alone, silent and thinking and coming up with no solutions.

And this solitude that used to comfort now haunted her.

She was sipping cold coffee when the door swung open and Mick entered on a chilly breeze that filled the small apartment. Caked in mud from boots to knees, fingers to elbows, his face streaked by sweat or tears, he yanked off his knit hat and flung it against the wall. He turned slowly to close the door then stood in his coat, unmoving, one hand tangled in his hair, eyes lost.

To ask what happened seemed like a gruesome invasion. She set her mug down and stood. His eyes raised, meeting hers, as if he'd just realized he wasn't alone. Wherever his mind was, the return path was a struggle out of a deep and dreadful place, and she watched him travel it until the Mick she knew snapped back into his frame. His shoulders squared. His eyes cleared. If he could speak, he'd be telling her to stay put, take it easy, she should be in bed, but all he did was put up a hand as if to halt something. A hibernating part of her shook itself out, rearing up to return to the place he'd come from, to fight alongside him.

Teaming with Mick had never been a good idea, no matter how right or natural it felt. But watching him stand there immobile, his hand in the air to stop her, his eyes still glazed with a hint of that lost look—

She didn't plan her path on the obstacle course toward him. Intention gave her balance, and she made it to him as if healthy muscles carried her. His arm fell around her. She folded against him. He sucked in a deep breath against her hair and held it, his heart thudding against hers. She could sense a sob building in him and his resistance against it. He bowed against her, clutching as if she could hold him up. And she did.

But her strength waned. She nudged his scratchy chin with her cheek, allowing space to unzip his coat and help him out of it. She removed the knife from his belt. Then she took his face in her hands, smearing the lines from his cheeks.

"You oughta be—" he started, his voice rough.

"In bed. Yeah, I know." She left it at that, unsure what question to ask.

He detached himself from her, went into the bathroom, and closed the door.

Whether it was the food she ate and the coffee she drank or his presence, she felt some power had been returned to her. A hot breakfast would help him, no matter the ailment. She cleared her dishes from the table and laid new ones. Brewed fresh coffee, fried eggs, buttered toast. Hoping Isabel would stay asleep and give her some time alone with Mick, she loaded Mick's plate and sat across the table to wait. By the time he emerged from the bathroom his food was nearly cold.

He'd stripped to a white T-shirt and bare feet, jeans still muddy to the knees. His hair was damp from washing his face.

"I'll warm this up." Waapikoona scooted her chair back from the table, but he stopped her with a hand on the shoulder.

"It's all right. I don't got much appetite."

"It would be more appetizing if I warmed it."

"I threw up twice in the woods. I think I'll start with coffee and see how that goes."

She crossed her arms and leaned back, watching him.

He sat down, elbows on the table, face in hands. The sound of water rushing through pipes upstairs reminded her of her bath in the herbs and salt. Specific spots on her body came alive, tight and tingly and aching to be scratched.

"Mick."

He shook his head as if to fend her off, face still buried against his hands.

Wanting to leave him, yet eager to care for him—she wasn't sending mixed signals, she was receiving them from her own mixed-up needs. "What were you doing in the woods?"

When he lowered his hands, she could see he'd returned to the dark place he'd carried home with him. The anguish on his face could only come from there. So unbearable, it scored her heart as if a part of her knew exactly where he'd gone. Like she'd been there herself and had escaped—but not without memories that scarred her bones.

"I'm gonna have to ask you a favor," he began, finally looking at her. He smoothed his hair back off his forehead. "And I don't know what I'll do if you say no."

Foreboding fell upon her. He did not need to say this favor might be too impossible to ask.

"I'm in no condition to do many kinds of favors, Mick."

He put his hands on the table, palms down and fingers spread as if to keep the world steady. "I need you to take my baby niece's bones to The Silent One to be revived."

She broke eye contact. His desperation, his tangible trust in her—it was too much. She entered the grim space her foreboding had warned of. The answer came straight and obvious, but she wrestled with it despite the truth she knew. The Silent One would not see her. She was cut off. She'd failed him—no, she'd committed treason. She could ask no more of him even as she must continue to do his work. His powers had been snatched away from her, and there was no way she'd ever retrieve them.

"The Silent One will only raise my people."

His breathing changed. He looked away, deceptively placid in body. If he shifted and tore her apart, it might explain the volatility that laced the air. The danger didn't seem aimed at her, although it should be.

"I'm not lying," she said. "Hammond was an exception. I have no idea how Jeremiah got—"

"I made a promise to my sister. She gave up and let her baby die because—" He shoved away from the table, stricken, his chair screeching across the floor. "Tell me there's a way."

There was no proven way. No uncomplicated way. The Silent One did not revive dead bones to bring good to the world. He built bones into soldiers who shared a common history which he'd exploit to create unrest. The force generated by this unrest would be used to power a gateway that would release the underworld across the earth. She'd used these reasons to raise her sister, a Native girl who matched The Silent One's criteria for a soldier, but it could not be so easily used on a white man's child who was far too young to be any help to the great demon's cause.

"There is no way." If she hadn't shielded herself, it would have stung her as strongly as it appeared to sting him.

Heartless. Selfish. Ignoble.

Well, that was okay. It made her feel like herself again.

CHAPTER
4

Mick rested his forehead against the cold shower tile and let the lukewarm water run down his back. Every minute he nudged the handle colder, hoping it would wake him up so he could do what he had to do: visit The Silent One in his cave and demand he raise baby Helen's bones. And if that didn't work, he'd offer a deal. His eagle's servitude in exchange for a living, healthy—and cured—baby girl. By tomorrow, instead of working to save the world, he'd be working to destroy it.

"Damn it all," he muttered, turning off the shower. There was no other option.

He tugged the shower curtain open and jolted at the sight of Waapikoona standing in front of the mirror staring at her reflection. A background process in his brain recognized she was as nude as he was, but that thought was immediately overcome by what else he saw. Runes. He remembered her mentioning them but hadn't associated anything malicious. It was Old Mae, for crying out loud. What he saw in front of him now were what he suspected were runes, but they marked her in angry charred slashes and loops, her flesh sick and rotting.

"Yeah, I know," Waapikoona said, still viewing her reflection. "I don't think my undead skin is taking too well to that woman's medicine."

"Oh my god," he said, feeling like he'd already said it a moment ago but hadn't had time to process it yet.

"I probably should've asked what was in that paint, and the herbs—"

He grabbed a towel. "I'm goin' up there."

"For some reason I feel like she'll be as surprised as we are." She rubbed the edge of a mark as if it itched but she was afraid to scratch.

He stepped out of the shower and got a closer look. Down both arms and along the vertical line of her backbone, strange symbols necrotized her skin—toxic, blackened, but somewhat contained within each design. Nothing seemed to be invading her healthy tissue. With the tattoo of the lightning strike, she looked like a victim of some kind of demonic torture, and he couldn't escape the grief that it was all his doing. Maybe it fit. Soon he might be doing the work of a great underworld demon. Perhaps he had just gotten started early.

"Does it hurt?"

She rubbed a different spot, more adamantly. "No, but it itches like hell."

Something made him lower his face and breathe in the scent of her arm where she rubbed—his eagle thrashed so hard he could almost feel talons tearing him up on the inside, trying to get out. The urge to buckle and fight it off consumed him. He set a hand against the sink to find the world again and lowered his lips to her ruined skin. Let his eagle scream. He'd have to get used to the underworld and all its creatures. Soon he'd be a part of it.

She tried to ignore the kiss, but he hooked an arm around her waist, drawing her closer. Her skin smelled like dank cave air and stone weeping the earth's purest water. Another kiss gave him cold rune scar and warm female skin at once, a juxtaposition that enraged and calmed his eagle in the same heartbeat. This combination could tear him in two if he let it. He needed to be in full human mind when he raised his head, turned her to face him, and kissed her mouth. The pain of wanting her—of needing her—bloomed so heavily in his stomach he couldn't imagine ever pulling away.

As much as he needed her, she seemed to need him because now she was kissing back, and the heft in his stomach fell lower. Between their bodies, the knot of his wrapped towel dug into his hip where he'd tucked it. He reached for it— but so did she, halting his hand for a moment of thought.

This was bad timing. No way would he take her to bed with her skin in such shape. His bed wasn't even empty right now. And god, what he'd just done in the woods—

Imagery crashed upon him. Baby Helen's frail little body wrapped in a white sheet. Morning sun thawing the earth and warming him through the trees as he dug and cursed and choked on his own bile. It was a blessing the ground had not been frozen, that this day was the first day that felt like spring could really happen and he wouldn't be stuck in a lifelong winter.

It was no blessing. It was all part of the same damn nightmare.

He turned his hand over, enclosing hers in his own, and released his hold on her hip.

"I'm not stopping you, I'm just ... " She turned her ear toward the door.

He strained his own ears. Dog nails ticked across the kitchen floor, a chair scooted.

"Isabel," she said.

Gravity reversed, pushing the weight that had just settled low a moment ago straight into his throat. He coughed, forcing it down. From the high of sex, to the low of death and his work required to undo it, on to his responsibility for Isabel—the transition through emotions left him dazed. He couldn't forget Waapikoona, with new damage on top of her already weak and healing body. Come to think of it, he'd been diverted. He needed to have a talk with Old Mae.

As Waapikoona slid back into her—actually, his—robe, he stripped off the towel and dried off. She sneaked through the cracked door and left. He could hear her speaking to Isabel about breakfast while he finger-combed his hair back from his forehead, got dressed, and tried to subdue the harsh words ready to unleash on Old Mae. Surely she didn't expect to scar Waapikoona like that. Surely her goal was to help. Surely she wasn't a witch.

Outside felt like true spring. A wide spread of sunlight, close and warm, drying the dewy grass. For once, Old Mae's porch steps were bone dry. Leftover salt from the last time he de-iced them crunched under his boots. His knock on the front door sounded like a bang. Inside, he heard a thump on the floor and a creature tearing away. Great—he'd startled the cats. He was pissed off, and now, so was Old Mae.

He turned around to confront the yard with his anger and let the scene calm him before he did something he'd regret. Shaking out his arms, he watched birds flitting in the trees. Cattle from the farm to the north called, their bellowing distinct. As a child, he knew if he could hear them, they were right at that boundary fence, and if he hurried he could catch them there, chewing grass and ogling him like he was their entertainment for the day. Once Kari dared him to jump the fence into the cow pasture and he'd done it, nearly getting trampled in the process. On his scramble back to safety, he'd torn his shirt and Kari had cried, knowing the trouble he would get in was her fault. Neither found any trouble because Old Mae fixed his shirt and told them mistakes could be fixed if they fessed up.

"You probably woke them cows with your banging on my door."

He turned around, halting the apology that was so automatic. "You seen what you done to Waapikoona's skin?"

"That ain't what I done. That's what's been done to her, gettin' drawn out."

"Looks like witchcraft to me."

She put a hand on her hip. "Ignorant people might call it that."

"You sayin' I'm ignorant? I think I know more than—"

"Hush, Mickey. It looks bad 'cause it is bad. You just make sure she comes back every third night for my bath— she tell you that?"

"You think you're gonna—"

"Every third night. And when I'm through with her, she won't have a mark on her. And she'll be welcome under my roof." Old Mae backed into the house and closed the door.

"Are you for real?" Mick asked the tarnished brass knocker. He'd grown up with this woman. The road out front had been his and Kari's bus stop before and after school until they were old enough to be left alone at home until his mom or Pop got off their shift. Early on, she was like a mother to his own mom and a grandma to him. When he graduated high school a couple years after his mother's death, the longing to be on his own clashed with his need to be there for his newly widowed father suffering the early signs of dementia and his sister who'd lost a mother so young. Old Mae's partially finished basement offered Mick independence and proximity to his family. So he made it inhabitable and moved in, never finding a new reason to move out. If she was a witch, she had a real expert way of hiding it.

A shuffle on the driveway caught his ear, and he turned around to find Waapikoona catching herself against the Jeep. His life was full of stubborn women of all ages. He stifled the need to hop down the steps. Urgency would only get him Waapikoona's angry eyes and bitter tongue, and he was in no mood. When he reached her side, she'd taken a bag from the back of the Jeep and slung it over her shoulder.

"You want some help, or are you plannin' on passin' out so I can haul you inside again?" Apparently, his own tongue gave no shits about his mood.

She slammed the door and eyed him.

"Never mind," he said. Before he could take one step toward his apartment, she tossed the backpack to him. He caught it by the strap.

She picked her way over to him and hooked her arm in his.

"Wow," he said. "Who are you?"

"Shut up."

Bringing a bag inside meant good news—unless she was bringing it in to reload with her and Isabel's things from his apartment. He needed to talk to her. Lay it all out. He just wasn't sure what he had that could be a worthy enough proposal.

At his apartment door he stopped to look at her. A slant of light fell across her from the side, deepening the brown of her eyes, highlighting a spectrum of tones in her dark hair, glinting off the tiny aquamarine jewel nestled in her upper ear. She was so familiar to him, so perfect. Maybe he loved her because he'd saved her from death, and some primitive part of him recognized the cost of that emotion he'd endured in that moment. Maybe he simply remembered what she'd bargained to save his own skin. Life, death, longing, heartbreak—he'd drowned under endless fathoms of emotion over her. But despite its cost, he wouldn't feel any of that so deeply if he didn't love her.

"I know I got no hold on you—"

"Mick—"

"Hold on, I need to say this. I will … I'll rearrange my life to fit you. Whatever I gotta do—"

"You don't know what you're saying. My baggage—"

He felt the backpack hanging against him. What she spoke of was not so tangible. "I'm well acquainted with your baggage."

"My baggage is literal flesh-eating demons that will eat us all if I don't continue feeding them new corpses."

He turned so he could fully face her. "Let me kill them."

"You? Or your eagle?"

"Either one."

"That's not going to do anything but worsen my crimes against my maker."

"Let your maker try to do somethin' about it. What's he gonna do, come above ground, try to find you? There are thunderbirds all over just waitin' for him to do that."

"So they can do what? Peck off an antenna? You've seen how big he is. He's poisonous to you, and he can shapeshift into whatever he wants. It's not a fight you'd walk away from."

"See, this here's the problem. You're seein' so far down the road you're not even giving a chance to today."

"And you don't plan for anything. It's one day at a time. No thought to a year from now."

Mick felt the low blow deep in his gut just the way her words intended. She was right. He made no long-term plans, not out of choice but necessity. He could barely manage what the day threw at him, for longer than he wanted to admit. Every day got squeezed for its last second, every pay check wringed of its last cent. He saw no way out of it. It wasn't anger that swelled in him. Sadness and desperation, left over from his painful morning, took a jarring hold. He clenched his jaw against it. He would not find new loss with Waapikoona leaving again for good. He wouldn't accept it.

"You want me to plan? I'll make one." He was shocked by how angry he sounded. He didn't feel it at all.

Waapikoona pulled her arm from his and opened the apartment door, one palm steadying her against the frame. Her hand looked colorless and frail, white knuckle bones visible through the medium-brown skin. He could take her by the arm and help her—and surely get an elbow to the face. So he let her go in alone and filled his chest with air before going in himself. He was going to make a plan. He'd get a notebook and put the whole damn thing in writing. And the first item on the list was to pay a visit to a great underworld demon and get his baby niece back out of the grave.

WHILE MICK FILLED notebook pages with a bullet list mind dump of his planned future, Isabel sat next to him at the kitchen table and studied his nephew's *North American Birds of Prey* coffee-table book. Doug had brought the book to Mick's place so they could help identify Isabel's other form—or the closest upperworld equivalent. Being born of both upperworld and underworld made her thunderbird like a ghost of its real form.

"Was it this one?"

Mick stopped writing. Her strong little voice was so rarely aimed at him he, at times, forgot she'd ended her silence. A direct question like this was still so new he had to smooth the astonishment off his face before answering. "Let's see, yeah, that's it. Prairie falcon."

She turned the book so he could view the page straight. Then she looked up at him like she needed further confirmation.

Mick scrutinized the photo. Pointed wings with dark tips, pointed tail, and a lighter line above the eye. "Yeah, that's the one all right. Or the closest to it, considering … " He didn't finish, worried she might take issue with him reminding her she was rebuilt from bones.

"Where are we on this picture?" She pointed to a United States map showing the habitat of the bird.

"Missouri. At the bottom of it, near Arkansas." He watched her make sense of that, feeling the urgency of talking to Waapikoona about getting the girl enrolled in school. It was on his bullet list already, but he needed to move it to the first page.

"Then it's wrong."

Mick looked closer at the map. The colored area showed the prairie falcon habitat being more out west, but no one here in Wyona would ever spot her and find it unusual to see the bird in southern Missouri. They'd be more distracted by the translucent body that looked more phantom than material. That is, if they could even see her at all. To the human eye, she'd be nearly invisible in the sky. "I don't know if the map matters. You ain't no ordinary bird."

She frowned, pulling the book back in front of her. He felt eyes on him and looked up, directly into Waapikoona's hardened gaze as she leaned a hip against the back of the couch. It was an obvious halfway resting spot on her path across the room, no matter how casual she made it appear. She looked like herself again, or what he remembered her to be, minus twenty pounds of healthy weight he was determined to put back on her with good food and rest. Her clean hair brushed to a silky shine, she'd dressed in well-worn jeans and an oversized sweater in a colorful weave that must have come from the backpack he'd carried in from the Jeep.

"We're studying North American raptors," he said to kill the charged silence.

"That's a new topic."

"Yeah, figured we might want to read up. There's a big golden eagle that's been comin' around, tearin' up all my clothes."

Her gaze morphed to a glare in its effort to suppress the emerging smile she could hide from others, but not him. He'd tuned himself to that subtlety long ago.

"And a dirty rotten peregrine falcon," she countered.

Raúl. God, he'd almost forgotten about Raúl. He glanced at his list, wondering how he'd handle him in the plan he was forming. His chicken scratches didn't look like a plan. It looked like a mess.

A distinct crunch of dead leaves outside the apartment door had Mick standing fast. Too easily he remembered the group of bad men he and Waapikoona had killed, their car that had come down his driveway. The meth-addict brother of his sister's ex who Waapikoona had killed for him last December. Kari's ex was in prison, but not forever, and if he found out his youngest girl was dead, buried in an unmarked grave in the woods and kept secret, he'd have a good reason to pay Mick a visit and demand to know why.

Before Mick could drag his stupid leg across the room, the doorknob turned and the door swung open, revealing Kari's other two children. Doug held Janie's hand to help her into the apartment and then let her go so she could run to Mick—straight into his bad leg before he thought to stop her. She smashed her face against him and clung on. Mick pried her loose and picked her up so he could hug her back. A cold throb coursed through Mick's tibia. Across the room, Doug took off his coat and hung it on the knob as if in a sleepwalk.

Mick felt his throat go thick. He cleared the roughness from his voice. "Dougie, where's your mom at?"

"Up with Old Mae."

"Why's that?"

Doug shrugged. "Dunno. She was takin' us to church and just all of a sudden turned around in the road. Said she changed her mind and we were goin' to see Old Mae instead."

Mick restrained himself from asking if she was okay. No one was okay. He was not okay, and now seeing the brother and sister of the dead baby he'd just buried, he wasn't sure anyone would ever be okay again. He hugged Janie against him and held his free hand against his mouth, panicked that a scream, or sob, or curse would push its way out. He saw Waapikoona looking at him but couldn't make sense of the expression on her face—then she was sitting stiffly on the couch, facing away, no longer a mystery to solve.

"Did you see Old Mae?" he managed to ask.

"Just for a minute. Then Mom told us to come down here."

"You two want somethin' to eat?"

Doug pulled out a kitchen chair and sat, not answering. Mick peeled Janie's arms from his neck and set her on her feet. The sulk was severe, even for Janie. It wasn't just sadness and grief, it was deeply hurt feelings. Her hair seemed unusually messy, considering they'd been on their way to church before the change of plan. He welcomed the topic—anything but a discussion of their dead sister right now.

"Janie, why's your hair not done?"

She kept her eyes glued to the floor, the frown wrinkling her chin.

Doug piped up. "She threw a fit when Mom tried to brush it, 'cause she wanted it braided but Mom said there was no time. So Mom said she goes with tangled hair."

"Come here, little birdie." Mick took Janie by the hand and tugged her to the couch where he sat, positioning her in front of him. Having Waapikoona so close beside was like a blanket on a fire. He still burned with the urge to curse at the world, but her presence was snuffing it out of him, making him feel like calm was achievable if he could just settle down long enough to find it. Janie's hair wasn't too bad off to gather up and run his fingers through the ends to clear the tangles.

"Two braids or one?"

She held up one finger.

He started at her crown and began to braid. Maybe it was too early to call the whole day gone, but with two more kids in his apartment, he couldn't get away anytime soon. Hunting the great demon in his cave to propose a bargain would have to wait. Come to think of it, he might be better off going straight from work so he wouldn't have to tell Waapikoona where he was going—or lie about it. Reaching the end of Janie's hair, he leaned to check the side table for a spare hair tie and found Waapikoona holding one in the air between them. The raised chin and slight quirk of one eyebrow meant she was impressed by something, but she didn't say what.

He fastened Janie's hair then spun her around to look her in the eyes. "Better?"

She nodded.

"You need to teach your brother to do that. That's how I learned, ya know. Your mom taught me. Brothers and sisters got to take care of each other. Especially now, when your mom has such a big hardship." By some miracle he got it out without his voice breaking.

"Did your mom have a hardship?"

"Yeah, she had a few."

Doug walked up and stood on the other side of the coffee table. "Mom don't know about Isabel. She don't know how you can bring Helen back. Isn't that what you're gonna do?"

A barely contained curse nearly fell out of his mouth then, not due to anger but surprise. He tore through his inventory of stored conversations—but even if he hadn't come out and told Doug, the kid had probably put it all together. No use in covering up something that was already out in the open.

Unless this was a test.

"I'm gonna do everything I can to help your baby sister."

It was another test not to catch Waapikoona's eye. And from the prickle he felt in the back of his brain, spilling like carbonation all along his skin, he knew she'd turned her glare up to war. Let her think what she wanted. He didn't enlist the kid for a shakedown. He didn't doubt Waapikoona either. If she said her demon boss wouldn't raise his niece, he took that as truth. But he also took Hammond as an exception that had set a precedent the great demon could not deny. All he'd need was a little convincing.

"Is Helen dead?" Janie asked.

He took her by the shoulders and looked into her eyes. She shrunk a little in his gentle grip, as if preparing for a scolding. Clearly she'd been afraid to ask her mom that question, and here she was, presenting it to him. All he had to give her was the truth, even if it was an unfair answer for a child. Even if it came back to destroy him. "I really hope not."

Chapter 5

S NUGGLED IN A pocket of warmth, Waapikoona woke to the murmur of voices. Coming back into consciousness near other people meant bad news for longer than she could remember. It meant feigning sleep, keeping her breathing even, finding some way to feel around for a weapon. But these two voices she knew like her own. They were the warm, dry place out of the storm, a refuge she could count on. She sat up on the couch, not remembering having put herself there. The small windows near the ceiling of Mick's basement apartment were two dark rectangles of night.

"Good. Now which one's east of Montana?"

She peered over the back of the couch and found Mick and Isabel sitting in the kitchen, their heads bent over something on the table.

"Idaho?" Isabel said, squinting her eyes at Mick.

"That's west. East is this way, remember?"

"Nebraska?"

"Close. This one's Nebraska. Can you write out Nebraska?"

Mick reached to the other end of the table and picked up a notebook. He handed a pencil to Isabel, correcting its position in her good hand after she took hold.

"No, capital N. Erase it and fix it. You'll learn it better if you fix it, I think."

Isabel flipped the pencil to press eraser to paper, her little tongue resting on her upper lip like she used to in the Indian school. Waapikoona saw it all again. Pine tables, dust motes in the slant of sunlight through the smudged windows, Native kids in ill-fitting white man's clothes and badly butchered hair. The rap of a ruler on the edge of a desk to wake an exhausted pupil and send him off to Gilbert Hammond for punishment. Isabel had hated that collar on her dress nearly as much as she hated her bobbed hair, and no matter what Waapikoona did to adjust it, her sister was never comfortable. Now the girl's hair was in two braids tight against the back of her head, and her bangs were pinned back with yellow barrettes. She could let her hair grow back out, and no one would ever hold her down to cut it off again. She was alive. Mick had found her, fed her, clothed her, kept her warm. He'd braided her hair for her and was now schooling her at his kitchen table.

The man did too much. He'd started a new branch off Waapikoona's path in life, and she wasn't even sure *he* knew where it headed. He was just doing his thing, never mind her. No plans for where he'd end up, just one righteous foot in front of the other. How could she be mad when the whole thing didn't even seem intentional?

"That's pretty darn good. Let's do a couple more letters and call it a day."

Waapikoona pushed the blanket off her legs and eased herself up. No dizziness this time. Her vision stayed true. She eased her way to the backpack she'd pulled from the Jeep and retrieved her plastic zipper bag of cash. Mick gave her a brief glance as she neared him in the kitchen. He seemed to be playing the indifference card since she'd cut him down, and that was fine. It made things easier when he didn't look at her like she was a gift from his god.

She set a stack of cash in front of him. Fifties and twenties, but she didn't count it because no one could put a cost on Isabel's care.

"You don't owe me money," he said after a distinct pause.

"It's grocery money. You're feeding us. You've been feeding Isabel since she came back."

"I'm a tad more frugal at the store than that."

"Groceries and rent."

He pushed back in his chair, wove his fingers together, and put his hands on top of his head, facing her straight on. His look was severe indifference now, if that could even be a thing. With the T-shirt sleeves riding up his biceps, she could compare her wasted muscle health to his toned power and decide she owed him even more. Protection against the Thunder-Beings out to destroy her and Isabel would be his other service, because right now, she was useless.

"Have you been working out?"

He held the position, watching her, his face taking on a strained look from the physical perusal. No doubt he expected her to say something else, some surly comment that should follow that line if it was meant to tease him. But it wasn't. He looked strong, probably because he was working his ass off to kill underworld demons and dig graves and handle the world.

She said nothing else, hoping to draw a response from him.

"You think I got time for that?"

"Maybe I've just never seen you in a T-shirt."

"You seen me in le—" He shifted his gaze to Isabel, who was diligently working on her writing.

Yes, she had seen him in less just this morning, and she'd seen him in even less than that before she'd gone and gotten herself lost in Oklahoma and stuck in a second grave. His hair had gone shaggy enough to fall in his eyes if he didn't brush it back, flipping up at the ends behind his ears. How long had she been stuck between life and death?

"I made chili," he said, getting up. "Canned beans. Nothin' special. But your sister liked it. And let me tell ya, she's a tricky one to feed sometimes."

Waapikoona took a seat next to the little girl. Slowly writing the final capital G in a whole line of them, Isabel said, "His food is weird."

"My food ain't weird. Your palate is weird."

Isabel smiled at her letters on the paper like this was a well-rehearsed exchange and started a new row with a capital H.

"Your letters look good," Waapikoona said. "Do you remember?"

Isabel paused her writing to stare distantly at the page. Waapikoona wasn't the only one who remembered too much. After a deep breath, she said, "Mighty Eagle taught me while we were waiting for you to find your body again."

Mick set a bowl of chili in front of Waapikoona. "Isabel, didn't I tell you to call me Mick?"

"Pop calls you Mighty Eagle."

"Pop gets confused sometimes. And he ain't your pop, he's my pop. So you can call him—"

"Grandpop." Isabel's eyes lit with pride for having pieced together the right English term.

Memory stabbed Waapikoona. She took for granted all that she knew now, and the work spent learning it when she was a little girl, newly raised, transported out of time. Vocabulary, relationships, technology—the culture shock was devastating.

Mick looked a bit stricken. "No, he ain't your grandpop neither."

"I can call him Grandpop if Dougie calls him Grandpop."

"Dougie ain't—" Mick looked at Waapikoona for a lifeline.

"What's 'ain't'?" Isabel asked.

"A real bad habit. Don't say 'ain't.'"

"You say 'ain't' a lot."

"And I shouldn't. You need to say 'isn't' or 'haven't' or 'aren't'—"

"Which one?"

"It depends on what you're sayin'."

Mick slid a spoon across the table to Waapikoona, but she couldn't eat just yet. She was getting too much enjoyment out of watching Mick drown.

"Tell you what," Mick said. "If you can spell 'Grandpop' and write it to the bottom of the page, you can call him that."

"And if you can spell 'Mighty Eagle,' you can call *him* that." Waapikoona pointed her spoon at Mick.

Isabel went to work on *Grandpop*. "I can call him that anyway because it's true."

"Fair enough," Waapikoona said. "And he *ain't* gonna have a thing to say about it."

Isabel aimed a smile at Waapikoona like a little conspirator. It seemed she understood English well enough to know when someone was wielding it exactly right.

"That's great," Mick said. "Make fun of me. I never asked to be an English teacher."

"Should I bring over more cash to cover that?"

Mick's eyes hardened. She hadn't just spoiled the moment, she'd gone too far. He thrust a plate of cornbread in front of her, avoiding her eye. She knew a person didn't pay a friend for kindness. From what she and Mick had survived together, she also knew they were more than friends. But she was determined to keep herself out of debt with him, even if they were beyond that.

In truth, she didn't know what else to do. Mick eyed her, his back rigid as he leaned against the counter.

Silence had never bothered her so much. "The other kids left?"

Mick let his response lag just long enough to show he was in no mood for speaking. "'Bout an hour ago."

She decided the silence would be an easier opponent and left it at that.

As she ate, and Isabel practiced writing, and Mick tidied the kitchen then walked around the apartment gathering laundry in a basket, her thoughts took a hard turn. What if Mick did plan, and his plan was to indoctrinate Isabel into his family and his way of life, really get her dug in deep? So that when Waapikoona did wake up she had no easy way to leave? Suspicion curled in her stomach. She closed her eyes to breathe. It was wrong to pin this on Mick, the man who'd saved her life.

Would he do what she suspected? Could he?

"Be right back," he said, leaving the apartment with a full basket of laundry.

Fragrant evening air hit her a moment later, just cool enough to wake her up.

Mick was a good man, a Thunder-Being, a god—and she was crazy. Warped by her history. Fabricating evil where there was only vivid wholesomeness. Determined to ruin a good thing, just for the sake of ruining it.

Mick wasn't without flaws. He trusted too easily, that was for sure. He made decisions based on now instead of what would come. He worked hard without any evidence of getting ahead, stretching himself too thin, saying yes to everyone when he should learn to say no. And he was broke, and getting more broke, even though he seemed to be constantly working.

She looked at the stack of cash on the table. He needed it, but he wouldn't take it. She got up and went over to the coffee table where he'd left his unopened mail. Credit card bill, junk mail, there—bank statement. Footsteps on the concrete outside, and the door opened. She was too out of practice with any stealthy activity to do anything but freeze.

He stopped just inside and nudged the door closed with an elbow. "You lookin' for somethin'?"

She hated being caught more than anything. Hesitation looked weak, though, so the truth was the only option. "I need somewhere to deposit my cash."

"You really that bent on pissin' me off today?"

"I have another bag of it buried in the cemetery near the tomb and another in your dad's woods." This she hadn't planned to expose, but now that she'd said it, it gave her a rich relief. All that cash, stolen from her victims, weighing on her every day. Anxious that she'd forget about it, dreading that she'd always remember. "You'd be doing me a favor. I'd like to get it off my conscience."

"And load it onto mine? God knows I got enough." He dropped onto the couch next to her, elbows on knees, face in hands. A deep exhale, shaky on release. "And since when do you have a conscience, anyhow?"

"Give me your ATM card."

"Funny."

"The machine will take a cash deposit."

"So I can get my account flagged for fraud?"

"I'll do a little at a time. No one will notice."

"Cut it out."

"Why, because you know you need it?"

Heavy, silent hesitation told her more than any words would. She watched him harden himself against it.

"Money's not so important to me right now, not when I made a promise to my sister, and her little girl is buried in the ground. Not when you got burns—scars—whatever that is—all over your skin. You're so thin, and I..." He ground the heels of his hands against his temples. "I got no idea what to do about any of it."

"Don't concern yourself with my skin."

"Why not? If it was me, wouldn't you?" He watched her face, and she was determined to keep it neutral. His eyes turned hard, yet vulnerable. "Don't even lie."

Something about his words, paired with those glacial blue eyes, sparked her fight response. She hated how much she adored him, how cleanly he could undo her. How his anger could burrow so viciously into her and make her feel more strongly than she did when plunging her flint knife into flesh and gutting a man. How human he proved her to be, even though she was outside of time, undead, raised by the underworld. She should be above all this, able to kill and steal carelessly, without guilt, without burden. Mick proved all that to be wrong. He called her to it, made her feel it, chained her to who she was and what she'd done.

And he was a fool to believe they could live happily ever after. It was naïve. It pained her, and angered her worst of all.

His face darkened. He pressed a fist into the couch cushion between them, his arm rigid. Of course he saw all this on her as if she spoke it. Shared trauma had opened that connection between them, and she'd never be able to sever it.

"Isabel," he said to the little girl without taking his eyes off Waapikoona. "Why don't you go upstairs and say goodnight to Old Mae?"

The chair scooted against the kitchen floor. Isabel stepped into a pair of rubber boots by the door and turned the knob.

"And take Spot with you."

Mick whistled, and a hard thump hit the floor in the bedroom. A groggy but excited dog joined Isabel by the door and they both left. As soon as Waapikoona returned her attention to Mick she realized something she'd missed before.

The man was about to snap.

His fist sunk deeper into the cushion. He took a breath as if to steady himself, but all it did was make him look like a wild animal. Not the eagle, with its watchful glare and predator's confidence. This man in front of her appeared to be more like a wild dog—crazy eyes, bunched muscles, teeth ready to tear out a throat.

"Ain't no reason you should want to leave here." It was indeed a growl, like it came from a low place he could barely keep shackled.

Missing any kind of setup for this comment, it seemed he'd been saving it up. Strange, since this conversation was so old and rehashed she could have easily rolled her eyes—if he'd been Mick, in his right mind, instead of this creature before her.

She knew her tone would be harsh to match his, but she did nothing to fix it. "Mick, I've told you—"

"You know what I think? This…" he motioned with a finger between them "…scares you. 'Cause it could be a real good thing. And you're one of them people that gets off on being miserable."

"A masochist?" Funny, she'd had the same thought about herself too many times.

"Whatever. That, and you can't stand to see yourself with me because I'm white. Maybe that makes sense because of your first life, but in this century we call that racism."

Her anger, once in check, now flared. "I'm familiar with racism, thank you."

"I don't doubt that you are. But there's none of that here, not from me, or my family, or that 90-year-old woman upstairs. She don't want you here because you're undead, not because you're Indian. I don't care what color people are or how their face is shaped. I—"

"How is my face shaped?"

She hadn't realized how close he'd gotten until he leaned back, away from her. He turned his eyes on some indistinct space in the room like an imaginary person had spoken out of turn and ruined his train of thought.

"You're beautiful. So much … " He faced her once again. The animalistic anger had faded, returning a bit of humanity to his clear blue eyes. "It hurts to look at you sometimes. Because I know you're gonna be gone."

Without her consent, her mind took her back to Oklahoma, to the kitchen in the home of the people who took her out of the snow and raised her with love in a new time. And Sam's steady words, urging her to see what was in front of her face the whole time.

I bet you don't have to look all that hard to see these worlds you talk about aren't as different as you think. Life's too short to deny yourself happiness.

And she knew it to be true, because Josie didn't argue, and if Sam and Josie agreed on something, it was fact. Together, they were a right fit to chisel into stone.

Mick shifted forward on the cushion, as if he was ready to stand and walk away and end the conversation. But instead of getting up he turned to her again. "With you here, I feel like the weight I carry is lighter. You don't even have to help me out. Just havin' you with me … and knowin' you're safe … " He looked away, as if taking in the room with new eyes. "I feel like I can breathe again."

Still addressing the room, he nodded slightly, like some reckoning had just happened in his head.

"Okay," she said.

"What?"

"Okay, we'll stay for a few weeks." Maybe she was a masochist. All they'd do is make each other miserable.

His expression didn't change. "You're just agreeing to make me mad."

It was her turn to ask, "What?"

"You don't really mean it."

"You think I'm being dismissive?" She had to chuckle at that.

"Yeah. You're gonna say that and then pack and leave in the night. Sounds familiar, don't it?"

They were certainly going to make each other miserable. And she had a new thought that would push the test of trust even further. "And yes, go ahead and kill my Helpers. Mine and the orphaned ones. We'll live like you. No plan. No preparation for whatever consequences we call down upon ourselves."

"See what you're doin'?"

"It's what you want."

"It's patronizing. And you're just … You're settin' it up to fail. You just agreed to stay with me and then threw a wrench in."

She couldn't help but raise her voice. "*You* offered to kill them."

He stood as if fire sparked at his feet. "You're only allowin' it because you sense some disaster."

For a moment, disaster felt worth it. She'd been cut off from The Silent One. She was sure of that. Being in possession of—or possessed by—her Helpers was a burden she expected to carry to her next grave. When Mick had initially offered to kill them, she hadn't dedicated any real thought to it. She couldn't be free that easily. Mick had saved her life. He couldn't save her from this too.

But if he could, *she would be free of it.*

He was back on the couch with her again, closer than before. He took her hand in both of his, and when she looked up at him she realized she'd spoken that last thought aloud. Her eyes were wet, her voice stuck behind an unchecked emotion that had been denied for too long.

"Come outside," he said softly. "Release them."

"Disaster," was all she could say.

"The hell with it. We'll deal with whatever comes. Can't be any worse than what I'm dealin' with right now."

She rose to her feet, sobered beyond words. This was a dream—the whole night was. The awakening from the couch when she hadn't remembered lying down, the familial banter between Mick and Isabel, the strange up-and-down fight with Mick. His words to her, which she could've said right back to him if she'd taken the time to mull over her feelings and put them in English. Being with him, her burden also felt lighter, her trials easier to take on. She could acquiesce to it for now, but being stuck in his life long-term would only drown her.

Outside of her body, she watched it happen: Mick, opening the door for her but remaining inside. Her, walking up the few steps to ground level where the pale moonlight fell against her like a mother's hand. Mick's Pontiac sat silently, Rain's Jeep behind. Mild air swallowed her. A breeze played in her hair. She reached for The Silent One and found only a void. One chain broken, a manacle loose on her wrist. Her Helpers were her last ties to The Silent One and his world. She couldn't stop feeding them without them turning on her, so what if she turned on them first?

In the shadows against the tall grass at the edge of the yard she spotted a set of eyes, a hunched bounding shape, a wicked flash of teeth in the night. Ever loyal, they waited for her next kill. She'd accepted the task, knowing her work would one day build enough credit with The Silent One to request that he raise her sister from the grave. But now her sister was here, guarded by a Thunder-Being, as safe from the underworld as a girl could be. Another bounding shape joined the other. These were the ones she'd orphaned, and they'd followed her here to serve her, without her request.

She had only heard what the Helpers would do if not kept fed. Eat their keeper alive then go after every loved one. But she had no proof. Which was the greater risk—allowing them to remain or killing them off? Could she really turn Mick loose on these creatures who'd done nothing to wrong her?

She turned around. "I can't."

Mick came out from underneath the overhang to stand before her. "You don't have to. Just release them, and I'll do the rest." He looked toward the tall grass where the orphans waited.

"They've done nothing but do their job for me."

"They ain't your pets."

"They only go after the dead."

"And what'll they go after, if you stop givin' 'em that?"

The warm glow from the apartment lit one side of Mick's face, leaving the other side darkened by shadow. As she studied him, she imagined his eagle looking out, human blue eyes turned to a piercing amber with flecks of gold. Seeing her for all she was, all she had been, all she would be.

"You goin' soft?" he asked.

Of course he'd voice the question she'd been too afraid to ask herself. And with that tone, a little bit teasing, a whole lot hopeful. A change in her ways would count as a success for his eagle. One less minion of the underworld to disable or destroy. Or so she assumed. Too many times she'd found peaceful camaraderie with the bird. It hunted and attacked her Helpers, but never had it gone after her.

"I'm allowing flesh-eating demons to live. I think that makes me certified evil."

He watched her a moment. "My eagle don't need your permission." He canted his head toward the orphan Helpers, vulnerable outside of her palm.

"Maybe not. But take a guess who I'd hold responsible."

Mick closed the distance between them. Now overstepping into her space, it was a good way to trigger a fight—if the look on his face matched that intention. There was something else, something that brought focus to how their eyes and lips aligned, how despite being so close, he was too far away, and how easily that could be fixed.

He brushed past her, leaving her tingling and warmed by an overly zealous heart. His limp looked more pronounced than usual as he walked away. Instead of following him into the apartment like a puppy, she went up the stairs to Old Mae's door and collected Isabel and Spot.

"Bedtime," Waapikoona said, tugging Isabel down Mick's steps as the girl looked wistfully at the clear night sky.

Inside, Mick was on the couch, phone trapped between shoulder and ear as he tied his boots. "Don't go out there, you or Pop. Just hang tight till I get there. Promise?" Mick caught her eye then looked quickly away. "Okay, just keep the doors locked. I'll be right there."

He ended the call and went for his jacket, expression cleared and body angled away. So of course she had to ask, "What's going on?"

Pocketing his wallet and keys, he ignored her. She planted herself in front of the door.

"Really?" he said.

"Where are you going?"

"To my dad's. And since you're not gonna let it go till I tell you, apparently he's got a bunch of people campin' out in his woods. So I gotta go make 'em leave."

"What kind of people?"

Mick smoothed his hair back and tugged on a baseball cap. His deep exhale of annoyed resignation confirmed her suspicions.

"I'm coming with you."

CHAPTER

6

M ICK AIMED THE GTO in the direction of Pop's house and tried not to think too hard about the bubble of peace contained inside his car when outside there was so much pain. Waapikoona leaned an elbow on the center armrest, so close he could smell his shampoo in her hair. Buckled in the back seat, Isabel watched the moon out the window, one arm around Spot who sat beside her. They were like the family he'd never had time to think about having but now wanted so badly it made his insides flutter and his heart sing. He struggled against a feeling he'd never encountered before. That the world was shit, but as long this woman and girl were safe with him, he could take on anything.

This—he had to lock it down. Waapikoona didn't want a domestic life with him. And it didn't matter how much progress he'd made with Isabel. She didn't belong to him and never would.

So he said something that had nothing to do with any of that but he had to let out before it gored him. "Seems my sister would rather be anywhere than her own home right now."

Waapikoona turned to look at him, but he kept his eyes on the road.

"I can't decide if I should talk her into takin' the kids home or let her stay with Pop."

He felt a warm hand glide under his, fingers weaving in and holding tight. Something about that simple motion, unexpected, in the dark, made his eyes burn with tears.

"I think people need to be around their family when someone dies."

He allowed a moment to collect himself, to steady his voice. He didn't feel like crying and didn't want to. There was more anger spinning up inside him than anything else. But he could feel wetness on his cheeks despite that. "So, just let 'em be, then?"

"Hard concept for you, I know." She released his hand to blot his face with her sleeve. She wore her fleece jacket, the one he'd rescued from the mausoleum and washed for her, hoping someday to return it. Here she was wearing it, with him again. He had to figure out some way to make it not too good to be true.

Maybe Kari staying with Pop was not so much a depressing thing as it was a silver lining. Pop's dementia had seemed better lately, but it could go downhill anytime, and having someone in the house with him might unload a bit of stress from all of them.

He parked in the flood of light on Pop's driveway and killed the engine. "I got work in the morning, so this'll have to be quick. You two can stay right—"

"I'm going to talk to them." She popped her seat belt and pushed her door open.

By the time Mick had released Spot and Isabel from the back seat, Waapikoona had rounded the corner of the house and disappeared. There was no confirmation these people camping out in Pop's woods were her undead brothers and sisters, no way she could be sure what she was walking into. He took the girl and dog inside, passing Kari with a squeeze on her shoulder as he made a beeline for the back door. He heard Pop say to Isabel, "Now look who come to visit me?" and then he was halfway across the backyard and out of audible human range. He was suddenly very aware of human limitations and eagle strengths.

"Don't shift," he told himself. He'd had no time to mentally wrangle the eagle into submission.

His human senses caught the fragrance of woodsmoke and saw the orange undulation of a campfire in the distance. As he breached the first layer of trees at the far edge of lawn, a creature scattered dead leaves in a frantic burst away from him. In the dappled darkness he pushed through saplings and sticker bushes that tugged at his jeans, the shadows becoming too thick with the larger tree limbs blocking the moonlight. He unpocketed his phone and turned on its flashlight, angling it toward the ground. A deposit of limestone provided a natural path ahead, where Waapikoona's voice carried. She was using the same steady tone she used when making some demand of him where compromise wasn't an option.

He shut off his light. Human eyes adjusted slowly to the soft glint of moonlight on the limestone stretching in front of him. Her upright outline stood dark against the flicker of a healthy fire burning in a level spot ahead. An unfamiliar voice called back to her; others joined in, a few of them shouts. She raised an arm. From the play of firelight and perspective against the dark, it took a moment for him to realize her arm was raised toward him, not the people in the woods. Her palm open to him, fingers splayed. *Stop.*

The hasty, desperate motion of her arm plugged straight into his eagle and charged him up.

Dropping to a squat, Mick laid a hand against the cold stone and allowed a sharp edge to bite into his flesh. His heart beat in his ears.

Don't shift. Later, maybe. Not now.

Waapikoona had this under control. He had to trust her. He wouldn't screw this up. He pressed until the sharp rock bit in harder, dead center against the fleshy part under his thumb. *Yes, feel that. Human skin. Full of nerves. Hands, not wings. Feet on the ground.*

Her jean-clad legs and cowboy boots entered his line of sight.

"All their Helpers are loose. They're all around us. At least…" she pivoted, checking her surroundings, he guessed, since he hadn't gathered himself enough to raise his head and look at her face "…thirty of them."

She offered her unbandaged hand, and he took it, hoping he wouldn't pull her down to the ground beside him. Her warm skin gave him the perfect connection to his human side to rise and fill the space his eagle was eager to claim. He wanted more of her—all of her—but he wasn't sure the time would ever come. Now standing, the expected thing to do was release her hand, but he couldn't do that. Not yet. The delicate moonlight had turned clear and white— no, more than that. A spectrum of color glanced off everything before him, layering the view with new dimension. He saw how openly she grinned, making no attempt to hide how charmed she seemed to be. She likely believed the night would cover for her. Right now, she didn't know his brain was halfway tapped into eagle vision, and there was nothing she could hide.

"They're not going to bother anyone if no one bothers them—the people, or their Helpers."

"What about my niece's bones that are buried out here?"

"They'll watch over them."

"Bullshit," he said before thinking how harsh it would sound. She wasn't just indulging him, she was straight-faced lying—and more loyal to those people in the woods than to him. That was how it looked, and his disbelief felt miles high. He was missing something, had to be. And being caught between his two forms consumed too much processing power to think it through the right way. "There's no way you'd have known to ask 'em."

"They asked *me*."

He caught her bruised expression before she hardened herself. His trust in her wasn't so easily dismissed even if it looked that way. Why had he even said such a stupid thing? Standing out here in the chilly night wasn't the best place to have stupid miscommunications, and his leg was killing him.

With his eyes on hers he offered a hand, hoping she'd see how tired, how overwhelmed, how dead his brain was—and how much trouble his eagle was adding to the mix. If he opened his mouth to explain it, he'd probably say something else he wanted to take back.

"You go," she said. "I'm heading to them." She backed away from him.

"What for?" Surprise made it come out too loud.

"Just to chat a little more. I won't be long."

She turned; he caught her by the sleeve. A bad move, but too late to stop himself. He expected combat, but to his surprise she simply looked at his grip on her fleece as if talking herself out of kicking him in the nuts. She stalled long enough for him to feel the shiver in her. If he'd known she was planning to hang out in the woods, he'd have insisted she wear something heavier. He thought he was going to be the one dealing with the trespassers.

He released her sleeve, took off his jacket, and slung it over her shoulders. Allowing her to go talk to those people seemed like a terrible idea. But not allowing her—as if he even could—was undeniably worse. "Too cold out here in just that fleece until you get some more meat on your bones."

"Thank you for getting my fleece. I know where I left it. You didn't have to go back there."

"I also got your gloves. You oughta be wearin' those too." He'd found her mica crystal as well, but he wouldn't be able to return that to her just yet.

She wrapped his jacket tight around her and turned her gaze away from his. "You can't be in love with me, Mick."

He frowned at her, but she was still gazing off into the distance, unseeing. He should probably be careful here, but his response was automatic. "I can and I am."

"No." She turned back, suddenly fierce. "I'm telling you that you can't."

Was he hearing this? The woman had some nerve telling him what he could feel.

"Maybe I should come clean with you," she said. "Yes, I said I'll stay. But I know how easily people can be ripped apart. Right now, I have Isabel, and she's the only one who matters. I can't take the risk on anyone else."

"You're wrong." They were stronger together. He felt it in the car on the way over there. He felt it when he drew the blanket over her so she could rest while he helped Isabel with her writing. He felt it when she refused to surrender to Jeremiah in the mausoleum, when she called on his eagle to help them. He felt it when he dug her from that muddy grave. He felt it right now. Waapikoona was stuck, reliving the trauma of her past, equating it to their present. Her baggage wasn't just her flesh-eating demons.

"I'm committed to Isabel. I can't commit to you."

"I never asked you to commit to me."

She turned to face the house, the inviting glow of its windows warm in the night. "Especially not to you," she said, as if dismissing his response. "Look at all the people you come already connected to."

Meaning … his family? She'd just alluded to the importance of family a few minutes ago. He could now see her point. The more people you love, the more there is to lose.

"Nothing's gonna happen to me."

She looked directly at him. "I was forced to choose between you and my sister once. I won't put myself in that position again."

"No one's gonna put you there again."

"Exactly."

"I mean, ain't no way that'll ever happen again."

"Right."

He was thoroughly confused now, and his leg was nearly numb. Through his half-man half-eagle vision, she looked like an angel of darkness standing before him. If it weren't for his jacket wrapped around her, he'd feel infinitely unworthy. There was no way he could deny how delicately they'd imprinted themselves on each other, and neither could she.

"I got you stayin' with me and that's all I'm askin' of you right now."

"It's not permanent."

"Can't see how it could be since I only got one bed." He intended it to lighten the mood, but she tilted her head in a way that made him wish he hadn't said it. Instead of mess it up worse with words from his misfiring brain, he laid the back of his fingers on her cheek to gauge her warmth. A practicality, and an assurance, so he could go back to the house and leave her there without taking on more worry—but then she moved in close and turned his baseball cap backward before softly touching her lips to his. He might discount it as a platonic thing, but she let it linger. Long enough to inhale, take the kiss inside him, slow the world. When she pulled away, her eyes were carefully fortified. Against what, he could never guess.

"You shouldn't be so … " She seemed to get stuck there as her eyes lost focus. "Kind," she said finally. But on that last word the fortress broke a little, and he could see a depth of emotion, so immeasurable and startling he couldn't even name what it was.

"Okay," he said, unable to invoke any other response. He turned to go. He thought about adding, *See you back at the house?* But instead of sounding light in his mind, it sounded desperate, so he headed toward the inviting gleam of Pop's windows without another word.

CHAPTER
7

I*T'S NOT PERMANENT.*

Waapikoona heard the words again in her head, knowing they had to be true, feeling they were a lie. That was the problem with Mick. He'd felt permanent the day he'd walked up on her trashing Soto's car with that crowbar. It was like she'd been living in the fury of a storm, and he was its calm, steady eye, gliding toward her and taking her inside.

Now he was walking away, his shoulders stiff against the cold.

She'd attempted finality with that kiss, and it had backfired.

She clutched his jacket closer, grateful for it. No matter how she fought, she still managed to find herself cocooned in his comfort. Inside his Pontiac on that first day, she should have recognized that feeling of permanence—and opened the door and bailed. And even as she learned to recognize how easily he drew her in, she was still making the same mistake because here she was, standing in the woods inside his warm jacket. Too late to decline the offer. Too late to give it back. Now she was seduced by its warmth, clothed in his scent, and on her way to talk business with the people who could get her out of the inescapable permanence of Michael Svendsen. There was no way she could think clearly of a future without Mick with his jacket around her.

Maybe he'd done it on purpose. Ownership, possession, or even just a simple reminder of his existence.

Nonsense. If he was that conniving, she'd have found a way to hate him a long time ago and wouldn't be in this situation.

She picked her way across the stone path, avoiding the wet spots that would surely take her legs out from under her. Her limbs felt heavy, like she trudged through water instead of air. Moving around was the best way to regain her strength. She couldn't spend any more time at rest in Mick's place while The Silent One built his army. Without a firm foothold, she and Isabel might find themselves on the wrong side, or worse, collateral damage.

The radiant heat of the fire ahead warmed her cheeks as she neared the group of people. Faces swiveled toward her, relaxed bodies turned alert and rose to standing. It was an equal mix of men and women, all within fifteen years of her age in both directions. Tents flapped in the breeze at the far edge of the clearing, where smaller fires burned. She raised both hands to show she wasn't armed, watching their firelit expressions for any sign of hostility or fear. One came forward to pat her down, and she held steady against the pressure of the woman's rough hands. Visible weakness was not an option here, no matter what. The woman snatched the wrist of her wounded hand, gave the bandage a quick look-over, and sent an unreadable glance toward a man sharpening a knife near the fire before stepping away.

Waapikoona wasn't sure if she'd just been cleared to proceed, but she wasn't going to stand there and wait for an invitation. She combed the crowd for the ones she'd spoken to earlier from afar, but they were no longer present. Most likely they'd been tasked with following Mick to make sure he kept the form of a man and retreated to a less threatening distance. A twig snapped in the woods to her right. She fought the urge to get an eye on what it was. It was only natural they'd surround her, cut her off from any others like Mick who trailed her. Their strategy proved exactly what she'd returned here to confirm. They were warriors in The Silent One's war. Now all she had to do was find out what side they fought for, and if she should join them.

"I need to speak to someone here who knows English." She kept her voice low and level, knowing it wouldn't reach those who were farthest away. Raising her voice earlier had dried her throat and made her weary. She had a cache of strength that wouldn't last long, and she needed some in reserve to make it back to Mick's Pontiac.

The woman who'd patted her down regarded her before walking over to confer with the man sharpening his knife. They exchanged words too guarded for Waapikoona to determine if it was a language she could understand. Her own language was lost. It had either died or branched into something new. In Indian Country she'd learned some *Myaamia* and a bit of Spanish, but there were hundreds of Native languages that were as foreign to her as English had been in her first life. The little *Myaamia* she knew had gone so long unused in this life she'd nearly lost it as well.

Now in her peripheral vision she could see the people closing in behind her. Two flanking either side, probably more behind her. Mick's jacket turned heavy and stifling. Adrenaline erupted from her core, flushing her limbs. Neither fight nor flight would suit her here. She had no backing from The Silent One to help her fight through a crowd. And she had no desire to kill people like her who'd been raised from their graves to survive a new life. She was glad Mick had left. His eagle would complicate things here.

The man tested the blade of his knife against his thumb, sheathed it at his waist, and advanced toward her. He stopped a few paces away to watch her, his face giving nothing away, his hand resting on the handle of his blade. He wore his lined denim coat open, like this bitter air was nothing but a harmless breeze. Her height matched his, but his arms were long and thick, his shoulders double hers. She realized the unexpected help of Mick's jacket—to make her frame appear more substantial than its true withered shape.

She set her gaze on his knife. "If you'll be using it on me, I prefer it sharp."

He said nothing to that. He seemed to be waiting for something, and Waapikoona had no time for guessing games. "I need to know if you fight with our creator, or against him."

His eyes remained fixed and harsh despite the new smile. He swiveled, keeping his attention on her. The woman who'd patted her down came to stand beside him. He spoke to her in an unfamiliar tongue; she gave a curt reply back. Waapikoona noticed the woman's features swayed a bit Caucasian, her lighter skin contrasting with her dark eyes.

The woman turned to face her. "We can't give that answer to a person we don't know."

Understandable. Waapikoona felt her backbone relax a little, even though she still sensed the people behind her like they each held a gun to her head. "My name is Sarah Clarke.

I'm raised, and my Helpers…" she took the opportunity to glance over her shoulder into the eyes of the people at her back "…mingle with yours out there in the dark. I've split from The Silent One, and I'm looking for m—"

The woman raised a hand, silencing the word she realized then was too brazen to speak aloud. *Mutiny.*

Feet shuffled behind her as if new, more powerful stances were being formed, but she ignored it. She had to be clear with these people, especially since she was sure they already knew what she was about to disclose. "I've teamed with a Thunder-Being, but he's…" She lost her momentum in an effort to find the right word. When it came to Mick, lying felt like a crime she'd rather not carry on her record. "Not working out."

The half-Caucasian woman nodded in the direction of Mick's father's house. "Him."

Waapikoona said nothing. It was answer enough.

A voice spoke up from behind, causing a fresh shot of adrenaline and a new trickle of sweat down Waapikoona's spine. Foreign words, their angry tone universal. Instead of turning around to acknowledge the attack—whether it was aimed at her, or the man and woman in front of her— she watched the body language of those who had wandered closer to this meeting. Crossed arms, shaking heads, untrusting eyes. Her teaming with Mick would sink her.

The half-Caucasian woman tilted her head at the people behind Waapikoona as if they'd spoke out of turn. Another spoke up from the sidelines, and now the hand of the man in front of her was lying heavier on the handle of his blade. He watched Waapikoona, as if she were the one shouting.

"They want to know whose bones lie in the grave … " The woman gestured to her left.

"A little girl who died too young."

"… and what you plan to do with them."

"Nothing." It was a truth that pierced Waapikoona in a place she'd never felt before.

"But they're important to you."

Waapikoona weighed another lie, decided it was yet another she couldn't face. She offered a small truth instead. "It's important that you leave them at rest."

"We … " The woman looked around, catching the eye of every person around in an act of solidarity that made Waapikoona feel like an outsider more than ever. "We think you anger The Silent One more than would be safe for us."

Waapikoona wanted to laugh. What could be more angering than mutiny?

"And you have ties—"

"I have no ties."

Isabel, Waapikoona thought, shocked by the act of remembering—or forgetting. She had lived untethered for so long that she'd forgotten—but did it matter? Where Waapikoona would go, Isabel would go. She'd make it safe for both of them. She suddenly remembered another reason Mick's apartment would have to be temporary—Soto knew she was there and would find out about Isabel. Soon he'd grow tired of waiting for Waapikoona to join him, and his Thunder-Being would end both her and her sister.

The woman bowed her head, taking a breath, releasing it. When she returned her focus to Waapikoona, a look of unguarded sympathy broke through. "We can't accept you. It's too much risk."

Anger and rejection heated Waapikoona's chest, deepening the beat of her heart. She'd come here to decide if these were the people she should join, not to be interviewed for a place with them. The choice was supposed to be hers, not theirs. And they were basing it on flimsy claims of risk—

when each one of them was a risk—and false ties they'd completely misunderstood.

"I'm no more risk than each one of you."

"We all still work for him. He has no reason to suspect any of us as doing anything more than socializing."

"Socializing isn't allowed."

"True, but it's a mild betrayal, and becoming too common for him to look twice. If he sees you among us, he'll question us all."

The time and space of Waapikoona's nightmare while she recovered in Mick's bed fell fast upon her. If it was a glimpse of the future, these people must know—but when had she ever had visions? It couldn't be anything more than a dream. Waapikoona felt the cold gripping her jeans and Mick's coat shielding her from it. She thought of him standing at the back door of Pop's house, looking across the yard and waiting for her to return. She should walk in the opposite direction. She should go to the road and hitch a ride to his place, pack her things into the Jeep and drive far away. There was no place for her anymore. Not with The Silent One, not with her raised brothers and sisters. Not in Indian Country with her foster family who lived solely in the upperworld with no knowledge of her undead bones. And certainly not with Mick. Her world would destroy his, and she would not fight her raised brothers and sisters to protect him.

These people in front of her were The Silent One's raised, but they were not family.

I belong nowhere, she thought, the heat of humiliation prickling and building up in Mick's coat. The people guarding her back parted when she turned, hands sliding toward concealed weapons. If her face was that severe, she would have to somehow fix it before Mick saw it. She could not answer his questions right now.

Instead of returning to Pop's house, she walked to the Pontiac in the driveway and let herself into the passenger side. She snuggled down in Mick's coat, grateful for the lingering heat from the engine. *I belong nowhere.* The first time it was a jarring realization; now it was an oath. She would choose this, just like she'd chosen solitude before. She worked best alone. Other raised people had only felt like a family she could always choose to join because she hadn't thought it through. Now she knew. It stung like a vital lesson. She didn't need anyone. She didn't join others. People were a complication whether they were living, dead, or undead.

Isabel.

Except Isabel. It would be good for her to stop forgetting about Isabel. To the little girl, she'd have to be sister, mother, teacher, friend—everything. And she was bad at all those things. She raised her bandaged hand from the shadows of the car into the hazy light, noting the stab of pain as she turned it, the sharp edges of white knuckles visible through skin, the weakness in her grip. Isabel also needed a protector, and she couldn't even be that.

Light fell across the yard, and the old man came out on the front porch in his robe and socks, waving her inside. But in that house wasn't just the old man, Mick, and Isabel. It was also Kari and her kids—a whole family grieving a child's death Waapikoona refused to even try to undo. Too clearly she remembered that jagged hole in her chest she felt every day before her sister returned. The loss of young life somehow became more tragic with each year she grew when her sister did not. The more time passed, the more she felt like a mother than a sister. And she was grateful she wasn't really Isabel's mother, because the hole would surely cut unimaginably deeper.

The old man stood waiting, more stubborn than her. If he were Mick, she could refuse him. If Mick insisted, she could tell him where to shove it. This wasn't Mick but his father, who had taken her in as a stranger walking across his land. He'd offered warm clothes and coffee. He expected nothing in return—not even an explanation. And when she declined the clothes and coffee to go back out and search his woods in the cold, he hadn't even called her crazy. He looked at her like a human being instead of an object to be managed, mocked, dismissed. Whipped, raped, torn from her home, erased. Centuries muted it, but too much of that was alive and well.

She swung open the door and used it to get her legs under her.

"What're you doin' out here by yourself, girl?" he said as she rounded the front of the car.

"I'll just grab Mick's keys and get the car warmed up."

"You look like you're fittin' to drive off, with the man's car and his coat."

She'd take off the coat and hand it to the old man ... if she wasn't so cold and tired.

"I told Kari them people ain't gonna hurt nothin'. She's a bit sensitive right now, 'bout everything ... "

"Would you mind telling Mick I'm out here? I'm not coming in." She took a step back, ready to turn away, when Mick appeared in the doorway behind the old man.

His eyes were sunken, his face drawn and tired. He looked like he'd been in the house for years, not minutes. But when he caught her standing there, he raised his eyebrows to ask, *all okay?* And she felt the question hit as if the words themselves had fallen on her eardrums. Her steady gaze was answer enough for the way he dropped his brows and put a hand on the old man's shoulder to squeeze past him toward her. Isabel came through next, her good hand tight in Mick's.

"Drive safe, Mickey."

"Okay, Pop. Call if you need anything else."

Waapikoona found her own cold hand enveloped in the warmth of his, and with it, a painful fracture of the oath she had made moments ago. She couldn't choose solitude, not when her hand felt so right in his. Not when they understood one another without speech. Not when Isabel looked so content and safe with this man who would forget his own self before he forgot her.

Maybe she didn't have to choose between them. Maybe they came as a pack now. Maybe she could choose them both. She'd gone so long with so little, it seemed like too much to ask.

Isabel broke away to open the car door for Spot, and Waapikoona stopped walking so Mick would stop too. She could never admit he was right, that yes, this choking breathlessness and shaky feeling in her limbs meant she was afraid. After facing monsters of all types in two separate lives, she'd conquered fear and never expected to encounter it again. Now she'd been called for a rematch, and before her stood a truth she must face. This accord with him wasn't simple teamwork. It was a belonging so real and strong it bound her. This was the fear that filled her, fear for what she'd be responsible for, for what she could lose. Blind chance, free-falling out of the sky had connected her path to Mick's. How could something so arbitrary be so resolute, so true?

It had to be unnatural, wrong, a mistake, and a hazard to both of them. But no—it was sound. Perfect. And too precious a thing to put near the danger that closed in tighter each day. She was terrified for how it had caught her and would never let her go, for how much it would break her when it ended because she knew it could be ripped away as easily as everything had been ripped from the child she once was.

Being at Mick's side felt right. As right as taking her sister's hand in their first life and hurling themselves off that cliff. She'd been terrified of that, too, but here they were, alive and whole.

She turned to Mick, unable to put anything into words except, "How are we going to do this?"

This encompassed so much, but she knew he would understand.

He gripped the lapels of the coat she wore as if he was going to kiss her, but instead he closed it tighter against her. "We're gonna put one foot in front of the other until everything has worked out right."

"How can you expect that?"

"I can't. But I'm gonna work my damnedest at it, and keep at it till we're there."

She couldn't be so optimistic and had no idea how he could. "You'll die first."

"Then at least I died tryin'."

Chapter

8

The alarm on Mick's phone went off right next to his head like a kick in the face. It was his normal Monday morning wake-up, turned punishing from the late bedtime from the night before. He swiped it off before it woke Waapikoona and Isabel and rolled off the couch. If he knew he'd feel this hungover despite not drinking a drop, he would have allowed himself a beer or two. At least then it would feel justified. Now, it just felt like he'd missed out. And the day ahead of him was going to be a long one.

He showered, dressed, and ate two overripe bananas and a bowl of cereal at the counter while packing a lunch. Coffee would have to wait. Time seemed to be on double speed, or he was moving at half and having trouble keeping up. At the door he remembered he'd worn his last pair of coveralls home and hadn't had a chance to wash them. The hunt for a clean pair stole all his spare time with nothing earned, so he grabbed the dirty ones from the laundry pile and left rubber on every road heading to the shop.

Virgil had already flipped the OPEN sign by the time he arrived. Because Mick hated coming in the front entrance if customers were already inside, he pulled to the rear of the building and reversed the GTO against the brick wall. He let himself in the back door and changed into his coveralls, still funky from the last week. No point in dwelling on that—from the spread of sunlight outside it was going to be warm again, and even clean coveralls would be ripe in no time.

He headed to the office for some coffee. Voices carried to him before he got there, someone talking Virgil's ear off.

"… and my church started stockin' up too. Nobody's got any idea where these people are comin' from, or where the disappeared folks are goin'. It's almost like they're being switched, if you think about it. So, I'm just sayin', if I were you—"

"I'll consider that. Maybe we'll start a stockpile here in the shop. I'll get Svendsen on that." Virgil caught Mick's eye like he was sharing a joke.

Mick easily recognized Virgil's dismiss-the-overtalk-ative-customer act and knew better than to get himself stuck too. He busied himself by replenishing the stack of paper coffee cups beside the coffee maker. The stack was nearly out, and he'd be hitting the coffee all day long.

The customer's ride showed up, and he cleared out. Virgil chuckled as soon as the door jingled closed.

"Should I ask what you're gettin' me on?"

"Collectin' a stock of canned goods and toilet paper like it's Y2K all over again. Ol' Larry has gone nuts like the rest of 'em."

Mick let a few seconds tick by to keep his question casual. "What's he think is goin' on?"

"The end of the world. Just like last time. Only this time it's the real deal."

"Well, in that case let's forget the canned goods and go for junk food and beer. We can go down partyin' while everyone else is eating green beans."

"I like the way you think." Virgil handed Mick a worn-out Honda key fob. "Lost his muffler again. His buddy's gonna drive him down 29 to see if they can find it."

"I told him last time—"

"Yeah, we both told him. He ain't gonna learn. Might as well pull it in the bay, 'cause you know he's gonna find it."

Through the shop door Mick saw Andy pass by, shoving an arm into his coveralls. With no overnight drop-offs and Andy showing up, there was a chance Mick could clock out on time and get a good start on what he planned to do. Getting out early would be better yet, and he even had it in him today to hope for that.

AT THREE O'CLOCK it was quiet enough for Andy to take a seat on the curb outside and play games on his phone. Mick had learned long ago that putting away tools early on a slow day meant some emergency was going to roll in, followed by another. Today felt like the day to tempt fate. He started winding up his air hose.

"That's bad juju for all of us, man," one of the afternoon mechanics called to him across the garage.

Mick wasn't going to tell him he planned to cut out early. He didn't want anyone else to get the thought before him. The part-timers always got the idea first.

One hour later he was out of there, aiming the GTO toward the cave Waapikoona had led him through with his arm infected by a demon bite. He had no way to warn her he'd be home late, but he figured his whereabouts were an overstep into commitment territory she clearly didn't want. His goal today wasn't anything more than a test run through The Silent One's cave, just to feel it out. To see if navigation was possible without Waapikoona. To prove that he could travel near such a powerful presence without triggering his eagle. A couple hours were all he'd need before he got himself home. A few passes would familiarize himself with the paths and turns so when the time was right to confront the great demon, he'd be just as at home as he was.

Okay, maybe not at home. But it felt good to say that.

The sun hung well above the horizon as he parked in the weeds on the shoulder of an abandoned dirt driveway curving off the main road and got out of the car. At the shop he'd changed out of his coveralls so he wouldn't have to fight his way out of them inside his car. He got out of the GTO, zipped a waterproof jacket over his T-shirt, and popped the trunk to retrieve the old backpack he'd tossed in there. Into that he loaded some bottled water, a small crowbar, a flashlight, and two giant rolls of fishing line. From the back seat he retrieved a second flashlight, which he stuck in the back of his jeans. Too easily he remembered the first time he'd gone underground; Waapikoona had briefly lost the only flashlight, prompting too many helpless seconds of unfathomable darkness.

With one last look around the trunk, he shouldered the backpack and slammed the trunk lid closed. There was one major thing he was forgetting: the woman who could safely lead him through the underworld. He'd have to prove he could make do without her. He felt his pockets—phone, keys, pocket knife, and Waapikoona's mica crystal he'd saved from the mausoleum.

She thought he couldn't plan. Well, he could prepare for a reckless trek through a demon-filled cave. The only thing he hadn't packed was common sense.

Standing on the shoulder of the road, he appraised the wall of trees and underbrush, thick even without any greenery. He and Waapikoona had taken a deer trail the first time in, which should still be visible, but he wasn't sure if he'd parked at the right spot. He walked up the road until he found a narrow entrance of long-ago snapped branches and packed earth. With no way to determine if this was the right one, he figured it was as good a trail as any to check out and angled his shoulders into the opening. He ignored any smaller paths that branched from the main one, keeping an eye on the sun's position. Getting lost in the woods was no big deal—he could always shift, take to the sky, and locate the GTO—but it would cost him time. On the day Waapikoona had led him through these woods she'd walked crow-flies straight. If he could remember nothing, his eagle mind could remember that.

Now he just had to recall how far in they hiked. Memory of his dying arm overwhelmed all other details of that day: demon venom crawling through veins gone black, graying his skin, downward from the bite into numb fingers, upward into his shoulder; the contrast of his living side against the dying side nearly cleaving him in half; and his bewilderment at Waapikoona's unconditional help. There had been no discussion of it. She'd not just led him to a healer, she'd put herself in danger to do it. He stopped, reaching for more from his memory of that day. It had been snowing, tiny flakes that swirled through the air but died before landing. She'd gone ahead, but she'd turned when he spoke her name. Her real name, which had been new to him. Then she'd handed him the mica crystal—he fished it out of his pocket as if replaying his actions on that day—which was when he'd spotted the limestone slanting gently from the earth, hiding a cave under its lip.

He raised the crystal to his eyes and squinted, forcing his vision through the disorienting haze of the crystal until his path ahead and the trees flanking it sharpened into recognition. And there, not more than fifty feet away, lay a shadow against the ground. A few careful steps forward gave him a better view of layered slabs of rock, the color and texture of limestone. Beneath its lowest lip hunkered a darkness so absolute it seemed an impossibility with the sun still lighting the sky.

Nothing was this easy. Something was wrong.

He lowered the mica crystal and found what he expected, a featureless earthen path curving through dense winter woods. No limestone, no shadow, no darkness.

"Well, shit," he said, raking a hand through his hair. Serendipity visited him so infrequently he didn't know how to welcome it. Was that why he suddenly felt so uncomfortable? He schooled his expression, muting all triumph and awe. He swiveled, checking three-hundred-sixty degrees of run-of-the-mill Missouri forest. He felt as if he was now under extreme surveillance.

He looked up, into the blue sky. His kind would have every reason to watch him right now. It was a good reason to raise the crystal and find that opening before a passing raptor got an eyeful of what he was about to do. Using the crystal to locate the opening beneath the limestone, he headed for it and slid his hand along the edge. He pocketed the crystal and could now only sense the stone by feel. At his elbow stood an adolescent tree with a perfect limb for tying his fishing line around. After securing it, he clipped the roll to his backpack so his hands could remain free. Then he reached for the invisible limestone. Walking his hands down, he found the lowest slab and pushed the collection of leaves and branches aside before shoving his boots through. Then it was a seat on the ground, a turn onto his stomach, and a slide in, where gravity took over and yanked him inside.

The fall was shorter than expected, and his knees took the brunt of it. Tomorrow, he'd feel that, especially in his bad leg which had miraculously held him up. Because he didn't want a headache on top of a sore leg, he found the ceiling with his fingers before he stood fully. He tried not to wonder how the darkness could be so complete just inside the opening like he was. Scrambling for the flashlight would only get it dropped and lost, so he did nothing but breathe. Listen. Let his eyes adjust.

Dampness coated him. He felt the weight in his hair, on his jeans, like a frisk from a rival gang. The cold seeped across his hands and face, intimate, searching, testing. He was an intruder of the worst kind. An enemy, invading a space sacred to others. With a guide from this world like the first time, he'd had a ticket through. This time he had no ticket, no map, no welcome. This must be how his ancestors felt … or not. Perhaps they felt entitled, like the whole continent was a prize they'd won.

He was not in The Silent One's cave to win any prize. He was there to stay undetected, to learn a safe way through and out. Later, secure in his familiarity and path of escape, he'd return to bargain with the great demon, to make an appeal. There would be no invasion, no threat, no violence. Just a negotiation between an underworld demon king and an upperworld … whatever he was.

More god than man. It's what Waapikoona had said to him right after he got her home.

He felt anything but godlike right now. If he was a god, he could save his baby niece himself. He wouldn't be standing in this dank void contemplating who he was.

The darkness couldn't be this absolute just inside the entrance. A check above him, and around, offered no speck of light. The tiniest pinpoint would be visible in such pure ocean-bottom darkness. He felt his pack, found his roll of fishing line, gave it a tug. It held. The relief gave him a foothold. He drew the flashlight from his waistband and flipped it on.

For a moment he truly felt as if he were at the bottom of the ocean. The definition of his beam of light appeared as if under water, and it went forever, losing intensity before it found anything to reflect off. He swung it to the side, then up, then behind him. The room had no walls, no edge. If the upperworld entrance to this cave had mimicked the one he and Waapikoona had entered together in search of the healer, it had tricked him. Just inside the door, that resemblance ended. This was not the same cave.

"It's connected. It's all the same cave." He said it just to hear his voice over the thunder of his heartbeat. He couldn't let panic be the only sound. Fear was only helpful to avoid danger; once danger arrived, the fear would have to be put aside.

He shined the light to the floor in front of him and began to walk. The fishing line unspooled behind him. It was a comfort even though there was no point in marking his trail, for he was pretty sure he'd just come through a one-way door. The only way out was to move forward, blindly, into the edgeless obscurity, with hope as his only guide.

Story of my fuckin' life, he thought, helplessly angry. This right here was why he never took the time to plan.

CHAPTER
9

WAAPIKOONA DIDN'T NEED to be reminded why she'd be better off with no attachment to Mick. It was past midnight, hours after he should be home, and he was missing. She couldn't come to terms with why it mattered, other than it simply being odd. The likely explanation had been rejected by Isabel over dinner. Tonight was not Mick's second-job night. First, because it wasn't, and second, because if it was, he'd have come home first to check on her, set out her dinner, or take her up to Old Mae. And she'd refused bedtime so she could sit up watching the door, waiting for him. Waapikoona had left her at it and tackled the dishes.

Hours passed and still no Mick.

"He probably got called in to his second job and had no time to come home first. Let's get you in bed where it's warm."

"I can look for him from the sky."

"Not a chance. Now get up. I'm still too weak to move you."

Waapikoona got Isabel tucked in bed and lay down beside her, but sleep wouldn't find her. Her concern for Mick worried her. She knew she was attached, but she'd never felt it threaded so deeply. Tearing it out—whether she did it, or the universe did—would disembowel her. She'd have to find a way to slowly unravel herself from him. The first step was to end the worry. She had no reason to wonder where he was, none at all.

But it was still very odd.

She extracted herself from Isabel's warm clutch, slipped off the bed into the cold air, and used the wall for support on her way out of the room. With the bedroom door closed behind her, she flipped on a table lamp and collapsed onto the couch. Mick would scold her for overdoing it today, and without him here, she could admit he'd be right. Her nerves flared, raw and aggravated from being upended from much needed rest. She fought the urge to curl into a ball, contain the bone-deep ache. Instead, she stretched against it and grit her teeth against the chilly air and waves of hot-cold that traveled every nerve. Her tolerance for cold had been lost. Now she craved warmth like a snake coming out of hibernation. She found a blanket and wrapped herself to the chin, her knees against her chest.

On the couch she waited. Against the window in the door, the pale moonlight turned to purple, pink, then gold as dawn arrived. Still there was no Mick.

WAAPIKOONA WOKE, GROGGY from a dream of squeaky refrigerator doors and kitchen faucets. Sitting up too fast pinched something in her neck. She paused long enough to realize those dream sounds continued into reality. A chair scraped the floor, a plate settled on the table. Someone was in the kitchen making breakfast. Mick was back. She braced herself and stood.

"Where were—"

Toast popped from the toaster. Someone much shorter than Mick retrieved it and set it on a plate.

"Oh, hi," Isabel said. "Hurry and eat. We're going to find Mighty Eagle and make him come back."

Waapikoona took a moment with that, unable to decide how she felt about Isabel thinking Mick was purposely staying away. Deeply she felt discomfort—and the need to correct her. Mick would never leave. It wasn't her place to defend Mick's character, no matter how much she wanted to.

"Where will we look?"

"The place he fixes cars. Then Grandpop's house, and his other job … " She said *other job* as if it should be capitalized. She stopped buttering toast, tilting her head to think. "But I don't know where that is. We can ask Dougie." She finished buttering and handed Waapikoona the plate.

Waapikoona would need more than toast if she was ever going to recover her strength. It wouldn't make sense to release her attachment to Mick until she could once again hold someone his size against the blade of a knife. It was a good goal, one that made her smile. "How about some eggs?"

"We're not allowed to use the stove when he's not home."

"I think that's a rule for you, not me."

Isabel shrugged, her expression saying, *your funeral.*

And Waapikoona's smile widened, imagining Mick laying down that law in his polite, gentle way. Dread fell through her so unexpectedly she had to grab the back of the kitchen chair. She saw Mick in a puddle of his blood, bound in that tomb while Jeremiah brought a hammer down upon Isabel's delicate white bones. Forced to choose, one or the other. Two to love, two to protect. She could never do it, especially not now, severed from the powers of the underworld.

In her first life she'd loved so many. Mother, father, sisters, and brothers. Aunts, cousins, neighbors, friends. They were all ripped away. The only one she'd been able to hold on to was her sister. She couldn't expect this life to be any different.

It was too dangerous to love them both. Today would be proof of that.

DRIVING AROUND TOWN was easier than walking across Mick's apartment, even with her bandaged hand. And it reminded Waapikoona what it felt like to be free and alive.

"Car fixing place first," Isabel said.

It was hard to imagine how an eight-year-old girl could be so confident when so newly raised from bones. Waapikoona had been reborn with an extra three years of age—but maybe it was those three years that had added more burden, making new life harder to accept.

"Does this one open?" Isabel fumbled with the window control on her door.

"Yes. Press it—there you go."

The window cracked, releasing fresh spring air into the Jeep that provoked goose bumps all over Waapikoona, but she refused to acknowledge it.

She didn't want to spoil the morning, but she had to say something, if only to put to rest a big chunk of grief. "You have a good grasp on this time."

Isabel turned to look at her. "Grasp?"

"You fit well. Better than I did when I came back."

Already cradling her malformed hand against her belly, Isabel hugged it tighter. "The white people here are nice to me."

"Do you remember the ones from before, in the school?"

"I don't want to remember," Isabel said softly. "I decided to forget."

"Did you forget what we did—what I made you do—on the cliff?"

Isabel said nothing, only stared straight ahead.

"I lied to you. I said we could jump off that cliff and soar like eagles. You trusted me, and … " Waapikoona didn't want to pass along a memory that her sister may not have carried into this life. If it lay dormant, it was best to leave it that way. Ignorance could be freeing, could spare a person from torment.

"You didn't lie. I can soar like an eagle now."

The Jeep was losing velocity, and Waapikoona found the pedal her foot had released and brought her speed back up. "I suppose you're right." She couldn't be pardoned so easily. This chain would not break free as easily as The Silent One's. "But I had no idea then. It was a story meant to trick you."

"You didn't trick me. I knew we would fall."

"But you jumped."

"You were with me. And I didn't want to go back—" She scrubbed her face, hanging her head.

Right now, Waapikoona was making her go back, and she had to end this. Not before she said what she'd had in her mind for so long. "I gave you a new name in this life because I couldn't remember your old one. I imagined you floating to the ground like falling leaves, so I named you Pinepakatwi."

"That's what you called me when I saw you again."

"It's what I've been calling you since I came back. I remembered so little."

"You remember our people's words?"

"Some of them. The people who found me taught me a language I think was similar to ours—"

"Our family is dead." The finality in Isabel's voice touched upon a very old pain Waapikoona had long ignored.

"Yes—"

"And never coming back to be with us. Mighty Eagle told me that."

Waapikoona had no reason to be angry with Mick for telling the truth. "He's right."

"I asked him if all our people are dead. He said no, that there are many. Where are they?"

Waapikoona turned into the automotive shop parking lot, scanning the cars for an orange Pontiac. Even though she knew he wouldn't be here, her heart dropped. She pulled into a spot. They needed to talk about where else they were going. The U-Fill was okay. But she wasn't feeling right about paying a visit to Mick's grieving sister and her kids. Isabel had turned her face toward her, waiting for an answer.

"Mick wasn't talking about our people. He meant all Native people, from all the Nations. And yes, there are many."

"What happened to our people?"

"It's hard to know. We were forced to move by the white man. Some tribes moved together. I think our people died out or merged with the ones who live in Oklahoma now, but I can't be sure. That's where I lived until … " Joining up with Jeremiah, abandoning the foster parents who cared about her, pledging herself to a great underworld demon, killing a ton of people. "Until I came here."

"I know Oklahoma. Mick taught me that one."

"Well, it looks like Mick isn't here." Waapikoona pointed out the window. "No orange car."

Isabel released her seat belt. "We have to go talk to the white man with the white hair and glasses."

"You've been inside?"

"Uh-huh." Isabel opened her door and hopped out.

Waapikoona killed the engine and joined Isabel who took quick hold of her unbandaged hand as if suddenly afraid. Isabel's steps were impatient, slowed by Waapikoona's own careful ones. It was a long walk on pavement with nothing to hold onto but a little girl's hand. Her legs felt weak and heavy, like they'd both fallen asleep. She locked her eyes on the bright entrance of the auto shop and dragged herself there.

Inside, the old man who worked the counter was standing at the window that looked out into the shop, one hand over his mouth. Waapikoona headed for the counter, just to have something to lean on. The man gave no response, just kept his back to her, statue-still.

"Hello," Waapikoona said.

He started, spinning around quickly. "Sorry, didn't hear you come in." His gaze dropped. "Oh, hi there, Isabel." When he returned his attention to Waapikoona, something had changed. A series of emotions crossed his face—recognition, relief, then a stiff hold as if bracing for some hard news.

"Is Mick here?" Waapikoona said.

"He ain't. Didn't show this morning. Very unlike him. I suppose that means you don't know where he's at?"

"He didn't come home last night."

"Not at all?"

Waapikoona shook her head.

"Any other guy and it wouldn't worry me. But Mick hasn't missed a day—hell, without callin' in? Never. I rang his phone a dozen times already and it just goes to voice-mail."

"We have a few more places to look." It was a stretch, but she had nothing else to say.

"With what's been on the news … well, to be honest, I didn't believe the hype. Not till today. If you find him, would you mind lettin' me know?" He took a business card off the counter and handed it to her.

A weight settled in Waapikoona's stomach, weakening her already feeble knees. To take over the upperworld, The Silent One would need to exterminate all Thunder-Beings. If he succeeded, it wasn't a matter of *if* Mick would die. It was a matter of when. It could be now.

She slipped the business card into her back pocket and nudged Isabel toward the door. When she found Mick, she'd make him call the old man because he'd be alive and per-fectly able to do it himself. She'd kick herself for getting so worked up about what was sure to be nothing at all, and she'd sock him in the stomach for making the old man worry.

Her hand found stability on Isabel's shoulder, and the girl took the hint and slowed her stride. Suddenly light-headed, Waapikoona focused her breathing and swallowed a tremor of panic. She'd walked the steps in there, she could walk the same back. There would be no collapsing in this shop or the parking lot outside, where police and paramedics would be called. The core of her weakness had been found in that muddy grave, when she'd given herself to imaginings because all her fight was gone. It didn't matter how she was sprung from that place. She was no longer there. Its grip had been broken. Right now, her boots crossed pavement. They did not sink into earth determined to swallow her. She'd been forced into that grave. She didn't belong there, no matter how much it felt like she should.

The Jeep's door handle was a mercy, a crutch. She pulled the door open and hauled herself into the seat, wondering if this hopeless frailty was the stain of Death's hand upon her and if she'd ever be clean. She didn't start the engine. She needed to catch her breath and think.

"Grandpop's house next," Isabel said.

That grieving household did not need more bad news. "We can drive by and check for his car. But we only stop if it's there."

"Grandpop might know something. Or Dougie."

"If his car isn't there, he's not there. And we're not going to bother them."

"We have to ask about his other job."

Waapikoona started the engine. "I already know where that is."

Chapter 10

As Waapikoona drove, she watched the shoulder and the woods for signs of a car that had run off the road. It was more likely she'd find Mick crashed against a tree after falling asleep at the wheel than at his U-Fill gas station job in the daytime. At the turn-in that led to Mick's father's house, she pulled to the side so she and Isabel could peer down the driveway and found no orange Pontiac, just as she expected. At the U-Fill, she circled the fuel pumps then the quick shop just to make sure his car wasn't in back. Isabel insisted they go inside, but Waapikoona couldn't trust her legs to carry her.

"I'll pull up close to the front. We'll see if we can see who's in there."

She rolled past the glass wall. Isabel yanked her seat belt off and kneeled on her seat for a better view past the stacked cases of soda and posters in the windows. There was a man behind the counter—not Mick. Isabel sat back down and crossed her arms, sulking.

Exhaustion doubled the weight of Waapikoona's arms as she turned the Jeep around. She had to get home and rest before she fell asleep at the wheel and drove the two of them into a tree. This day was over, unless …

"Would you recognize his car, if you saw it from the sky?"

Isabel's tightly crossed arms loosened. She looked over, pensive.

"There aren't a lot of cars the color of his."

"My bird won't see the same colors. It's … all different."

"It's worth a try, right?"

"If I didn't see his car, I might see his eagle."

Waapikoona turned the Jeep out of the U-Fill lot and accelerated onto the road. "We'll go home first. And I don't want you flying too far—"

"You sound like our mom."

Such a simple statement, provoking a deeply complicated feeling. She focused on the road ahead, the shadows like crooked fingers across it, now dappled by the heavier screen of a group of evergreens blocking the late morning sunlight. "I don't mean to."

"It's stupid."

"To want to keep you safe?"

"You're not her."

"I know that."

"You're just my sister."

Not anymore. She had to be more than that, whether Isabel liked it or not. And she wasn't going to argue about it, just like their real mother would have never entered an argument about her own rules.

"Let's see what we can find to eat at home."

Every time she said it, she didn't mean to call it *home,* but it was always too late to catch.

At the entrance to the driveway, Waapikoona took a breath to keep herself from holding it. As far-fetched as it was, she couldn't resist the expectation of seeing that orange Pontiac. The feeling didn't abate until they'd rounded the turn and made it far enough to see Mick's empty parking spot. Pulling into the space felt too much like a bad omen, so she parked beside it.

The apartment felt more than empty. It was sad and still, as if missing its soul. As if … dead. This is what it would feel like for Mick to be dead.

"Hungry?" Waapikoona asked her sister, just to fill the void with sound. "You sit. Find something to watch on TV." She located the remote and powered on the TV, chilled to the core.

On her way to the kitchen she plucked one of Mick's jackets from the clean laundry basket and pulled it over her own, hood raised. She knew it wouldn't warm the worry out of her, but at least it would warm her blood.

AT DUSK, SHE followed her sister outside and watched her turn from girl to raptor and ascend into the darkening sky. As soon as she lost the sight of the moving wings, she lost the bird entirely. The porch light flipped on above her, and she stepped out from under the overhang to find the old woman waiting for her. Isabel would be gone for a while. She may as well spend the time with Old Mae and her witchcraft.

She made it up the porch steps on her own, only to be half-tripped by Eros once she crossed the threshold into the house. He was so desperate to rub her legs she had to stop and let him do it before she could continue inside. Old Mae scolded him as she led the way down the hall to the bathroom where the tub was already filling by the light of several candles. Herbs floated on the water, creating a grassy scent in the room. Old Mae sprinkled salt over the water as Waapikoona undressed. She was shivering before she was finished, cold feet against even colder tile.

Old Mae laid a soft hand on her wrist, gently turning her arm to inspect the inflamed skin running from wrist to shoulder. "I see why Mickey was sore with me. You tell 'im he oughta be sore with the one who got you into this mess."

"That would be me."

"Good people don't get mixed up in bad stuff without someone to browbeat them into it."

Waapikoona had nothing to say to that.

"I'll put my money on someone who sees a young woman in need of a friend and sees her for a sucker instead."

"I guess I'm a sucker then."

"We all are at some point, especially when we're young. That don't give anyone the right to take advantage. Now, all you need is a good soak this time. I think my runes are still doin' their thing."

"I've been trying not to scratch."

Old Mae released her wrist and shuffled over to an antique cabinet. "Let's put in some oatmeal to help with that."

Waapikoona sat on the edge of the tub and swiveled her legs into the water. The heat went straight through her. She wouldn't be able to stand it unless she eased into it slowly. Eros jumped up beside her, four paws landing perfectly on the porcelain edge. She envied his confidence, his balance. She used to have that. Someday she would find it again.

"Mick is missing." She hadn't prepared for this conversation with the old woman. She shouldn't have said it.

Old Mae set a cup of powder on the ledge. "Here's your oatmeal. Sprinkle this in after you've soaked for ten minutes."

Waapikoona wasn't sure if she should repeat what she'd said. The running faucet could have covered her voice enough for old ears to not hear. It was also possible those old ears had chosen to ignore it. And now, as Old Mae reached and the faucet squeaked off, Waapikoona wondered if she'd even voiced it aloud. Those three words had been on repeat in her mind with every fraction of the earth's turn. Perhaps they'd just gotten strong enough to feel like speech.

"Holler if you need me," Old Mae said, pulling the door closed until the width of a cat's body remained.

Waapikoona ripped the bandage off her hand and slid into the water until it reached her chin, the shock of the heat a welcome diversion.

With her eyes closed she imagined a map of the roads she and Isabel had searched that day, from Mick's apartment to his father's house, the auto shop, the U-Fill. Tomorrow they'd drive the roads they hadn't taken. They'd look around the grocery store and Mick's sister's. Even the cemetery and the tomb needed to be searched. The radius of Mick's daily life was a small dot on the enormity of this country. The Jeep would make it quick work.

Eros began to purr. She opened her eyes and found him gazing at her. He inched forward, dipping his head, a study of perfect balance.

"Yeah, I know," she said to him. "I could always call Soto." She had no phone. But she was sure Old Mae would let her use hers.

She would have to be beyond desperate to ask Soto for help finding Mick.

TWO WEEKS LATER, desperation attached itself and wouldn't let go. She'd checked every road, every store, the diner, the bar—even behind the bar, where she'd executed the scumbag Mick couldn't kill himself. The cemetery, the tomb, the abandoned gravel lot where she and Mick had joined—underworld and upperworld—and turned a whole mob of guys into feed for her Helpers.

She'd consoled Mick's sister on the steps of his apartment, unable to give a solid reason why Kari shouldn't call the police. The sheriff and a deputy had come to speak with Old Mae who told them, no, they could not take a look in Mick's apartment or search her land. She stopped at the auto shop several times to open the door to give Virgil a headshake and receive one in return.

Now it was dusk again, fifteen days deeper into spring since she'd last seen Mick. Cool night air circled the day's airy warmth, pushing it upward toward Isabel's falcon as she climbed the sky and disappeared. Tonight could be the night she found Mick's eagle.

Tonight could be the night she found his corpse.

This is what I did to him when I left. No, it wasn't, and she wasn't sure why she kept thinking it. Her departure had been known. Expected. Witnessed by Mick, both human and eagle. Because of that, her absence was understood. *His* absence made no sense.

That's probably what he thought about mine.

"Stop it," she said aloud.

Now with Isabel busy on the hunt, Waapikoona took the steps up to Old Mae's front door where she tapped to signal she was here for her bath—but not until she made a phone call. She let herself in, but instead of heading for the bathroom, she stopped in the kitchen and slid the paper Soto had left for her in that motel room out of her back pocket. "May I use your phone?"

"There's an extension in the front room," Old Mae answered.

Waapikoona turned around and tripped over a shadow on the floor—Eros, who let out a loud bleat and ran ahead to lead her where she needed to go. The front room was dark behind heavy curtains over the large front windows. She felt around on the wall for a switch before she saw a table lamp at hip height and turned it on, illuminating an old desk phone. Its cord limited her to the armchair beside it. She sat and punched in the number.

It went to voicemail. No one answered unfamiliar numbers anymore. She'd just have to annoy him until he did. After three more times, she got a brusque, "Who is this?"

"Sarah Clarke. I need your help."

"You do?" It was both gloating and hopeful.

"Mick has been missing for over two weeks."

"What?"

"Mick has been—"

"*Sí, sí, entiendo*. It's just … isn't that unusual for him?"

"Yes. So I need you to—"

"You should have called me sooner. I'm not in the States. I can fly up, but it'll take me … " A woman's voice spoke rapidly in the background. "Hold on a minute while I consult my manager."

A rapid-fire argument in Spanish carried through the phone line, even though it seemed Soto had muffled the phone. Waapikoona couldn't catch a word, but from the tone it sounded like Soto was backing down. He returned with a long sigh into the microphone.

"I've been reminded we can't spare any time right now, even for you."

"For Mick."

"You and Mick."

"I wouldn't be calling if I wasn't desperate."

He sighed again. "I get that. But I can't fly up for at least three days. Maybe two." He paused, as if reconsidering. "You have a lot of resources I don't. You sure you've exhausted them all?"

She didn't want to tell him she'd been severed from The Silent One if he didn't already know. Her connection to the underworld, along with her partnership with Mick, made her useful to Soto. Missing one piece of that might give him reason not to help her at all, not now or ever again.

Since she had no answer for that, she hung up the phone and looked at Eros, watchful and still except for the flicking tip of his tail as steady as the second hand of a clock. A countdown hounded her, gaining intensity with each day. Now she felt it hanging right over her head.

In her bath, she thought again about what Soto had said. Even without The Silent One's influence, she remained tied to the realm of the dead. Unquiet spirits begged her to be liaison between worlds. A nuisance, mostly … but could she appeal to them for once? Was she in any position to? Her Helpers still took her commands. And her best resource was already at work and would soon be home from her nightly search from the sky. As soon as Isabel landed, Waapikoona would look into her face and judge her level of weariness. Tonight, she would be traveling to the cemetery—again— and this time, she would seek out the unquiet to ask a favor, and she didn't want to go alone.

After her bath, Waapikoona sat on the old woman's front steps to wait for her sister's return. The mild night rested before her, the waxing crescent moon high and bright. Months ago, she'd be enjoying the crisp breeze, but tonight she did her best to endure it. Yes, spring hadn't yet arrived. Yes, her hair was still damp from her bath. That alone shouldn't create such an arctic shiver. She could go inside Mick's apartment for his fleece-lined flannel that she'd decided might have to be hers since she'd been wearing it every day in his absence—but that would break her battle of wills against her new fragile self. Regaining her stamina to the elements would never be achieved if she didn't toss away her crutches.

She played with the edge of her new bandage on her hand. The skin had sealed, but the scar still looked fresh, as if threatening to tear open all over again. It would be concerning if she didn't have so much more on her mind—like why she wasn't capitalizing on this opportunity to pack Isabel into the Jeep and head west, away from the complications of Mick.

This time she'd leave a note. A destination, a number. Some way for him to find her again should he need to. Should he not be so angry she'd broken her word. Should he come back at all. These thoughts felt like they were from her, but not of her. Old thoughts hanging on, the death song of the old Waapikoona. The one who thought she could meet someone like Mick and walk away from him. Now she feared—especially now, with him missing, possibly dead— she couldn't walk the circle of time without him.

"It's too late," she whispered. He'd been missing too long. Hammond was dead but there were too many others who could want Mick's death. The Silent One had never commanded a hunt of Thunder-Beings, but she knew it to be inevitable once his army grew. Since she was cut off, she'd never know when that call was made.

Isabel needed to stop her nightly search. It was too dangerous now, and it was futile. Mick was gone, probably dead. There was nothing for her to do.

Mick never gave up on me. If he had, she'd be decomposing in a muddy grave. Whatever had driven him to find her, she didn't have it. She was no Mick.

A shadow crossed over the moon, followed by another. Waapikoona stood, resting a hand on the railing for support. Silent black sky widened over her as if she hadn't noticed its breadth before. A sound beat down, more of a feeling than a noise. A colossal beat of air, a flap of giant wings. She ducked nearly too late as something came at her, tearing her cheek. A falcon cried—she knew it to be Isabel—and another larger voice screamed in response. The sound curled through Waapikoona. This wasn't friendly. It was a battle.

Waapikoona reached for her flint knife—of course it was missing. She wore Mick's cotton pants right now, and hadn't armed herself since she'd woken in his bed. How could she be so careless to ever be unarmed? Bending to avoid another set of talons, she hopped down the remaining stairs and threw herself under the overhang to the apartment door. Chaos continued in the air beside the house.

"Isabel!" She hoped the bird would understand her signal. When she opened this door, she only wanted one creature to enter beside her. "Now!"

She flung open the door. Wind rushed against her; feathers brushed her arm. She jumped inside, falling against the door frame, the handle out of reach. As her toe hooked the edge of the door, she spotted a shape falling out of the sky toward her. An impossible wingspan, sharp curved talons, a yellow eye trained right on her own. She kicked, slamming the door as a shriek outside broke the night.

Isabel had made it inside. She couldn't have mistaken that.

"Where are you?" Waapikoona pried herself from the floor and got to her feet. Isabel crouched beside the couch, holding onto the leg of the end table. She watched the door as if something was about to burst through.

"We're okay. Let me get you a blanket." She jerked a quilt off the couch and wrapped it around the little girl, helping her to stand. Her dry, rapid breath was that of a girl who'd just run for her life.

There was a moment of relief, of gratitude, of calm. But only a moment. It took a few beats of Waapikoona's heart to understand the danger Isabel had been in, and was still in, with those birds outside. As Isabel had hunted for Mick, these birds must have hunted her—and chased her all the way home.

A current ran through Waapikoona. No one threatened her sister and lived. Not in this life.

She traded Mick's flip flops for her cowboy boots and snatched her flint knife from beneath the couch cushion. As she went through the door, she picked up the baseball bat Mick had leaned against the wall. Its handle settled against her bandaged palm in a perfect reminder of how far she could go. Just as she had caught her enemy's knife by the blade not long ago, she'd catch these birds by the talons. She'd hold them against the tip of her flint and demand they turn human so she could properly look them in the eye while she gutted them.

The door slammed shut behind her. She took the steps up into the yard, losing the cover of the overhang. The sky yawned above. The moon had vanished behind clouds pushed in on wind that had since gone dead. Silence had never felt so perilous. Against its backdrop, her own breathing sounded hysterical. She took a deep breath and let the exhale slowly seep through her lips.

"Face me." No more than a whisper, but they would hear it. If Thunder-Beings didn't understand the words, they would certainly recognize her intention. "You want us, come get us."

She'd fought in worse condition, for lesser reasons, and if she didn't exterminate these Thunder-Beings, they would come back. For the first time since waking in Mick's bed, she felt right again—unforgiving and alive. Her duty was clear, and she felt her back straighten and her knife at one with her hand. This fight is what she lived for, and she finally remembered how it felt to be strong. To know her way. To strike at the right time. There was no reason to back down.

Except now there was. Isabel waited inside, reliant on Waapikoona to stay alive. Recklessness had no home in Waapikoona's life any more. She had to shift things around, make room for caution, responsibility, sacrifice. For being not just a sister but a mother, a guardian, a teacher. She was tethered to a home, to stability and warmth and safety. And if she could find a way to become this, perhaps she could find a way to keep Mick—if he still lived.

Too long she'd been idle, repressed by infirmity as disaster loomed.

Next time, she thought to the wide, waiting sky and the Thunder-Beings that had disappeared as quickly as they'd arrived but were sure to return. Tonight, she had a visit to pay and a favor to call in—and her own Thunder-Being to find.

IT WAS STRANGE entering the cemetery via the road enclosed in the Jeep rather than on foot. So strange, she decided to back into the grass by the crumbling stone pillars and leave the wheels there at the entrance. Isabel hopped out and ran for her hand to grip tight. The girl's eyes hadn't stopped watching the sky since they'd left Mick's apartment.

"We're fine here, Thunder-Beings won't attack with so many witnesses."

And now it wasn't just Soto who'd have eyes on Mick's apartment. Isabel had been followed. She would never be safe there.

A faint curve of moonlight hid behind lazy clouds. They walked hand in hand up the dirt path she'd tread so many times alone. Waapikoona relied on Isabel's superior night eyes since she'd seemed to lose hers after The Silent One cast her away. She didn't want to think about what work her sister could be doing for him or how deeply she was bound. What could he possibly ask of an underworld Thunder-Being?

The spirits, so familiar before, were slow to recognize Waapikoona. A few hung close to the first row of tilting gravestones. Weathered by time, they'd been abandoned by the current century so their cracks remained unrepaired. Left alone so long, many of their inhabitants wandered, unremembered and unquiet and seeking Waapikoona's attention since she seemed to be the only one who noticed them. Now they seemed hesitant, even shy, just as they had the first time she'd set foot here. She knew their memories were forever, and even though they should know her, the Jeep and Isabel had probably thrown them off. They were naturally curious, desperate for any kind of attention from the living—or the once-dead who had recovered their bones for a second shot at life. *Or a third.* And the thought gave Waapikoona added strength in her step, because it was Mick who'd granted her that third chance, and now it was her turn to help him.

Beyond the graves in darkest shadow stood the tomb where she'd cooked and slept while she worked for The Silent One. The sacred space where Mick had kissed her and she'd kissed him back. Where she'd failed to stop an evil man from crushing Isabel's hand bones that now left her crippled today. Where Mick had chosen to die, so the rest of Isabel could be spared.

"Please come close," Waapikoona called out. "I need to speak to you all."

At the sound of her voice, the wavering forms seemed to straighten. A hum carried from one to the next, and they came from all edges of the darkness to gather in front of her and lend new dimension to the air. The waver of light through gentle water, gliding along earth, each spirit independent of the other but more understandable as a collected group.

"The man who was here with me, do you remember?"

As one they shrank away, a recoil of disgust and fear dimming their forms so they nearly faded into the night. She felt the burden of race upon her. This was a Christian cemetery, inhabited by white corpses and their unquiet spirits. She hated bringing race into this, especially with Isabel present, but it was the easiest way to distinguish between Jeremiah and Mick.

"Not the one who started violence here. The other one, the white man. The one who bled into the stone and earth. The man who's also the eagle."

Her audience returned, upright and brightened almost to the point of creating their own light.

"They know him," Isabel whispered, like she was witnessing a dream turn real.

"He's lost somewhere," Waapikoona told the assembly. "We're not sure if he's with us or with you. I'll offer you my ear tonight if you find him and send him home."

All these forgotten spirits ever wanted was for her to listen. So until the sun's rays tinged the horizon pink, that's what she and Isabel did.

Chapter 11

Mick's legs no longer felt attached to his body. Even though he knew he was moving forward, he wasn't aware of the bodily process that made that happen. He'd been in the belly of the cave for at least an hour, circling the same set of caverns, reencountering his own taut fishing line so many times he was ready to snip the thing and call it a failure. The dampness had saturated him, even his feet were soaked from wading through six inches of slow-moving water that crossed his path more than once.

It was time to find the exit. It had been time for a while. As long as he didn't commit to the idea of full-on panic, he could hold it off.

He checked his phone—again—only to be reminded that the clock had frozen on the same time it had been the last time he'd checked. Or had it? With all the circles and monotony, he wasn't sure of anything anymore. Except for one thing: he was quite sure he was lost and had been since he'd dropped into this cave.

Time had ceased to exist, along with his dry throat and grumbling, empty stomach. The coldness and uniformity had numbed him so much he couldn't even hear his boots on the stone floor anymore—or could he? A trickle of water to his right, shift of his pack against his back—but that couldn't be, because he no longer had his pack. And that fishing line connected to him? Also gone. His mind certainly hadn't numbed because he could remember everything from his life. Pop's hand on his shoulder, Doug and Janie giggling into their cereal bowls. Summer wind catching in his hair as he steered the GTO into that hairpin turn behind Bryson's farm. Andy tossing a tire to him at Virgil's shop. The register at the grocery store ringing up so high he had to look over his stuff and decide what to put back. Helen's cold body, dirt falling against a white sheet. And Waapikoona. God, Waapikoona. He remembered so much about her, it hurt. He was all mind now, all memory. His body was drifting; time had forsaken him.

This must be what it felt like to be an unquiet spirit.

He ducked through an opening he was sure he'd dragged his fingers along fifteen other times and saw them.

Speak of the devil. He wasn't sure if it was thought or words. That was how disassembled he'd become.

Even though they stood still and upright like the human beings they once were, their shapes wavered slightly as if he was viewing them in the reflection of wind-rippled water. His brain expected to see the characteristics that would make them living humans—eyes, mouth, shoulders—but these features were imagined. Filled in by his brain because if he focused, it all went away. He saw his mother like this once, and he'd made a desperate bargain to return her to the peace of her grave. Recently? Or a long time ago? He couldn't remember.

He passed his flashlight across the group. Where the beam hit, the hazy wavering shapes disappeared, leaving only the shiny dark cave wall beyond. Hallucination, then. Not a good sign. He turned, shining his light toward his intended path—but there was nothing in his hand, no beam of light, only darkness.

Panic, he told himself. *Curse. Scream. Now is the time to freak out.* Instead, he felt nothing.

And patting his pockets, his belt, his back proved that he had nothing on him, and now that he thought about it, he'd had nothing for a long time. His flashlight, backpack, and phone were all memories, and he wasn't even sure how distant. Five minutes, five years, it was all the same. He was standing alone in the unending dark forever.

I'm more god than man. That's what she said once. He could shift into eagle, gain better vision, call for The Silent One, demand to be led out of here.

He couldn't. All that was lost. He'd chosen to go alone, and this is where his world ended.

He felt for the wall so he could slide down it, rest his back. It seemed like the right thing to do even if he couldn't sense his back needed rest. The darkness took on dimension, and he could see them again, their wavering shapes, their steady persistence gathered before him as if waiting for him to do something.

Die and join them in death? Or was he already there?

Already standing and unaware of the movement that got him there, he took a step toward them. A lodestar in the hole of black, they were the only thing for his eyes to focus on. Another step brought him closer but them farther away. He moved forward with purpose now, numbly irritated by the game. His steps went on, a few feet or forever, until his boot met something that softly gave, and he reached to pick it up. Why he'd leave his backpack so far away—or so close—was beyond him. He swung it to his back and followed the spirits as if towed by an invisible rope until an arc of light pulsed into his cave-blinded eyes, pounding into his skull.

So death, then. People spoke of walking into the light. It must be true.

There would be no walking toward it until he could open his eyes and straighten from the crouch he found himself in, braced to withstand that skull splitting brightness. As the pounding eased, he slitted his eyelids, recoiling from a new type of percussion. Now it wasn't just in his head but also on his face. Its blanketing warmth awoke a deep-seated memory of skin touched by sunlight. He thought of his family, his home. Something to fight for, giving meaning to his life, and life to his meaning. Like Waapikoona.

Standing, he reached into the warmth. The toe of his boot caught an unexpected ledge and he pitched forward, catching himself on a cold wall with both palms. Above him, that spill of light filled the ceiling, brightness shooting into the dark. Dust motes swarmed. A puff of dry air crossed his face, and he saw movement against the edge of the light. A flutter of dead leaves, a dance of shadow and sun. The upperworld. The exit.

He gripped the top of the wall and felt earth crumble against his fingertips. Soon he could be back on earth, instead of inside it. All he had to do was find the strength to pull himself up.

BEHIND THE WHEEL of the GTO, he tried to affirm it wasn't a hallucination. He knew the feel of this seat, the push of power as he pressed foot upon pedal. He could smell the cherry candy he kept in the cupholder for the kids. That cave had been the hallucination, not this. To ground himself he tried to calculate what time it could be. The car had come to him missing its stereo head unit, so there was no help from a digital clock. Dusk had arrived during his hike back to the car, which gave him an idea of the hour, but being in that cave had mixed up his sense of time so thoroughly he wasn't even sure it was still the same day. The car battery wasn't dead, so it hadn't sat for too long. There was no ticket on the windshield or tow notice from the sheriff, but there was plenty of dust—probably pollen at this time of year—and a tree branch he'd had to remove from the windshield, which could have fallen five minutes after he parked and walked away. His phone was dead, but that meant nothing. He didn't remember the battery level when he'd entered the cave.

So the dark had played with him, and he'd lost his mind a little. But now that he'd found himself again, he could put it all together. He hadn't had time to go very far into that cave if the walk to the exit was so quick. The water bottles in his backpack were full. If he'd been in there for long without water, he'd be dead. What day had he come out here? Monday. He'd left work and come straight here. That meant it was still Monday, and he'd be home in time to strip out of these soggy clothes and make dinner.

OLD MAE'S HOUSE was strangely bright, like she'd turned on all the lights in the house to ward off the dark night. Even the porch light was on and the floods out back. He parked beside the Jeep and decided he was too tired and disoriented to unload the car. Losing the soggy clothes would be first priority, followed quickly by a hot shower.

He could hear the noisy television as he unlocked the door. Waapikoona would wonder why he was coming home from work soaked to the bone, and he had no answer other than the truth. As he turned the knob, he weighed telling her. It might be best to say nothing. If she took issue with him going into The Silent One's cave, he had no energy for that conversation. He was completely out of gas.

The door swung in. He closed it behind him and flipped the deadbolt. The TV lit the area by the couch with flashes of color. Beyond it, in the steady warm glow of the kitchen, Waapikoona paused in her gathering of dishes from the table to look at him.

"Ya'll eat without me?" he asked.

She dropped the stack of plates and utensils onto the table so hard they clattered.

He felt his heart squeeze, as if he was missing something. A pang of amnesia overcame him—just the feeling itself with no basis because there was nothing to forget. Unless— had he forgotten something? Had she asked him to run an errand, bring something home, do something he'd completely lost sight of?

Her eyes held an intensity he'd never seen. Not agitated but stunned, taking him in like she'd never seen him enter this apartment before. She crossed the room straight toward him, too fast for him to grab a weapon because he knew without a doubt she was coming for him. Then she was on him, but instead of a strike he got an embrace. Arms tight around his neck, her warm cheek crushing his chilled one. She breathed hard against him, her heart beating heavy and frantic.

"Hell," he said. Just when he thought he had her figured out, she was giving him a greeting like this. "I'd hug you back if I knew who you were."

"Do it," she whispered.

He wrapped his arms around her and held, her warmth puddling against his wet clothes. He felt the fervor of her heart and breathing die down, loosening her frame. Her death grip on him slackened, turned affectionate instead of suffocating, and he turned his face and set his lips against her hair. Being underground in that damp unmoving air must have reset his brain and turned these everyday scents overpowering. Clean skin, fresh soap mixed with something herbal, the fabric softener in her shirt—which was *his* hoodie, now that he thought about it. When he'd walked through the door, he'd been cold and exhausted, but now he was waking up.

She tilted her head, allowing him room to kiss her cheekbone—and he stopped, because against his lips her skin felt soft and fleshy. Normal, not sharp like it should be. Come to think of it, her walk across the room had been strong and solid, more like the old Waapikoona than the new damaged one. In the span of a day she had gained noticeable health, and he had to pull away and verify it with his eyes.

"How—"

She looked at him so fiercely he decided to shut up.

"Mick." It came out on a heavy exhale, almost a growl. A scolding so vicious it wasn't even his name anymore.

Letting her go so he could put a space between them seemed like the right thing to do. "Did I miss somethin'?"

"Seventeen days."

"What?"

"Where were you?"

"At work. Then I had to—"

"At what job, Mick?"

He rubbed a hand over his bristly jaw, unsure where this was going.

"Human job, or Thunder-Being job?" she prompted.

"I was at Virgil's most of the day—"

Her eyes set harder on his. "I've been checking in with Virgil, and the last time you were there was over two weeks ago."

It was her idea—no, her demand—to have no domestic ties to each other, and she was going to check up on him like this? Sounded like he'd somehow landed in a relationship with all the cons and none of the pros. Except for that greeting—what the hell had that even been? And what was she saying about two weeks?

"I've looked for you every day—"

"What do you mean, every day?"

"And Isabel. You put her in danger, Mick."

"Where's she at?"

"Upstairs with Old Mae. She's gone out searching every night."

His hand went to his phone in his pocket. He took it to the kitchen counter, plugged it in, and waited for the screen to light up.

"I can't fight the other Thunder-Beings like I used to. And without you here—"

He held up a hand. With her talking, he couldn't understand what he was seeing. The phone had started up, and not only was the date way off, but he had so many missed calls and unread texts, going back days—weeks?—from everyone. Kari, Pop, Virgil, Amanda, his boss at the U-Fill. Now the email notifications were popping in. Available statements, missed payments ... if what Waapikoona said was true, he'd not only have overdue bills but he'd be out two weeks of wages for both his jobs. Oh god, he'd been a no-show for both his jobs.

"I went into that cave, the one you and I—" He turned so he could see her confirm the idea that was ricocheting around inside him. What she'd said when they first traveled through that cave. What he'd forgotten.

"You went in there alone?"

The wet clothes already had him on the verge of a tremble, and he succumbed to it, feeling the quake weaken his bad leg. Over two weeks away from work. From Pop, Kari, and the kids, right after he buried the baby. From Isabel who'd grown to trust he'd be there. From Waapikoona as she recovered.

"Mick, I told you it's not safe to go in there without an underworld guide. Time gets mixed up—"

The hit of adrenaline he'd gotten from watching his phone start up had died, leaving a weary anger in its place. He didn't care what she'd told him about that godforsaken cave. He had to go in there to help his baby niece. He wasn't going to sit here and get scolded for doing what he had to do.

"Well, I'm back," he bit out. There would be no apologizing, not right now when he had other things to do, like come up with a believable way to explain ditching both his jobs with no notice. A lie. He was going to have to lie to everyone.

After a heavy silence, she matched his tone. "You need to call your sister."

"I figured that." He needed to get out of these clothes first and into the white noise of the shower to help him think.

CHAPTER
12

IN THE SHOWER Mick rehearsed every possible conversation with Kari and realized a vague explanation would do more harm than good. He needed to see her with Pop present, to take advantage of the old man's inexplicable understanding of Mick's purpose. Mick would apologize, hear Kari out, and let Pop settle her down. Pop had done it once when Mick was tongue-tied about how he'd bring the baby back to life, and Mick was sure he'd be there to help him out again.

"Coward," Mick muttered to himself as he shoved his stiff leg into clean jeans.

His request for Kari to simply trust him felt more like a trick than anything.

When he emerged from the bedroom, Isabel clung to his arm. Having a child attached to him was so normal he didn't think anything of it—until he realized which child it was. Isabel wasn't a hugger, at least not with him. So his absence had meant something and would mean something again when Waapikoona decided it was time for them to pack up and move on. He couldn't dive into that right now. There was another difficult idea he'd wrestled in the shower—he'd have to speak to Isabel later. Privately. Without Waapikoona.

He peeled her off so he could squat to her level. It killed his leg, but he was beyond caring. "Sorry I was gone."

"You didn't tell me."

"I know. I would've, if I knew I'd be so long."

She stared him straight in the eye. If she wasn't so small, he'd be taking a step back. She lunged so fast he could do nothing but absorb the blow—another attack turned embrace that he couldn't have expected. This girl had never hugged him like this, and it choked him up so much he wasn't sure if could find his voice. "Sorry," he managed.

"If you leave again, I'm not talking to you any more ever."

The girl's silent treatment was infallible. Not long ago he'd been convinced she had no knowledge of English whatsoever. "I believe that."

She let him go and hopped to the couch where she burrowed under a bundle of blankets. Waapikoona was nowhere in sight. He found a jacket, deciding if the Jeep was missing outside he'd take Isabel up to Old Mae until he returned from a visit to his sister.

Old Mae was going to tear him in half.

Floodlight created an unfamiliar sight outside. Now he remembered Old Mae had forbid him from replacing the bulbs that lit the side yard as they burned out, in the spirit of 'letting night be night,' and from the day that last bulb ticked and went out, the night was exactly what he saw outside his apartment, its only changes painted by the seasons and phase of the moon. Those variations had become normal, unlike this directed beam of harsh light. He'd have to find out what changed her mind, and who replaced those bulbs.

The woman had no business on a ladder at her age, and Waapikoona—

He spotted her at that moment, a dark shadow in the middle distance just outside the blanket of light. Tall and motionless, feet planted apart as if facing a foe. Her ability to keep so lifelessly still placed her securely as a creature of the night. She'd lost that effect after he dragged her from that grave. While she recuperated, she seemed more human than ever. Now he saw her how she really was, how she had been, how she'd always be. It put a warning tingle on his skin, a flash of cold in his veins. But when those impulses reached his head, they transformed from fight and fear to excitement and passion, to the feel of her weight against him, the smell of her, the taste. If being with her meant grappling with his eagle every moment of his day, he would welcome that fight.

"I'm headin' over to Pop's for a bit—"

A shadow lurched from the corner of the house, flitting into the floodlight's beam for a fraction of a second before all went still. Mick grabbed his own face at the temples, covering his eyes against the rush that screamed through his head. No eagle tonight, for god's sake. His eagle needed to back off.

"Just so you know, Isabel's in there by herself." It sounded raspy, like he was on edge, but vocalizing human words would keep him from taking flight and hunting whatever scurried in the shadows.

Waapikoona made no move that she'd heard him. If she was still mad, that was all right with him. He had bigger fish to fry.

"I got my phone with me." He waited for some kind of acknowledgment.

Her body language—or lack of—wasn't abnormal for her, so there was no reason to walk out there and get a look at her face. Her sister had to have learned that extraordinary silent treatment from someone, and it was nothing to Mick but something to shrug at. He had no room in his life for this kind of game.

But walking out there to her side was what he found himself doing. To his surprise, her eyes were closed, her face solemn as if in prayer. He felt like a jerk for calling out like that, but how was he supposed to know she was locked in some kind of meditation? This was new to him. He'd never seen the woman pray before. He turned to leave. She reached and caught his hand. The contact stung him so fiercely he fell to his knees, his eagle filling his belly, his arms, his heart. Mick pounded the ground with a fist, dispelling it. Months ago he'd been enslaved to the whim of the bird. Now he had a modicum of control.

His palm still tingled as he got to his feet. He rubbed it against his jeans, feeling a wet grit wipe down and away.

"What the hell's that?"

"My Helpers. The ones I carry." She held her hands out to him as if presenting evidence. They were streaked with ash, one dark circle on the heel of each hand streaking down to her fingertips. "I tried to release them, but—"

"They're right over there." He thumbed toward the corner of the house. He had to get out of here before his eagle spotted them again. One rejection had been used up, and with this level of exhaustion he worried it was the only one he'd be allowed.

"That's the orphaned ones. Mine ... " She looked down at her hands, curling her fingers to enclose the dark streaks of ash. "This came out instead."

He remembered the black runes on her skin, Old Mae's insistence she come for her baths.

"Let me see your back."

In her eyes were the words, *you don't want to see it,* but she swiveled, offering her back to him. As he raised the bottom hem of her shirt she gathered her hair over her shoulder—and what he saw made no sense. In the harsh light, it was a crime scene. A police photo in an evidence folder. His hands went to her shoulders to hold her, ground her, keep her and him together. The runes glistened wetly, a mix of red blood and liquid black. Where it had run across her skin and dried it had left a crackly band of discoloration from her neck to the small of her back. If this was the underworld weeping out, how much of her would be left once all was said and done?

"Old Mae—"

"She hasn't seen it."

A yell filled his chest. He took a breath, counting to three. "You think you oughta show her?"

"No, because she'll call it off, and I have to go through with it. Especially now."

He lowered her shirt and turned her to face him. Space inflated in his head where words had been. He had nothing to say, nothing he hadn't already said. Nothing that would change a damn thing. But he held onto her shoulders hoping somehow he'd pass the understanding through the grip of his hands. How much he cherished the team they made, how troubled his struggle in life felt without her. How it felt to kiss her on top of that great mound in Illinois, hold her hand in the car after he'd dug her out of the rain-soaked earth.

"I'm just surprised it affected my Helpers. I planned to free them." She was studying her palms again, eyes lowered so Mick could no longer see them. "I suppose they weren't mine to free."

And if the Helpers belonged to The Silent One, so did Waapikoona. She was not Mick's, or Old Mae's, to free.

Would he wake up one day and find a pile of ash where her body had been?

"I think you got no choice but to quit the baths. Let all that heal. Then maybe—"

She looked up at him, twisting her shoulders to break his grasp. "I'm finishing it."

Of *course* she was. But she couldn't stop him from talking to Old Mae and describing exactly what he just saw. First, he had to get to Pop's and talk to Kari and the kids because the only way he was going to handle all this was one crisis at a time.

Kari burst out of Pop's front door before Mick had even set the parking brake. The GTO had broadcast his arrival and stolen his last minute to prepare—as if he had anything to say at all. His sister stood under the porchlight watching him get out of the car, both hands over her mouth like she was holding back a scream. This time it was his turn to embrace someone. He crossed the driveway and wrapped his arms around her as she gave in, crying into her hands.

"You won't be happy with my explanation," he said.

She stayed put, letting him hold her a moment before she finally gasped, "Why not?"

He didn't answer right away. This exchange he hadn't rehearsed, and he wasn't sure why since it came out of him so naturally. It was yet another reason why he didn't plan. Nothing ever turned out the way he expected. His idea of doing this in front of Pop to engage his help wasn't even working out for him.

"'Cause it makes no sense."

She pushed away from him, scrubbing her face with her sleeve. "I thought you were dead, Mickey. I thought you were one of those missin' people, that we'd never see you again."

"I'm here now, and I'm sorry. If I'd known what would happen, I wouldn't've ... " It occurred to him then that being lost in a cave wasn't just an excuse. It was the truth and an explanation that made sense. No need to mention great demons or unquiet spirits or falling outside the boundary of time. Someone could survive in a cave for as long as he was away as long as there was clean water to drink—and there was.

"Wouldn't've what?"

"Got myself good and lost inside a cave." He added a smile, just to soften the memory of that cave for himself. He didn't want his anxiety coming through, or she'd be the first to pick up on it.

"For two weeks?"

He shrugged. He had no way to explain how he'd survived without food and water. "There was a spring running through, and—"

"You're tellin' me ... " She angled herself away from him, rejecting the smile he'd just given so she could welcome in some wholly justified anger. The idea of him exploring a cave on a whim right now was preposterous by itself. She needed some good reason, and he had to offer it before she came up with a more pointed question he wouldn't be able to answer.

"It was for Helen. I had to go in there to find somethin'. This is the part I asked you to trust me about."

"Oh, for heaven's sake, Mick."

"I know I'm askin' a lot here—" He didn't know how to finish.

She stared at him. "I was certain you were dead. Even though Pop kept sayin'—" Her voice cracked, and she covered her mouth like she would cry again.

Pop had already helped him with Kari, had probably been the whole time he was away. And would continue to tomorrow. Mick was done here with all he could do right now, and if he didn't get home to bed, he would be dead for sure.

Back at home his midnight adjusted eyes burned at the affront of near daylight bursting from all sides of the house. He parked the GTO and got out, shielding his face on his walk to the apartment door. It was unlike Old Mae to be fearful of the night and even more unusual for her to waste that kind of electricity on something so unfounded. Tomorrow he would talk to her about unscrewing some of those bulbs—after he told her about Waapikoona's back. That image lit brighter in his memory than the light that confronted him now.

Inside his apartment he found Waapikoona sitting stiffly on the couch, watching the door. A table lamp was on but unneeded due to all the light spilling through the windows from outside. He'd have to get the ladder right now. He'd never be able to sleep like this.

"I'm gonna have to unscrew some of them lights—"

"Isabel's upstairs sleeping with the cats. You can have your bed."

Stretching out in his own bed for six whole hours of uninterrupted sleep? He nearly collapsed with the thought of it. But that left Waapikoona on the couch, and he couldn't stomach that. "Bedroom is yours."

She flipped on the TV and turned the volume low. "My hours are off. I won't be tired for a while." When he didn't budge, she lifted her legs and folded them beside her. "Go to bed, Mick."

As he stripped down to his underwear in the bedroom, he thought back to that scene he'd walked in on. Waapikoona, sitting alone in a quiet room waiting for him to come home. For seventeen days had she done the same? More apologies would serve no one. He hadn't meant it to happen. Guilt was an unpleasant bedmate, but he was too tired to kick it out.

In the lull of night he woke, turning to embrace a woman's soft form beside him, and his brain discovered what his body already knew. He breathed her in, falling into a sleep so tranquil it redefined the act. She turned her face toward his, waking him long enough to discover her presence all over again. He rolled her to her side so she aligned perfectly against him—heart aligned with heart, pelvis to pelvis, his knees locked behind hers. Now that he'd had this, he'd never achieve this level of rest without her.

He woke again later, before the alarm, the repetitive chirp of a rowdy cardinal infiltrating the stone walls of his basement apartment. Birdsong promised a warm sunny morning outside … and brought him solidly conscious to the feel of Waapikoona sleeping against him. His arm tight around her ribs under her breasts, the backs of her bare legs against his own. Her skin—soft, amazing, cool against the heat of his. He thought of her ruined back, hoping the layer of cotton T-shirt between her damaged skin and his chest was protective and not irritating it worse because he could not let her go.

Then he registered how hard he was, pressing into her backside. He took a deep breath and tried not to press harder. He was just drifting back into a doze when she turned over in his arms, hooked a leg over his hip, and took him inside her.

This couldn't be a doze, not with a dream like this. He drowned in the soft strength, the hot slippery grip. It built an aching hunger that was too bad, too good—had he ever fit inside a woman this precisely? For the first time he appreciated the mechanics of the fit as much as the feeling of it. He had two views: aching male desire layered beneath distant eagle precision. Never had he found sex so effortless, so uncomplicated. It struck him then that without mental preparation he wasn't going to last two seconds, and if she so much as moved one muscle …

Her arms now around his neck, she pulled him in deeper.

His breath caught; he went for her wrists to unlatch her and look into her eyes for some answers because this was not a dream. She gazed back steadily, her intention plain and perfectly readable: desperate need, a heaping load of dare. This was insane. *She* was insane. No lead-up, no warning, no protection, and no way in hell was he going to risk bringing a child into his mess of a life. This was anything but uncomplicated.

He pulled free. It felt more like he was ripping off a limb.

She came for him again, undaunted, and for a breath he wondered if she was sleepwalking—sleeploving?—if that was even possible. Her eyelids were open but heavy and slightly unfocused. He shoved away—and fell off the edge of the bed onto his knee.

It wasn't the first time she'd attacked him, but this time was worlds away from the first. And he liked it. Too much. He couldn't let on just how much because then it would be out in the open and he'd have no choice but to act on it.

She propped up to look at him, tilting her head like she wasn't sure how he got himself so quickly off the bed.

"You on the pill?" he asked.

No answer, no change in her expression.

"Yeah, I thought so." He sounded mad. Was he? He must be, but he couldn't feel it for the fire burning through him and the amorous woman right there in his bed. The woman he was stuck in love with. The one who'd accused him of not being able to plan his future.

If the turmoil in his life wasn't a good enough reason to end this right now, even worse would be the risk of putting a baby in a woman who might so quickly leave him. About that, he could plan.

CHAPTER
13

In silence Mick ate cereal and prepared a thermos of coffee. Waapikoona watched his post-shower hair dry and take on its slight wave, his absentminded hand combing it back off his forehead only for it to fall back into his eyes moments later. He ignored her scrutiny. He ignored her presence altogether. Sipping her coffee at the table she wondered how long he would be upset with her. Sex had never really meant anything to her, but what she'd just done with Mick, as brief as it was, had been … different.

He was shrugging on his jacket now, grabbing his keys. She couldn't let him leave with this discord hanging in the air.

"I'm not used to being rejected like that."

He looked at her hard, as if trying to dissect the meaning in her conversational tone. "You forget the world might be ending. Not a good time to be careless about—"

"You're anything but careless, Mick."

"Awful lot a trust you put in me. 'Cause underneath me, on your back, you got no control over what I do."

"Is that how it would go?"

He took a moment, as if pondering more than that. "This time."

She couldn't remember being witness to such bitter lust. She'd call him repressed but knew it was wrong. This man was simply biding his time. Somehow she'd find a way to explain what she'd just done, and why—but at this point she didn't understand it herself. In bed with him she'd been warm, content, a feeling so new she'd accidentally reached for more. In that moment it felt necessary, and so longed for she had to have it. It had somehow ended up with Mick jerking away from her, and she hadn't yet defined the weight it left her with. "I like how you think."

If his thoughtful glance toward the bedroom meant that comment had given him a few ideas, he wasn't alone. How simple it would be to go back in there and finish what she started, pregnancy and the end of the world be damned.

"Good," he said. "'Cause it seems I'm the only one thinkin' right now."

"You worry too much."

"You don't worry enough."

It took her back to the nights she watched that door. He had no clue. "I worried plenty."

He watched her as if searching for proof. If he hadn't caught her waiting up for him last night, perhaps he'd never be able to picture it, and probably wouldn't believe her. She scarcely believed it herself.

"I gotta go see if I can get my job back."

The door closed behind him. The lock slid home. She got up, opened the door, and walked into the yard. The grass was dewy and slick on her bare feet, the warm sunlight slanting against her with newfound determination. She called his name. He stopped in the open door of his Pontiac and looked at her, his eyes harder and more shielded than before. She crossed the ground toward him, unsure of what she'd say once she reached him. She knew she couldn't let him drive away like this.

She stopped a few feet away. "I don't know how…"

They both looked toward voices on Old Mae's front porch, at Isabel who was hopping down each step one by one with both feet. Spot followed, taking them in one long leap. Waapikoona returned her attention to Mick, forgetting everything she wanted to say.

"I don't either," he said, and he got in his car.

Waapikoona backed away to make room for him to turn around as Isabel joined her side.

"Is he coming back?" the girl asked.

"He better be."

WAAPIKOONA'S RESTLESSNESS COULD be cured by nothing inside the apartment, not even the oversized kids' activity book Isabel lugged from Old Mae's, as if it would solve all their boredom. Many of the yellowed pages had already been completed by another child's uneven writing. When Waapikoona flipped to the first page and saw *Michael Svendsen* written in blue crayon, she had to slap the book closed.

Isabel frowned up at her.

"Let's go outside for a walk." Waapikoona picked up the book. A white square slid out from the pages onto the table. She flipped it over, still distracted by the image of Mick's childlike handwriting and the heady collection of regret she seemed unable to stomp down. What confronted her was a hundred times worse. It was a photograph of two kids sitting on peeling porch steps. A boy grinned widely at the camera, squinting one eye closed against a sun that turned his shaggy hair white-blond in the captured image. It was the same gentle wave she saw on his head that morning. The girl beside him had thrown her head back, laughing, as if the camera's shutter opened just after some cracked joke. Her braids were messy, her knees skinned and muddy. The boy had a sunburned nose and his own set of scabbed knees—and no visible cares in the world.

Waapikoona could not handle the fondness that bloomed in her then.

"Is that Mick and Kari?"

"Looks like it." Her voice sounded far away. This was Mick from another time. Mick who had carefully written out his full name, his heart unburdened and free. She felt overcome with a desperation to know more about this version of him, about what his life was like, what he'd said right before the shutter snapped.

"How old are they?" Isabel asked.

"A few years older than you." She had to figure out how she could recover that boy's carefree grin. There was a gouge in the world without it.

She rushed Isabel into her jacket and shoes and out the door. Gloom pulled at her, presenting her with enough dirt to bury the reality in that photograph. Rehashed images of the death she'd created, the bodies, the hate. Of her previous life, the large-scale abuses against her people, the more directed and painful attacks to her and Isabel. The unrelenting homesickness and sorrow, the fall to their deaths. The world she'd seen in two separate times, a hundred years apart, with the same unsolved problems, undeserving of that boy's grin. She slid Mick's hoodie over her head and ushered girl and dog out the door. If she didn't get moving, she'd crumple into a kitchen chair and remember too much.

There was something heavy in the pocket of the hoodie. She brought the object into the light. It was her Jeep key fob fastened on a well-worn *Wyona Automotive* keychain with another key attached. It looked like a house key.

She followed the girl and dog outside and tried the key in the door. As it slid into place, she felt the click of metal reverberate inside her. She imagined him prying that key ring open and sliding her key fob on. Making room for it just as he had for her. Instead of presenting a house key to her and expecting an answer, or her gratitude, he'd stuck it in her pocket like it already belonged.

Permanence like the one she faced now, with this key in her pocket, would have clashed with her life serving The Silent One. She couldn't hunt people and feed them to her Helpers and remain in one place. The only solution had been to stay on the move, never settle, always look ahead. Everything she felt since waking up in Mick's bed came swiftly together as one cohesive thought: she'd died twice now, and this was her third life. For once she felt like a fixture in time rather than a specter blowing through it. This place could be hers—was hers, unless she chose to cast it away. The underworld was draining from her; she could feel the itchy rawness down her back. Would it have been possible before Mick had dug her from that grave?

She no longer had to travel between two worlds, never feeling fully welcome in either. Real choice presented itself. Her plans could be built on desire, not circumstance. She could choose this, right now, with two feet planted firmly on upperworld earth and a key to a warm home. She could distance herself from all the death and all the hate inside her. She could stop running. She could choose Mick.

Intentionally or not, he'd helped make this place for her. Waking up in his bed had begun her third life, one where she no longer felt so alone. She hadn't expected to find belonging in this time. She hadn't wanted to.

Where panic should have loomed, she felt that boy's grin in the photo like it was a real thing. Like it was something the world could own again, and she would be there to witness it.

Outside, the air was light, the sun divine. The sky stretched into a deep afternoon blue with a tumult of rounded white clouds on the western side where the sun burned bright before it ended its day. Good could be found in the world—could be made. She'd never forget her pasts, but she could jump once again and leave them behind. Her happiness only felt like a betrayal because the spirit of her people had hung over her for so long. There was no longer anyone to betray. Isabel was here, content and alive. Their people were lost forever. Her brothers and sisters of the underworld had already disowned her. So had her creator. Her foster family had encouraged her to come back here. Just because this town with this man and his key in her pocket hadn't been in her plan didn't mean it couldn't be.

Was there something wrong with her? Why couldn't she just accept the good things life had brought to her and stop feeling like it was some monstrous con?

Ahead, Isabel petted Spot's head as he stood stiffly watching the edge of the woods. Waapikoona caught the low growl as the wind shifted, a warning that quickened her stride.

"What does he see?" she asked, joining them.

"Squirrels. He's not fast enough, but he tries anyway." Isabel withdrew her hand, and Spot took off for the trees.

"Let's walk. There's a deer trail on this side that leads to a little meadow. Some early flowers might be blooming."

"How do you know that?"

"I used to walk a lot before I lived with Mick."

Isabel stopped and turned, her yellow sneakers squeaking on the wet grass. "You didn't always live with Mick?"

"No." She heard it again: *live with Mick*. The flush in her gut made her change the subject. "Where did you get those nice shoes?"

"When you were sleeping, he took me to a place that had lots of them. And other stuff too. So much stuff. Have you been there?"

A sudden contrast of memories held Waapikoona so tightly she couldn't answer. Crouched by a fire in a cold stone tomb in the dead of winter. Sneaking into a warm bed beside a warmer Mick in a cozy apartment in the peace of night. And now she was seeing that firelit tomb with Mick inside it, his presence warmer than any blaze. The stark loneliness of her life before him was distant enough now to compare to something new. It was the type of isolation that turned a person into something not human. She hadn't felt afraid then, but the thought of returning to that existence fueled a fear she couldn't abide. Worst yet was the idea that putting that life behind meant she had lost her grit.

Isabel had started walking again, her attention span too narrow to wait any longer for a response to a question Waapikoona had forgotten. Together they pushed through a knee-high wall of grass at the edge of the lawn and squeezed between saplings into the filtered light of the woods. Waapikoona stopped, unable to match the visual to any memory she had. She'd walked this route often—once with Mick, after demanding he return her second Helper after he'd killed her first. Now it was a different place. Tiny insects flitted in slants of golden sunlight; emerald green sprouted above and below. Birds and squirrels played in the branches, driving Spot into a near frenzy. Her boots crunched acorn cups as she looked up into the wide arms of an oak gleaming in rebirth.

Waapikoona hadn't lost her grit. She had shed it during hibernation. And if the forest could wake with new growth as if winter never happened, so could she.

DUSK LOOKED DARKER than it ever had for Waapikoona, causing her to misjudge the time needed to return to the house without the aid of a flashlight. It was a stupid mistake for a big sister, a ridiculous failure for a parent, and both roles belonged to her. Cold had crept in behind the sun's retreat, and their slow pace in the dark didn't move their blood enough to keep them warm.

Waapikoona slid her arms out of the sleeves of Mick's hoodie. "Come here, let me put this on you."

"I'm not cold."

"You only have that little jacket."

"Are *you* cold?" It sounded like an accusation.

Freezing, Waapikoona almost said, trying to keep her teeth from chattering. She had lost her underworld eyesight and her resilience to the cold. "You tell me if you change your mind."

Isabel gave her a thoughtful look before pushing ahead to take the lead. The girl's superior night vision doubled their pace, and Waapikoona had to work harder at not clocking a shin against a log or taking a branch to the face. Now she understood why Mick seemed so clumsy in the dark. Normal human eyes were trash.

"I think Spot ran home," Isabel said. "I can't even hear him anymore."

Which meant they had to be close. Waapikoona peered ahead. The pattern of trees appeared better defined than what she'd been seeing, as if a bit of daylight remained ahead. She looked over her shoulder, where shadow melded with forest into one smooth pattern of darkness. They were nearing the edge of the woods for sure. Once they stepped out from the trees into the open yard, her human eyes would be able to make sense of the world again.

Isabel stopped abruptly. "Do you hear that?"

She hadn't before, but now with their footfalls silenced she could. A high-pitched whine, broken by—breath? Panting? "Yes, what is—"

The girl took off toward it, hopping objects in the dark that Waapikoona couldn't see until she was right up on them. If she didn't slow down, they'd quickly be parted, and Waapikoona would have no way to find her. She cupped her hands at her mouth to call her back. In the silence of that moment, underbrush rustled to her left. From the space where Isabel had disappeared came a clipped gasp, then a cry, and Waapikoona ran toward it.

She spotted the little girl, hunched over a white shape on the ground. That unknown sound was now an animal's whimper of distress punctuated with labored breath. Somehow her brain made sense of what her eyes could barely see. Spot on his side, unnatural darkness seeping from his fur. He wagged his tail but didn't move from his prone position against the ground.

"He's hurt, Sarah. Really hurt bad."

"Let me see." She knelt beside her.

Up close it was the metallic scent that gave it all away. She'd seen many wounds like this. Multiple punctures, serrated flesh, too much blood to make sense of where it was coming from. She'd caused them, received them, watched Mick almost die from one. Isabel turned her face toward her, eyes reflective in the dying light. Nothing could be done out here. They'd have to somehow get the dog home without harming him worse. As she ripped her hoodie over her head, she wondered how they'd missed the commotion of the fight between Spot and whatever had done this.

"Here, help me get this under him." She tugged the material under his dead weight, smearing warm blood up her arm that cooled in the air and sank its chill through her skin. Now their exit from the woods would be stalled even more. Soon it would be too dark for even Isabel to navigate them out.

They yanked and stretched the hoodie underneath him as his whines became more desperate. She balled the bottom corner of each side in her fist, prepared to hand them over to Isabel before she remembered the girl's crippled hand. It wouldn't be easy to carry an improvised stretcher with only three good hands. They needed help. Even though Mick might not be home yet, she had to bank on that because she had no other ideas.

She put a hand on the girl's arm. "You run home and get Mick. And a flashlight. Don't—"

A heavy blow knocked her sideways, cracking hip and elbow against hard ground. She ripped her knife from her belt and swung her legs around to face her attacker even though she was down. All she saw was darkness. Branches snapped around her. On her back she swiveled again, following the sound. A gust of air pressed down, whipping her hair against her face, filling her nose with the smell of damp earth and rotting death—the unmistakable scent of her Helpers. A shape rose above her, invisible except for its movement of pumping wings and glassy texture—and then she put it all together. Spot, attacked by her orphaned Helpers who were back now to finish him off. Isabel, turning into falcon to protect them. She couldn't do that. The Silent One would find out. She'd start accruing a tally sheet like Waapikoona had, and then—

"Isabel, no!"

Waapikoona rolled to her knees, her free hand against the prickly forest floor, and heard a rustling, scampering creature gaining on her. She swung around, seeing nothing. Pain seared through her hip and knocked her back to the ground. She twisted to cover the creature with her own body and protect it from the swoop of the Thunder-Being. Sharp teeth grazed her bare arm, but she trusted her own Helper wouldn't bite her—but hadn't it already? Her hip pulsed raw, soaking her jeans. She got one of the creature's legs in her grip and tried to pin the other with her knee. Its jaws snapped, seeking a second purchase. If she wasn't certain her hip was a victim of those teeth, she was now certain she could no longer trust. The Helper strained toward her, its teeth aimed at her, sharp in the night.

Air beat above her and she rolled, dragging the creature away with her. Calling to Isabel again was pointless with the bird not just set on Thunder-Being duty, but also working to protect them all. It wouldn't stop until this creature was dead. She couldn't kill one of her Helpers, but she had to, before Isabel did. She rolled again, pinning the powerful creature between her body and the earth. It created the perfect position to bring her flint down toward that soft belly—and for those snapping jaws to sink teeth into her ribs. She ignored the pain and stabbed so close to her body she recoiled. The contact she felt was still teeth—double rows of teeth, but only teeth, not blade—so she stabbed until the knife fell from her hand, too slippery to hold onto any longer.

All at once she became aware of her arm as the only movement. Her frantic breath the only sound. She was alone on the cold ground in an unending pool of darkness. It felt so much like The Silent One's cave that she had to steel herself, remember where she was.

"Isabel." She'd never be able to make out the translucent bird while forest canopy and clouds shielded the night sky.

Her injuries bled into the gore of her Helper's body beside her, blurring the boundary where her blood ended and the creature's began. No longer its caretaker, she was its murderer.

She felt along her hip, where mangled jeans exposed cold slippery flesh. Above it, torn T-shirt and more ruined skin. She did not feel bone, which was an improvement over previous wounds. She could lie here and bleed out, or she could get up, find Isabel, and get them home.

She'd made it to hands and knees when she heard Isabel calling her name.

"Here," she called back. Her voice sounded faint.

Isabel helped her up. "I found my clothes. My eyes are really good right now, but it's not going to stay like this so we need to get Spot and walk fast. Oh, Sarah, you're bleeding."

"I'm okay." Waapikoona took what was left of her shirt and wrapped it tight around her, holding it with one hand. "Not sure if I can carry Spot, though, unless we can get him over my shoulders."

"We can do it. One hand each. I'll show you."

They managed to bundle him, the hoodie stretched between them like a hammock. Waapikoona held her mangled side with one hand and the dog's weight with the other. His whimpers had gone growly and indignant. Her breath came hard and fast. She felt blood leaking down her side, running in little rivers down her legs where they cooled as they slid into her boots. Isabel dragged her through the ever-darkening woods, black on darker black, until grays blended in and they stepped into open field awash in the faintest tinge violet light from the western sky.

And the orange Pontiac sitting there like something she'd dared to count on, and it actually came through.

"I have to stop." Her legs gave as she said it. Thankfully, Isabel was already lowering Spot to the ground.

"It's not much more. Come on, Waapikoona."

It was the first time Isabel had called her that. *Yes, Waapikoona, come on.* She wound her grip of the hoodie around her fist and got to her feet. She'd returned to her bones after a cliff jump, a burial, a lightning strike. It would take a lot more than two underworld demon bites to defeat her.

CHAPTER
14

FOR MOST OF his adult life Mick had lived alone in this apartment. There was no reason for it to seem so painfully quiet now. He'd never used the TV as background noise before, so he wasn't sure why he felt the need to flip it on. The dread that lurked in every room was his own paranoia, remnants of his episode in the cave. It was a modern affliction of wondering where someone was and not having the instantaneous gratification of sending a text to check up. It wasn't the trigger to panic and start searching for two people who weren't lost.

The Jeep was here. Their things were here. His childhood activity book lay on the table as if awaiting someone's return. Waapikoona didn't subscribe to the always reachable, always connected model of life and never would.

Could he buy her a phone? Sure, if he wanted a phone shoved up his ass.

And obsessing about their absence surely meant he was some kind of overbearing prick, exactly the kind of guy

Waapikoona would gut, rob, then drag into the woods as a sacrifice to the underworld.

"Dinner," he said to the open room.

Inside the fridge he found an assortment of vegetables he never bought because he didn't know what to do with them. In the cabinet he found the gourmet pasta sauce he'd only splurge on when it was on sale and five different kinds of expensive salsa. He dug in the back for some spaghetti and put a pot of water on the stove. He couldn't wait to see what Waapikoona had planned for those vegetables. If she got home before the water boiled, maybe they could forgo the pasta and he could find out.

A charge buzzed through him. He turned to look across his apartment at the door. Still closed, the window dark. Just like it looked a few minutes ago when something propelled him to check it out then.

"You know what … " he said to the stove, turning off the burner. He'd do a quick perimeter check of Old Mae's yard. Make sure all the flying underworld creatures were tucked away in their caves and not dive-bombing the house. Shoo away any wandering spirits. Tell any of Waapikoona's undead friends to get lost. He threw on a jacket and went to the door. It opened against him, pushed from the other side.

"Mick! Spot's hurt. Sarah too. We were … "

He lost track of the little girl's voice when he looked at Waapikoona. Strands of her hair clumped against smeared blood on her face. Her eyes burned with sheer will. He took hold of what she gripped to relieve her of the weight that seemed to be moments from pulling her to the ground. Then he saw the blood leaking between fingers that held her side.

"I'll allow you to call them demons now," she said.

"Kitchen," he replied. There had been enough blood and guts lately for practicality to overtake panic, and he'd rather clean wooden chairs and vinyl flooring than couches and rugs. Plus she was talking, walking, not unconscious, not buried alive. It was good to have something to compare to.

As soon as she was seated under the light, he could see the wound and had a good guess for what created it. "Your pocket demons."

"But I'll not allow you to gloat."

His eagle had already risen to attention, but it was no match for the fuel of human testosterone. He kept his voice low, knowing his next question would come out in a way that might scare Isabel even though she hadn't followed them into the kitchen. "Where are they?"

"See to Spot. I'll take care of myself."

When her eyes caught his, he knew she'd recognized the barely contained threat in his voice and was prepared to hold her ground. There'd be no answer until she was ready to give one. That was fine. He could hunt those demons without any clues from her, and at this point he needed no permission.

At the front of his apartment Isabel bent over Spot, stroking his cheek. Mick pulled a chair over to avoid having to squat with his bad leg and drew the hoodie off the dog. If it weren't for the rise and fall of Spot's ribcage, he'd have thought he was viewing death. Something about a wounded animal seemed so much more dire than a human—maybe it was the helpless feeling that went along with it. Most people knew basic first aid. But on animals? He didn't know how to clean and bandage skin with fur. He didn't even know what he was looking at or where the most critical organs and arteries were. And all that gored up fur made the whole thing look more hopeless than it probably was.

"I'm no vet," he said.

"What's a—"

"But Old Mae used to work with animals a long time ago. Can you stay with your sister and I'll take 'im upstairs?"

"I can help—"

"I'd rather you stay here with Waapikoona."

It was true what he'd said about Old Mae, but that wasn't the main reason he wanted to take Spot to her. If the dog died, he didn't want Isabel to have to witness it.

He kneeled beside Spot and slid both arms underneath him, hoping he didn't have more wounds on his other side. Practicality overcame him once again, ensuring he could get the dog upstairs and into better hands before he succumbed to the lump in his throat. Rural life could be hard on pets, a lesson he'd learned more than once. Danger tempered the freedom to roam. State highways abutted front yards; bobcats and bears prowled the nights long before the underworld showed up. Yet every time the lesson returned, it felt new, like a stab in the back he should have seen coming.

IF WAAPIKOONA'S IDEA of taking care of herself was limited to that wad of paper towels she had smashed against her side while she rifled through the fridge, he was about to take issue with that. First, he had to ask a favor of Isabel that was sure to land him in hot water with her sister. It was a risk—and a fight—he'd have to bring on. He had no other options.

As he untied his boots, he caught Isabel's eye. She looked at him expectantly, surely wondering what Old Mae said about Spot. He tilted his head toward the bedroom. She rose from her nest of blankets on the couch and followed him in.

He pushed the door until it was almost closed and made sure to keep his voice low. "Spot's in good hands. Now, I gotta ask you somethin'."

She climbed on the bed and sat. Her bangs had grown long enough to tuck behind her ears. With her looking so much like her sister, Mick felt ill-prepared for what he was about to do. On top of that, with Waapikoona wounded—again—and Spot on his deathbed upstairs, this was rotten timing, but when would a thing like this ever be suitable to bring up?

"All the times you leave, where does your falcon take you?"

All emotion drained from her face. In those few seconds, she returned to the girl she was when he'd first found her—withdrawn, mistrustful, mute. She started to slide off the bed, ready to bail on this conversation.

"Isabel." He laid a hand on her head, hoping she'd look up at him. "I ain't accusin' you of anything. I just need you to ... I need to be sure it's what I'm thinkin'."

She kept her eyes on the farthest wall.

"A cave?" he tried.

Her gaze moved to him.

"To meet with The Silent One?"

She dropped her mouth open a little at that before closing it tight again.

"It's okay to say so. I've been in there with your sister. I tried to go again the other day but got lost."

Now her mouth opened and stayed that way, but he wasn't sure which part of that had her so surprised.

"Look…" he sat beside her on the bed "…I have to go back and talk to him. But I'm not like you and your sister, so I can't make sense of that cave, or even find him, without one of you. So I was hopin' you could help me."

The girl broke her silence as if she was unable to keep the thought to herself. "He wouldn't want you in there."

"Too late. I've already been and I'm goin' again. I have to talk to him."

"He'll kill your eagle."

"My eagle won't be around."

"Why don't you ask Sarah?"

"I did. She told me no. So now I'm askin' you."

Isabel glanced at the door as if trying to deduce her sister's reasoning. "She thinks you'll get hurt."

Mick had to take a moment with that. Had Waapikoona said The Silent One wouldn't raise his niece because it was the truth or had she dissuaded him because she feared for his safety? Now he was the one with his mouth stuck open, and he couldn't decide if the possibility of that lie had flared his temper or his affection for her because right now they were both on a hard simmer. His heart beat a little harder, unsure if it wanted to kiss her or throttle her.

Isabel slid off the bed as if the conversation had ended.

He tapped her shoulder before she could get away. "So whadda ya say?"

"I don't want you to get hurt either."

"What if I promise not to?"

She narrowed her eyes, watching him a moment. "A promise won't do anything."

Why had he expected this girl to be an easy sell? Her spine was stronger than her sister's. "A promise is all I got to give. And it was all I had for my sister, when I promised I would help raise her baby from bones, just like what your sister did for you. Only The Silent One can do that, and only if I ask him. If I go in there by myself again, I might get lost for good."

The waver in his voice had put a bit of shock on her face. There was nothing more terrifying to a child than the threat of tears from a grown-up.

"What baby?"

"Dougie and Janie's baby sister."

To play on her friendship with the kids was a dirty move, but it was too late to take back. He was going to hell—or at least to the depths of Waapikoona's bad side which would be remarkably worse.

She brightened. "Then I have to help."

"You don't, but I'd be real grateful if you did."

"Then okay."

"And if it gets dangerous, we leave. I can definitely promise that."

"Fine."

"And your sister can't know." Yes, he was going to hell for sure. "Which reminds me, let's go get her bandaged up."

Mick felt eyes on him as he and Isabel reentered the living room. Guilt pressured him to keep his head down, but he fought it and returned the steady gaze across the apartment. She stood against the kitchen sink, one hand pressing the wad of paper towels against her side. With that glower it was clear she'd caught him at something. With the glower he returned, most people would decide to back down.

"I can't hold pressure and chop peppers at the same time."

"That's surprising. I thought you could do anything while bleeding to death." He took a detour into the bathroom to grab bandages and ointment. When he caught his reflection in the mirror, he paused to run a hand through his hair and collect himself. The clash of love and anger for this woman wasn't new. The guilt from lying to her was. It turned the emotional mix unstable, fed him imagery and sensory recall he had no room for right now. Her gently stroking the neck of his eagle, sticking his feather in her hair. Her eyes, daring him to kiss her again in that mausoleum, the hot press of her lips, the flick of her tongue. The eagle's view of her walking away from him, the feel of her when she took him inside her that morning.

The woman had brought him unrelenting confusion—trouble—heartbreak. Violence. Death. She'd sucked him into a world that shouldn't exist, but one he must now navigate, with or without her. He thought of her day and night; he couldn't envision a future without her. She threw fuel on his temper and disrupted every aspect of his life, but despite all that, her presence felt right. He wanted to chop her peppers; he wanted to keep her safe. He longed to walk beside her in the woods, to fly above her in the night. And the next time she started something in his bed, he'd be prepared. Even if the underworld was spilling from every cave, he would have her. He would prove to her how good they could be together.

He snatched up the bandages and joined her in the kitchen. When he saw her chopping at the counter with the blood-soaked towels on the floor, he decided he would have to throttle her. The laugh that came out of him didn't fit the impulse.

"Would you mind sittin' down over here so I can doctor you up?"

"I'm hungry."

"Okay, but ... priorities."

"Food is my priority right now." She continued chopping.

He took the knife out of her hand. "Well, it ain't mine. Go have a seat. As soon as I get you patched up, you can go back to it."

Knowing she'd never submit while he watched, he turned away to wash his hands. He heard her move away and slide into a chair at the table.

"It already clotted," she announced.

He pulled up a chair, took hold of her knees, and swiveled her wounded side toward the light. As he picked shreds of T-shirt from chainsaw-like lacerations a new kind of anger grew. The creatures that had done this should have been killed by his eagle long ago. He should have insisted. Waapikoona didn't need more wounds—she'd had enough pain. And Spot? He was dying because Mick had not acted.

Together they got the rest of the shirt off. New blood wept from the torn skin. He squeezed ointment over the mess and started laying bandages across the worst parts of her side and hip. He tightened his jaw so he wouldn't curse. This was his inaction, his fault.

"Is it dead?" His voice came so rough and angry he couldn't bring himself to look at her.

She took a breath to speak but halted, watching him instead.

"Is it?" Now he sounded angrier. If she thought it was aimed at her, he couldn't help it. He had no time to sort it out. It seemed she wasn't going to respond until he made the effort to look at her, so he lifted his eyes, careful not to look too deeply. This place he'd gone to in his head—he couldn't bring her there.

Her answer was direct and steady. "I'm not sure."

If she was going to lie, she'd have told him yes.

"Lift your arms."

She laid both wrists on the top of her head, still watching him. He wrapped her midsection with rolled gauze and pressed a piece of cloth tape to the end to hold it in place. This time it had been Waapikoona and Spot. Next time it could be Isabel or Old Mae. He'd asked her before if he could kill her demons. This time he wasn't asking.

Armed with a pry bar he dug from his tools in the utility room, he avoided Waapikoona's eye and walked outside into the night. His human thirst for vengeance could never be satisfied by his eagle's stoic precision. This he would do himself.

CHAPTER 15

Since there would be no comfortable way to get her arms into another T-shirt, Waapikoona borrowed one of Mick's button-up flannels, rolled the sleeves to her elbows, and returned to cooking. She'd carved the stomach out of that attack Helper. She'd lay beside its motionless form. It was no danger to Mick, and there was no reason to follow him into the night. It was a mantra she'd have to keep repeating for how wrong it felt that she was not out there at his side.

The two others could be nearby and might be rattled by the death of the other. Before tonight, she'd have expected them to take cover and hide in the shadows, awaiting her return. They feasted on death, not on the living. There was no reason for them to attack an able-bodied man. But there had been no reason for them to attack her or Spot either. She was made from the same underworld fabric they were. Their bite to her flesh was nothing but a bloody wound.

To Mick and his Thunder-Being, it would be a lethal toxin. His eagle would be poisoned—which would poison Mick.

All that only scratched the surface. A different sentiment cut deeper, one she'd experienced before and was sure to encounter again. To Mick's life she was a toxin herself. What she brought to him, what he had to do for her ... it changed him. Once a moral, well-mannered family man, now a vengeful murderer.

Waapikoona and Isabel ate in silence, sharing wordless worry for both the man and the dog. Neither spoke of how easily the grief of their past flowed into the room, blanketing them. Waapikoona knew her sister felt it as keenly as she did. Where a woman like her who'd faced it so many times could make it a familiar, comfortable sort of pain—a guilty pleasure, a fuel for her purpose—the little girl instead held her breath against it.

"Breathe, Pinepakatwi. Old Mae will take care of Spot, and Mick will take care of himself."

She'd seen candles in one of these kitchen cabinets once. She got up to find them—too fast, for how the motion spun the room and pulled at the gash in her side. After lighting one she switched off the overhead light. Warm candlelight softened the room. She placed the lit one on the counter and struck a match for another, setting it between them at the table.

"That's better," Isabel said.

"I was afraid of lights when I first came back. My foster mother burned candles for me instead."

"I was afraid of Mick's phone."

Waapikoona smiled. "I was afraid of phones too, the kind that hang on the wall. She had to turn down the ringer so it wouldn't startle me."

"I was afraid of Mick. I thought he was going to take me back to the school."

The same raw fear clutched Waapikoona then, as acute and helpless as a child's. "I see how you'd think that."

"I saw Grandpop before that. I thought the same thing about him. But I was cold and didn't know where else to go."

Waapikoona tilted the candle so its flame would even out the wax. "I'm sorry I wasn't there. I should've been."

"Where were you?"

Running. It sounded so childish. She could say she was hunting Hammond, or releasing Mick from her dark influence, but had that been just an excuse to leave? And she didn't want to bring up Hammond, not with Mick in danger outside and Spot fighting to live.

"I was visiting my foster parents, my home. Trying to decide if I should go back there."

"But Mighty Eagle found you."

"He did."

"He saved you from a bad person who hurt you."

"Did he tell you that?"

"No, but I figured it out. You had a bruise on your arm like fingers. And your face had been hit. Mighty Eagle would never do that. He loves you."

Waapikoona set the candle down so hard it spilled hot wax across her fingers. "I don't think—"

"He was sad when you weren't here."

Waapikoona thought of Mick's mud-streaked face after he buried his niece. When he begged for her help raising the little girl from bones, and she'd refused. "I think he's pretty sad now."

Isabel looked away, considering that. "Yeah, but it's different. When you were gone, he was like a bumblebee in the fall when it's first getting cold. Even his eagle was like that."

Sharp curiosity pushed her to ask. "Like what?"

"Slow and crumpled. Like he was breaking."

Waapikoona felt a sudden need to clear the dishes. Clear her head. Focus on anything else. What she really wanted was to go outside and find him, help him, bring him home. She couldn't do that without proving something to herself she wasn't ready to prove.

Could she really want him, now and forever, even if it ruined him?

The door opened across the apartment. She and Isabel spun toward it as one. Mick entered, wind-beaten and grim, shiny wet pry bar hanging from one hand.

"It's dead now," he said.

The silence that followed was marked by a single drop splattering the floor at his feet. Waapikoona measured its origin to his unencumbered arm hanging in a rigid clench, the blood darkened fist, the torn shirt sleeve. Another drip fell. It hit the floor like a gavel on Waapikoona's fears, proving everything to be true. Loving her sister was inescapable. Loving him was a choice and a liability.

"You've been bitten." Anger peeled through her, at him, at herself. He was stupid and careless. He remembered just as she did what a demon bite could do to him.

"No." He said it so fast it could only be a lie.

She shoved the kitchen chair out of her way and crossed the floor toward him. As he raised the rigid arm and growled at her to stop, she grabbed it, wrenching the sleeve up to his elbow. A shudder ran through him, head to toes, discharging into her like static on steroids.

"Back *up*," he ground out.

He'd shaken her off, but she snatched his arm again. The pry bar clanged against the floor as he bent double. She was sapped from that electric discharge, every nerve misfiring, every muscle sore and limp, but she had to see how far the poison had spread, what his chances were. Now he was on his knees. She flipped on the light switch and fell beside him, wrestling his clenched arm loose so she could see the bite.

"Waapi—"

"Damn it, Mick. Just let me see."

"I said—" he looked up at her, panting "…I ain't bit."

She stilled at the sight. Under the overhead light his irises had gone amber around the edge, horror-movie strange. She felt herself in full view of her absolute predator. Thunder-Being to her undead bones in this life, white invader to her Native self in another. She dropped his arm but did not relax her gaze. This was a fear she'd mastered, and she would not allow it to return.

"I'm tryin' to…" he swallowed, clearly straining to recover himself "…keep my form."

All at once she understood. Now in the light she could see the otherworldly shade of black in the slick up his arm. She breathed in the scent of buried bodies, decay, death— so much, she could taste it. "Demon blood."

"Yeah." He put a hand on her shoulder for support. "It's a lot."

"Me being here probably isn't helping."

"Actually, it does."

The hand on her shoulder slid up her neck to her jaw. Fingers touched her unadorned earlobe, the corner of her lips. Probably leaving a trail of gore, but she was no stranger to that. She watched his eyes return to their deep arctic blue, the strain in his face release, a smile begin to rise.

"Thinkin' about you brings me out of it sometimes."

She placed her own fingers against his neck where his fast-hitting pulse had started to slow. Loving him wasn't

as much of a choice as she thought. "Thinking what about me?"

He glanced toward the kitchen where Isabel had returned to her meal. He lowered his voice. "All kinds of things."

"You'll have to show me."

His eyes roamed her face, touching on every feature. "I plan to."

MICK WASHED UP and ate, standing at the counter with plate and fork and a hard furrow between his eyes. Waapikoona made no conversation and neither did he. It was difficult for her to imagine settling on the couch with Isabel when Mick looked like he was about to go to war. She thought of something she could ask and spat it out before she could talk herself out of it.

"Did you get your job back?"

He downed an entire glass of water. "For the time being. Virgil's cuttin' hours. Might close the shop."

"Why?"

"Not enough business. People are scared."

"What will you do?"

He shrugged, dismissive. "Try to stop the world from ending." He set the glass down on the counter and looked at her, hardened against a fight she didn't realize they were having. "How many more are out there?"

"Two."

He removed his shirt and handed it to her. She took it, grateful the man in him had nothing to prove this time. This hunt would be safer. Her Helpers were no match for his eagle.

She followed Mick outside where he shed his jeans and then his human form. With one great thrust of wings, he launched into the blank overcast sky. Her remaining Helpers would be drawn to her if she followed him. It would simplify the hunt but add to her grief. She wouldn't do it, couldn't even offer it. She was glad he hadn't asked.

The cold night grazed her wounded side. She felt her bandage for seeping blood and found it clean and dry, thanks to Mick. He was the first man who didn't use his protection and care as some kind of weapon or debt to be paid. She understood now how much easier it was to live with assholes. Her own crimes could never weigh on her when in the company of a worse character, when she could ditch those guys and never look back.

Back in the apartment she tucked Isabel in bed, kissing her forehead and promising they'd check on Spot in the morning. She grabbed her flint knife and a quilt from the couch and went back outside. If she couldn't walk with Mick's eagle, she would share the night with him. She sat on the cold ground and drew the quilt around her, watching the shadows for the creatures Mick was destined to kill.

Try to stop the world from ending.

She'd seen that end as she lay unconscious in Mick's bed. She'd struggled to recover her place in time, join her human body with her spirit so she could return to him instead of be forever parted, wandering and restless. It could have been her own mind's creation of what she expected to happen, but it felt too real, too much like another piece of the circle of time where she didn't want to belong but easily could have. She'd fought it. She'd woken to Isabel's soft hand on her cheek, sunlight sparkling through the bedroom door, and the scent of Mick heavy in the sheets. She'd fallen back into her limbs fully, her heart picking up speed, her lungs opening wider to take in more air and ensure she would stay awake, alive, beside that little girl, in that man's apartment.

Not before she'd seen all the rest. A rotten spill of underworld encapsulating green forests, rolling Missouri mountains, rocky western deserts, the lake-filled north. Ruin and death spoiling the beloved flatness of her first life in Illinois, its incoming storms, majestic and terrifying on the horizon, the rushing wind at the top of the mounds, puffy clouds in vast blue sky. It should have taken eons to change the world in such ways. But in those images while she slept, the time frame was much shorter. It was months. Weeks. Viscous black liquid rose from underground, swimming with horned serpents. Winged demons flew along the flow like summer insects over a lake. Thunder-Beings fought in the skies above, throwing electric death to the hordes but still more swarmed. And on the remaining bits of land, undead soldiers animated by The Silent One destroyed everything they touched. There was no fight against a flood of liquid death. No war against soldiers who were already dead.

The missing piece in this nightmare was the people who'd been raised like her, the ones who planned to mutiny against The Silent One and disrupt it all. She could not see them or sense them, and in her reach toward them she felt her hold on Mick and Isabel slip. In her unconscious mind she'd arrived at a painful reckoning. It was the man or her undead brothers and sisters. And she'd fought her way back to Mick, to the feel of his sheets on her skin, the memory of his fingers changing bandages, his arms dragging her from that muddy grave.

An eagle's cry sheared peace from the night. Mick's Thunder-Being declaring victory or calling to her? She could wait until he returned home, but she was tired of waiting. She stood and tightened the quilt around her shoulders, allowing one hand free to brace her wound. After gathering Mick's discarded clothes, she crossed the yard toward the wall of trees. A bright moon had emerged from dwindling clouds to lay a path her very human eyes could see. Mick's eagle would spot her before she found him. She wondered if she would feel the predator's gaze as she once did, or if she was human enough to unknowingly walk beneath him. If she was far enough removed from The Silent One's world that she was no longer a Thunder-Being's prey.

She entered the woods under deciduous branches still bare enough from winter to allow moonlight to trickle through. Just weeks ago she could've called upon The Silent One to lend her some night vision. Without that option, she had to slow her pace, ducking under limbs that seemed to move into her way as she neared them. Weak human vision awoke human fears of stalking night creatures and shadowed woods and all the things she could not see that rustled dry leaves just paces away. It was too late to go back for Spot—grief shot through her at the lapse. Spot was dying or dead. It seemed like a bad dream—but that was her fault for befriending him. Even if he was still healthy and alive and able to be her scout and protector in these dark woods, going back for him now would prove a surrender to her new weakness. She may as well stay inside until Mick returned. Something hard fell from the canopy, hitting branches and wood until it hit the ground. Probably a squirrel with a nut, but without the ability to see, it could be anything. If she was no longer enemy to Thunder-Beings … if her own Helpers had attacked her … if she'd joined the side of the upper-world when she woke in Mick's bed … then every under-world creature would be stalking her tonight. Good—then she'd have a reason to be out here. She stuffed Mick's clothes under her arm and drew her flint knife. She'd never recover her grit without a little practice.

A shadow passed across the trail of moonlight ahead. She looked up, finding a clear view of sky—then the moon was snuffed out by a large moving object. Long body, outstretched wings, fanned tail. It swooped down, buffeting her with a gust of wind she refused to duck for. Talons caught her hair and released with the gentlest tug.

"Jackass," she said, hoping the tease would cover her reverence.

The eagle chirped back. An innocent, almost sweet sound coming from such a deadly animal. He fell from the sky, reaching for a limb beside her that swayed against his weight as he landed and folded his wings. Feathers ruffled on the back of his neck, he turned his head to eye her.

"Try that again in a couple weeks when my reflexes are better."

He released another bright chirp, a daytime sound so out of place in the quiet of the night.

She sheathed her knife. "You sound like a songbird."

He opened his wings and fell straight down, dark talons lengthening into muscular legs, open wings lifting high into human arms, hands catching the limb. Where a great bird once perched, now a man hung. He was so fair in the moonlight he almost reflected it. With a short swing he hopped down, one hand going to the ground to absorb the force for his bad leg.

She tightened her grip on his jeans. She wouldn't give up the quilt either. She wanted to admire him.

He stood and walked until he was just a step away. "You shouldn't be out here."

In his human form, he was just as vulnerable as her. "Neither should you."

"All your underworld cousins have crawled back into their caves tonight." His teeth were dark. He wiped a hand across his mouth, smearing black goo across his cheek. "Ain't nothin' out here that could hurt me, except maybe a mountain lion."

His eagle must have made an example of her two remaining Helpers. She swallowed a sudden cold grief. She would not think of them or of the consequences for allowing this.

"Then it's just as safe for me," she said. How it felt to admit that, she wasn't sure.

"Is it?" He snatched his jeans faster than she could counter. Thunder-Being still ran hot inside him. He coughed and spat into the underbrush, wiping his mouth again. "Next time bring me a bottle of water, will ya?"

"Instead of the jeans?"

He stooped to put a leg through, lithe and perfectly balanced, empowered by the best of both his forms. "Sure."

Once he was upright again and buttoned into his jeans, she closed the space between them. He tightened his lips, watching her with those strange, not-quite-human eyes. She wanted to kiss him before his eagle fully retreated. She imagined conquering that power, diffusing it into herself. She wanted to join him, pull him inside her like she had that morning in his bed. If that had been a sleepy accident, now she wanted it awake and with purpose.

She raised the corner of the quilt still around her shoulders and wiped his cheek clean.

"I'm not really sure," he said hesitantly. "Why my eagle never tried to kill you." With those eyes, his lowered chin, his powerful stance, and the short, rapid breathing, he seemed on the verge of attack.

"Do you want to kill me right now?" It seemed like more of an admission than a question.

He shushed her, slapping a fast hand over her mouth. She felt her knife slide free from its sheath and then he was spinning away from her, the flint in his hand. Now against his back she understood his move was protection, not attack, and the heavy silence of the woods around her came alive in her ears. Not even a breeze dared to stir the branches above them. Out of habit she reached for The Silent One's help—and clamped it off as soon as she caught herself. If he could sense these attempted connections, it couldn't be good. She would be broadcasting her existence and her need of him while reminding him of her betrayal. At the least it built his ego—and his power along with it. At the worst, it built more of a case against her.

Mick stalked forward on the path, closing in on the darkness that wouldn't be so dark to half-eagle eyes. He seemed fixated on something she couldn't see, a spot on the ground several feet away. With another step he rotated the knife in his hand to aim downward. An abrupt hiss leaked from the dark and Mick lunged, stabbing toward earth as the hiss turned to a screech and the blade struck flesh with a sucking, wet sound that Waapikoona knew well.

The rotting stench of the underworld surrounded her. She covered her nose with the edge of the quilt, noting how much more offensive that scent had become.

Mick struck again, going to his knees to finish the job. His forearms were lost to the shadow, but from the position of his shoulders she could tell one hand held his foe while the other made use of her blade. One final screech marked the end. With a bitter curse, Mick swung the corpse from the darkness to the path in front of her feet. Its long dark body lay like a threat in front of her, even in death. The human mind had a primitive sensitivity to a serpent's form, even missing half its head like this one. A horn curved from the other half, proving Mick's belief of safety wrong.

"I thought your eagle had scared them all away."

Mick remained on his hands and knees, panting like he'd just grappled with a creature his own size. The horned serpent had been easy; now he was fighting his eagle, voracious and working to reclaim its form and continue the night's hunt.

"Me too," he gasped.

She went to him, offered a hand to help him up. He knocked her hand away. If he was irked with her, she couldn't decide which reason was the culprit. She'd done too many things to make a lesser man tell her to pack up and get out.

Her flint blade lay on the ground beside him. She snatched it up and returned it to her belt before turning to find her moonlit path, now dimmed by the veil of an incoming cloud. She could accept the more challenging solitary route home and prove her recovering grit. Or she could pause her return until Mick found his legs again and led them home with his half Thunder-Being eyes. Remembering his bitter rejection of her offered hand, she decided waiting for him would mean something other than trust or friendship. It would feel more like subservience.

"Jackass," she said again. This time, it was barbed.

She stepped over the slack length of the horned serpent's body and headed home, feeling the sentiment of that word—*home*—ringing urgently in her head.

Chapter
16

Waapikoona followed behind Mick and his new halo of gloom. Whatever had come upon him—or between them—as he butchered that horned serpent seemed to be his problem, not hers, and she had no interest in bringing up new issues before they hashed over the old ones. He'd recovered quickly when he saw her walk away, and she had no practical reason to balk when he'd taken the lead. Now his bare feet found a trail off the moonlit one she'd used to get into the woods, leaving her completely dependent on him for vision—until he stopped so abruptly she collided with his back.

"Shit," he said. "I just lost my good eyes. You're gonna have to lead." He stepped back, allowing room for her to pass in front of him.

He'd led them under a thick canopy of monster pines where no moonlight touched the human eye. His form was a vague shadow against swaying dark as the breeze rustled through the surrounding wood. She reached to confirm that it was indeed him so close, and found warm skin on a muscled arm. Even her earlier trail would be useless under the clouds that had rolled in and erased the moon.

"Just turn eagle again."

He released a tight breath. His outline shifted as if he'd looked away. "I'd rather not."

She walked her fingers up his arm to bare shoulder, neck, jaw. If she couldn't see his expression, she wanted to feel it for how loaded that answer sounded. But when her thumb found the corner of his mouth, he brushed her away, his hand so rough he caught her again as if to apologize. Only a moment he held her hand before he dropped it. She sensed his weight shift away.

"Well, I can't see either," she admitted. "So it's eagle or we wait for the sun."

"Stop playin'." He sounded very far from playing.

And she didn't feel like explaining just how much she'd lost when The Silent One cut her off. "Let's just keep walking. I'm sure you had the right direction. It can't be far."

He turned as if to check behind them and probably saw what she saw—an expanse of black upon black, the idea of movement, of swaying underbrush and leaves fluttering as the breeze hit, but when she squinted she realized it could just as easily be her brain filling in the void with imagery based on what it expected to be there.

"I'd rather not break an ankle on a tree root," he said.

"We could crawl." She almost laughed at the absurdity of it.

With a muttered curse he turned again, brushing the quilt off her shoulder. A visceral awareness lit the night between them. She needed no moon or sun to sense his place in relation to hers, and she reached again, her fingertips finding his mouth without the need to walk them there. The quilt slid perfectly back to its resting spot on her shoulder, guided by him with an accuracy that could only work in daylight. She heard—and felt—his intake of breath, and then his mouth was on hers, the tip of his tongue in perfect contact with her own. The spice of otherworldly blood mingled with the simple sweetness of Mick, a taste she craved more each time she had it. She could cleanse that blood from his mouth just as she'd wiped it from his cheek, but she could never wipe away all the things he'd done for her. His arms enveloped her shoulders completely—the only way to hold her and avoid her wounds. He seemed to remember this more than she did.

Something about the pure dark, she thought. In the cave, in his bed, now here in these woods. Something about this level of blackout absolved them from their impossible pairing. If the dark could strip away his world and hers, their histories, their pain, then she'd gladly stay here in the darkness forever.

She lost the contact of his lips, but his arms did not release.

"If I turn eagle again … " he whispered against her cheek. "If I do it too much … "

She laid a hand on his waist, fearful of his next words but hungry for him to continue. This was confession, his soul bare before her. Something inside her longed to hear it, to claim it, to store it away so that maybe someday she could speak so openly to him.

"… the more I do it, the harder it is to come back."

He allowed no chance for a response before he kissed her again, fiercely, desperate, his shoulders hunching, his body arching, as if he fought the urge to find a closer connection. She needed no hand against his waist to sense his change in position, but she left it there just to be sure reality wasn't hallucination. Darkness could lie. This could all be a dream.

"And now..." he broke away again, breathless "...I got to worry about you bein' attacked by thunderbirds *and* by demons."

You don't need to worry, she heard in her head because his mouth came upon hers too fast for her words to escape. If he was any other man, she'd think he was silencing her, and she'd be kneeing him between the legs and drawing her flint. But this was Mick. Collected, responsible Mick, losing his shit while blind and adrift in a sea of night. If she could be his anchor to grasp, she would let him sink her. She'd been to the depths. She knew them well.

"I should've killed your demons the first time—I fucked up—"

She dropped the quilt so she could hold him with both hands as he bent even more wildly against her, his face pressed into her neck. Allowed to continue, this would be no sleepy accident. It would be crazed calamity, and its memory tomorrow might just tip Mick over the edge.

With a yank away he released her shoulders. Hands slid onto her face, cradling her jaw. She sensed another incoming kiss by the proximity of his breath on her mouth. Instead, his forehead rested against hers, and he held her face a moment while he labored for control.

"Mick—" An attempt to help him, but she wished she'd simply shared his silence. His features began to materialize before her—the hard line of his jaw, a flip of breeze-touched hair caught in a steady silver light against his ear. Above, the clouds had parted, allowing the moon to shine through an opening in the canopy straight to them.

"My baby niece," he choked. "My fault."

"You don't control nature."

"Her skin was gray, her little fingers—"

"Death can sometimes be mercy. And you—"

"I told Kari to let her die and I would fix it."

Waapikoona had no answer for that. It was an idea too hopeful for the world around them. A person would have to be blind and naïve to say it and even more dim to believe it. Or maybe they'd just have to be desperate. None of this would be helpful outside of her thoughts. What was done, was done. So she tipped her face, breaking the contact of their foreheads to press her lips against his. She passed comfort, empathy, a deep understanding of that special pain of children dying under your reckless hand with no way to fix it. Even if a child's death was mercy, it was hopelessly unfair.

He broke the kiss, still holding her jaw with both hands. His eyes reflected tears in the new light. "Isabel's gonna take me to The Silent One. I went around you and asked her."

She put her hands over his and curled her fingers around, ready to rip herself free—but she stalled the motion. How could she be angry when she'd have done the same thing?

"I can't keep it from you no more. It's gonna break me."

The darkness still puddled around them even as the barest light filtered down. She thought of how it could smother these problems between them because right now she didn't want to be angry even as the feeling swelled. He'd rejected her refusal and moved on to a little girl who had little understanding of her placc with a great underworld demon.

He drew his hands away from hers. "I promised her, and I'll promise you, that if it goes bad, I'll get her out of there."

It sounded like another reach into fortune that did not exist. Mick had been battered by life, and still he carried on like good luck shined on him every day. Clearly it did not. He knew what Waapikoona knew: that she could control a little girl, but she could not control the girl's Thunder-Being. A yes from the girl was a yes from the bird. Mick had taken his request above Waapikoona, into a realm where she had no authority.

He took a breath to speak, but she didn't want to hear any pleas or promises, and she certainly had no desire to hear his excuse for bypassing her in recruiting Isabel. There was a slim chance it might not match her understanding or her sympathy, and right now she only saw his desperation, his limitless fortitude. She admired it all too much.

"I forbid it, Mick. You can't use my sister." Because if there was a person to help Mick pursue some reckless dream, she didn't want it to be anyone but herself. "*I'll* take you."

He raised his head to look at her. Moonlight played in his hair, rested on his unclad shoulders. She stooped to retrieve her quilt from the ground and avoid his eye and the worship she saw there. She was unfit for such a thing. The downward motion slowed time, gave her a moment with the plan unfurling before her. In sleep, or in some daytime autonomous process, her brain must have worked it all out without her consent. Mick's request for help, and her refusal, had laid out the need. She knew exactly the bargain they could present. A real, solid plan, destined for success. An idea she couldn't possibly agree to and wasn't ready to voice aloud.

Mick covered his face with both hands, breathing slowly into them. She watched him wrestle elation and relief as she braced herself against the trial she'd soon face. If The Silent One didn't agree he owed her for the work she'd done, she'd have to bargain with something new. Knowledge of the people building a mutiny. She'd sell out Jeremiah's father and the people at the commune who left her to die, but she'd also sell out the raised people like her, the ones she'd met behind Pop's home. Being rejected as a member of their group was not a good enough reason to expose them to The Silent One, but it was a sure way to get her killed in both his world and Mick's.

But could she even draw that line anymore?

"I'd kiss you again," Mick said. "But I'm afraid I'll wear out my welcome."

Never. "Let's get home, Mick." Before they lost the moon, fell back into darkness, and did something he might regret.

This time she led the way through dappled moonlight and a new heavy chill on the breeze. Mick's silence matched her own, weary and resigned. To betray her allies so completely to satisfy the needs one of man—but she had to admit he'd made similar sacrifices for her. As they emerged from the woods into an expanse of moonlight, he came forward to walk beside her. She sensed him about to speak, but nothing came but a heavy released breath. And she was relieved, because if the glow of the big old house's porch light made him remember Spot so did she, and speaking of it would do nothing to reverse it. If it had been a simple clash of upper-world predator and prey, she could find peace with it being Mother Earth's way. She had no answer for how to cope with this.

"We don't know he's dead," he said quietly.

Waapikoona felt her eyes fill but refused to wipe them.

"And it ain't too late to check."

She knew Mick spoke of the clock, but she answered as if he'd meant the arrival of death. "It is."

He took her hand and pulled her to the wide front porch steps sitting under that warm welcoming glow. She would never engage in battle with this man's hope. It was an unbreakable force. Instead of leaving her at the bottom to wait, he dragged her up with him. She wanted to be no witness to this. She wanted to cram it against all her other bad memories and push it down and away. Then they were going through the door, and he was flipping on a hall light, calling out to the old woman.

"She's asleep," she scolded.

"She don't ever sleep," he said.

A shadow slid down the stairs and brought itself to Waapikoona's feet, chirping a hello with soft paws reaching to plant against her leg. She extended a finger for Eros to sniff before he rubbed his cheek violently against her.

"I'll check the kitchen," Mick said, heading off down the hall.

Waapikoona sat on the bottom step to let Eros love on her while Mick got his answer, and then they could leave. Eros trampled her lap and purred until she petted him. He wound around her, butting the length of his body against her as if trying to rouse her. He didn't know which side to avoid, and she had to keep an arm against her bandages to fend him off her wounds. They stung now from overexertion, leaking weariness into her bloodstream. She felt the centuries in her bones.

"Stay in the house," she told him. "There are too many monsters out there."

His response was a purr-filled meow and headbutt to her chin.

Loving animals was a setup to heartbreak—but so was loving a man.

Eros settled his belly upon her, his front legs hooked over her thigh. She closed her eyes and absorbed his vibrating warmth, feeling an urgent need to curl in a ball and rest.

"Waapikoona."

Mick stood before her with an offered hand. She wasn't sure how many minutes were lost behind her closed eyes. She took his hand, thinking of the warm bed beside the warmer sleeping girl and how soon she could be in it. Too sleepy to correct his direction, she let Mick lead her to the back of the house instead of out the front door. They crossed through the kitchen into a small sitting room where a dim lamp cast its glow onto the old woman in an armchair, a quilt across her lap. At her feet on top of a pallet of blankets lay a softly breathing Spot covered in clean white bandages.

"He's gonna be okay," Mick said in her ear.

She yanked her hand from his. She was still on that bottom step in the front hall, dreaming with Eros on her lap. Mick caught her shoulders to prevent her forward motion.

"Mae don't want him bothered though. She got him to sleep."

Waapikoona looked at the old woman, finding disappointment and a severe tongue lashing on temporary hold. Whether it would be aimed at her or Mick, she didn't care. She would endure it. She would rest, heal, and regain her strength, and then spend every day and night monster-hunting so the land around this house could be safe for Spot and everyone else. If she was going to betray The Silent One, she may as well burn his whole house down.

CHAPTER 17

A T T H E S T E P S leading down to his apartment, Mick laid his hand on Waapikoona's arm to stop her. "Sorry 'bout what I did out there."

"Don't apologize to me, Mick."

"I lost my cool."

"You're welcome to lose your cool on me anytime."

A sweep of headlights across the side yard caught Mick's attention. Any car coming so late at night down this secluded driveway could only be bad news.

"You expectin' someone?" he asked, knowing it was rhetorical. Together they'd killed both men who wanted Waapikoona dead. Jeremiah, Hammond—and he'd do it all again if he had to. Could there be another?

She stepped stiffly in front of him as if to get eyes on their visitor first.

"There somethin' you forgot to tell me?" he asked.

"Yes. Jeremiah's father. He's … "

Mick's ear fixated on a familiar sound, and he lost track of Waapikoona's words. He knew that aftermarket exhaust note, and there was only one car it could be. "Raúl."

"Go inside," she said.

He looked over at her. She was the one who was injured and needed rest—*she* should go inside. Instead, she walked out into the driveway to meet the car head-on. As it rolled to a stop, the passenger door swung open and a raptor burst out. Teresa hopped from the driver's side, hollering for them to get inside. She snatched a tennis racket from the trunk and strode toward them.

"We're tracking a swarm and it's headed this way. You need to either get in the sky or get inside." She then looked at Waapikoona. "Are you armed?"

Waapikoona gazed back. "Are you?"

Teresa swung the racket with the power of a pro player then stomped a combat boot against the gravel. "Best method for the flying ones. And there's about a thousand coming here now."

Raúl's falcon screeched overhead.

"And then we need to talk to you. Sorry for the late hour." She turned around to survey the sky.

Mick turned to Waapikoona and caught her eye. His admission in the dark woods had released him from carrying that burden alone, but had there been any point to outing himself? She could not help him. No one could. One more shift meant one step closer to living his life as a golden eagle. Staying human put him in danger of another poisonous demon bite that had nearly killed him. With a small tilt of her head, Waapikoona silently indicated the door he could put himself safely behind.

And leave her and Teresa out here to deal with a demon swarm alone? "Forget it," he said.

Something large struck the window above them like a songbird in flight hitting the glass. Sizzling demon flesh rained down instead, and Mick registered what had been too quick to see. A peregrine falcon diving at breakneck speed, snatching up the disoriented intruder with electrified talons and ripping it apart.

"Here they come," said Teresa.

"Any harder of a hit and they're gonna go right through the glass." Directly into Old Mae's first floor where she and a recuperating Spot dozed, unaware. A voice inside told Mick that was the exact intention. There was a stack of old plywood in the crawl space. He had to get his drill.

"If ya'll can hold them off—"

"Yes," Teresa said. "But hurry."

He saw Waapikoona and Teresa share a glance before he ran inside for tools. Let them worry. They could use it as their fuel. God knew Waapikoona needed it. She had been half asleep on Old Mae's staircase, and the quicker they worked, the faster he could get her inside to rest. Remembering Isabel asleep in the bedroom, he eased the apartment door to lessen its squeak. From utility room to kitchen to front room he rushed, gulping water, shoving feet into boots, throwing a hoodie over his head. He loaded his pockets with screws, tucked the drill into his waistband, and carried his baseball bat outside.

"Watch my back," he said to Waapikoona, handing her the bat.

She accepted it with her bandaged hand while drawing her flint blade with the other, her grin wide in the gleam from his apartment.

Teresa took position in the open, eyes locked on something circling the expanse of dark sky. The falcon cried a warning from high above. Mick didn't need to be in eagle mind to understand.

Waapikoona covered him as he dragged plywood from the crawlspace.

He remembered her earlier unfinished thought. "What you said before, about Jeremiah's father—"

"Forget it."

He paused longer than he should have in order to shoot a look in her direction. Forgetting a comment like that was no option. Neither were secrets between them. He'd have the info now and not the surprise later.

Whatever showed on his face prompted her to give it up. "He's alive. He was there, at that commune where Hammond was."

He rested his ladder against the house, grabbed a sheet of plywood, and climbed. Old Mae's floodlights were coming in handy. "Hold the corner of this. Does he know we killed Jeremiah?"

She dropped the bat, put her flint blade in her teeth, and raised both arms to hold the bottom of the plywood in place. Mick couldn't understand how she could move like that with that wound across her hip and ribs—and her hand, still not fully healed.

"I never admitted to it. I'd have to go back to Oklahoma to find out if he suspects me."

He didn't want her going back to Oklahoma. He jumped from the ladder and moved it down the house to the next window. Teresa's tennis racket hissed inches behind his head. As Waapikoona skewered the fallen demon's body against the ground, his eagle pressed against him. He squeezed a screw hard enough for it to bite his palm and focus his human form. "Keep talkin' to me," he gasped.

"We could go to that commune together. Kill them all."

The ladder creaked under his weight as he climbed with another board and raised it into place, Waapikoona bracing it before he had to ask. He dropped a screw from shaky fingers and went for another from his pocket. His eagle couldn't hold a damn drill and needed to back down. "We got too much other crap to do."

"That could've been them coming down the driveway."

The idea singed through him. "Pick a different topic."

He felt her grab at his waistband then the ladder tip. He dropped his hold on the plywood to slam a hand against the house to keep the ladder upright. She was perched behind him, hissing curses, one hand clinging to his jeans, the other jabbing at the air behind him. He couldn't see the attack— and was glad. The ladder shifted again. He got a grip on the window edge and locked his arm to hold his weight and hers on a tipping ladder.

"Don't move, Mick!"

Trying not to! he wanted to holler back, but the unholy screech of a winged demon took his human voice away. He closed his eyes, focusing on the rough contact of Waapikoona's body against his. Of his straining elbow, muscle and bone, nerves and blood. The give of her lips between every one of his impulsive confessions out there in the dark. He could feel foolish and regretful, or he could own it and feel gratitude. She was his salvation. Consciously or not, she unchained him.

He lived to do the same for her.

Something slid up his leg and around, bunching and twisting his jeans as it advanced. Reflex opened his eyes even though he already knew what it was. There was no holding his eagle, not on this night. Waapikoona would have to jump down so he could let the ladder fall as he shifted, but he had no way to speak the command. As he felt the shudder build, she slashed down, flinging a long sinuous black body away from them as his nose filled with the sting of underworld serpent blood and the grip on his leg disappeared.

"Back to work, Mick. I just bought you a few minutes at least."

She released his waistband and hopped down, sending the ladder in a direction his human hands had no choice but to counteract. He took his drill as she handed it up, the weight of it pinging deep into human memory of building things with his hands.

"Thanks," he bit out.

The plywood hung by one corner. He swung it into place and drove more screws through, fixating on the sound of metal shrieking through wood instead of Waapikoona kicking a path through the mangled rodent-sized bodies littering the ground below him. He finished and climbed down, his eyes focused on the house's mortar lines and Missouri red brick wall as he moved the ladder through the cleared path. He could so easily look up, or down, or out into the yard. He didn't dare.

"How many more?" she asked behind him.

"Two around the corner. I'll tell Mae to close up the other side of the house. The second floor is already locked down."

"Sarah?"

They heard Isabel's voice at the same time and turned toward the apartment doorway. She stood barefoot where the top step met grass, her face tipped up toward the sky. Teresa stood watching the girl a few paces beyond, hair escaping its tight knot, pale face sprayed with demon blood. Mick felt his struggle against his eagle slip. He could not acknowledge the chaos he heard above and around, a cacophony of wings pounding air, the hiss of demons, the whoosh of a falcon's dive. Isabel trembled, dropping into a squat, good hand against the ground.

"I have to get her—" Waapikoona shoved away from the grip he'd unknowingly taken of her arm.

Lightning illuminated the sky in a blue-white fork, rocking the ground with a deafening hit of thunder as Mick was forced to see what he didn't want to see. Winged demons swarming like a net above them, dodging beams of crackling electricity, creating chaos for one thunderbird who worked alone.

Not for long. Isabel's sleep shirt lay crumpled on the ground, and a translucent bird rose into the sky with an uneven beat of mismatched wings. Mick knew how impossible it was to stop his eagle's hunt once it had started. For Isabel, it would be the same.

A creature broke from the swarm and fell toward him. There was not even time to shift. He swung, knocking the demon from the air with the butt of his drill. Waapikoona had made it back to his side in time to stomp a boot over the body.

"We have to get her down," she said.

"Ain't no gettin' her down until that whole swarm is cleaned up."

She turned, aiming her gaze at the yard. "And the serpents?"

"Them too."

Wind pushed her hair over her shoulder, revealing a leak of blood down her neck. "Well, get to work so I can get both of you inside—"

"Hey." He pushed her hair aside and traced the blood to a pair of dark holes on her neck. "You got bit."

"So you didn't have to. Now hurry and finish so I don't have to take any more fangs aimed at you."

MICK PRESSED GAUZE against the weeping bite on Waapikoona's neck in the harsh light of his kitchen. His eyes hadn't yet adjusted after being so long in the dark of night. Raúl and Isabel had followed the remaining handful of winged demons that bailed once their horde was crippled. Teresa was in the bathroom, showering off the blood and grime that coated her. For the moment, Mick had Waapikoona to himself.

"It's nothin' like the bite I got," he said, remembering that night in the road, the snake-eyed shark-toothed winged demon turning his human arm gray with underworld toxin. "It looks more like a vampire bite."

"Maybe I'll develop a thirst for blood."

"You don't already got one?"

He pulled a chair to face her so he could sit and enjoy the weathered smile before it fell. She watched him sit, her sleepy eyes reddened by fatigue. A complicated thought played across her face, one he wasn't sure he wanted to hear right now.

"Hold this here for a bit." He lifted her hand to replace his on the gauze held against her neck.

"You held off your eagle out there."

It was true. He could be reassured, even emboldened by it if he wanted, but accepting a premature victory could also be a reckless thing that would make him slow to defend himself the next time.

"You're still in charge," she added.

"It don't ever feel that way."

"I see it."

He wondered what else she saw. In him, in her thoughts, in the muddy grave before he'd dug her from it, in the place she went while unconscious in his bed. He looked squarely at her. "What else do you see?"

She averted her eyes as if caught at something, an action he'd never seen from her since the moment he met her. He could blame his demanding gaze, a power move he had to play here or he'd never know where she truly stood. Being on the same page was crucial. He could not face The Silent One beside her if secrets dwelled between them. He'd already divulged all his own. So he kept his eyes on her face and refused to back down.

When she finally looked at him, the energy between them changed. Instead of seeing avoidance, he saw reluctance. To offer her some space, he stood. If she needed a moment, fine, but there'd be no dismissal this time. She owed him something—he just hoped she knew what it was because he sure didn't. All he had was a feeling, a vague sense of a hazy wall that hadn't been there months ago during the time they spent together. Wandering the woods as eagle and woman, killing scumbags, crawling through caves, sharing an impulsive, blazing hot kiss in a firelit mausoleum. Even as strangers he hadn't sensed this distance. Even as she'd walked away from him that final day and disappeared.

At the counter he sorted through bandages to find one for her vampire bite. He needed to put her in bed. He wanted to curl around her, tuck her against him. With bandage and ointment in hand, he returned to the chair facing her and removed her hand from the wound on her neck. Meeting her eyes wasn't in the plan, but he couldn't ignore the haunted, distant look that had come across her—eyes slightly downcast, unfocused, lips pressed. She raised her wounded hand but seemed disconnected from the action even as the fraying bandage flapped off. There was no doubt it pained her after how she'd used it outside to help him board up the house. He'd have to rewrap it. But he couldn't let it be a distraction.

"Where did you go, while you slept? Did The Silent One take you … ?"

She began to unwrap her hand. "I saw the world as he wants it. Slashed, gutted, turned inside out."

"A dream?"

She laid her hand on the corner of the table between them, palm up, fingers curved. He could see the exact edge of new pink skin joining red-purple scab with healthy light brown. Damage repaired, a tear closed, except at one corner where a shiny spot of bright new blood leaked through.

"More like a vision from his consciousness. He and I shared that space many times. When I was unconscious in your bed, I was inside him."

Mick dressed the bite on her neck, careful with his expression. The emotion that turned his stomach and raced through his blood wasn't simple jealousy—how could he be jealous of a giant millipede from hell? The simple explanation was sharing Waapikoona with anyone. The more complicated one was his territory in threat. He didn't own her and never would. He also couldn't abide her sharing space with the king of demons, whether she volunteered or not. He moved his doctoring to her hand, dabbing ointment on the new break in her skin before starting a new bandage. "Then you know his secrets."

"I know his ambitions. There was a time I longed to see this world turned upside down, in my old life and in this one. I wanted to watch it burn." She lifted her eyes to his. "But then I met you."

Now it was his turn to avert his eyes, and he wasn't even sure why.

"I realized something after seeing the world he wants so clearly. This is more than Isabel and me getting a second chance. This is Native people being ripped from their quiet graves, used and discarded, nothing but collateral damage in a new colonization of this same soil we suffered on not long ago. Mother Earth remembers—we remember—and he's using our anger and suffering to fuel a new war. It's a nonstop cycle of Native people stripped of human rights. It never had a chance to end the first time."

"We can stop it," he said quietly, hoping it didn't sound as naïve to her as it did to him. When he aspired to prove to her that he could plan for his future, it never included saving the world.

"Stop a fracture between the two worlds? Underworld cracking open, a flood of demons, The Silent One walking the earth?"

"That's what you saw?"

"I saw masses of the dead wake from their graves with no humanity or free will. Not raised and built with flesh like me and Isabel—something else. Soldiers, an extension of him. Centuries—no—millennium of dead bodies reanimated, overrunning the earth all at once and leaving no space for us. Think of the mass graves of Cahokia before your kind even arrived. And the millions massacred in the name of colonization. All the tuberculosis deaths in the schools in my first life. They built cemeteries next to the schools, Mick."

"Those would be children—"

"You think The Silent One won't raise children to fight? I saw them. If he hasn't already, he will. And his power will grow with each person he can extend to. Every person who's died in this country and rejoined Mother Earth through all of time. He will raise them all."

"They won't be able to do anything. In modern America? They'll all be … lost."

"They'll be powered by The Silent One. He's learned how to live in the upperworld through me, through all of us. He'll command them to spread out and destroy everything that's here."

He got an image of pioneers crossing the planes. Wagons, then trains and highways. Settlers from a different world clearing land, animals, people, to make way for a different civilization. Wide open land now divided up, doled out, owned, with no attention paid to the people who already had claim. Treaties drafted and signed in a show of peace then quickly broken. Fences, cattle, crops. Genocide. History only told one side in this country, and he could imagine how young Waapikoona in her first life would have seen his kind—not that much different from an underworld demon. As he thought it, he spoke it. "Like history repeating itself."

She leaned toward him a little as if finally she had him on her side. "But on a much larger scale. Indian Country survived when it happened to us. This country as we know it today will not. All living humans will be wiped away. You can't fight what you can't kill. You can't kill what's already dead. And no one will believe it's happening until it's over."

"You saw what Raúl's talons did to those winged things outside."

"Multiply that swarm by a hundred. He'd be overpowered in a heartbeat."

"He ain't the only thunderbird out there."

"And you have a family to think of. What you have to do, because of me … what I am, what I've done … it's going to poison you if it hasn't already. The bad energy I've created follows me around, and you're too good—"

"Don't." He couldn't stand to hear her praise his goodness, not now. There was no such contrast between them, and there never had been.

"You and I, Mick, we aren't meant—"

"I don't want to hear that."

"At least admit it's true."

"It ain't. You've got this idea you're a bad person when the truth of it is all those guys you've been killin' … well, you've been doin' the world a favor. Leo Boyle? Hammond? Any decent person would be glad they're dead. Only difference between us is you found a way to get away with it."

"Before you met me, you would have never thought to kill them."

"You wanna test me? I could make a list of people I wanted dead. I just didn't feel like goin' to prison for it."

"I don't believe you." Her eyes held his in challenge.

He accepted the test and let his silent gaze be his answer. She would not have recognized him in the days of Kari's bad marriage and worse divorce, the nights Mick sat by himself trying to come up with reasons not to hunt the bastard down, his visits to Kari's hospital room, the nonstop court dates that followed. Satisfied she understood, he got up from the table.

She caught his sleeve. "In this life I've never felt I belonged anywhere. With anyone."

He heard what she didn't say: *until now*. And maybe his temper was already hot, but he couldn't understand a comment like that when she was so dead set on proving how incompatible they were.

"My instinct is to run."

He pulled free of her grip. "You tried that once."

"I ruined your life."

"You opened my eyes."

"I've brought death—"

"Death was already here. You're helping bring life back—"

"Your niece may not ever be raised."

"But you give us a chance."

She dropped her forehead into her good hand, releasing all her breath. "Mick … "

He sat again in front of her, both hands gripping her knees. "You gave me eagle vision and wings. A form that's above human laws, free to rid the world of human garbage. You give meaning to every daily task, from buying groceries to boarding windows against monsters. You give me someone to come home to."

She hadn't raised her head from its cradle in her hand, but she lifted her eyes as if memorizing every word.

"And if today's the day of me comin' clean, I have to say this too. Every other woman I've been with has felt like just another job, and I sure got enough of those. You're the only one that's made the work feel worth it. Like it's work I want to do, work that makes life good. And now, after all that's happened, I think you're the only woman that could ever understand me."

She straightened, letting her hand drop onto one of his. Unexpected tenderness touched her eyes. "Someday you could put all this behind you."

"We both could. Together."

Reaching across the table, she slid something toward them. "I want to see your face like this again."

He picked up the photo. He and Kari sat on Old Mae's front steps, two grubby, silly kids. For some reason that ordinary moment had created a crisp memory that never faded, and he wasn't sure why. Maybe the photo was the key, and without it and the glimpses into that moment he had through the years as he held it in his hand, he'd have never remembered that day. Or maybe it was just one of those random things that stuck with a person. His ever-patient mother insisting they sit down nicely even though he and Kari couldn't hold it together long enough to hold a polite smile. Instead of getting mad, his mom had given up and snapped a candid shot. He couldn't tell Waapiloona that smile died with his mother. Instead, he gave her an impossible mission.

"You'll have to stick around long enough for it to come back."

And the smile he gave her just then made him wonder if it wasn't so impossible after all.

CHAPTER 18

WAAPIKOONA HELD TERESA'S eye through the dancing orange light of a vibrant fire while Soto tossed demon bodies into the flames. Mick stood at his apartment steps, watching the sky for Isabel and fighting his eagle. Everyone but him had cleared the bodies from the yard. Soon the evidence—and the temptation—would be gone, and he could join them.

Soto broke the staring contest with thick arms around Teresa's shoulders and an inescapable kiss. "*Hueles bien, bebé.* But you should go inside with that wet hair."

Teresa snatched the knit hat from Soto's head and put it on her own. After her shower in Mick's apartment, she had helped herself to a pieced together meal from his fridge and gone outside to wait for her man to return, saying not a word to Mick and Waapikoona as she ate and washed her own dishes. When they joined her outside, they found Soto had returned, half dressed in the driveway with no sign of Isabel. Waapikoona could choose to believe he'd lost her near the entrance to The Silent One's cave as he claimed, or she could be realistic. An upperworld Thunder-Being's duty was to destroy all underworld creatures, and it would be especially easy to kill one with a deformed wing. She hadn't yet decided how she would kill him.

Soto released Teresa and announced, "I'm starving."

Waapikoona gestured toward the dead bodies crackling and charring on the fire.

He chuckled. "I prefer them raw."

The squeaky hinge of Mick's apartment door carried through the crackle of the fire. Moments later Soto caught a tossed object, and Waapikoona recognized the shiny wrapper of the toaster strudels Isabel had become obsessed with. Mick stood halfway between house and fire, no doubt testing the strength of his human form in the presence of so many burning underworld bodies.

Waapikoona's patience had run out. "You didn't come here to help us with that swarm."

Soto chewed, swallowed. "No. But it's a show of good-will."

"For what?" She felt Mick approach. Then he was beside her, his jacket skimming her arm.

"For the deal I'm about to give you."

The fire sputtered between them, pushing the scent of charred demon flesh into the night. Mick turned quickly away, a hand over his nose and mouth. She could suggest they move somewhere else for this discussion, but this would be good for him. The more his eagle was tempted, the more he could practice keeping it down. She couldn't bring him into The Silent One's cave if he couldn't control his form.

"No deal until my sister returns in one piece."

"Two o'clock," Mick muttered behind his hand.

She looked in that direction and found a tree branch bobbing as if holding new weight. Darkness clung below and around it, masking what created the movement—especially a translucent falcon.

"The deal is banking on your sister's return. There can't be one without it."

"I've already told you no, and that extends to her."

Mick took gentle hold of her elbow. "Told 'im no to what?"

"To joining us," Soto answered. "We're looking for someone who can travel into the underworld, get us close to what rules the caves. Someone who wouldn't be out of place there."

She trusted Mick would not give up her secret. That severed from The Silent One, cleansed by the old woman, freed from her Helpers, she was no longer eligible for this deal.

"A double agent," Mick said.

"A secret weapon," Soto said.

Waapikoona turned away from the fire to stare at the lit square window in Mick's apartment door. She'd explained to Mick all the injustices Native people had suffered. He wouldn't see this as another notch on the wall—sometimes it was hard for her to see it, since Soto was indigenous himself. He spoke the language of his oppressors just as she spoke that of hers. His culture had been forcibly erased just like hers. Her bitterness confused this topic so much she'd pushed the idea away every time it was offered.

"Looks like it's still a no," Mick said beside her, still facing their guests across the fire. And that tone—she'd heard it before. He'd used it on her long ago. A threat, packed in soft, well-mannered words, just daring someone to take the first strike.

"It wasn't long ago you called me and expected a favor, Sarah."

Expected a favor and received one in the form of advice that may have been what had saved Mick's life. Was he suggesting she owed him for that? Mick's life in exchange for hers, or her sister's? She couldn't be back to this place again so soon.

"Other thunderbirds plan to take your sister, whether she chooses to join or not," Soto said.

"Which thunderbirds?" Mick asked.

"And if that's not enough, I have something else. There was an explosion at an abandoned lead mine. You both should know the place."

Waapikoona saw it. Power lines cutting through heavy forest, a deeply rutted road leading to an old water tower surrounded by broken-down buildings. She'd walked right into captivity and her second death until Mick had found her. Then he'd broken both Hammond's knees and Waapikoona had finished him off.

She couldn't let Mick speak for her, so she turned back around to face the fire.

"Used as a hub for some unusual activity," Soto continued. "Not a safe place, which explains the explosion."

Teresa snorted. She busied herself throwing sticks on the slowing flames. Waapikoona guessed which one of them had been the one to detonate the bombs, and she fought a spike of envy and lost. She wanted nothing in common with these two. They might be allies to Mick, but they were nothing to her, even if they helped her recover Mick and fulfilled her dream of torching that commune until nothing remained.

"One survivor. Has a tattoo on his arm. Horses running through fire. He'd love to know where you are."

Waapikoona found herself one step closer to the pyre. "You piece of shit."

"I thought he'd be useful in convincing you."

"Let him find me. I'll send him where I sent his son."

"He might find your sister first."

"You sic him on my sister and you don't get your secret weapon."

"*Exacto*. You see my dilemma. And here's the other thing. That injured hand transfers to her bird. It's a liability. You join us—you and the girl—and I'll take you to someone who can fix it."

If Isabel's malformed hand was a natural part of the little girl, Waapikoona would tell her guests never to set foot here again unless they wanted her flint in their throats. A human-sized pyre was just as easy to build as the one burning in front of her. But she knew Isabel's broken hand was her own fault, for not protecting that sack of the girl's bones, for allowing it to fall into enemy hands, and for indulging a softness in her heart for Mick that turned his life into something worth saving. She'd refused to choose between her sister's bones or Mick's life. And if his eagle hadn't heeded her desperate call, she'd be left with neither man nor girl. Once she avenged them, she wasn't sure what she would have done. It was better not to imagine.

"Steal some good bones from a child's hand. I know that's not beneath you. Call me when you're ready and I'll take you and your sister to someone who can help."

Waapikoona glanced toward the branch that held the invisible falcon and instead found a bright face that watched from the ground, bare shoulders catching light from the house. Isabel had regained her human ears and heard it all. Stripping off Mick's hoodie, Waapikoona crossed the grass and pulled the warm top over the little girl. "You okay?"

"Just tired. I want my good hand back, Sarah."

"Soto isn't the kind of man we can trust."

In the driveway the Nissan's doors slammed closed—an engine roared awake. Mick stood alone beside the fire, hands in pockets, watching the car back down the driveway. He caught her eye. Something tightened between them; she felt a tug, a twist, a strange apprehension. It wasn't clear how she could so easily discern he was angry with her.

She could feel its unseen force in the apartment as she helped Isabel wash up and tucked her into bed. She could see it as Mick paced between living room and kitchen like a caged animal on a marred leg. Whether she and Isabel joined Soto was none of his business, and she hadn't even decided if it was worth a second thought. When she'd kissed her sister's forehead goodnight she'd followed with a kiss on her malformed hand, and the little girl had been too tired to notice. It wasn't worth fixing if she had to agree to Soto's terms … was it?

If she ignored his threat of releasing Jeremiah's father on her, would she regret it?

In the bathroom she released her hair from her braids and wiped the scent of smoke off her face. She looked into her own bloodshot eyes in the mirror. There would be no easy answers without a good night of sleep. She flipped off the light, opened the door, and turned for the bedroom. Mick caught her arm.

"If your leg is bothering you, you need to sit down."

His lips parted—and a loud bang hit the apartment door followed by two more. A sideways fist, not knuckles, the type of knock used by aggressive cops or people set on murder. Waapikoona knew it well. Jeremiah's father with his horse and fire tattoo must be early. Soto hadn't even allowed her time to give him an answer.

A muffled bellow carried through the door. "Svendsen, I know you're in there. Get your ass out here."

Bewilderment passed through Mick's eyes before they hardened into pure eagle ferocity. He snatched the giant wrench he'd used to break Hammond's knees. "Get back. Don't let him see you."

Mick opened the door so fast it swung and hit the stop. A white man stood outside, fist raised to bang again. He recovered his balance and Mick took a step onto the threshold, forcing the man back.

"My wife said to ask you where our baby girl's at."

"Not your wife. Not your baby girl. When'd you get out?"

"What'd you say?"

"You been to see Kari? You don't go to see Kari."

"I go see who I fuckin' wanna—"

Beyond the shaft of apartment light there was a scuffle followed by a thud—a body hitting those concrete steps outside, and Waapikoona knew it wasn't Mick. She snatched Mick's pocket knife from the table and edged toward the open door, mindful of Mick's line of sight. It wasn't the demand to stay out of sight that she aimed to obey, it was her desire to keep him undistracted because whoever this guy was needed Mick's full attention. She reached the wall and peered around the door frame to see a set of boots on scrambling legs as the body it was attached to was dragged up the steps. At the top Mick stood to his full height, releasing the guy's collar so he fell hard to the ground. Mick saw her then, and the hardness in his eyes broke. His chest deflated. There was a snap of visible fear on him before it quickly smoothed away.

"I gotta kill 'im," Mick said, a resignation almost too quiet to hear. He could've been talking to himself or his god. He could've been talking to her. "Ain't no other—"

The fallen man surged toward Mick's legs too fast for him to move away, but Mick rolled into the impact, curling around the man like a cat with a toy. Waapikoona spotted the wrench on the ground an arm's length away—Mick must have tossed it there when he needed both hands to drag the man—but she halted her motion toward it. There was a wet gurgling choke coming from Mick's prey. They rolled into the slant of light, allowing Waapikoona a clear visual. Mick's chokehold was foolproof. He could hang on and choke the guy out, or he could tighten harder, longer, and kill him. She wasn't sure he wanted to do that.

She climbed the steps outside, avoiding the wild jumble of the man's legs, and opened the pocket knife so Mick could see it glint in the night. "I can do it."

He shook his head, tightening his arm with a hard jerk. The body stilled. Sometimes it was a feint. Mick knew this. He kept his hold.

"Test that blade on him," he gasped, fighting to catch his breath.

She pricked the man's thigh. No reaction. Mick released his arm and dragged himself out from under the dead weight. Squatting, he checked the neck for pulse and looked up at her.

Reading Mick's eyes, she said, "Still alive."

Mick stood and brushed the heel of his palm across his forehead, mussing sweaty hair. "I still gotta kill 'im. They let 'im outta prison, and now he'll—" He turned away to spit curses Waapikoona had never heard him use.

She could guess who this man was. Kari's violent ex, locked up for domestic assault, a behavior that prison rarely cured. By the look of Mick's hardened jaw and determined stare into the dark woods, she could also guess what he was planning. "Your eagle can't carry a whole body."

"I'll have to tear him up and scatter the pieces. Won't be the first time. Just takes a while."

This wasn't her business and shouldn't be her job to fix, but she couldn't let Mick do it alone. Too many bad jobs should have been her own grisly solitary work, and Mick had stepped up to help. Now it was her turn. "I can help."

"There's nothin'—"

"Do you have a chainsaw?"

He turned his hard attention onto her. "Can't ask you to do that."

"Tell me what he did to Kari, and I might enjoy it."

The dark woods drew his gaze again. "Not just Kari."

"The kids?"

"Yep." He covered his face with both hands, scrubbing across his cheeks, fingers into his hair, as if wiping away actual dirt. "The last time, he beat her up, broke her wrist, held a thirty-eight to her head and made her apologize for some stupid thing that wasn't her fault. She ducked away just before the gun went off. Dougie called 911 from a closet."

She watched his face as he relived it and breathed it back out, holding in cleansing cool night air for a three heart-beats before pushing it back out through gritted teeth while angry tears collected in his eyes. If she were making the call, they'd be doing more than killing the guy, but in the end it would only bring Mick more grief.

She remembered his confession in the woods. "If you shift again today—"

"Don't matter right now."

She reached for practicality. The only emotions needed for cleansing Mother Earth of human garbage were deter-mination and, at the end, relief. "I'll need the chainsaw and a tarp."

"Crawlspace. Just kill 'im first."

He was out of his clothes and in the sky quicker than she could respond. A good thing, because she hadn't processed what she was about to do as her fully conscious self. She could no longer mentally check out and let The Silent One take over these messy tasks. This one would be all her, experienced fully and dedicated to vibrant memory. It was a line she'd soon cross and, once on the other side, she could never deny that she'd do anything for Mick.

Allowing The Silent One to do these tasks through her was servitude. Doing them voluntarily for Mick could be nothing but love.

CHAPTER 19

Mᴵᶜᵏ ˢᵀᵁᴹᴮᴸᴱᴰ ᴼᵁᵀ of his bedroom, sweat-soaked and confused, wincing against the spread of sunlight blasting through the single unboarded pane of glass in his apartment door.

"Whoa," Waapikoona said, appearing from thin air. She guided him by arm to a kitchen chair, pulled it out with a foot, and oriented him into it. "Let me get you some clothes."

Clothes? He'd boil alive. All at once he realized he was buck-naked. He looked around for Isabel. Shorts and a tee dropped in his lap, and Waapikoona was back without him seeing her approach. He opened his mouth to ask what happened, where was Isabel, what day was it—but his tongue was locked and his brain pounded away the impulse. He lowered his forehead against the cold tabletop and breathed.

"Just take a minute," she said above him. A chair scraped the floor then creaked as her weight settled. "We're alone. Isabel's with Old Mae. I already talked to Kari."

Something bad related to Kari—something new—and he could make no sense of it. "Kari ... "

"Yeah, she's fine. I thought to plug in your phone last night. It was dead. She'd been calling, and was still calling, so I picked it up and told her you took care of it."

Forehead against table, Mick closed his eyes. That rich scent of human blood came rushing back. He'd flown back and forth all night, from here to nearby lakes and rivers, dumping body parts, shredded clothing, and finally, a blood-soaked tarp. He felt a caress on his head, her fingers woven into his hair, stung by a sudden stark recollection of what she'd done for him. He raised his head.

She withdrew her hand. "Let me open the door for some air to cool you off."

He tugged the tee over his head and stood to slide on the shorts. The tightness in his bad leg brought him fully into himself, away from the blood, the dark sky, the stars reflecting upon black water. The clock above the stove said it was late afternoon.

"What day?" he gritted out.

"Saturday," she said behind him. "You slept most of it away."

He spread his hands in front of him, fingers splayed, gazing at them. At some point last night he didn't think he'd see them again.

"I carried your eagle inside to the bed and shut the door. I wasn't sure—" She came around to face him. "Tell me what to do next time."

Mick wasn't sure there could be a next time. Yes, it was tedious work to scatter a body, and he'd already been exhausted after the day—week—he'd had. Never had he failed to shift back. On purpose or involuntarily. Never had he tried to, found himself unable, and simply given up.

More accurately, he'd fought his eagle to the point of collapse, and his eagle had deflated at Waapikoona's feet. And he was remembering now, back to before that mess last night when he realized just how much he'd trusted her and how much she'd betrayed that. It came in clear, sharper than any memory of the past night or previous day. If it had been a simple lie, it might be easier to digest. It was more like a trick, and he'd been just gullible enough to buy it. He'd been angry, waiting for his time to confront her, trying to remain calm, keep his voice low, not attack her. He needed the truth for why she'd agreed to take him into the cave to bargain with The Silent One to raise his baby niece from her grave. Why had she agreed to that, after allowing him to kill her Helpers? Without them, there'd be no way to collect flesh, no way to raise dead bones. After learning his plan she'd sabotaged him. Helping him into the cave was nothing but an empty promise.

"Mick?"

He looked into her eyes, finding the haunted look that surfaced in her most tired state. Now he knew it wasn't just the burden of chopping up a body with his chainsaw and every other horrible bit of reality she'd survived. It was the predicated end of the world, its plan already in motion. Neither of them had the option of looking away, taking a day off, pretending there was some other person to handle the job of whatever it was they were supposed to do to stop it all. He'd slept all day, but how much sleep had she allowed herself? Had she kept vigil over him, after carrying him inside to safety? It was beyond screwed up—all of it— but he couldn't keep this anger inside him a moment longer.

Seeming to sense his attack, she turned away. He took hold of her arm. "How does The Silent One rebuild people from bones?"

Her eyes had darted to his abrupt grip. Now they returned to his face. "From the flesh we gather."

"With your Helpers."

"Yes. Do you mind?" She yanked her arm from his grasp.

"You let me kill your Helpers."

She pushed past him. "You wanted to kill them."

"Yeah, but you let me."

"What's your point?"

"Why bother takin' me into that cave if you got no Helpers I can feed?"

"*You* can feed?"

"How else is the baby gonna get raised?"

She crossed her arms on her chest, watching him. He heard it with new ears. She hadn't sabotaged him. *He* had. Too much stress and new ridiculous issues to solve, like Kari's ex being released from prison, swarms of killer demons trying to break into the house, Spot getting attacked, Waapikoona's injuries, and Mick getting himself lost in a cave and going full deadbeat on both his jobs. He'd scribbled a plan for his life on paper to prove to this woman he had his future under control, and then he went and rashly exterminated two creatures that were a crucial part of that plan. Raise baby Helen was number one on his list. No longer possible because he'd gone and fucked it up.

But hadn't she already known what he wanted to do? Then she'd baited him. She'd taken advantage of his overstressed brain—and his trust—and he'd walked right into the trap.

"Sit down, Mick."

He felt the clench in his fists, the rapid heartbeat in his ears. He needed to get away from the crush of this apartment and think. But that was his eagle mind, feeling imprisoned under this ceiling and longing for the open expanse of sky. A long look at the open door got him one step closer. Waapikoona took a fistful of his shirt and repeated her command for him to sit. He ignored her. The beam of outside light took on new dimension, filling with colors his eagle saw but his human couldn't name. She curled her leg around his bad leg, buckling it so he dropped into the kitchen chair.

"I'm going to make tea, and you're going to keep your human ass in that seat."

After a long glance to root that idea in place, she moved away. Her trust in him to stay put fed both eagle and man. They competed for her affection equally. Inside him, they squared up.

"I think you just broke my ass."

"Your Thunder-Being has no such sense of humor, so am I right in thinking I'm speaking with Mick?"

A vibration passed along his skin. "For the moment."

"Then put your mind at ease. We don't need my Helpers to raise your niece."

"Then how'd you—"

"I had a quota to fill. It had no bearing on raising my sister. That was something I asked as a favor, that she be one of the next to be raised. We can all make that request. It's just a matter of whether he chooses to do it."

Mick felt his anger retract, along with his eagle. He'd already figured the great demon would need convincing to raise his niece, and he had a bulletproof offer.

"Taking you into the cave won't be easy. I don't belong to him anymore. But it won't be impossible." She took a breath and looked away. "What's impossible is to fix Isabel's hand … I'll have to kill a child and steal its bones."

"Not happening."

She turned a harsh gaze upon him. "You don't make that call."

Panic climbed through him. There was no way she'd do it, no way he could stand by and allow it, no way he could stop her.

"I told you, Mick. Sometimes death is a mercy. It was for me in my first life. So I just have to find—"

Mick raised a hand to stop her from going down that morbid path. *Death can sometimes be mercy.* She'd said that to him in the woods when he was breaking down over Helen's death, and now, inspiration flashed hot and bright. There was already a dead child buried secretly in the woods. They could take the delicate bones from her hands and donate them to Isabel. Could he knowingly cripple his niece, should she live again, in order to heal another girl who might help them save the world?

"Helen's bones." Someone else may not have given it up so easily, but Mick had no time to hold information and wait for it to be more advantageous later. "They're from a smaller child—" He wasn't sure if they needed to match in size. Building dead bones with new flesh seemed like more art than science. Accuracy and specifics couldn't possibly matter.

Waapikoona opened her mouth as if ready to oppose him, but nothing came out. She looked toward the open door, where the slant of sun had lowered and shadows encroached. Mick recognized her silence as surprise, a reaction to an unexpected answer she hadn't thought of. Now this plan she'd been set on explaining was not just unexpectedly changed, it was solved.

"I won't ask you to do that," she said finally. She wouldn't look at him.

"I'm offering." He couldn't make a suggestion like this without Kari's agreement, but he felt certain if she knew all he knew, she'd be proposing the same thing.

"You can't. Because then your niece will be raised with a broken hand like Isabel's."

"Better alive with a broken hand than in a grave."

She watched him a long time then, with eyes that grew more sober as he studied her in return. It was a good plan—a great one, really—invented by a guy who apparently didn't know how to plan. With effort he kept the victory out of his expression. This moment was too important for gloating. He wanted her to experience the ever-tightening strings that bound him to her, as real and palpable in the room as her steady dark eyes. Soul-deep trust. Comfortable, meditative silence. Wordless understanding. This is how it felt to find a lifelong companion. He was sure of it.

"Then we'll pass the rest of your niece's bones to The Silent One as my sister," she said quietly, averting her eyes in thought. "I'll convince him it's a debt he still hasn't paid."

"Your sister's already raised."

"He doesn't know that."

He felt a clash of eagle disagreement. "She goes to his cave, Waapikoona. My eagle has seen it."

She turned again to face him. "He doesn't know she's my sister."

Man and eagle tossed that idea back and forth and found no reason the girl could have been identified. Even if she had, the demon's memory spanned ages. He couldn't possibly keep track of where one girl belonged. And Waapikoona had fled Wyona and disappeared before Isabel returned to life, so the timing was off, unexpected, or completely random. The demon surely raised too many dead people for one to hold his attention.

"How will you convince him?"

"You'll have to trust me."

He hoped he wouldn't regret saying it. "I already do."

"Your niece's hand, in exchange for my help in raising her from the dead." She said it quickly, as if to erase his last statement.

He extended a handshake which she took and held with her eyes locked on his. Knowing what he planned to offer the great demon, he worried what she herself planned to pledge to him.

As NIGHT ENCROACHED, Mick cleared a space in the utility room at the rear of his apartment to unfold the ladder in the ceiling allowing entry into Old Mae's first floor through a trapdoor. At the top of the ladder, he found the edge of the panel and pushed upward slowly. Even though this door had been covered for decades, he knew which room it opened into and was pretty sure there was no furniture in the way. Slight resistance above him had to be a rug. He opened more and saw a fringed edge flap into the opening.

Isabel's face appeared. "Hi."

"Hey. Do me a favor and pull that rug off."

The girl reached for the rug and peeled it back. Mick stepped up one more rung so he could see into the room. Two cats stared back, heads bobbing as they cautiously advanced on silent paws. If he left this open, he was going to have an apartment full of animals.

"Come on down," he said to the girl. "We got a big day ahead of us."

"Why are you coming through the floor?"

He backed down the ladder, holding a hand against Isabel to steady her as she climbed down with her one good hand

and her opposite elbow. "'Cause it ain't safe to go outside at night."

"It used to be."

"Well, it ain't no more."

Chapter

20

Exiting the bathroom after his morning shower the next day, Mick found Waapikoona doing pull-ups from the rafters. He took inventory of her known injuries and felt a sympathetic tingle roll through him at the thought of her gored side under strain. He'd doctored her up enough lately for those wounds to be his business—and he needed her somewhat healthy and not actively bleeding to lead him through the cave.

Of course she already sensed his scrutiny. She dropped to the ground. "Save it, Mick."

He pulled on his T-shirt. Buckled his belt. Eyed her back with the same amount of heat she gave him. He wasn't sure which game they were playing—animosity, lust, or both. Cereal bowls clanked in the kitchen where Isabel was setting the table for breakfast. The game would have to wait.

They ate enough to cover both breakfast and lunch, and then Mick went outside to load the GTO with tools for the day ahead. Grave-digging, demon-killing, cave-crawling …

He stood at his trunk as a warm sun emerged from behind heaps of blue-gray clouds edged with pure white and tried to think of what else the day might bring. This was the time of year to tune up the old riding mower, for Old Mae to scold him for trimming too close to her daffodils. For Pop to dig out his push mower from the garage, for Kari to fuel up hers, and for Mick to somehow find time to mow three lawns and work on saving the world.

Waapikoona came outside with her hair braided, wearing cowboy boots and jeans, beaded earrings, fleece zip-up, and a dark denim jacket over her shoulders that must have come from the Jeep. He felt both disappointed and relieved the weather called for something lighter than her brown puffy coat because if he'd seen that along with everything else, he might fall headfirst through time to last December, when this all began, then ended, then began again. Isabel trailed behind, two short braids in contrast to her older sister's one, a folded canvas drawstring bag clutched under one arm.

The last time he'd seen a bag like that had been in the mausoleum, his leg ruined, foot burned, wrists bound to the wall. Body nearly numb with oncoming death. Waapikoona's face bloodied, ear torn, her eyes demanding he find his eagle and save them. And that canvas bag full of a child's bones, the horror that followed, and his awakened fight against it.

Winter was over. True spring felt so close he could smell sunlight and the fresh bite of rain in the air. Waapikoona and her sister were here, alive, climbing into his GTO like they belonged with him. He slammed the trunk lid and tried to subdue the gush in his heart. When he got in beside Waapikoona she looked at him, pensive, as if what she had to say would be ruined with speech so she'd chosen to keep quiet. He wanted to kiss her—a casual, sunny Sunday morning kiss—but wasn't sure if he'd earned the right to an impulse like that. "How's your demon bite lookin'?"

"Fine."

"You up for this?"

"Drive, Mick."

"Yes, ma'am." He started the GTO and gave it a hefty hit a gas as he backed up to turn around in the driveway.

"Wait," she said, a hand on his arm that thrilled him more than it should on a day lined with such gruesome tasks. "We should take the Jeep. It's—"

"Less noticeable. Good call."

"And not registered to you. In case we need to leave it somewhere."

He pulled back into his parking spot to think on that. He was not going to get stuck in another cave, that was for damn sure, and taking a more dumpable car seemed to admit that was possible. But she and Isabel were already out of the GTO. She tapped on the trunk lid, and he hit the release. Together, they moved all their gear to the Jeep.

She tossed him her keys. "You're still driving."

He helped Isabel into the back and slid into the driver's seat.

When the tires met the lip of road, they encountered police cars, spinning lights, and uniformed officers on foot around a pickup with a rusty camper. Waapikoona stiffened, her hand moving to the door handle as if she might run. Mick grabbed her free wrist on instinct, and accidentally met the gaze of the same police officer that questioned him at Virgil's not long ago. His own guilty self should be turning onto the road and flooring it away from this scene, but the old Mick who trusted folks and had no habits of murdering people would be getting out to ask what the heck was going on so close to Old Mae's place, so that was what he had to do.

He unbuckled his seat belt.

"Mick." Waapikoona's voice spiked his own unease with more warning and alarm.

"It's all right," he said, getting out.

A semi screamed past on the road, stirring road dust into the air as he rounded the back of a squad car parked on the shoulder behind the camper truck. Now he could see the ground beside it, and the numbered yellow markers positioned near large rusty stains on the pavement. This wasn't just an abandoned vehicle.

"What's goin' on?" he said to the group, keeping his distance.

The officer who'd caught his eye earlier separated from the others. "Mr. Svendsen, right?"

Mick felt like asking questions, not answering them. "Whose truck?"

The cop checked his notepad. "Registered to a Ronald Ramsey. Is this your driveway?"

"You know it's my driveway."

"Did Mr. Ramsey pay you a visit last night?"

Mick felt bulldozed by the memory of who had actually shown up at his door. Eddie Boyle, high school friend turned brother-in-law, domestic abuser and convict, now feeding the fish of several nearby lakes. Even though Mick didn't feel like answering questions, he knew what it would look like if he didn't. "Never met him."

"You know him?"

"It's a small town. I know *of* him." Another meth head who ran in the same circles as the Boyle brothers, more closely acquainted with Leo since Eddie had been locked up for the past couple years. They'd all been decent guys once, or so Mick thought. It wasn't just the drugs—that seemed to have come later. The disgruntlement and abusive stuff came first. He'd never understand how normal kids could grow into angry men who targeted their own wives and children. If it was a disease inherited from angry fathers, Mick was grateful for the one he'd been given, dementia and all.

"He didn't come by here last—?"

"Not to my place. I told you I never met him. Is that blood?" Mick knew last night's real visitor hadn't been bleeding when he'd banged on the apartment door, and there was no way for his corpse to have leaked all the way out here on the road. His eagle had flown the opposite direction.

"Was this truck here yesterday?"

"I didn't see it." And neither he nor his eagle saw another person on his property. If Ron Ramsey had been in this truck, something else must have gotten him. "You think it was a hit and run?"

Unlikely without a body. But Mick couldn't think of any other way to prod for more information.

The officer adjusted his belt and glanced toward the other police circling the camper truck like he was about to go off the record. "Or maybe another Wyona missing person connected to you?"

Mick held the other man's eye a bit harder than he should. Accusing him seemed way out of line considering all the missing people all over the news, not just in Wyona. Of course this guy knew that and was using it to bait Mick into talking. "That's quite a reach, don't you think?"

"We're investigating." The officer's attention fixed on the Jeep. He lifted a hand to shield his eyes from the sun for a better look inside.

"Good luck with that." Mick didn't intend it to sound so mocking, but it was too late to take it back. He returned to the Jeep, put it in gear, and pulled onto the road, passing the line of squad cars with their flashing lights. With Isabel in the car, he wouldn't be able to ask Waapikoona if she killed a second guy last night. The little girl watched him in the rearview mirror, and he knew he had to say something. "Just an abandoned truck. Cops are probably gonna have it towed."

"Is it broken?"

"Could be."

"You should fix it."

"Nah, I'll let the cops handle it."

"That was his ride," Waapikoona said softly as the engine's RPMs gained volume. A back seat passenger would have trouble hearing over the sound.

He shifted into fourth and the sound waned. A glance in the mirror at Isabel showed a girl contentedly gazing out the window. He accelerated up to the speed limit, and when the RPMs offered enough cover, he said, "You see the blood?"

In his peripheral vision, she nodded.

"Had to be a second person." Now at cruising speed it would be difficult to talk.

Waapikoona's silence marked her agreement. He'd have to wait for a safe opportunity to ask if she knew anything about that second person. They'd also just lost the anonymity of the Jeep, if they did have to abandon it somewhere.

As he slowed for the turn onto the road that led to Pop's, he noticed the wide stretch of packed dirt beside the church that should be parked full on a Sunday morning. He braked harder to read the sign. *Service canceled until further notice. Trust in the Savior, for He will lead us.* It left no space for the pastor's weekly scripture selection.

"Do you want me to drive?" Waapikoona asked.

He found the correct gear and centered the Jeep in the lane. If she worried he was distracted due to suppressing his eagle—well, it was more dire than that. First Baptist of Wyona had never canceled a service in his life, possibly longer. People going missing, underworld creatures swarming the earth, the world ending … if there was ever a time for church service, it was now.

"Real strange time to close up the church. You'd think right now people would need it more than ever."

"Your god is only a comfort to some. To others, he's a weapon."

Or painfully absent, as Mick had learned the hard way when he'd begged God for help with his dying mother, his father's mental decline, and every impossible thing that happened to his family once those things were in motion. At some point in his early manhood, a drain plug had been pulled, and he had spun down and around, scrambling for hold, only to find slippery walls and darkness. In the end Mick wasn't even bitter. He was relieved to know that fixes would only come from his own hands. He was the owner of his life. And he got up every morning and made it all work. No longer was he dependent on some plan he had no access to.

His mother had always believed. Her brand of God had given her comfort until her last breath, and his gratitude for that held him from asking Waapikoona to elaborate. If religion had been used to torment her in her first life, Isabel would know the same. Mick swallowed against the sickness that rose whenever he imagined what horrors were done to that little girl. There was no way to travel time and seek justice—or revenge—and even if he could, how could he ever claim the task as his own if Isabel wasn't his to begin with?

AMONG BUDDING TREES in the dappled sunlight, he searched Pop's woods for stones laid upon loose earth marking the grave he dug for his dead niece. If his stomach and heart survived burying her, he could survive digging her up. As he worked he wasn't sure what to pray to, but out of habit he prayed to God that she had turned to bones. If there was anything more inside the grave, he wasn't sure how he'd endure the heartbreak of seeing someone so fragile and helpless and loved reduced to gruesome ruin.

"Here," Waapikoona said, the tip of her boot brushing dirt from under a pile of fallen leaves.

Together they kicked away the pile to expose the grave. With a glance at the trail they'd taken out there, he stabbed the shovel into one end as Waapikoona began to remove stones. Even though they'd left Isabel with Pop, he couldn't be certain the girl would stay put.

"She won't follow us here," Waapikoona said. "She minds you."

"Probably 'cause I'm the new toy."

"Nonsense. She respects you as an adult. I'm not sure she'll ever see me as anything but a big sister." She spread a tarp beside the grave. "How is your niece buried? We don't want to lose any pieces."

Mick recognized the weighted change in subject. If Isabel's obedience to him versus her was a touchy subject, he'd love to jump on that. It would do him good to put something else to mind right now. "Or maybe I'm just better with kids."

She paused her flattening of the tarp for a long moment. Brushing her hands on her jeans, she stood, avoiding his eye. "Seriously. We lose one bone and—"

"Or better with people in general."

Then she did look at him, and the thrill of those hard eyes settling on his pushed the morbid task further toward the edge of his mind.

"Are you picking a fight with me, Mick?"

She was the only one who used his name like that. From her lips it was a different word, addressing a different person than the one he knew. The name she spoke didn't belong to just another blue-collar nobody living near the poverty line in rural America. The Mick on her tongue was someone of importance, someone who stood for things and fought beside her. They came from opposite worlds, but each day since the moment they met he was working toward her side and she was working toward his. Soon they'd meet in the middle, and he wasn't sure if that would be the beginning of them or the end.

He shoveled a heap and dumped, feeling sweat prickle his back and neck. A symptom of panic and approaching doom, not exertion. "You want me to pick a fight with you?"

"It might mess up your plan for the day."

"Nice of you to admit I got a plan."

"I didn't say it was a good one."

The heck it wasn't. He dumped a heap of dirt on the tarp and turned to face her. "You got a problem with my plan?"

Waapikoona had no problem with Mick's plan until he'd led her down this trail across the land behind his father's house. Last winter she'd searched these woods for a different little girl. She'd crossed through the same gathering of ancient sycamore, their white trunks like the bones she'd hoped to find. And on the ground below their branches, where no underbrush grew, a ripple of limestone had jutted from the earth to mark an entrance to the underworld. Too small for her human frame to enter, but large enough for a swarm of winged demons to pass.

Here on this walk with Mick, she'd found no limestone. No opening. Just the sycamores towering over a strange clearing empty of the smaller trees and woody vines cluttering these forests. Her connection to the underworld must have fully drained away—either from her severance from The Silent One or from the old woman's medicinal bath and mysterious runes. She couldn't act as Mick's guide through

The Silent One's cave. She wasn't even sure she'd be able to find the entrance.

Perhaps it was harsh to call his plan bad. He didn't know about any of this. If she truly couldn't perform her side of their bargain, then there was no use in unburying his niece. Her old self would wait until she had the hand bone in her pocket before she revealed her bad news.

What was she thinking? Her old self might have been able to do that to someone else. Not to Mick.

"Maybe you should stop digging. Leave her at peace." She kept her eyes on the glimmer of sunlight through the trees, unwilling to witness the hope drain from Mick's eyes.

"Where's this comin' from?"

"I'm not sure I can be your guide. I'm not part of that world anymore."

"No one has to know that but us."

"Yeah, but if I can't see the doors anymore—"

"You'll see it." He turned back to his work.

"I'm saying I can't. There's one under a slab of limestone back there where the sycamores are. I saw it last winter. We walked across it today and it's as hidden for me as it is for you."

"What limestone?"

"Exactly."

"You just now tellin' me this?"

"Would you rather I have waited until you opened that grave? I didn't know until five minutes ago, Mick."

He flung the shovel down and walked away, hands shoved into his hair. They couldn't ask Isabel. If The Silent One saw them together, it would ruin the ruse. Mick's niece wouldn't be raised, and Isabel would undoubtedly be punished. If they didn't come up with a better option, Isabel would be their only choice along with their impossible risk. Mick paced in a slant of sunlight, thinking, fuming, or both. The only other raised person who might consider her a friend was living in Oklahoma, doing what he could to fill his quota for The Silent One, keep his head down, and maintain a normal life. His wife thought his nighttime outings were a second job to help pay the bills. She wanted upperworld things like a college degree and a baby. Waapikoona couldn't imagine asking him.

"Hey," Mick said, drawing near. "The ghosts in the cemetery—"

"Hey—" The parroted word went straight to her mouth without thought because that was a damn good idea. "Okay, let's think about this."

"'Cause if I can see 'em, then you can see 'em, right?"

Unquiet spirits walked the realm between upperworld and underworld. Once someone became aware of their presence, it was hard to unsee. How many days, or more importantly, how many of Old Mae's baths had passed since the day she begged the spirits to help her find Mick and bring him home?

"You can see 'em," Mick announced, as if just holding that belief made it so. He picked up the shovel and plunged it into the earth like the passing time was a new enemy they must overcome.

When the shovel exposed the first glimpse of dirtied white sheet, Mick excused himself and pushed roughly through a patch of young evergreens. Waapikoona watched him retreat, shovel in a tight grip, unaware he was leaving her without a tool to continue the job. She went to her knees and clawed the dirt free. It was damp from misty spring rain, loose from its recent disturbance. Neither Mick nor she had the skill to identify which bone was the one to cure Isabel's broken hand, even with the skeleton at rest as it would be. She found the edge of the sheet at the head and feet and peeled it from the ground, collecting the remains in a pile toward the middle. She was well acquainted with death. To her, this girl was unknown, just a pile of remains returning to Mother Earth. She could spare Mick from this task, and she knew he would do the same for her.

She carried the bundle to the hose behind Mick's father's house and cleaned the bones. In the side yard she found a patch of sunlight out of view from the house's windows where she laid them out on the sheet to dry. Then she took a seat in the warm rays and stretched out her legs, keeping watch over the bones, waiting for Mick.

Not much later his form caught her eye emerging from the woods, shovel over his shoulder, tarp folded under one arm. The sight of what lay next to her in the sun caused no waver to his step. He reached her, dropped the tools, and lowered himself beside her in the crooked way determined by his bad leg.

He aimed his gaze in the same direction as hers. The far distance, beyond the downy green carpet of new grass, through the trees shimmering in dew and morning light. "It's a hair less gruesome like that."

"The healer will know which bone she needs for Isabel."

"Good, 'cause I got no idea."

"Me neither."

"Thank you." It came out fast with not a moment's pause, as if he'd stored it up to say and couldn't keep it back any longer.

He kept his eyes aimed ahead, but she knew they'd be dewed just like those trees. The magnitude of that *thank you* impacted an unfamiliar place inside her, and every response she tried in her head sounded wrong.

It was nothing.

Don't mention it.

No problem.

The gravity of it wasn't even his thanks. She didn't need those words from him. The honor was all hers. A difficult task she could shoulder for him and give him relief. The bittersweet pleasure of it encased her like the sunlight on her clothes, making her want to thank him. She was practically high from being useful and alive and able to lend a hand to someone so loved. In her language there had been a word for this feeling, more heartfelt than anything she could think of in English. It was more than *you're welcome* or *my pleasure*. It carried longevity, that it was one of many things a person would freely do, that it wouldn't be the last, and it only skimmed the surface of how a person might serve another—not out of servitude, but love.

Dying for someone was easy. Walking beside someone through life's hardship and pain proved truest, unbreakable devotion. All of this, packed into one word she no longer remembered.

I walk beside you always.

All she had was the English translation, missing the context and depth it once had in her lost language. A word viciously stolen from her by the ancestors of the man who sat beside her, the man who'd revived the feeling for this missing word into her head.

"What?" Mick asked, scanning her face like he'd been watching her awhile.

She straightened her back, catching the breeze in her hair, feeling the sun's warmth on her skin through her jeans. In the fleece jacket he'd rescued from her tomb and kept safe, knowing someday he'd find her again, she slid her fingers against the ground to connect with his.

"I walk beside you always," she said, because it was all she had left. The worst of his kind could destroy her language, her culture, her people, but they could never destroy her soul.

"PRISON BREACH," POP said when they reentered the house to collect Isabel. The bones were dry, safe in a canvas bag in the back of the Jeep. Mick had cleaned off the shovel and loaded that up too, and then he'd paused at the rear bumper of the car like he wanted to kiss Waapikoona but wasn't sure if she'd accept it. Instead, he'd asked if she'd come inside, and she'd followed him in.

Kari stood at the kitchen sink, watching it fill with soapy water. "You can't be serious." She wiped her hands on a kitchen rag and turned, her gaze snagging on Mick before moving to Waapikoona.

"Pop's sayin' he got out in a prison breach, Mickey." She gave her brother a long look, a wavelength of understanding between siblings that Waapikoona had no access to.

"What prison breach?" he said, eyeing her back.

"Lookie here," Pop said, turning the volume up on his little kitchen TV.

… security breach at a Missouri penitentiary leaves two hundred thirty-nine prisoners unaccounted for. So far there's no explanation for how this breach occurred, but News Six caught up with …

"We need to call the police and tell them he was here—"

Mick caught Kari's reach toward the table for her phone. "He wasn't here."

"If they catch him, they can lock him back up." Kari looked at Mick's hand on her arm and frowned. "What're you—"

"Listen, the world's about to turn upside down. The police got more important things to do than search for a guy they won't ever find."

"He's in Wyona!"

"He ain't. And none of us saw him. If you gotta lie, lie."

Pop spoke up from across the room. "I ain't seen him."

Kari looked at her father, her frown deepening. "Don't confuse him, Mick. Shame on—"

Waapikoona elbowed against Mick, forcing him to drop his grip from Kari's arm and step back. He'd asked her to come inside, so she was going to make herself useful and fix this mess. She couldn't stand to see him reduced to lying about the world she'd brought down upon him. His sister couldn't live without the truth any longer.

"Your ex is dead. Torn to pieces and scattered among every lake in southwestern Missouri. Mick doesn't want to upset you, but I think believing that man is alive is more upsetting than knowing he's been killed."

Mick's eyes tore into her, his mouth a tight line.

"We have your daughter's bones in my Jeep, and we're going to take her to the same underworld demon who raised me from my grave."

Pop's voice carried across the room. "Knew it."

"Are you okay donating two bones from your daughter to heal Isabel's broken hand?"

"Killed?" Kari hadn't yet caught up.

"And disposed of," Waapikoona said.

Kari put both hands on the table and bowed her head. "Who killed—?"

"Take a minute to think if you really want to know that. It makes it harder to lie."

"Okay," Kari said, taking in air through her nose, releasing it slowly. "I think I ... okay."

Mick turned away roughly, muttering an unusual combination of *fuck* and *god* and *shit*. His footsteps stomped toward the front of the house. The door opened and slammed closed. From across the room, Pop whistled like someone was in trouble.

Still bent over the table, Kari turned wet eyes toward Waapikoona. "How well do you know my brother?"

"Better than I thought I would."

"He's never really had anyone, you know." Somehow, a threat leaked through her weepy gaze.

"He has all of you."

"Are you going to break his heart?"

"I already did."

And then she sat Mick's sister down and told her everything—except the part about breaking her brother's heart.

WAAPIKOONA EXTRACTED ISABEL from Janie, Doug, and a scatter of coloring books and crayons in the spare bedroom at the end of the little hall. Taking her hand, she walked her to the door and said, "Fair warning. Mick might be upset with me."

Outside, he leaned against the rear of the Jeep, arms tight across his chest, eyes hard on the road beyond. She closed Isabel inside the back seat before she approached him.

His frown remained. He didn't look at her. "You don't do that."

"I'm not going to stand there and watch you lie to your family for me."

"That ain't your choice to make."

"It's my choice to free you from it, though. If you want to fight with me, we can do it in the car on the way." As she crossed in front of him toward the passenger door, he caught her jacket sleeve.

"Knowin' the truth puts 'em in danger."

"They're in danger either way. At least now Kari knows to keep the kids inside." She twisted her arm to break his grip and stepped against him until their belt buckles clashed. He could take it as aggression. She meant it as intimacy. Even though she was aware of her mixed signals, she had no clue how to fix them. "No more lies."

"I'd never lie to you."

"To your family." Her words sounded gravely urgent, and she had no idea how to deflate them. For the first time she realized how important this was to her, and how much it had been eating away at her.

"You tryin' to redeem me?"

Close enough to kiss, but he wasn't taking the offer. Instead, she touched her fingertips against his lips. Trailed them down his scratchy chin, across his jaw. Laid them against the pulse in his neck where she'd once held a blade. "I tried that when I left you. It didn't stick."

He took her hand away from his neck and pressed a kiss against her palm. His eyes had gone sad. "You bein' here don't mean ... "

The end of that thought needed no words—or maybe they were lost like so many of her own. She saw the feeling heavy on his face. He'd never believe she was bad for him, that they were headed for a painful end. But she didn't want to see her hopelessness reflected in his face. It was enough to find herself wrapping arms around his neck to allow him to pull her in. His breath warmed her ear before he planted a soft kiss against her lobe, another on her cheek. She turned her face and gave him her mouth. The tenderness he gave back proved she wasn't the heartbreaker. He was. Her chest skewered, life drained out, her knees weak, breathless, limp. The world was doomed, and he was bringing her bliss. Something else to mourn later when everything collapsed. And if he kept kissing her like this, there would be nothing of her left, not even bones.

Or perhaps he was giving her something to fight for.

A shudder rolled through him. He pulled away, hands going to her shoulders, eyes closed as if he was trying to ground himself.

"That's weird," he whispered.

She was about to ask what when she saw the answer. Three Helpers, their eyes reflecting brown-red in the daylight as they hunkered in the shadow at the edge of the woods past the detached garage. She pitied the hardworking creatures who knew nothing but servitude. The girl's remains had lured them, and it was only luck they hadn't arrived sooner.

"Let's go before your eagle takes you."

Mick controlled a breath. "What is it?"

She dug the Jeep key out of his jeans and put a hand against his chest so he'd release her. "Your eagle's favorite snack. I'm driving." And she gave him another push toward the car door.

CHAPTER 22

"My eagle's favorite snack are the snakes." He said it more to test his human voice than anything. It had taken him miles of meditation to find it again.

"Mine too." She drew her hand from the clutch of his.

Mick's knuckles felt raw from the strain. He hadn't realized how tightly he'd been holding onto her. She maneuvered the Jeep along a packed gravel road he rarely used, and he was surprised an out-of-towner like her had found the shortcut. Finding a direct course like the one his eagle might fly could be tricky in the Ozarks. The bends and twists ate up a lot of time. Traffic was never an issue unless he found himself behind a tractor in a no passing zone. And speaking of traffic, he hadn't seen another car on the road since they'd left the house. Folks really were bunkered up. The number of missing people had skyrocketed, along with sightings of roaming outsiders. The escaped prisoners sure didn't help.

"You think there's somethin' behind that prison breach?"

"It's a diversion. One of many that will come. Law enforcement will be too busy to notice the world falling apart."

"I'm pretty sure they already noticed."

"And they'll be stretched thin dealing with upperworld issues like loose prisoners. The world will be overcome from above and from below. The Silent One feeds off that unrest. Why do you think he pitted my kind against yours?"

The pitched slate roof of the old mausoleum flashed through a gap in the tree line, and Mick fell hard back into his human brain. His head swirled with the altitude plunge. He'd been having a human conversation with Waapikoona while partially in eagle mind—more concerning evidence of his fast-approaching doom he'd have to push aside for now. He checked the time on his phone and wondered why every little thing he had to do took so damn long. "We gotta make this quick."

"The dead can't be rushed. Especially when it's us asking them for favors."

She turned the wheel hard to narrowly avoid a set of ruts, causing Isabel to cheer from the back seat. Quite a change from the day Mick and Dougie had to strong-arm the little girl in and out of the car. After rounding a bend, the trees fell away to reveal the first crooked gravestones hidden in tall winter-browned grass. This was the northern edge of the cemetery, farthest from the entrance on the main road, where the maintenance was lax. No one had the time or money to get a mower back on this slope behind the mausoleum, so the landscape got a bit wild. In a few months, poison ivy would be too thick for any visits. These were the loneliest of the unquiet.

Waapikoona pulled the Jeep to the edge of the road and killed the engine. Mick found himself outside the Jeep, cataloging every tree limb, blade of grass, rock, and cloud, with no recollection of putting his boots on the ground. A gust of wind threw his hair in his eyes. The air smelled thick, like it had blown in from some faraway rain storm. He turned around to help Isabel.

"Piggyback, so you don't get lost in them weeds."

"What's piggyback?"

He turned his back to her and squatted. "Hop on."

When he straightened up with the girl on his back, her one good hand latched onto his shirt, he caught Waapikoona's eye across the hood of the Jeep. Adoration, quickly covered by a narrow-eyed judgment.

"Uh-oh. I think we're makin' Sarah jealous."

Isabel cackled in his ear. He remembered his tease about being better with kids and shot a wide grin at Waapikoona that broke her persisting scowl so fast she looked away before he could see her so mollified. She slammed her door and cut a trail through the knee-high grass, ditching Mick without a glance. Isabel's added weight disrupted his balance, giving his bad leg a harder task on unkempt land with hidden trip hazards, so he took his time following. This job was all hers, anyway. He'd do nothing but add pressure as he tried not to look at the clock. His presence could also make the spirits shy or wary, and he'd prefer to avoid any delays.

"What's in there?" Isabel pointed at the rear of the mausoleum. Morning sunlight glinted off the textured glass in the small porthole window under the upper peak. The structure seemed less ominous at this end of the graveyard, where a person could stand on its level on the height of the incline instead of approach from below. Here at the rear, it appeared cloistered, safe. He couldn't tell Isabel what was inside.

A whole lot my blood, Mick thought.

"Can we go in?"

"It's boarded up," Mick said, hoping it was still true. He couldn't see the entrance and didn't want to. "Where's your sister at?"

Isabel pointed down the hill to where a large conifer hung over several broken headstones, unrolling its dark shadow on the ground. Waapikoona knelt in a bed of pine needles, watching and waiting.

She's gonna see them. She has to.

He couldn't watch. His bad luck would jinx it. And now he was thinking about a different graveyard, a different bed of pine needles where he once laid Waapikoona so he could use his wings to find the GTO and get her somewhere warm and safe before Death took her a third time.

"Know what? Let's see if we can get in." He negotiated his way around a fallen headstone and its crooked neighbor. A rabbit burst from the tall grass, ricocheting through the graveyard. Inside, he felt his eagle lurch. It was a first. No normal woodland creature had ever caused that reaction before. More evidence for how quickly his eagle was taking over his everyday life.

He deposited Isabel on the stone wall remaining on one side of the mausoleum so she could walk it to the front where it joined the stone steps. He followed beside her until he faced the wide wooden door with the two-by-four he'd nailed across the front, which now hung by one nail. His intention had been to seal up this space where bad things had happened, but maybe that was where he went wrong. Maybe whoever removed that other nail knew it should be opened up, aired out, cleansed. Sun-warmed spring air could trick a person into thinking it was a fix for anything.

Now Isabel was pushing against the door, trying to get it unstuck from the floor. Mick shouldered it open. He'd done that before, the night he returned the demon's corpse to Waapikoona and stole a kiss along with it. She had wanted him that night, as much as he wanted her, and he'd deprived her of a second kiss—and more—just for the power it gave him.

"It's cold." Isabel hugged herself and walked further inside, looking up at the cobwebs floating in the intruding breeze.

Everything in the mausoleum was just as he'd left it. Circle of ash where Waapikoona's fire had burned, the pile of old sleeping bag, blankets, and clothes. Dry leaves kicked around, covering the dark stain of blood in the stone floor. The fraying rope that had bound his arms to the wall. The damp cold of the place clung to him like it had that winter day as he bled his life into the stone floor.

Isabel rested her hand on one of the coffins and peered into the crack exposed by the askew lid. "Are there people in here?"

Mick's gaze rested on a crushed Ramen cup. Sickness clenched his stomach. "Imagine so. Maybe we oughta … "

"Can you help me put this top on right?" She braced a hand against the edge and pushed.

… get outta here. Strange how it was what he wanted to say but not what he felt. How dare this place hold onto such a dark moment in his life so perfectly. And who was he to allow it? None of it would ever be purged from his memory, and that wasn't even what he wanted. He had the power to undo the visible remnants of what happened here, return the space to its previous state of quiet and peace. He could fix this.

First, he went for the Ramen cups—the worst reminder and the most out of place. Trash, representing the trash that fed from them that day beside the fire while Mick struggled against the rope and worked to bury his eagle. He smashed the Styrofoam pieces into one bunch and shoved it into his pocket. With his pocket knife, he cut the rope and tore it free. As he started collecting blankets and clothes, Isabel began to help. Arms loaded, they returned to the Jeep and dumped everything in the back. Mick got a trash bag for Isabel and a shovel for himself. Then it was another piggyback ride through the weeds to scoop the ash from Waapikoona's many fires and other debris.

"Now give me a hand over here." Mick put both hands on the crooked coffin lid and waited for Isabel to add her own hand. He counted to three and they shoved together, her effort matching his but of much less consequence. With a mighty scrape the stone slab slid back into place, and Mick held a fist up for a bump.

They backed against the wall to admire their work. Sunlight shifted from behind a cloud outside, turning the small circular window into a forceful glow. What had been vague dimness now danced with dust motes and sparkling light. Shadows dissolved from the corners and edges, highlighting the darkest spot in the room: the large rusty stain in the center.

It wasn't just Mick's blood. There was a bit of Waapikoona's there too. And a whole lot from someone else, the one who ruined Mick's leg, broke Isabel's hand, and had tormented Waapikoona for too long. Mick closed his eyes against his eagle's memory of torn flesh, hot blood pumping from a fresh artery, eye sockets scraped clean. And a woman—his woman—telling the bird to stop toying with the prey and end it. He couldn't remember where his eagle had tossed the man's heart, and he didn't want to.

"Someone died here," Isabel whispered.

A shadow fell across them. Mick turned to find Waapikoona standing in the doorway, backed by pure perfect light. The glare on her face now was not a cover for any other emotion; it was not directed at him in play. It was concentrated and needed no words to explain itself. They'd reached an accord where the most refined feelings no longer needed words. She didn't need to scold Mick for bringing her little sister to this godforsaken place. He already felt it. And he didn't need to meet that attack with his own. He'd cared for this girl when Waapikoona had abandoned them. He'd been there during her hardest hour. Waapikoona knew this girl in her first life, but in this life, Mick knew her better.

Waapikoona surged forward, took the girl's hand. "You brought her in here ... " She breathed the sentence away, too riled for words.

And Mick knew fury wasn't working alone. If Waapikoona's grief from that awful day in this mausoleum was anything like his own, he knew what it could fuel. He suspected she had a bit of guilt adding its own heft because she hadn't just walked away from Mick that day. She'd walked away from them both.

Isabel tore her hand away from her sister's. "We fixed the broken lid." Built into the statement was a hurtful, *why are you mad?* Mick heard it and figured Waapikoona didn't. He could acknowledge it and twist the knife of what she didn't know, or he could leave it alone.

"Your sister's upset because bad things happened here." He looked at Waapikoona as he said it. He was an asshole.

"We fixed it though." Isabel scrunched her face at Waapikoona, not understanding.

Someday, if told the whole story, she might understand that to Waapikoona, this mausoleum wasn't just the place where she and Mick fought for their lives. Before that, it

had been her quiet haven among the dead. And on that terrible day, it had been soiled and invaded, stained with violence, a cycle that repeated in both her lives in little and big
ways. To Mick, all that just gave him more reason to scrub
the place down. Make it something new. He didn't have the
weight of her pain, and he wondered if what he'd just done
was the equivalent of a *get over it.*

Waapikoona took the girl's hand again, this time steer-
ing her out the door. Over her shoulder to Mick, she said,
"What you think you can fix … " The harshness of her eyes
finished the sentiment, and she left him alone in the room.

Mick never felt such a streak of defiance, and he knew
someday he would be back here with chemicals and tools
to nuke that heinous stain out of the stone floor. And when
he did, he'd drag her back here to kiss her against the wall
like he had that night, before a terrible man unleashed hell
into her hard-won quiet.

He would never apologize for fixing things. It was what
he lived for.

On his way out, he tore the two-by-four off the front wall
before yanking the door closed. He carried it like a crude
weapon back to the car, where he found Waapikoona leaning
against the rear of the Jeep, scowl muted but still hanging
on. Isabel chased a grasshopper across the gravel.

"Call Soto," she said. "We have a guide."

His relief seemed tainted by the bad vibe between them.
"You think I don't understand you."

"I think you don't understand a lot of things."

He got out his phone. "I could say the same about you."

She pushed off and headed for the passenger door, calling
Isabel to get in the car. Mick opened the rear door and tossed
the two-by-four in and found the little girl at his side.

"Is that Dougie and Janie's baby sister?" She poked the canvas bag sitting on its own in the closest corner.

He nodded, unable to put anything into words.

"Does she have to ride in there with all that junk?"

"It's probably safer … "

"Can she ride on the seat with me?"

Staring at the canvas bag among the tools and junk, he released a hard exhale. He saw what she meant, and if he indulged her, Waapikoona would probably kill him. It was a death he'd surely enjoy.

He lifted the bag from the back and helped Isabel into the back seat, settling his niece's bones next to the girl before buckling her up. When he opened the driver's door, he caught Waapikoona's prolonged appraisal of what he'd just allowed and decided to make that phone call outside before he sat himself down next to a lit fuse.

Wandering away from the Jeep, he waited until Raúl picked up. "Hey."

"Hello, Michael." Not Raúl but a female voice. Teresa.

"Where's Raúl, on a hunt?"

She said nothing. The women of this day were about to do him in. He squeezed his eyes shut, a reaction to quell voiced pent-up irritation. It would only make his life worse.

"Guess that's a yes. Tell him we got the bones. We're ready to meet, and I don't got all day."

The call dropped. He checked his reception—full bars. So not a dropped call. She'd just hung up. God save him.

Now he had time to kill, waiting for one impossible woman to call him back while he sat inches away from another impossible woman who might also be out for his blood. He walked to the nose of the Jeep and faced it, staring inside at the woman who met his gaze and refused to look away. A staring contest to kill time? Sounded good to him.

He crossed his arms and held the stare, taking in the slant of light across her neck and collarbone, her hair resting along her shoulder. Her anger made him physically hot. He basked in it, letting his own irritation burn from within as hers scorched from the outside. They were about as dysfunctional as it could get, but instead of worrying him it made him more eager to find that common ground he knew they'd found before.

His phone rang. He answered it, his eye still on hers. "You tell him?"

"She did." It was Raúl this time. "The entrance to the healer is direct, but it's one way. You'll have to take the catacombs to a different exit. I may have forgotten to mention that."

Catacombs. Strange for him to call it that. "Through The Silent One's cave."

"You up for it?"

"Figure I'm a pro at this point. We're on Valley Spring Road behind the old cemetery. You know where that's at?"

Mick heard a question in Spanish directed away from the phone. The only words he recognized were the name of the road he just gave.

"Twenty minutes," Raúl said.

Mick ended the call and slipped his phone into his pocket. Angry eyes still watched him through the windshield. If she wanted to know the result of the call, she was going to have to ask nicely.

THEY ENDED UP meeting two miles down the road where the gravel turned to blacktop.

Not tearing up my suspension on this shit, was the text that came in from Raúl, and Mick wanted to ask Waapikoona if she'd taken this road just to needle the guy. He felt it more important to match her belligerent silence. If they got lost in the cave for seventeen days like he had, it was going to be a very long seventeen days. Or not, because had he even felt the time when he was there? He couldn't spare that time away from his life.

As they tailed the dust-coated 300ZX farther away from Wyona, he forgot the battle of silence in favor of panic. "You got us a guide, right?"

"We have three."

"All right. I just don't want a repeat of—"

"It's fine, Mick."

If she used his name like that, she couldn't be too mad at him.

CHAPTER 23

Soto led them to a strip of concrete in front of a derelict roadside restaurant, its sign hanging by one rusty hanger. Two cars unloaded—Mick tugging a baseball cap over smoothed hair, Isabel struggling with the weight of the canvas bag, Soto tossing his keys to Teresa as he turned to face Waapikoona. "A short hike from here."

Waapikoona had no idea where they were going. After a brief glance at Mick to communicate that, and a tight nod from him in response, she took the bag of bones from her sister and slung it over her shoulder. Mick retrieved a backpack from the Jeep. Soto led the group around the broken building and across the back lot. As Mick joined Waapikoona's side, he slipped the Jeep keys into her hand.

"Just in case," he said.

In case he lost the fight against his eagle.

"No," she said, handing them back. If he knew they were counting on him for their safe ride home, he'd have more reason to hold fast to his human form. She lengthened her stride to catch up with Soto and Teresa, knowing even if Mick's bad leg allowed him to match her pace, he wouldn't leave Isabel behind. She needed a little space from him, from them both.

Teresa hung back until they walked side by side. "You look like you want to gut him."

Waapikoona knew how this woman felt about her relationship with Mick. "Would that make you happy?"

"Depends what he did."

It was more than a single action. Inviting Isabel inside that tomb, trying to erase what happened there … carrying her over the tall grass instead of expecting her to plow through it—or even thinking about how a little girl would manage to begin with. Their father-daughter rapport that appeared more natural than cultivated. Waapikoona was too old to be a big sister, too self-centered and inexperienced to be a mother. She'd been guided so long by the goal of reviving her sister, she never considered what she'd do once she had her. "I guess he's just really good at exposing my faults."

"Like he's perfect?"

Waapikoona had to chuckle at that. "Maybe he is."

"*Dios mío*. Don't be so fooled." Teresa broke her stride and hung back, turning as if to wait for Mick and Isabel to catch up. Once they did, she made no effort to lower her voice. "Hey, Michael? This party only has room for one insensitive prick, and he's up there in the lead."

A burst of laughter from Soto stole a bit of the taunt's payload. Waapikoona looked over her shoulder to catch Mick's baffled expression before he locked it down.

He adjusted the rim of his baseball cap to sit lower over his eyes. "Great to know the womenfolk are getting along."

"We easily ally against the male ego."

"I think you mean 'conspire.'"

"When we start conspiring, you'll know. Isabel, go catch up with your sister."

Waapikoona heard the gallop of little feet and slowed to make it easier for the girl to gain on her. She tucked Isabel's hair into her hood and took her hand, spotting Mick on the path many paces behind, blocked by Teresa whose voice had now lowered enough to be whisked away on the breeze. Tilting his face down to the shorter woman put his eyes into the shadow of his baseball cap, impossible to read. He thrust both hands into his jeans pockets and shifted his weight to his good leg as if settling in for a lecture. His good manners would have to serve him, because she was in no mood to save him from Teresa's sharp tongue.

Ahead, Soto squatted, one hand flattened on the ground, and disappeared. The heavy thud of his body landing against earth came a moment later. Isabel broke free to run forward. It wasn't until she stopped short that Waapikoona saw the slippery rock ledge at the girl's shoes. A shout of her name lodged in Waapikoona's throat. If the girl hadn't caught herself, it would be too late anyway.

Her need for Mick had never felt so glaring. His expert safeguarding of children, anticipation of their needs, understanding of their little minds—she'd never reach that level in time to care for Isabel on her own. How she needed him couldn't be summed up as a simple craving to share a bed and home with him. She needed his childrearing skills for Isabel.

Isabel sat on her butt and pushed off. Waapikoona did shout her name then, but again it was too late.

"Got her," came Soto's voice from below.

She steadied herself with a hand against a tree trunk. Air rushed against her face. The day's breeze, not the wind from a lethal jump from a cliff. Her heart pounded, remembering Isabel's hand pulling free from hers a moment ago, a lifetime ago. It was the same feeling, one trivial, the other devastating. Separated by a hundred years, but the helpless panic and failure was the same.

Now Mick was at her side, asking where Isabel was, what happened, and Teresa was at the ledge, hopping off. Waapikoona couldn't find a way to catch her breath. Mick walked onto the spread of stone and looked down. He shrugged off his backpack and came over to face her.

"Hey."

She closed her eyes, letting the canvas bag slip to the ground as she bumped into the tree hard enough to feel the rasp of bark tug the jacket against her back. Several paces ahead was a small ledge, not a cliff. She was here with Mick, not escaping the terrors of the Indian school. "I'm fine."

"You thought—"

"Yeah." She couldn't hear him say it. It was stupid. It was all too real.

"Okay." He took off his baseball cap and turned away, knocking it against his leg. "I can't go in there today not knowing what's goin' to happen … with you mad at me."

"I'm not mad at you."

He blew out an exasperated breath, gave a tight smile. "Well, I just got my ass chewed out for nothin' then."

"I'm sorry I missed it."

"If I'm bein' insensitive—"

"You're being … " Insensitive to how much it killed her to be so tied to him. She'd been alone so long, even when she was with Jeremiah she was alone. Now she'd found a place she belonged, a person she longed to be with, and it didn't fit her life. How could she ever make it fit?

"I hate you for how good you are with Isabel."

He raised his eyebrows a bit, working to subdue the surprise evident in how he straightened his spine. He crossed his arms, an attempt at nonchalance that was fooling no one. "At least you're bein' honest."

She didn't want him to misinterpret this. It wasn't so much about him. "I'm not a mother."

Watching her, he took a moment to chew on that. "There's all kinds of mothers."

"I would've let her walk right into those high weeds."

"What high—" He looked around for a culprit like he'd missed something. When he turned back, his face held understanding. "And she would've figured out a way around them or asked for help. She's a smart girl. Maybe I'm the wrong one, for babying her."

"She adores you."

"That don't mean a thing." He kept a steady eye on her like he truly wanted no part in disrupting the love between two sisters. "And if that's all this is, then I think we're good. Because you got nothin' to worry about."

He put his baseball cap on her head and pulled her off the tree by her jacket lapels. "Hang onto this, will ya? It won't fit my eagle, and I don't want to lose it."

She transferred it back to his head. "Your eagle stays far away today."

He turned it backward, grinning at her like he was prepping for a kiss. It wasn't the same unfettered grin in the photo of young Mick, but a fabrication modeled after the same design. His face remembered it, even if his heart was too burdened to properly back it. With the shaggy hair curled on the ends behind his ears and faded flannel jacket and work boots, he looked like what she'd once called a redneck. A white guy at a truck stop chewing a toothpick, catcalling her in bad Spanish as if mistaking her race was an intentional addition to the abuse. Riding in the back of a pickup through Indian Country with a bunch of other guys doing their impression of an Indian war cry. Too often they lived up to her bias. Too often they did much worse things than taunt, on reservation land, outside of their laws. Mick wasn't the only exception, but he was her exception, and she saw into his blue eyes and understood for a heartbeat where his optimism came from.

"If you stay human today, I'll kiss you later."

"That's a deal, ma'am."

She would do more than kiss him. And this time she wouldn't allow him to escape.

Mick stashed his hat in his backpack and picked it up. He gathered the canvas bag of bones, and she took it away from him. Together they walked to the edge of the rock floor and looked down. About six feet below, Isabel and Teresa bent over something on the leafy forest floor. Soto had wandered away, phone to his ear.

"Gonna kill my leg," Mick said.

"Let's find a path down." She took off through the underbrush, angling sideways to avoid thorns. "I guess Soto doesn't make her panic shift anymore."

Mick stopped to untangle his sleeve from a branch covered with stickers. "They found common ground in the sky that night we got rid of the demon swarm."

"I'm not sure I want her trusting him."

Mick said nothing. If he was schooling his comments about Isabel now to remain in some submissive place, she wasn't sure how she felt about that. This was why she hated explaining herself. With her problems now on offer to someone else, she couldn't handle them and move on. They would always lurk in someone else's mind and memory, to be brought up any time instead of buried alone in her own. No one ever lived up to that amount of trust.

She found a steep bank smoothed with erosion. Mick gave her a nod, and she eased down it, testing the difficult spots for a guy with a bad leg. Twice she lost her footing, catching an exposed root to slow her descent. At the bottom she called up to Mick, "Take it slow."

"I got it." His response was tight.

Her concern had irritated him. Teresa wasn't wrong about the male ego. She considered turning away to spare him but found the idea of slowing his inertia with her own body at the foot of the decline to be more appealing. He crashed into her, laughing, half-bent, hair in his eyes.

"I thought you said you had it."

He used her clothes as handholds to straighten up. A tug on her jeans, a brush on her hip, her breast. A delightful pawing, almost like foreplay.

"I did. You were in my way." He let her go to brush himself off, his voice no longer so taut.

Damp cold seeped from the rock opening fifteen feet away. Her spirit guides promised to find her, and since they hadn't yet appeared, she would either have to admit to Soto why she waited or find some other reason to stall. She should have taken more time to find an easier path down, but then she'd not have the heated patches of skin where Mick's hands had taken hold.

Soto ended his call and joined them at the dark entrance, gray rock edged in glistening dew jutting above their heads.

"It's one way in," Soto said. "Out through the catacombs. Pray you come out in the daylight so you're not attacked by demons."

Isabel looked up from whatever had captured her and Teresa's interest on the ground.

"And where are you gonna be at?" Mick asked.

"Wherever. We can't help you. There's no way to know where you'll come out."

Mick muttered a curse, turning brusquely away. Returning to the surface at night would be an inevitable shift he did not want. They'd still have their spirit guides, though, and Waapikoona could send them ahead to scout.

"I'll send word out to watch, but I can't promise any backup." He turned away and called to Isabel, who had remained at Teresa's side, attention focused on the cave opening like something would soon spring out. Soto waved the little girl over to him. "I'm not sure how soon I will see you again. I need to show you something."

He unzipped his jacket and pulled up his shirt. "See this?"

Waapikoona pulled the flap of his jacket aside so she and Mick could see. Tattooed across Soto's hip and stomach was a long serpent, its slender head eating its tail beside his navel. She walked around him, lifting the jacket as she walked. The tattoo encircled his whole torso.

"Ouroboros," Mick said behind her.

"This represents the endless cycle of time," Soto told Isabel. "I need you to find this."

"Why don't you?" she asked. It was the stubborn tone she used that gave Waapikoona a pit of fear in her stomach for the fragile control she had over this child.

"I can't. Only an underworld being can see it. You'll need strength to find it. It could be far away. Once your hand is healed you will be strong enough to fly great distance."

She backed away from him to face the cave opening. "I'm not going in there."

"This serpent is not in there."

"I don't care. I'm still not going in." She squatted, tucking her knees inside her zipped jacket.

Soto and Teresa shared a glance over the girl's head. Teresa squatted to her level. "Your sister will go in with you."

"Is Mighty Eagle going?"

Waapikoona had no time to shield herself against the gouge. It wouldn't hurt so badly if it weren't true. Mick was the one to protect her, not her sister. He was the steady, even-tempered, trustworthy one who would never leave her side. She saw on his face the position she'd put him in by admitting what he had over her—and clearly he had no interest in drawing out more of her resentment—while also being torn by Isabel's concern and wanting to ease her mind. She spared him. "Yes, Isabel. We're both going."

The girl turned back to the cave, considering. She stood and walked to Soto, poking his stomach for another look at the tattoo. He raised his shirt.

"Do any other serpents eat their tails?" she asked.

Soto glanced around at the other adults for mock consensus. Somehow he knew Isabel would not trust him alone. "No."

"And what do I do if I find it?"

"You tell Mighty Eagle, and he will tell me."

Although he hadn't moved a muscle, Waapikoona felt Mick's presence stiffen. He wanted no more tasks for his eagle, and this one, as indirect as it was, felt more like a command. If Thunder-Beings had a hierarchy, how would Mick's golden eagle rank against Soto's peregrine falcon? Size and strength versus speed and experience—or maybe none of that mattered in a supernatural pecking order.

"Where's this tail-eating serpent fit in?" Mick's question seemed directed at Soto, but he shot a look at Waapikoona: *what did you not tell me?*

She knew the symbol well. An ancient one, common to many cultures, and it pained her to realize she had no recollection of her people's word for it.

"We need to find it before Sarah's boss does." Soto tilted his head at the cave entrance.

"Or?" Mick asked.

"Or he gains command over the cycle of time itself."

"*La niña está escuchando,*" Teresa said.

Waapikoona knew Isabel was always listening. If she'd heard things today, or any day, to frighten her, she gave no indication. Or maybe Waapikoona had just failed to notice.

"Seems it could be anywhere in the world," Mick said.

"We've tracked it here. Up the Mississippi, then smaller rivers, to underground. So has The Silent One. His presence here proves us right. We just need to find it first."

Mick's eyes hardened on Soto's. "Seems there'd be someone better suited for the job than a little girl."

"If you find another Thunder-Being born from the underworld, you let me know."

"She ain't the only one who can see it. There's images of the ouroboros all over the world. People have seen it."

"Mystics," Soto said. "They're a bit hard to come by nowadays. Our best tracker fell to her own Helpers not long ago."

"So you started tracking me," Waapikoona said.

"It's not easy finding someone willing to work for both sides."

"So that's The Silent One's motive. To stop time? End the world?" Mick asked.

"Power," Waapikoona answered. "Dominion. Ownership and control. Exactly what your kind wanted when they arrived on this land."

Mick opened his mouth, but shook his head instead, as if he had no energy for this argument. Soto had the decency to shrug. A casual acceptance of her answer even as barbed as it was. She and Soto had never been allies, but on this they could agree.

An unearthly glimmer appeared beside a dark trunk past Mick's shoulder. Others of the same form settled beside it. Their guides had arrived.

And she was tired of talking. It was time to move. She went to Isabel and bent to her level, taking both the girl's hands in hers. One strong and perfect, the other limp, shrunken, a shell of flesh and tendon without its structure. "Are you ready, Pinepakatwi?"

The girl pulled her good hand away and extended it in Mick's direction. He gave Waapikoona a hardened look, took the girl's hand. Waapikoona snagged the canvas bag and led them under the shelf of limestone and into the dank air. Behind her, the three wavering forms followed. She and Mick had to duck until the earthen floor began to fall away, allowing them to straighten. As they stepped away from the slant of white light, darkness covered their feet and crept up their legs. Mick shuffled his pack; a zipper squawked.

"Don't let go," Isabel gasped.

"Just gettin' a flashlight. Hang onto my jacket, right here."

Waapikoona imagined him hooking the girl's little hand on his flannel pocket, and a bubble of warmth trickled through her chest. A chill quickly followed, pointing her attention to her own hand still clinging to Isabel. She was being silly. Isabel wasn't playing favorites. She simply needed them both.

She will always need us both.

Grieved by the deep truth of this, she wasn't sure how it would ever work out. She could not see a future that contained the three of them.

A beam of light flipped on, outlining Mick's height, the glistening ceiling inches above his head, and the black depth beyond. She could see a trickle of water along the ground beside his boots that disappeared at his toe, just like Isabel had on that ledge outside. Mick took a step; she grabbed his shoulder as he swung the flashlight down toward where the edge of wet rock met absolute pitch.

He jerked back, his free hand pulling Isabel back by the collar as he cursed his god.

"It's a drop-off." Her words sounded choked.

"Yeah, I'm just now seein' that." He went to his knees and eased toward the edge, shining the light down. "Holy … "

All at once Waapikoona felt warmth at her back. She and Isabel gained new shadows that quivered in light undulating on the cave floor in front of them. They turned as one. Instead of the darkened wide cave entrance with the daylight beyond, they were in a small room lit by candles melting on a thick wooden work table. Under a lantern hanging from the wall, a man bent over a straw pallet, his work out of view.

"Mick," she whispered.

His footsteps came to rest behind her. It was clear the instant he recognized they were not alone. The backpack slid to the ground. He took an easy step around Isabel, putting himself between her and the stranger. Waapikoona watched his gaze dart around taking inventory of the room. No visible doors or windows, no other humans, and now, where a cave floor and ledge stretched behind them moments ago, a cold stone wall stood at their backs. She spotted their guides beside her and felt grateful they had made it through whatever door they'd just entered.

The man working at the pallet wiped his hands on a rag and stood to face them. Closely shorn hair lay the faintest shadow on his head. His eyes were as blue as Mick's, level with his height and hers. In the candlelight the man's strong bones gave him eyebrows that would be too fair to see otherwise. Muscled and lean enough to display pronounced clavicle and ribs, he wore loose pants from another era and no shirt. He draped his rag across his shoulder and appraised his guests, rounded up and backed into a corner. It felt like a trap.

Behind him, something stirred on the pallet.

Mick caught her eye for one breath before turning his attention back to the man. "Afternoon," he said, holding up both hands, palms out.

She wanted to smile. Grounded, steady Mick, using a time-descriptive greeting in a timeless cave. It temporarily distracted her from translating that look he'd just aimed her way, but now she knew the plan. He would play it friendly, unarmed, the good cop to her bad cop. If this man really was the healer who could help them, that was all they'd need.

Another shuffle on the pallet sent an impulse to her arm to grab the handle of her knife—but no, she had to wait, let Mick do what he did best so she wouldn't have to do what she did best in front of her little sister. The man took a glance behind him, swiveling his shoulder out of the shadow and revealing the rag on his shoulder was covered in sooty black, dried brown, and crimson that reflected wetly in the light.

He turned back to Mick. "Who send?" His English was harshly accented, nearly a grunt.

"Raúl Soto."

"Do not know."

"Mighty Eagle," Isabel said, as if correcting Mick, not introducing him. She then shrunk behind Waapikoona as if regretting the words.

The man scratched his beard. "Why come?"

"First … " Mick seemed to be buying time. "You tell us who you are."

"You come here. You know."

Mick held a breath, looking around the room again. Dancing flames animated every shadow and reflected warmly in a line of glass jars organized on a roughhewn wooden shelf at the far wall. Some of the jars were sitting uncapped on a large central table with knotty wooden legs. Mick shifted his weight like he wanted a closer inspection of the room but wasn't sure it was a welcome move. "Can I be real honest? Truth is, I didn't expect you to be a man."

"You expect beast?"

Mick chuckled. "I expected a woman."

"I am not woman."

"Are you a healer?"

"Healer, witch doctor, *Nekromant*."

Mick shot Waapikoona a tight-eyed look. It was not her people's word, that she was sure. But she could take a guess. "Necromancer."

"I am work here," the man said. He took a long look at the space where the spirit guides had rested before he began to turn away.

"What work?" Mick risked a step into the orange glow of the room and within striking distance of the man, but he kept his arms loose at his sides and his eyes set on what lay beyond.

"Is your business?"

Now Mick settled an easy gaze on the man. "It's my business if I'm about to hire you for a job."

Waapikoona's hand slid toward her flint as the men assessed each other silently. The half of Mick's face she could see showed a new expectation of man-to-man trust, a contest of who proved more worthy of the silent bargain being made. Not a struggle of dominance but a mutual reading of intention. They had to believe they were equals or this arrangement would not work.

Of course it was Mick who made the first move of peace. He raised a hand, fingers pointing up, the more casual version of the handshake. The other man took it with an easy grasp, and then they were turning as one toward Waapikoona as if awaiting her approval.

She sheathed her blade, suddenly aware of it being in her hand. "We're all friends now?"

The man nodded. "I show my work, you tell what I do for Mighty Eagle."

Waapikoona offered a hand to Isabel and pulled her toward the pallet where now the men stood. Mick had rooted himself in place, a hand shoved into his hair. The healer stooped to arrange something on the pallet where the body of a large raptor lay. Or the pieces of a body. One leg lay to the side, unconnected, and one of the wings dangled like it had been completely ripped off and was in the process of being sewn back on. Blood stains and feathers littered the linen sheet, dark globs of flesh sat leaking through the fabric.

The bird's eye twinkled in the candlelight, alive but lost. The good wing raised in a half-attempt at escape before settling down again.

"Is it hurting?" Isabel whispered.

"It feels not a thing." The man dipped a long-handled spoon into a bowl on the side table. He gently opened the beak and poured the liquid in before folding the good wing back against the body. He took up a sinewy piece of flesh and fitted it into a crevice of chest, his fingers twisting and seeking as he bent closer and blew out a deliberate breath aimed at where his fingers worked.

Waapikoona flinched against a hand on her arm—Mick, pulling her aside, his warm lips against her ear. "We can't leave Isabel here."

She pressed her cheek against his and whispered back, "We have to."

He pulled away to glance briefly at the man, Isabel at his side, spellbound by the magic being wielded in front of her eyes. "If he was a woman—"

"It would be no different. A healer is a healer."

"You see them organs in the jars on the wall?"

"The woman who healed you had the same."

"Somehow it's different when it's a man."

As unnatural as his perspective felt, she knew it held more truth than it should. She had watched what happened when his kind had rolled into her land. Being female within her people had never marked her as prey. He'd been raised in a culture that not only believed that, but practiced it too often. In her first life she experienced it, with no armor or skills to avoid it or defend against it, and she now lived within it too. The only difference was now she used her role as prey to lure the predators and turn them into the hunted. "If he hurts her, we will come back for him."

"How will we—" His attention roamed the room again as if convincing himself it was a safe place.

She caught his sleeve so he'd look at her. "We will come back."

He rubbed the back of his neck, his eyes on hers, fighting an inner struggle. Yes, she saw the bowl of human teeth on the worktable, the wall of knives, the archaic surgical tools, the healer's white skin. She also saw how delicately he worked to repair the bird and how calm he had been when three strangers entered his secret domain.

"Only other option is take her through the caverns with us, right? And if The Silent One sees—"

She clamped a quick hand over his mouth. Speaking the great demon's name in here was not wise. "It's a bigger risk I refuse to take."

He pried her hand off and held it firmly in both of his. "So we blindly trust the skinhead with the medieval torture lair."

She couldn't help it—she smiled and had to bite down on it to keep from laughing. Ancient peoples shaved their heads for practical reasons, not to join a racist cultural movement. Laughing at the concept felt strangely cathartic, almost like humor could strip away all its power. If anything, it gave her a reason not to let it sink in. "I think he's a warrior."

"Well, shit, even better. Warrior-healer dude with the collection of people's teeth." He glanced at their host—and flung a hand to grasp her arm, an excuse to hold her back when it seemed more like he was stopping himself.

She turned. The healer had taken a break in his work to examine Isabel's crippled hand, and now he was pulling her toward his worktable to a brighter puddle of lantern light for a better look. Waapikoona felt a portion of her bias soften. Another exception in her list for this warrior-healer white man she had no choice but to trust, even though Mick, with his unending optimism and belief in humanity, could not.

CHAPTER
24

W AAPIKOONA PICKED UP the canvas bag from where it rested beside her feet and softly dumped its contents onto the healer's work table. "These are from a younger girl."

The healer began to sort through the bones. "With right bone, I make it work."

What he discarded, Waapikoona returned to the bag until she caught a hushed conversation happening behind them. Mick had taken a seat on the edge of the pallet where Isabel had retreated. With one palm braced carefully beside the sleeping bird, he bent his ear to her so she could whisper. If it truly was a stolen chance for a secret, Waapikoona couldn't join the huddle unless she wanted to alert their host of words being spoken behind his back, so she resumed packing unneeded bones and put her mind to offering her companions more cover.

"Her hand needs two bones." In crisp memory, she saw Jeremiah's hammer come down once, twice. Her breath caught—she remembered the impossible choice between Mick's life and Isabel's. His slumped body bleeding his life into the cold tomb floor while her little sister's only chance was smashed away one piece at a time. Jeremiah closing Waapikoona's hand tight over the handle of the knife as he forced her other hand into a cruel grip of Mick's hair, jerking his head back, exposing his throat.

She blinked, recovering the view in front of her, the flicker of the candle-filled room, the canvas bag on the worn table, the healer gazing at her with new intensity. Two tiny white bones nestled against his open palm. For the first time she saw the terrible scar that ran from his temple to his chin, carving a path through thick beard.

"What haunts you?" he asked softly.

Behind him she saw Mick and Isabel, their heads bent together. How the man leaned to keep weight off his bad leg, how the girl cradled her limp hand. They were both broken because of her choices that had brought them together. How would she keep them from being broken worse?

"Too many things," she answered.

"I have medicine. I trade for this." He laid his free hand on the full canvas bag.

This image of him making speculative claim pushed cruel fear into her, snapping back from a lifetime ago when his kind rewrote the rules of trade with blackmail and lies. A no from her simply meant he would take for nothing instead of offer something in return.

She tugged the canvas bag from under his hand and slung it over her shoulder. "I don't need medicine."

"Your terrors drive you." He said it like a voiced understanding. An explanation, not a warning.

For the first time she stared those terrors in the face and felt proud to carry them. "I suppose they do."

"You and I, we are same."

She saw in the space between them she was right. He had been a warrior. He'd taken lives, and in his grief he learned the art of healing, never able to undo those specific crimes but the dedication to this new life was his own healing. Punishment or penance, it didn't matter. His wrongs may never be righted, but he walked the road away from them and let their memory fuel his pace. Was he in limbo here, outside of time, sentenced to this labor? Or was he firmly planted in his own time that was not her own, to age and die and return to the earth?

"Thank you for helping my sister."

"Do not thank. I am here, and I am glad to do."

She looked toward Mick who sensed the finality of their visit and stood, but his eyes seemed troubled. He rubbed his jaw with one hand as if preparing for a conversation no one was going to enjoy. When Isabel got to her feet beside him and clung to his arm, Waapikoona understood at once.

Mick turned his attention toward the healer. "We're gonna stay while you do your work."

The answer came quickly. "Only girl stays."

"She don't want to be here by herself."

"My work cannot be watched."

"Then we'll gladly look away."

The healer crossed his arms, stiffening shoulders and spine into a greater height that might assert dominance but would only turn him into a more frightening figure to Isabel. Waapikoona knew the little girl's fear and felt it like her own, but staying with her here would only validate something unfounded that needed to be proven wrong in the girl's mind. In their first life, there were few exceptions to what they'd learned from the white man. She could not have her sister growing into this life with a belief that no longer held widespread truth.

She went to her sister, untangling the girl's arm from Mick's and pushing between them so he had to step aside. She kneeled beside the pallet so their eyes were level. "There's no reason to be afraid."

Isabel turned her face away from the room. "The white man—"

"Hurt us before, yes. A lifetime ago. Sometimes, they're good like Mick." The slight widening of Isabel's eyes made Waapikoona wonder if the girl had forgotten what color Mick was. "And sometimes we need to trust them. This man is a healer, and he wants to help you. He can't do that while Mick and I are here."

"Why not?"

"I don't know, but it's his rules. And even if we did stay, we can't travel the cave with you. That would put Mick in too much danger, and I know you don't want that."

She shook her head.

"You don't have to be afraid. You can be brave."

"What if you get lost?"

"The spirits won't allow that."

Isabel cast a glance beyond Waapikoona's shoulder to where the spirit guides lingered.

"And they're ready to get moving." She kissed the girl's forehead. "We will see you on the outside. Now say goodbye to Mick so we can go."

With a hard look at him, Waapikoona stood and moved aside. Isabel climbed onto the pallet to give Mick a hug. As soon as he straightened, Waapikoona caught his elbow and hauled him toward a dark blot on the far wall that had not been there before. The spirits had collected before it, their shapes fluid with impatience.

Mick tried to pull away as they passed the healer, but she kept him moving so all he could manage was to aim a death glare at the guy on their way out. She might not have his ease with children, but she knew how to hand out tough love when its need was clear. The wavering shapes of their guides disappeared against that dark smear on the wall. She followed, tugging Mick through. Warm open room fell away behind them and chilly walls pressed in, drawing the scrape of their boots and sound of their breath into more intimate space.

"All right, cut it out," Mick barked, yanking from her grip.

She blinked and found them bathing in pitch black, the warm glow of candlelight from the healer's room not just snuffed out but utterly erased from existence. It felt like a faded memory, not a place they'd just walked away from. She swallowed, awash in unease. Isabel wasn't mere footsteps away. She was unreachable.

Cold brushed past her, forming a glimmer before her eyes—shapes, three of them, independent yet moving almost as one. Light burst against her. She turned her face away from it, cursing.

"Sorry." Mick tilted his phone so it shined against him. "Would you mind grabbing the flashlight from … "

Waapikoona was already unzipping the outer pocket of his backpack. She located the flashlight, handed it to him, took one for herself, and zipped everything back up. "Keep it aimed on the floor. We need to follow our guides."

"Yeah, I've done this a time or two." He felt above him for the ceiling a few inches above his head before he began to move forward, away from her. "And did you know that guy back there or somethin'? Because it's a lot of trust to put in—"

"I don't know him. But I do know toxic men, and he's not one of them." As she walked, frigid water dripped onto her hair, sinking through to her scalp where it trickled down the back of her head. An involuntary shiver shook her shoulders. "And we can't go back, so let's focus on getting through the cave for Isabel."

He snorted. "You know what? I don't like you behind me in the dark. Go on ahead." He paused, flattening against the wall so she could pass.

"Afraid I might stab you in the back?"

"Not hardly. I'm imaginin' what's back there, and I'd rather be the one it tries to pick off." His light shifted like he was switching hands. "But now that you mention it, yeah, that too."

"My sister would kill me if I hurt you."

His lengthening silence took the lightheartedness out of her comment, and she wished she could take it back. Now she wasn't so sure it had been lighthearted to begin with. She trailed her fingers along the wet stone ceiling, expecting it to be dipping down for how closed in she felt.

Finally, he spoke. "She told me your creator asked her to find the ouroboros too."

There was a note of overly subdued calm in his words that drew her thoughts back to the look he'd given her when they'd discussed the ouroboros with Soto and Teresa. Mick didn't seem eager to accuse her of withholding knowledge, but he did set it up for her to explain. If he wondered about her familiarity with the creature, she felt the same about him. "And what do you know about it?"

"Nothin' really. It's Norse myth, in one of Dougie's monster books. The enemy of thunder-god Thor. If it releases its tail, the end of the world begins."

"A story of your people."

"I guess," he said, a shrug in his voice.

To be descended from a people yet so separated from them … she knew exactly how that felt. It was not a commonality if he was dismissive, and it made her so helplessly sad. "If she finds it, she can't tell him."

"She's bound to him."

Waapikoona stopped to look at him. It was a worry she hadn't wanted to confront since Mick had tracked the girl's bird to The Silent One's cave. Now she regretted not addressing it sooner. "And how is she bound?"

"You'd have to ask my eagle."

"Your eagle doesn't speak English."

"And don't need no prompting to come out right now, so how 'bout if we change the subject?"

The spirit guides disappeared around a corner ahead, so she quickened her pace to catch up as Mick's flashlight bobbed behind her. Over the scuffle of their boots, she heard a faraway babble and had to pause, one hand held behind her to stop Mick so she could make out what it was. Mick took her hand and flipped off his light, a bold move that seemed to make them more vulnerable if something creeped up. But it would also make them disappear. Mick's eagle would sense an enemy long before one got within range. She flipped off her own light.

The absolute darkness narrowed her senses. She listened to the rhythm of the babble, trying to discern if it was human, demon, or something else. The sound played along the stone walls, too constant and unchanging to be human voices. With her eyes useless her nose came alive to the new element in the chill of the air. "Water."

"You think?"

"I can't tell if it's ahead or behind."

"Sounds so much like a faraway conversation. Sure had me fooled."

She readjusted the canvas bone bag so it crossed her back, knotting it tightly against her chest. "We might have to get our feet wet."

Minutes later they were wading through ice cold water in bare feet, their jeans rolled to their knees, socks shoved into boots they carried by hand. At the far bank she met a slippery wall higher than her head. Uneven layers offered many hand and footholds, but the entire thing glistened from the water trickling from the top.

Mick tied the laces of his boots together and hung them around his neck. "I'll give you a boost."

"It's too slippery."

He aimed his light along it. Different layers of rocks jutted, their edges smoothed by ages of running water. The slow flow of water turned the whole thing into a shimmer against black. "Not that far side. Looks dry there."

She handed him her boots, tucked her flashlight into the back of her jeans, and kicked through the water to the right side wall of the tunnel. Biting cold from the water climbed the flesh of her legs, making her steps slow and awkward. She braced a hand along the wet layered wall and moved toward the dry portion, anxious to get up and out of the bone-shattering water, her feet dry in her socks and boots. Her blood was thoroughly chilled now, bringing her back to that cold muddy grave and the nightmare she'd been locked in while sleeping the weeks away in Mick's bed. This here was just water, but she was not interested in facing the terror that was rousing in her right now.

All at once she felt her feet slide off a curved underwater edge. She hit a new bottom, too late to catch herself with her hands that would have no doubt slipped off the wall helplessly. Her stomach fell even farther. Now a foot deeper in the icy water, she'd soaked the bottom of her rolled jeans. She took a breath against the heartbeat in her throat that throbbed hot and dry. The depression could have been a bottomless hole, sucking her into a watery underworld death too fast for her even to scream.

Mick was hollering, snatching at her collar, the shoulders of her jacket, now hauling her back against him. Her foot slipped and she made a blind grab, tangling her fingers in warm flannel before she fell backward toward the freezing water.

"I got you."

"I had it!" She knew the anger in her voice had been powered by the frantic pump of her heart, but she had no way to calm it. He had caught her, kept her from plunging into the cold, but her gratitude couldn't be reached.

"You don't know how deep that goes!"

"My feet were on the bottom, Mick, so yeah I did."

"And how deep beyond that step, a hundred feet with a swift current sucking you in? You just scared the shit outta me."

She felt the current in the water then, pulling against her ankles, but had no idea how it could suddenly be moving so swiftly. "There's no better option up this wall, and I have to get on dry land before my legs go numb."

"Yeah, you and me both. But check the damn floor with a foot before you step into it, for god's sake." He nearly spit the words at her.

She jerked away from him. That tone of voice meant he was perfectly furious, and she couldn't even enjoy it for how desperately she needed to get out of this water. Easing back toward the hidden depression, she used her toes this time to feel out the edge and then step down. She kept one foot planted and felt ahead with the other until her toes met the wall.

Something sharp stung her calf. Her legs were so numb she wasn't sure how she felt it.

"There's something sharp—" It was more than a cut. There was a suction along with it, and a silky object floating against her skin. She leaned a hand against the wet wall and lifted her leg from the water.

Mick lowered the flashlight. "What the—" He splashed toward her.

Together they stared at the milky white sinuous body that was now attached to her leg. Impulse compelled her to tear it off and fling it against the far wall. A moment later she realized her error. Without breaking the suction or the clamp of its tiny sharp teeth, she'd just yanked out a dime-sized chunk of her flesh along with it.

"That was too damn big to be a leech."

She pressed her palm against the open wound. "Underworld leech. They have two rows of teeth. And if there's one there's many, and if *you're* bitten … " She didn't even work to keep the concern off her face. Her own terror meant nothing when confronted with what Mick would suffer if poisoned by another demon bite.

Immediate wordless understanding passed between them. Mick swung his backpack around to shove her boots inside. While he worked to get the zipper closed, she found a crevice in the wall deep enough for human hands and launched herself up, finding the driest fingerholds as her toes gripped each slab of rock. She heard Mick plunge into the deeper water below her as she climbed upward into opaque dark. He had to get out before another creature sensed his warm blood and penetrable skin that contained not only man but Thunder-Being.

"You ain't allowed to fall." His voice was muffled, strained. She imagined his fingers and toes finding hold just like hers and tried not to think about the cost to his bad leg. "'Cause if you do, you'll take me down with you."

"Don't tempt me."

She reached the lip of a flat stone that spanned far enough ahead that she could crawl on her stomach and turn over, pulling her flashlight free. She heard it roll away from her but couldn't see where. Beyond her feet, his light's beam darted all around as if clipped and dangling from his belt. One hand extended above her found cold ceiling high enough for her to sit up. She heard the scrape of Mick's ascent and leaned forward, latching onto his clothes once she found them. Scooting backward, she hauled him toward her until his light found rest, shining a beam into the blackness from which they'd come.

Walking her hands down his body, she found the clip and released it, taking the light in her hand to shine around them.

He'd wound up on his back with his eyes closed, back-pack flung to the side, one leg bent at the knee, the other flat on the stone. A stream of bright blood ran down her own leg, but his were clean below his rolled jeans. No wounds, no leeches, no demons.

She laid her hand against his jaw, clenched so tight the muscle jumped.

"Gimme a minute," he said, eyes still closed tight.

So his leg was bothering him. And now she had her own leg damage to add to the mix. She slid forward to lie down beside him. The cold of the stone seeped through her clothes, giving new focus so she could ignore her wet frozen legs. Perhaps it was an advantage to have her new wound numbed so well.

"You're gonna have to cover that bite."

"It's fine until we get—"

"No, I mean … the blood. It's too much."

It wasn't just his leg that had him so paralyzed. "Your eagle has never responded to my blood before."

"My eagle ain't usually so surrounded by the underworld. I'm not gonna make it."

"Yes, you are."

"Just cover it up." He gave the backpack a shove so it slid within reach.

Inside she found a camping first aid kit and got to work patching herself up, listening to Mick's meditative breathing against the watery gurgle below them. While he restored himself she repacked his bag, impressed with the thought behind each item he'd chosen to bring.

As she was pulling her socks and boots back on, he sat up and untangled his own boots from around his neck. "The guy who can't plan says you're welcome."

"Congratulations on keeping us alive for three days. If you're finished with your nap, we should get moving."

He watched her face as if to call her bluff. Yes, sometimes he surprised her. But he wouldn't be worthy of worship unless he survived the encounter with The Silent One.

CHAPTER
25

Their guides had moved so far ahead Waapikoona had to coax Mick into a quicker pace to catch them. When they'd told her they would not linger in the underworld, she hadn't fully grasped the meaning. At a fork in the tunnel she stopped, clicking the flashlight off so the absolute darkness might bring a hint of their guides once her eyes adjusted.

"This one," Mick said, pointing.

Eagle-eyed showoff. His Thunder-Being was worthy of worship any day. And Mick the man was worth every bit of trust she could award a person, so she powered her light back on and took the tunnel he'd indicated. Soon enough they came upon their guides, not lingering but moving as slowly as a spirit could move. The ceiling dipped, forcing a stooped walk that made Mick grumble. They took a sharp turn into a narrow slot that squeezed them down so much they had to remove their packs and drag them through the crevice behind them.

"Not a fan of this," Mick said.

"It's better than crawling."

"Except when you're crawling over me."

"Maybe we'll get to do that later."

The walls grew wet, smearing their clothes with what must be clay for how it smelled. It sparked a memory of Waapikoonu's first time in The Silent One's cave, with a different man. They'd been fighting—or, Jeremiah had been trashing her and she'd been sulking—and the shame she endured over taking that abuse when her foster parents had worked so hard to build her spirit felt worse than the abuse itself. Only one specific piece of that day stuck with her: Jeremiah had called her an "Indian coward," and she'd applied that label and carried it herself for too long.

If her memory was good, this slot led to a great room where The Silent One would entertain a visitor. She stopped in the slot. Mick came against her. She shined the light upward to confirm the space above was indeed limitless. Quite possibly, at some point in the year, sunlight might shine down upon them instead of the fine mist that fell, dampening her hair. She lowered the light. Minutes from now, Mick's eagle, and Mick himself, could be slain—one more victory for the underworld.

"We're getting near to meeting him." She turned her face toward his.

With the light angled down, she could only see the outline of his mouth. His eyes were in total shadow. Moisture glistened in the coarse hair on his jaw.

"Well, let's get movin'."

"Thank you for helping my sister. You didn't have to."

"Of course I did."

"If this goes bad—" As pinned as she was by the two unforgiving walls, she had no way to properly face him in this moment. When her fingers met the heat of his hand, she realized they'd been seeking that familiar touch just as he'd moved his own fingers to meet hers there. The steady warmth of his calloused skin closed around her hand and squeezed. For too long she'd been imagining Mick as a ball and chain, but now that she was about to lose him, he felt more like an anchor, a familiar comfort, a reminder of home. With Mick she'd always have a place to return to. He would never replace the people she grieved, but he could fill in the cracks they'd left in her heart. Families didn't have to be large and extended. They could be made of twos and threes, and he and Isabel could be hers.

If The Silent One didn't kill him.

And beyond that, she'd also have to shed her past. Forgive—and embrace—the world for what it was. Decide it was worth saving. And find some way to settle down with that, knowing all vigilante justice was over. It seemed too simple of a next step to validate the struggle she felt.

"No chance it'll go bad. My eagle can't negotiate with your boss, so I've got to stay human."

"Can't or won't?"

He was quiet a moment. "Figure it's both."

They pushed on. She sensed Mick working to control his breath even as they fought to advance in the tight space. The slot could go on for a few feet or miles. Just one minute in a space that allowed her to fully inflate her lungs would be enough to undo the frenzy that quickly approached her breaking point. She refrained from questioning Mick about his own mental state. The deep breaths he kept taking—slow in, twice as slow out—were proof enough, and his admission might prompt her to scream.

"If time's screwed up in here," Mick said, his voice stiffened to the point of removing most of his accent. "Then it don't matter how long we're in this—"

"Right," she gasped, strangely relieved. "It doesn't matter."

"So then hours are seconds. Nothin' to worry us. And if I'm bein' honest, there's no one else I'd rather be stuck in a miles long slot with, scrapin' all my skin off."

She pictured that as she shuffled along, holding her breath to squeeze through a tight spot before she asked, "What happened to your clothes?"

"Very well might be scraped off."

A chuckle trickled through the scream that still lodged in her throat. The fingers of her leading hand, instead of encountering the same flat stone, wrapped around an edge. She crammed the flashlight past her body to shine ahead. Instead of its beam reflecting off narrow walls, it lost itself in a dark abyss. She hooked her elbow around the wall edge and flung herself into open empty space with no care for what dangers awaited. The stomp of her boots echoed around her, the play of sound immense and impossibly wide.

Mick's scuffle between the walls sounded so distinct she needed no light to see his panicked reach for her into the now empty space. "Waapi—"

"Here." She aimed the light at the mouth of the narrow tunnel, illuminating his path so his ejection from that hell might be more graceful. "And you promised me no clothes."

He dislodged himself, righted his twisted jeans, and brushed his hair off his forehead. "I don't remember promising." Nearing her, he flipped his flashlight back on and shined it all around them.

The room was too large for the meager light. Vague shapes hinted of a ceiling three stories up, circular walls extending from the slot tunnel too far away to make any sense of actual distance. As Mick explored, she set her canvas pack next to his on the ground and stretched, savoring the movement of limb in the ample space around her.

"Can't find our guides," he said.

"It's the least of our concerns right now." A dark voice said, *you won't need them if you're dead*. Mick's life was her biggest worry, but if The Silent One caught onto her lie, death would be a certainty for her too.

"Now what?" he asked.

"We wait."

She switched off her light, closed her eyes, and gathered the cave against her. Damp, cold air numbed her nose and fingertips as darkness pressed all around. Utter silence swelled, until it didn't—a delicate trickle of water to her right, the creak of Mick's boot laces against leather, her own breathing. A normal everyday cave that would soon not be so normal, and when that changed, she hoped she would still have the power to know.

"I'm here," she called out, her voice strong and clear.

Mick came to stand beside her and flipped off his light. Even in the darkness she could sense the radiant force of him at her side. She feared what The Silent One would see in him and between them.

"Mick, I need to face him alone."

"You really think that's a good idea?"

"He knows I expect him to raise my sister. I've worked for too long to just forget, and what I've done for him up to this point, I've done all alone. To him, there'd be no reason for you to be here."

She heard him exhale. The light flipped on. "Guess I'll find a cozy spot to hang out."

Then he was gone. His absence lasted both seconds and days in the timeless obscurity. She sat on the ground, crossing her legs, one hand on the bag of bones before her. One heartbeat—or lifetime—later, Mother Earth's underground turned against her. Mick was no longer lost to her, he was right there, his skin pricking as hers did, his heart gaining volume in her ears.

"Shh." She said it to herself and him, knowing he couldn't be as close as he felt, but her voice would carry to wherever he was.

The vast room turned oppressive, more like the slot tunnel in how it constricted her breathing and felt like a fathomless hell with no escape. She strained to hear the telltale sound of the great demon's approach, the hundreds of legs hissing against wet rock as the giant millipede entered the cavernous room, dwarfing her so she became the insect.

But there was a different sound, gliding and meandrous, far away but gaining ground fast. She felt her pulse pump hot and raw against the fresh bite on her calf. The Silent One transformed as his power grew, and change swelled upon her. She stood, the canvas bag tight in one fist and the extinguished flashlight in the other. Her light would not touch him. She would picture him as the familiar giant black millipede, the wall of shiny body segments closing in beside her. There was no other shape she cared to see.

"Identify yourself." His voice was deeper than ever, the sound a creature itself crawling up her bones.

"Waapikoona."

"We have forsaken that name."

We. The word shot cold from heart to gut. New power had made him plural. She wondered if this new form was an evolution, or a second being entirely.

"When I first came to you, we had a bargain. My sister's bones are here. The one who brought them to you before was mistaken. She's not raised as you agreed."

"You cannot make claims upon a bargain you broke your-self."

"I have a new one."

A terrible new cold surrounded her, along with the sound of his new body. Wet, slippery, sinuous. She thought of the white demon leech and its rows of tiny sharklike teeth.

"Then speak it."

She had enough time to ponder this moment, its conse-quences, the shame she would take on. "There's a mutiny building. I have information."

It had to be her imagination to hear Mick's intake of breath. He wouldn't be close enough, and even if he was, she'd not hear him over the wall of body she knew to be cir-cling around her. She thought of her list. Some who deserved punishment, like Jeremiah's father, Jeremiah's cohorts. And some who did not, like the people sharing land with Mick's father. Descriptions and location would have to serve as names she didn't have. And when she was ready to speak, she had to force her spine straight for how the betrayal of those people already rotted inside her.

"I've got somethin' better." It was the echo of Mick's voice she heard as it bounced brightly off the ceiling into her ears.

The hiss that came then cascaded through the chamber. A large mass slid against her, cold scaly skin grazing her cheek, catching at her hair. She pressed a hand against it to ward it off and assert her position, distantly noting the dif-ference from the exoskeleton she remembered of his previ-ous form. A creature so large could plow over her, and she needed to remain alive to find Mick. It wouldn't be The Silent One who slayed him.

Now he'd flipped his light on, and she saw what she hadn't wanted to see. Black body segments had been replaced by grayish scales, silvery in a glance of Mick's beam of light. Millipede legs dangled, useless and shrunken like they were the last remaining body part of his previous form. The body had grown so much in size she had to tilt her head back to view its full height. The massive head arched even higher, raising like a cobra ready to strike. In silhouette she saw horns curving from cavities above milky eyes. So her maker was transforming into a great horned serpent, the true enemy to Mick's Thunder-Being in both intent and form.

The Silent One shifted his raised head to focus on Mick standing tall beside the rock he must have been hidden behind. A forked tongue lashed out, immeasurably long and fast. With those milky pupil-less eyes the creature must be blind, using its tongue to taste the air around its visitors. Something in Waapikoona burned red-hot over the thought of Mick being the target of that tongue. She was wrong to bring him in here.

"Douse your torch."

"But first I gotta ask," Mick said, aiming his light at the floor. "What's with your interest in my world?"

"You'd be wise to stop calling it yours."

A cough burst from Mick and he spoke through it, as if to overcome it. "You've got it made down here. All the space you could want. Why come above ground?"

"Our space turns foul because of your kind. Upperworld creatures have failed and your Thunder-Beings do nothing to stop it. We have waited. We now grow restless."

"Our Thunder-Beings are kept busy by you."

"Your land weeps. Her tears seep into my world, yet you do nothing. You poison her organs. You give her no voice. My domain has been breached, so I breach yours. Your kind is a plague that will soon self-destruct. I claim your land before you destroy it."

"That really ain't your call to make."

"The flesh I receive from the woman whose forsaken name I will not speak proves how depraved humankind has become. You were stewards of the upperworld and you have failed."

"Well, see, that's exactly what I'm talkin' about. If she only killed the bad apples, and that's all you see—"

"A shocking number indeed. There is no hope for humankind. The whole batch of you is soon to be spoiled. Better to claim Mother Earth now before you take her down with you. Now speak your bargain before I grow tired of you."

"If you raise the girl from those bones in that bag, you can have my eagle."

"I'll take your eagle now." The great demon bared fangs so long they'd pierce Mick's skull and skewer him to the heels before they ran out of length.

Waapikoona turned her flashlight onto Mick. He visibly shuddered and bent at the waist, hands on knees. When he looked up, wet hair hung like ropes in his eyes. "My eagle ain't here at the moment."

The Silent One's great head struck the rock beside him, creating a sound like one boulder smashing into another, a dusty crumble of debris flinging particulate so far it pelted Waapikoona and hit throughout the cavern. Now the great demon's body had shifted forward, coiling in a new way that cut her off from Mick. She could no longer see him and had no hope of reaching him.

"Like I said ... " Mick paused as if to steady himself.

She could now hear how he panted, and she swung her light against the wall to find a foothold that might get her up and around and to Mick's side.

"... you can have my eagle, but not till that little girl is raised, her heart beating, her feet on upperworld earth ... "

There was a shuffle of boots, one strong step followed by the irregular sound of Mick's limp. He'd come out to face the great demon head-on. "Healthy and perfect, ready to live a full life."

Said in such a way, this bargain ensured the girl raised from these bones would be disease free. Waapikoona wondered how long ago Mick had planned this. She found a ledge on the wall and stepped up, shoving the flashlight into her waistband before she felt for a fingerhold above.

The Silent One hissed a laugh. "One useless human child traded for an upperworld Thunder-Being. One might think this is a trap."

"Think it all you want. Truth is, my eagle's done fightin', and this little girl deserves to live."

"Your human emotions are foolish. Your world will soon be a different place in which to live."

"We got a bargain or what?" It came out rushed, as if Mick knew his voice was on borrowed time.

The giant body slid into a new coil, sandwiching her between snakeskin and cave wall. And what was she doing? Getting over to Mick's side would help nothing. She needed to sabotage this agreement, stop Mick from sacrificing himself like this. She sent a hard elbow into the serpent's body pressing against her. To the great creature it would be no more than a tickle, but its body slid easily away, providing her room to hop down.

"He's lying." Her voice was quiet, intended for the demon's ears because right now to her, Mick was out of it. "He offers you something he no longer has. His eagle is dead."

Her creator turned its massive head toward her, gathering a pile of body underneath it before raising to a height that brought it firmly within darkest shadow her light could not reach. "You know his eagle?"

This accusation would further condemn her, but it was of no consequence. "I killed his eagle."

"This is a man, not a spirit. You killed nothing."

She scrambled for a response. Now she had to work with all she knew about her creator, the underworld, upperworld, and the war between, and for the first time she realized how lacking her information was. Right now all she was … she was human, more human than Mick. "He shifted back to a man while in the throes of death. I revived him. We humans have that ability too."

A lash of tongue came too fast. She turned her face, earning a whip against her cheek so visceral she swayed, catching herself against the cave wall.

"The stink of lies surrounds you."

Her cheek lay open. She knew it. She resisted touching it to confirm the flayed flesh weeping blood. She could not encroach on Mick with an underworld wound so evil, so personal, or he would surely turn. She couldn't force him to rescind his offer if she couldn't stand in front of him, and she had no other tricks to nullify it herself. Stiff and numb, she slid to the cave floor. Across the dark room Mick choked against dry coughs, and she knew his human voice had left so there was no talking sense into him anyway.

The Silent One turned away from her, aiming toward the opening where he'd entered, and sent words toward the man she could not reach. "Lay the bones on earth. After the child rises, I will come for your eagle."

With her eyes closed and head resting back against the wall, she raged. Mick's eagle had made him senseless, imperious, reckless. She would not wait for The Silent One to come. She would kill Mick's eagle now. He'd be free from that influence. He'd be Mick, pure and imperfect and all hers—and he'd be dead.

Somehow she got up and crossed the room, now empty and returned to the sanctity of Mother Earth, open and peaceful and unthreatening. Mick's upright body leaned against the stone as if intoxicated, one hand holding a hard grip of the opposite forearm which was settled high against his chest. The scent of his blood joined her own. She grabbed him by the lapels, her force nearly pulling him down. "You don't get to be my white savior here."

He grabbed her in return, his force matching her own so their momentum jerked her aside and to a jarring halt. His voice was thick—anger, tears, everything. "Listen, okay? Listen!" He closed his eyes and gently shook her, as if dispersing energy into her would calm himself. "I offered my eagle. I got plans to banish the damn bird after all this is over, so if I can get through ... there will be nothin' for him to—"

"The Silent One doesn't separate you from your eagle. To him, you're one being. You offer your eagle, you offer yourself."

"He'll have to find me then."

"And he will."

"And I'll tell 'im where to shove it. If our shared history's shown us anything, it's that my kind are real good at breaking agreements."

"Asshole." She nearly growled it. Instinct sent her hand in search of a weapon she knew she could never use on him, and somehow that made her angrier.

Damn him for his flippant acknowledgment of something so disgusting. Damn him for bringing that up here, for twisting it, for using it for good. Damn him for planning this and hiding it from her until they faced The Silent One. The scent of Mick's blood rose against her again, and she saw fresh drips running off his elbow and dripping onto her boots. "Why are you bleeding?"

He tipped his head toward the ground where his pocket knife lay open and bloodied. "Had to feel good and human so I didn't change into something else. Self-control just wasn't cuttin' it."

He grinned, proud of his play on words. It sent a rush through her. Now was not the time to be playful, not after all he'd just done. She grabbed him by the collar, intending to slug him, make him feel fully human all over again. She kissed him instead, an unexpected muscle reflex controlled by some rogue emotion intent on sabotage. She hated him and loved him, as if such a contrast of highly potent chemicals could exist in a body without some kind of devastating reaction. His tongue pressed hers and yes, she was sure now, this kiss was punishment, not love, for what he'd never have. Tears stung her eyes, a stupid and unnecessary foreshock to some ripening explosion, burning her lashed cheek. He jerked away, throwing an arm out to keep her back.

"What's—" He snatched a flashlight from the ground and shined it on her face. "Shit, Waapikoona, you got a real bad—" He dropped like a helpless sack; she caught him before his knees smacked hard ground.

"I'll cover it, if you can keep your shit together for five seconds." She lowered him to the ground.

"Five seconds? Gimme some credit—"

"Okay, five seconds without performing self-mutilation."

"Did that just ... happen?"

Unsure if he was referring to her flayed cheek, his offered sacrifice, the ill-timed kiss, or the entirety of the meeting with a great demon of the underworld, she felt removed from the question by the hesitation within it that seemed to recover the perception of time. The Silent One had made his exit how long ago? Minutes, hours, it all felt the same. They were losing time, or time was losing them, and they needed to reach the upperworld before they were lost forever. She pawed through his backpack to find what she needed to hastily treat her wound. Halfway through she remembered his self-inflicted cut and tucked a rolled bandage under her chin before zipping everything back up. As if on the same wavelength, he offered his arm and she went to her knees to wind the bandage around, tucking it in tightly before helping him to his feet. She knotted the canvas bag of bones across her back, dismissing a new complication. They'd stalled too long. Their guides had moved on, well beyond reach.

It was of no consequence. She and Mick would find a way out together, even if he'd damned their future. It was a future she'd never believed in anyway.

CHAPTER
26

THE WOMAN'S ANGER burned so bright Mick was certain he could drop his flashlight and still find his way through the dark. His whole face felt bruised from her— kiss? If he could call it that. How he could enjoy something so combative he wasn't sure. He was supposed to be mustering the strength to release a bit of himself over to his eagle in the hope he'd sense their guides, not dissecting why anger would prompt her to kiss him, or how warm and wet her mouth had been, or why every time he found himself lost in a dark cave with her she managed to get him so aroused he could barely walk.

And he felt too wholly human to ever find his eagle.

"Anytime you feel like helping us out of here, Mick—"

"Like I said. Gonna be a few minutes."

"Minutes could be weeks on the surface."

"Oh, good. Pressure. That's helpful."

They'd explored every tunnel branching off The Silent One's living room, eliminating the slot they'd entered through and another opening that dead-ended against a wall several paces in. Two possible exits remained, similar in size and shape, seemingly opposite in direction. Since neither he nor she had seen which side their guides had moved toward after exiting the slot tunnel, they relied on his eagle sense to figure it out. Spirit residue lingered only so long. Waapikoona's badgering wasn't his only pressure.

"Come smell my calf," she said.

"That's a real weird come-on."

She laid the canvas bag on the ground and yanked off her boot. Mick's brain filled the rest in. Bandage unwrapping, wound revealed, tiny incisions around a large gaping hole, the skin around it purple. He remembered the smack of hard suction breaking, a lucid image of the creature's venom sliding through her veins. He didn't need to smell it. The heft of his eagle convulsed and his vision sparkled, laying image over image until he saw a streak of air in a color his human brain could not name.

"Effervescent." He wasn't sure how the word got out. Freed from his mind, it sounded like nonsense.

"What?"

"That way." He pointed at the tunnel to their left.

She swung her flashlight. In the fraction of a second it passed over him, his new eyes gulped the beam, firing explosions in his head. He reached for something to hold and found empty air then hard cold wall that clapped the heel of his hand and sent a charged throb from wrist to shoulder. No one heard his grumbled curse. He was alone in the room.

His own flashlight had been flung and now lay on the ground beside his boots, its beam shining into the opening where he'd indicated and Waapikoona had just disappeared through. Cursing her, he gathered his light and pack and followed.

The ceiling dipped a few steps inside, forcing him to bend with one hand raised to catch any low spots before his skull did. Far ahead, her light bounced around, moving at a pace he'd never catch. It would be a good thing if she caught up to their guides, a bad thing if she lost him. He was long overdue for a heart attack, and getting lost in this cave alone a second time just might do the trick.

"Déjà fuckin' vu," he muttered, wishing it was funny. And then, because he felt his stomach go cold, his heart throb hot, and his head swarm like he was on the verge of some terrible mental break, he hollered ahead, "Hey! Mind slowin' down a bit?"

Ahead, her light slipped around a corner, transforming the tunnel from perceptible space to obscure bleak nothingness. When he caught her, he'd strangle her, and he wasn't sure how that would satisfy this irritation because she just might like it.

His boots slapped through an inch of standing water as the tunnel walls drew against him. If this turned into another slot ... well, he'd be grateful it wasn't squeezing down from above and forcing him to slither through like a worm. "Been there, done that, not interested in repeatin' it. And talkin' to myself. Just great."

Something shuffled in the darkness behind him. He took a glance into the gaping void backward, then forward, and his brain decided to screw with him and tell him he didn't know which way was which. The pitch pressed from above and around as he analyzed his boots in the beam of light. His boots were pointed in the correct direction—or had he swiveled his feet when he stopped to check his back? He felt the ghost of the action in his legs. Crouching, he knocked the heel of his hand against his head in the hope it might disperse the brain fog. *Think. Remember. Which way?*

The cave had gotten to him, making him second-guess an instinct as simple as which direction he had been walking just a moment ago. The memory of being lost for those hours, which ended up as weeks on the surface, fed the disorientation. It could happen again so easily. As easily as it was happening right now.

"Mick!"

It echoed around him, coming from both directions at once. He couldn't even be certain it was her voice. Maybe it was a demon impersonating her, like the demon that had taken the form of his niece in her yellow nightgown in the road that night and bitten him on the forearm.

"Shine your light back to me," he called, switching off his own.

Absolute darkness closed so tightly around him he felt his lungs object, ready a scream. He stood and backed against the tunnel wall, allowing as much field of vision his human eyes would allow. Without the hard stone against his back and steady ground under his boots, he'd been swimming in a blackout. A fish in the earth's gut.

"Waapikoona," he called into the dark. At the same moment she called back to him, "Can you see it?"

"Can't see nothin'. Fittin' on havin' a heart attack right here, so—"

"Stay there. I'm coming back."

When light fluttered at the farthest point across his left shoulder he lurched toward it, not caring if it was The Silent One himself playing a trick on him. He'd rather fight demons and die than be lost and alone in this cave again. And then she had him by the sleeve, her latch so tight it was as if she was the one who'd been panicking. "Where did you go?"

"Me? You walked away—"

"You were right behind me."

"I wasn't."

She turned to stare at him, catching her breath. He wasn't the only one about to have a heart attack or the only one getting tricked by the cave.

"You in front," she said sharply, like he was a child who must be supervised.

As she began to squeeze past him to take the rear, he blocked her body against the wall and said, "No, you in front." In the expected indignant pause, he walked his fingers under her jacket hem and found her belt. With a strong grip he moved her back in front, keeping hold of leather and denim, her skin warm against his knuckles. "And this way you can't get ahead of me."

"You were right behind me," she hissed.

"All right." Because no damn cave was going to trick him into fighting with her. Arguments were his call. And if whatever had made the shuffling sound behind him earlier wanted to sneak up on them, he wanted to be the first one to give it a taste of his steel toe.

She moved forward, her pace accommodating to his. The movement of her skin against his knuckles got him thinking about that kiss, and he wanted to know but couldn't decide what he wanted to ask. "Thanks for comin' back for me."

"Like I was going to leave you in here?"

"Maybe. 'Cause I'm remembering that kiss, and it felt more like ... " A weapon? How could he say that, when just the mention of it got him excited for more.

"I was going to sock you. I changed my mind."

"For real?"

"And if you laugh about it again, I will sock you."

"Laugh? I didn't laugh—"

"You did. Trying to make light of what you pulled back there. I had a plan and you went over me."

He dragged her by the belt toward him, slowing her pace that seemed to increase as the anger built in her voice. "You're gonna kill my leg walkin' like that."

"You care about your leg? As soon as we raise your niece, The Silent One will take you. I'm trying to figure out how to undo what you did."

"I told you. He'll have to find me first."

She stopped, twisting around to face him. "He knows where you live. I let him possess me that night I tried to kill you."

The cave seemed to flex around him. Crucial information he should have known—but really, would it have changed anything? "He won't remember."

With each breath her naval pressed against his fingers that had slid around her belt when she'd turned, giving him solid hold of cold metal belt buckle. He wasn't going to let go of her, not while they were in this cave.

She seemed to forget the hold he had of her. "Your optimism is ridiculous."

"Ridiculous good or bad?" He fought a smile. Surely she would sock him this time. "I'm sorry I went over you."

"No you're not."

She turned around so abruptly it broke his grip. When he found it again, she moved forward, warm skin moving against his knuckles once again. He imagined yanking her back against him, an arm around her chest, a kiss pressed behind her ear. It annoyed him to admit she was right. He wasn't sorry he went over her, but he was sorry for upsetting her. It wasn't something she'd understand, so he decided to let it be. "When we get outta here—"

She shushed him. Her hand snapped backward to catch him by the arm, ripping his latch from her belt to hold him still. If something had made a sound, he was unaware.

Silently scolding himself for letting his guard down, he strained his ears and turned around to gaze into the pitch behind him. Her body language told him lighting up the tunnel to see what might be following wasn't the best idea right now.

Then he looked ahead, where the tight walls ended and an open room began. Her flashlight glanced off upright structures topped with a bulbous shape, their whiteness a shock in the dark. They varied in size but all followed the same form, and the unending quantity of them gave perspective to the enormous room. They stood immobile, locked in position as if waiting for command.

"Tell me that's not hundreds of human skeletons," he whispered at her ear.

"Thousands."

He couldn't think of his eagle. It would take him over. "Now I see why Raúl called it catacombs."

"They're in stasis. Waiting for The Silent One—"

"I'll never get through there. We gotta go back."

"It's the only way out, Mick."

"This is what's going to come out of the earth, to invade us?"

"This and countless others."

Mick took a minute to process the image of that. It would be a horror movie, a zombie apocalypse. Small town overrun by creatures that could fly, swim, and walk, every one of them teeming with deadly venom. What good were human weapons and deadly force if the attackers were already dead and attacked in such great numbers? If there was no antidote, no known upperworld treatment for their bite? This was one room, in one cave. They didn't even need to attack in great numbers. They could hide in the dark, behind garages, under beds, and pick people off one at a time. "Is this how you felt when Europeans came here? Like you were being invaded by monsters?"

"They were monsters."

He was glad she didn't say 'you.' And the thought of imminent invasion slithered under his skin, seeking the being that could disable these creatures before they awoke and end this before it began.

He grabbed her by the belt and hauled her backward. His skin had turned electric. He shivered with the fever of his bound eagle tearing itself free. *Warm skin against knuckles. Belt sliding around.* He opened his hand flat against her navel, felt the silky top of her underwear, the hook of his thumb on her cold belt buckle.

"You faced the greatest demon in this cave and kept your human form. You can do the same walking among his undead army."

Army. She said it like it was exposure therapy. Make the whole damn thing as worse as possible hidden in the safety of this tunnel so when he wandered between those skeletons it wouldn't be so bad.

She tore the bandage off his forearm and stabbed a fingernail directly into the wound. He let her do it, grateful for the human revulsion that tore through him.

"Those are the bones of people like me, ripped from the peace of their graves. Let your human heart see what it truly is."

So his eagle did not see the faceless undead bones that would soon illegally walk the upperworld.

"Give me your hand, Mick. I saw which direction our guides went. We have to catch up now."

He shook himself and offered the hand from his wounded arm, trusting her to give the split flesh another good stab should he begin to fall away from her. Finding his voice to tell her would cost too much effort. His focus narrowed to the simplest thing: maintaining his human bones and skin, his arms, his legs. He'd given up his voice. His human senses could shift—his thoughts, his soul. Not his human form. As long as he had a shell to put everything back into, he'd be okay.

She dragged him to the mouth of the tunnel. As one, they stepped from its safety. The skeletons stood facing away from them, intact bones standing erect with no musculature to keep them there. It was witchcraft and madness. It was a thousand Waapikoonas, a thousand Isabels, unearthed against their will to be used in another century by a dominating force.

Human beings. Not an undead army of bones. Just a mass grave, remains gathered in the underworld, just as they should be.

If soon they'd flood the upperworld, well, right now that wasn't Mick's concern.

She whispered to him not to touch anything, and the thought of it built a sickening quiver in his legs. He clamped down, repressed it, feeling the solid metal of the flashlight in his fist instead of the tease of air against him. Waapikoona sent the beam of her light upwards, lighting a ceiling thirty feet up. Now the shadow and light took on a dream quality, a nightmare he'd soon be out of if he could manage to put one foot in front of the other until they reached the other side. Pain seethed through the broken skin on his arm, a reminder from Waapikoona, sparking a gratitude he couldn't voice.

Now the light was aimed down, shifting around them. He saw what she'd just determined. There was no way around the horde, only through. She pulled him forward, between the shoulders of two skeletons, and Mick felt a tremor of fear down his back. If he could speak, he would say, *I'm not gonna make it.*

He'd succumb to the air against him, let the tease on his skin fill feathers instead. He'd crush every last bone with his talons; he'd fill the caverns with his cry. Then he'd fly from this cave instead of walk, and on earth in the sun he'd work to find himself again. He could succeed and be Mick, or he could fail and Mick would be gone.

It was not a risk he wanted to take.

He reached with his free hand toward her, finding silky hair, a strong shoulder. Down her back, over her hip, his thumb hooked her back pocket and his fingers followed. He shoved them deep inside, warm against her backside. She led him like a restrained prisoner through a sea of flesh-less corpses.

She stopped, tilting her head as if to hear a sound that had caught her attention.

Behind. Something coming.

Mick turned, his upper arm brushing the shoulder of a skeleton, the point of contact like a lick of fire. The knock of bones traveled down its form, a bedlam of sound in the severe quiet. Waapikoona's breath sucked in.

The room woke around them. Waapikoona's light bounced toward every wall then lit the ceiling. The night-mare turned real. The horde began to move in one direction, a chaos of movement and noise and rushing air. Mick locked his knees, one last effort against the inevitable, but couldn't hold the position because he was being dragged, choked by his collar, his boots scrambling on slippery stone. He went down, crunching a knee against rock. She was yelling at him, but he couldn't make sense of the words as he bent against his overtaking eagle.

Fighting out of his backpack straps he planted palms against stone. These were arms, not wings, muscles holding his solid human weight. Knees on hard ground, he curled his body into a ball of human that would not stretch out and find wings. His core burned hot, ripening, pushing against him.

He felt rough nails at the nape of his neck, a hard grip of his hair, jerking his head back. An errant, distant human thought: this action exposed vulnerable throat and next would be the slice of the knife, splitting his artery. A scent overtook him. Her. Seeking fingers followed by lips landing on his cheek. *Yes. More. Bring me back.* Her mouth found his, and he found his legs again—and lost them as she released the grip on his hair. Now her scent was all over him, the warmth of her body pressed against him, uncurling him, flattening his frame against cave wall. He felt a cushion of breasts against his chest, the rasp of her jeans against his. Lips, softly hunting his face in the dark and upon finding their target, her mouth, her tongue. He'd taken hold of her hips, how she moved against him turned distraction and ambush into intention. Cold wet cave wall dug into his back, reminding him where he was.

A foreshock of the delayed shift thundered through his bones, and she pressed harder against him, said his name on a breath between kisses, sent her hands under his shirt. He had to stop her. There was risk everywhere. Between them. Around them. The idea of *can't* pulsed through him, mutating into *have to, right now*. He found the button on her jeans at the same time she unbuttoned his. *Turn her around*, he thought. It would be easier, quicker, and then he was doing it and she was spinning with it and backing against him as if the idea had been her own.

Then he was inside her, every sense fixed on that single action. He reeled; his head spun.

"That's it," she said. "No more."

"No." He could not imagine what she said could be true.

"Yes. Don't move."

So he held himself in her perfect hot grip. Buried his face in her hair against her neck, the throb of her pulse against him, around him, through him. Even as he trembled with the effort of not moving against her, he knew she was right. He wanted her in his bed for hours, not here for five seconds. He gritted his teeth and closed his eyes, savoring the feel of her so he wouldn't forget and would know exactly what he had to look forward to.

Beyond the wall they'd retreated behind, a chaos continued. If he paid it mind, he'd forfeit the magic enveloping his body, the woman breathing in the space before him, the contact he'd been desperate for.

"*Mick.*"

"I know." Even contemplating what he might forfeit was pulling him away from her. She recognized that more easily than him. And some note in her voice sanctioned more, so he drew his arm around her shoulders, pulled her harder to him, and buried himself deeper.

She sighed, low with a slight groan, nearly sated. He tightened his arm, feeling the pulse in her throat throb against his bicep. "Don't—"

Because if she was going to make noises like that—

A new rush swept the room beyond the wall. More creatures, a second swell spilling from a deeper space. The sound burrowed into his ear and spoke a secret his eagle knew to be true. His shoulder hadn't jarred the mass awake. The Silent One had lied. There would be no wait until Helen's bones were laid out and she was raised. He'd sicced his army on Mick's eagle before it had a chance to exit the underworld.

Waapikoona reached behind her, hooking her wrist behind his neck. "Stay with me, Mick."

Yes. That was where his head should be. He would stay with her. Closing his eyes, he tightened his arm around her, feeling her intake of breath, her give, the force of her will in rigid hold against her need to move against him. He'd never had a woman in his arms who felt so much like his. The urge pushed past any desire of his eagle into a distinctly human animalistic depth, sandwiching his eagle from above and below and compressing it out of existence. As he breathed her in, he bore down harder inside her, imagining a circle connecting through them, an ouroboros. Timeless, unending, a crucial conduit he'd rather die than break.

She pulled free and turned around. The disconnection was indeed like a fracture in time until her mouth pressed his and he was there again, connected to her, in the place he should be. It was a mournful kiss, a last kiss, her arms around his neck squeezing him to her like she expected to be torn from him and had to hold tight. Too soon she was gone again, righting clothes, her hands encouraging him to right his own.

"They're gone," she said. "Let's go."

He struggled to zip his jeans, his fingers clumsy and body parts not wanting to fit back inside. "They're hunting my eagle. Your boss lied."

"I know."

They emerged from their hiding spot and found the great room drenched in lingering unquiet. It nearly turned him around, pushing him toward a desperate retreat behind the wall.

"We've lost our guides," she said.

He would not offer a reach into his eagle senses. He could not even think it. His arms trembled against the effort to take flight. Where were their bags? If he could find something for his hands to do, something human like carrying gear, slipping shoulders through straps, securing zippers with thumb and finger instead of beak …

"And our stuff," he gasped.

"Here."

He caught the object tossed to him—his backpack—its visceral collision against his chest reminding him of her lips on his, her body joined with his. The thought tapered his vision, turning it darker, concentrated, crippled by the absence of light until he spotted a triangular beam of dirty light against the ground. That would be his dropped flashlight, a welcome aid to his returned human vision. He flung the pack over one shoulder and picked up the light, sending its beam around the room to confirm with his human eyes what his eagle already knew. He and Waapikoona were alone.

Following her bouncing light, he found her at the farthest wall atop a four-foot-high ledge, ducking her head into the darkness beyond. He joined her at the base of the short wall, seeking a foothold to ease his climb. "Let's get the hell outta here."

"This is where I saw our guides disappear." She sat on the ledge and hopped off, landing beside him. "But it's a dead end."

Because every time they seemed to advance, they'd hit a new wall.

CHAPTER
27

T HERE WERE TOO many reasons for the unrest humming through Waapikoona's bones, and she couldn't stop wishing they'd joined the undead exodus from the cave. She could have, and would have, if she'd been alone instead of losing herself in that crevice with Mick. It would be a quick way out. She didn't even need to blend. She could've simply followed and felt the sunlight on her skin and wind on her face now instead of possibly never again.

In the fresh upperworld air she'd be able to determine if it was the cave itself enticing her to pick a new fight with Mick. Not just a verbal fight. A physical one, complete with hard-gripped clothing, his weight upon her, an unsheathed blade. She'd know if her anger was real or if it was a symptom of being stuck in the dark for so long, their hope to find an exit diminishing with each second that could be days on the surface. With her knife over his heart, she could decide what he meant to her and what she meant to him. In that crevice she'd intended to keep him human, nothing more. Meaningless sex was her specialty, and she'd never failed so badly. She was frustrated … confused … desperate for more of him. And wild with it. The fight she sorely wanted … maybe it wasn't a fight she wanted at all but to simply punish him.

If you raise the girl from those bones in that bag, you can have my eagle.

His eagle belonged to her. It was not his to offer.

"You hearin' me?"

She focused on the man himself. He'd stepped into her space, caution in his stance.

"You got that look in your eyes again," he said.

"You can't even see my eyes in this light."

"I said, all them skeletons went out that way. If the guides went up on that ledge, they either went through the wall or hid there till it was clear. Either way, we … missed it." He sent a hand into his hair, looking away sheepishly.

The man's sexual guilt made her want to cure him of it right then and there. She turned to face the room, seeing again what he described. The mass of animated bones had rushed past the crevice behind her left shoulder toward the space where Mick aimed his light. Replaying the image forced her to acknowledge the nightmare that lived to unnerve her. She saw this exact scene in her sleeping mind as she lay healing in Mick's bed. The hastily raised dead, fleshless, no longer fully human, sweeping across the upper-world. The Silent One had crossed a boundary where he no longer needed to slip his soldiers in among the living. He could boldly release them onto the world, unconcerned in how they'd expose his cause.

"I told you The Silent One's motive, yet you asked him the same question. Is my answer not good enough for you?" If she didn't put to rest some of the accusations she'd collected since their meeting with the great demon, she was sure she'd lose all control of the rage that grew since he'd stepped out from his hiding spot to offer his life.

"'Course your answer is good enough."

"Then what, Mick?"

He turned and walked away. "Let's at least try to go the way them skeletons went. See where it leads."

"Ignoring me is only going to piss me off."

"Okay, but my answer's gonna piss you off too, and if we're gonna squabble I'd rather it be in the light of day, in a time that ticks away in actual seconds instead of some god-forsaken—" He came back to her on a pronounced limp. "I'm real close to losin' it in here."

"Without the guides, we have no clear way out."

"Can you not say shit like that?"

"Answer my question."

He stared at her, his chest rising, falling, his hair a rumpled mess. If the quick walk back to her on a sorely fatigued leg didn't wind him, her push for an answer did. "You've got a bias. I wanted the answer straight from the bastard's mouth."

"Because he's so impartial."

"It really don't matter. I wanted his side. I got it."

"And then you sabotaged my meeting."

"Are we really doin' this here?"

A helpless terror rose in her, and she recognized how many different sources of anger were at play. Of course she was furious over Mick offering his life to The Silent One. His question to the demon after not accepting the answer she'd already given seemed trivial in comparison, but it bit just as hard and now she understood why. It was that answer that fueled the understanding that nearly tore her in two.

The Silent One was right.

Mother Earth did weep. She no longer existed in harmony with the people who inhabited her lands. Her lakes and rivers were a force of life for all but they were quickly turning to ruin. Indigenous legal systems gave a voice to these non-human relations, but those systems had been dominated by colonialism and overruled by money and greed for too long. Water was life, for itself and for others. It was a simple concept to her people. No longer so simple in the modern world. It trickled through equally ruined earth into the underground, its poisoned force puddling in underworld caverns like a glaring threat. Perhaps The Silent One's solution was the only way, but it was a nightmare she'd lived in her sleep, a tragedy she lived in her first life. A conquering force, bringing new ideals in a vain attempt to save the people from themselves. She could not live it again.

She swallowed to gain control of her voice. "We won't be able to stop this, Mick." What she didn't say: *I'm not sure I want to.*

He slid a gentle hand against her wounded cheek, around the back of her neck, fingers tickling her hairline. His gaze softened like he might kiss her. "We can't do nothin' till we get out of this cave. And first—"

His eyelids lowered, darkening his eyes. For a moment she mistook the wildness in them for his eagle until she remembered that look from a time before. Mick, storming into her tomb, kicking the door closed. His passion-fueled advance, the violent kiss. When they'd separated it was that look she remembered. The hooded eyes, the intention, the premeditation. He knew she wanted him, but he was going to make her wait.

"First I gotta get you home."

Home. The word nearly crumpled her. For once, she had a strong image to go along with it. A basement apartment in an old brick house. A well-loved couch, her jeans tossed over the back on top of a pair of Mick's coveralls. Three sets of boots by the door. A little girl and a man at the kitchen table, working on a spelling lesson. To get all that—and keep it—she had to stop the spill of the underworld and save a world that was not worth saving.

And saved or not, there was no world that would allow her to keep both Isabel and Mick. She'd been forced to choose between them once. Never would she be forced again. This decision would be hers, when she chose to make it, and would not be made under someone else's command. She knew the only answer. She simply had to commit to it.

Isabel would never be free of the underworld. Mick's eagle couldn't look the other way forever. Upperworld and underworld did not mix.

Agreeing to stay, even if temporarily, hadn't just led Mick on, but had fooled herself as well. Home used to mean two things—the one that had been stolen from her in her first life and the one created by her foster parents that felt as close to the original as she was going to ever get. Throughout this new life, the images had overlaid with each other, competing, never quite settling in, so the concept of home felt too complicated to ever nail down. The mistake had been allowing a new one to take form. There was too much liability in having a home. She had to fix it before the idea rooted deeper—into her and into him.

"I have Isabel and soon you'll have your niece. There will be no reason for me to stay."

He pulled his hand away from her hair but left it hanging in the air beside her, frozen and confused as if waiting for a blow. "No reason."

"Not unless I want to watch The Silent One come for you. And I won't stay for that."

"You're lyin'. To yourself mostly, but also to me."

"It's not a lie."

"Tell me to my face that I'm not reason enough to stay. In those exact words."

"You're not you anymore. You belong to him."

"Will you forget about him already? You don't work for him anymore."

"No longer working for the underworld, doing what I do—that makes me a serial killer in your world."

"But I'm sayin' you don't have to—"

"Okay, so what do you suggest I do the next time I reject a guy at a bar and he spits at me, calls me an immigrant bitch, and tells me to get out of his country?"

"You throw your beer in his face and tell him to eat shit like regular upperworld folks."

"So he and his friends can follow me out to the parking lot?"

"If you're not in the business of collecting bodies, you won't need to go into those places lookin' for guys like that."

"Maybe I want a beer."

"I got beer at home."

"Maybe I want a date."

"You mean a roll in the hay? I can provide that too. If you'll stop bein' stubborn and just see how it could be—"

"How it could be is how it is. And that same guy has a half-starved dog chained to a tree or a pregnant wife with a black eye. Without me, that guy carries on."

"I get that. But it's not your job—"

"That chained-up dog was Spot, Mick."

He took a moment with that, shoving both hands into his pockets, looking much sobered. "Anytime you see a dog like that, no one would blame you for stealin' it."

"It's not enough and never will be. You have the luxury of not seeing all the wrongs I see."

"So stay with me. Show me. I'm willing to listen."

"This world is unsalvageable. I can't watch you try to save it. I want to see it burn."

"You want to see Isabel burn with it? Spot? Old Mae?" He hesitated. "Me?"

She couldn't reconcile that and wasn't sure she'd have time to figure it out. "I don't know what to say, Mick."

"How can you not care?"

"No one cared when my world was overrun."

"And you see that's a real damn shame, right? That maybe people should care?"

Her statement wasn't exactly true. Of course people cared when her world was consumed, but theirs were being consumed as well. Her tribal nations and others, people who had systematically been stripped of power. New power structures had been erected before them without their consent. And people in this time were learning to care, but the damage was so long-term, so deep, and it felt like too much had been lost and the changes were irreversible.

But maybe that was her pessimism.

Remembering it all made her so weary she laid a palm on Mick's chest. A plea for an end. An agree-to-disagree. She had no more energy for this conversation, and she'd said what needed to be said. He didn't have to accept it.

Without another word, she took the lead, taking the same exit used by the mass of undead. When Mick stumbled and took a hard knock against a wall, she slowed her pace, caught his hand, and latched it onto her belt. She would not let the cave trick her into leaving him behind again.

Minutes—or hours—later, Mick called for her to stop and she did, recognizing how dim their lights had become.

They fumbled to replace batteries in the near dark. Her grip failed, dropping the flashlight to hit hard on the ground.

"That has to be broken," she said. Down a light made them one level closer to helplessness.

Mick found the plastic pieces and tried to secure the battery door, but it wouldn't hold. He calmly opened his pack. "Feels like it just cracked the edge off the threads. I got a fix for that."

And then he repaired the thing with medical tape and flipped the switch. The blinding new light dazzled her, and she moved forward into a room where water splashed with the power of an upperworld waterfall. They took a break to locate the source of the noise and found nothing.

"Above us?" Mick asked.

"Or in our heads."

"Ain't helpin'."

"Maybe we're close enough to the surface to hear a rushing creek," she said.

"Check you out, a ray of hope."

Her light grazed a shape ahead that shot her through with alarm. *Just a rock formation.* The beam had passed it up, and she had to find it again, make sure it wasn't moving. Mick released her belt and moved ahead to take the lead.

"Mick, wait." She swept the area, focusing the light on their intended path and there, ahead—

Mick cursed, stopping short. His flashlight beam joined hers. This rock formation looked exactly like a man slumped against the wall, his arm shielding his eyes from their approach. The legs stretched in front shuffled against the stone and moved as if attempting to stand.

"Stay the fuck down," Mick shouted.

If this was a stranded upperworld person, they were either close to the surface, or too deep in the underworld to ever escape.

"And let's see your other hand."

The arm raised higher. Ropes bound the wrist, hinting the other arm was strapped to it. The visible hand glistened darkly in the shadow.

"That's blood." She knew it without getting closer.

The man's sleeve fell down his arm to reveal an intricate tattoo they were too far away to see, but Waapikoona saw it as if her eyes were inches away. Horses rearing up with bulging eyes and bared teeth, surrounded by flames. This was the arm of the man she'd faced at the abandoned lead mine who'd left her beaten and bleeding to die in the woods. To be found by Hammond and beaten again then buried alive in a muddy grave.

"Jeremiah's father," she whispered.

Mick twisted around. "You sure?"

She nodded, one palm up to stop Mick in whatever he might do. Yes, Jeremiah had tortured Mick almost to death. But this man here was hers to deal with.

"It's in our heads. Like you said about the waterfall. Can't be real."

Hard pressure twisted the collar of her jacket. She reached to find Mick's attached fist. "Let go."

"It's a demon. A trick. Like Janie in the road that day."

She latched onto his forearm, an attempt to jerk free that wasn't working. He was too strong. "Demon or not, I'll slit its throat."

"If it's him, we can use him … find out how he got in, so we can get out."

She sent an elbow into his ribs, freeing herself.

"He told me you'd come," the man said, his voice gritty.

Waapikoona closed the distance, her flint knife already in her hand. She saw Mick's profile in his beam of light rounding the room to flank the man from the other side.

"You're lost," the man added.

She stood before him now, incapable of responding. He was indeed bound with dirty rope, ankle to ankle, wrist to wrist. She remembered too much about Jeremiah and what he did to her sister's bones, what he did to Mick. What he did to her in their life together when she was young and vulnerable. Of course this man wasn't responsible for the crimes of his son—except he was, because he was just like him. Soto dropped him here like a prize to be found.

Or a test.

"You need my help to get out," the man said. "Free me and I'll tell you."

If this was a test she was about to fail. "I'd rather die in here than take help from you."

"Yet you walk with this man, as a white man's slave, a traitor to your kind."

"Your son never understood and neither will you. You've forgotten who you are in the world. You gave colonialism exactly what it wanted. You're the traitor."

He spit at her. "A white man's whore should know to shut her mouth."

Mick's shouts filled her ears, but he was too far away to stop the blade she aimed toward tender throat. Her blade glanced off her intended target just before her shoulder slammed against hard stone. Mick's voice was against her now, quiet and easy as if the explosion in her could be calmed by words. She sent a fist into his gut, but he only pressed in harder, sandwiching her between his body and the cave.

"Knock it off." His breath warm against her hair, fingers walked down her arm in the dark, working to disarm her.

She shoved, ducking under his arm. Her dropped flashlight cast its beam against the ground where a bound man wriggled away. She lurched toward him, grabbing his forearm to hold him still. Wet warmth coated her hand as she stepped over struggling bound legs, gripped the head against her stomach, and felt the handle of her blade slip.

Her knife clattered to the stone floor. Mick had her by the shoulders, whirling her away from the thrashing man. She fell to hands and knees, the viscous coating on one palm causing it to slip out from under her, slamming her elbow into the ground. The metallic scent of newly spilled blood wafted against her, and she paused a moment, catching her breath against the ground until Mick got her by the jacket and hauled her back upright.

"What're you thinkin'?!"

She shoved him away. Someone was bleeding, and it wasn't her. Alarm rang through her. If she'd nicked him in the struggle, if her knife had any underworld grime on it—

Killing Jeremiah's father would have to wait.

"Whose blood?" she asked.

"Give me the knife!"

In the harshly shadowed light, he took hold of her again. She braced her feet but didn't fight him, which seemed enough to admit she had no weapon to protect. As the realization dawned in his eyes, he released her and snatched up a dropped flashlight. Let him find her blade. It wasn't her concern now. The pieces of her weeks-long nightmare she'd lived while unconscious in Mick's bed were coming together, given life outside her head. She'd already determined it was more than a dream. It was a premonition. It was The Silent One's unstoppable plan for the world. She could accept the underworld spilling above ground, the undead sweeping across like a great cleansing. She could not—would not—accept what might happen to Mick's eagle—

"You're bleeding." It numbed her to know what could so easily be brought into reality by an accidental scrape from her flint.

She watched Mick locate the blade and use it to cut the ropes binding Jeremiah's father's wrists and ankles. She said nothing when Mick jerked the guy to his feet and pressed a flashlight into his hand. She heard him tell the man to get lost, watched him push him toward a tunnel they hadn't yet explored.

When Mick rejoined her, she was so weary with fear she felt sick, trapped, and unsure she'd ever find a way out. She remembered how he'd thrown himself into the attack like she needed a savior yet again. Anger would consume that fear and give her strength.

"Always a fucking hero."

"Yeah, and I'm about done here." He thrust her flint at her so quickly she took a quick step to the side. "You can have this back, 'cause if you even try—"

"I know you're not about to threaten me."

"If you'd think just one minute, you'd see that killing that piece of shit down here is a wasted effort. He'll die on his own, and that won't be on you." Since she hadn't taken her flint from his hand, he grabbed her by the belt and sheathed it for her. "It's also a stupid risk. Even animals know not to attack unless it's life or death. You get hurt bad down here … "

She heard nothing else. Being compared to animals was a well-worn insult to her people, one she'd never learned to dismiss like her foster parents had. *It's the insult of an ignorant mind that doesn't understand each animal has its place. We aren't above nature. We are nature. The animals and plants of Mother Earth can live without humans, but we cannot live without them.*

The memory wasn't enough to call her away from the hovering images of her prognostic nightmare. Even as the insult burned, it could not burn through her fear for Mick's safety, even as he lectured her about her own. She held up her blood-coated palm. "Is this your blood?"

He jabbed a thumb toward the tunnel where Jeremiah's father had disappeared. "You cut his arm good when I tackled you. You might get your way if he bleeds out before he starves to death. We've got one flashlight now. Stay close unless you want to die with him."

Without looking back he set off, and Waapikoona decided she'd never seen the man so near the end of his saintly patience. She could worry that she'd brought him there, or she could worry about how narrowly she'd avoided living The Silent One's plan. A rebuilt world without Thunder-Beings, without Mick's eagle, without Mick.

I will come for your eagle.

The great demon would have to get through her first.

She picked up the canvas bag of bones before the only beam of light was entirely swallowed by the tunnel Mick entered as if determined to leave her behind. She caught up to him and took a rough fistful of his jacket, part retaliation, part lifeline. "Don't forget you're the animal, not me."

CHAPTER
28

Mick's eyes strained to find jutting walls, skull impacts, and trip hazards. His flashlight was so dim it blended with the surrounding darkness so eager to consume it. His phone was long dead. Waapikoona's hand was like ice through his jacket, and he knew her hair was as wet as his. The cave dripped on them, both insult and injury. He couldn't think about hypothermia when slow starvation or insanity seemed so much closer. Summoning his eagle's help had moved from a risky option to an impossible one. There was no strength left to do anything but shuffle along in the almost total dark.

He stopped to shrug off his backpack and rummage for fresh batteries a second time, as if the additional ten packs he should have brought had somehow found their way inside. Added weight was relevant on the surface but not relevant in a cave when the last set of good batteries were nearly dead and they could be weeks from the exit. Waapikoona stood silently above him. At this point, the spent ones he'd replaced earlier would have more juice than the ones he was using. Reaching into the pack, his hand closed on one of the batteries along with a different cold small object with jagged edges that had settled at the bottom of the backpack. A strange vibration scurried up his arm.

"Waapikoona," he whispered, drawing the object out. He opened his hand, squinting at the luminescence it seemed to emit in the dark. "I just found your mica crystal in my pack."

"Mmm?" Her voice was drowsy, severely fatigued.

He dropped the battery back in, yanked the zipper closed. Stood. As he brought the crystal up with him, it lit Waapikoona's eyes with a violet preternatural glow. She took it from him as if seeing was not believing.

"You just saved our lives, Mick."

They stared at each other in the strange light. It looked too dreamlike to be real, too present to be imagination.

"Had no idea it was in there."

"Lose the pitiful flashlight. We won't need it."

He flipped it off and tucked it into his backpack. Waapikoona raised the crystal to her eyes and turned around, scoping out every angle of the tunnel.

"We're going the wrong way. We have to backtrack. See if we can catch the trail left by our guides."

Backtrack how long? Mick didn't bother voicing the question because *how long* meant nothing and everything. It was as impossible to comprehend as it was to do. He rubbed his jaw, hoping to determine if his beard had grown, but it should be inches longer for how long they'd been in there. No human beings could walk for weeks without sleeping, and they hadn't stopped to rest. Or had they?

Waapikoona had moved away. He came against her and caught her by the belt. His eyes seemed stuck in the act of adjusting to the new source of light, and the more he tried to focus the more fake it felt. He would wake up from this in complete darkness soon. He just hoped this time, he wouldn't be so alone. They returned to the last fork in the tunnel where they'd had to choose blind, and Waapikoona jolted to a halt and passed the crystal to him.

"That's the way out. Look and see what I mean, in case something happens to me."

He didn't have the energy to argue that something was not going to happen to her, not while he still breathed, so he took the piece of mica and raised it against his eyes. What he saw was a cloudy, faint version of his eagle's vision when he was in human body and partial eagle mind. Textured blacks, unnamable colors of light, and a hazy lingering trail, like dust motes in a slant of moonlight, formed in three distinct lines.

He and Waapikoona would have been walking the wrong tunnel straight to their deaths.

"First dibs on the shower," he said, clasping her hand and leading the way.

WHEN MICK LOST the trail he passed the crystal to Waapikoona, praying that his eyes were just tired and that she'd have no trouble leading them out. What he didn't expect was the strange grayness hanging ahead, how it seemed to take the shape of the tunnel they were in, flanked by darker gray walls.

Without the razor focus of his eyes on the guides' trail, his ears perked up, drawing his attention to a distant white noise so earthly he barely recognized it.

"You hear that?"

"Yes, I think it's—"

"Rain," they said together.

"Shouldn't get our hopes up," she added. "Could be an underground waterfall."

"I'm okay with getting our hopes up."

They advanced, the grays ahead reforming in ways he couldn't comprehend until he realized he was seeing mild purplish light, now turning bluish, more vivid with each step. The cave's drips became a shower, soaking the shoulders of his jacket, running in thick streams through his hair and down his face. The stone floor collected an inch of water, then two. The noise was an assault on his hearing after being in the quiet for so long.

Splashing through the collecting puddles, they increased their pace, their eyes adjusting to the growing light. When the water reached his ankles, Mick ruled that he would not drown in a cave. The floor turned sticky, each step sucking at his boot. He couldn't decide if stone turning to mud was a good sign or a bad one. Rainwater breached the top of his boot, flooding the inside even though his socks were already soaked.

"Can you swim?" he asked.

"We won't need to."

He paused to study the shape of blue-gray light ahead. It lay just above head level like a horizontal slab of a miracle. After a short climb up a rain-soaked hill of packed mud, they were eye to eye with a dusky wide doorway into the pouring rain. Mick braced his fingers against the cold limestone ceiling and decided he preferred rainstorm to cave any day, especially since he couldn't tell if that dusk ahead would lead to daylight or night.

She brushed past him, tucking something sharp and cold—the mica crystal—into his jeans pocket, and walked out into the pouring rain, the pale canvas bag like his beacon.

As he followed into the downpour, a spread of wet warmth engulfed him. Spring warmth like a mother's arm, a heated home, daylight lingering on the air even though the horizon stood in the way. So this was evening, then, with an overcast sky that would make nighttime navigation impossible. To his cold, cave-coated skin, the rain was like a warm clean shower. To the defeat in his bones, he felt rebuilt. The return to daylight like a rebirth from the grave. He took a breath to ask Waapikoona if the feeling could be compared and decided it in no way could.

The canopy of the trees thickened, offering some cover from the pound of the rain, and as they walked, Mick's brain, and time itself, fell back into place. His stomach grumbled, a normal missed-lunch-and-late-for-dinner pang instead of the pain he'd expect from days-long hunger. He reviewed their conversations in the cave, their arguments, the confrontation with The Silent One. And the sex, a practical distraction from his eagle that felt like so much more. He remembered her promise of a kiss if he kept his eagle far away. Hunger might have to wait.

When they reached a border of woods and trimmed grass and he looked upon the back of Old Mae's house and rain-soaked GTO orange shining under the house light, he decided he must have lost his mind.

Waapikoona had stopped, likely as dazed as he was.

"How in the hell … " He lost the thought under a new wave of strangeness, like time had lied to him and he wasn't just vaguely hungry, he was so beyond it he'd grown numb to it, reentering his life through a wormhole, weeks or months after—or before—he'd left it.

"Our guides knew where to bring us." She untied the soaked canvas bag from her shoulder and squatted to unload the bones gently on the forest floor. "These are under the protection of the underworld. Predators will not touch them."

It was a question Mick should have thought to ask. Once the bag was empty, she tore it open at the seams, creating a thin cover for the girl if she awoke before Mick could figure out how to watch for her and be there when she opened her eyes. It was a problem too difficult for him to solve right now. Night had descended. Underworld creatures would soon rise. If his eagle took him, he'd never find the strength to be human again.

When Mick started toward the house, she pulled him to a halt by a fistful of his jacket. "We're not going in."

Mick felt stupid with fatigue and out of patience for anything that would block him from fully warming the deep underworld cold out of his bones. He pulled away and headed forward, but she grabbed his backpack to stop him a second time. He swung around, so ready to lash out it gave him a sickening jolt.

"The Silent One's soldiers will come straight here."

"Not my concern right now."

"You can't stay here."

"Bullshit." Hunger and exhaustion were making him angrier than he should be about a problem they'd already discussed. The contrast between cave cold and lingering sunlight had vanished, leaving him coated in rain that now felt as cold as it was and showed no sign of slowing.

"Your bravado isn't going to make him go away."

He felt his face harden. There was not an ounce of strength left in him to lighten up. "Glad to hear of your faith in me."

"Faith? This is your doing. I had a deal to offer him that he would have taken. You sabotaged it to put yourself in danger."

He expected to argue this to a resolution later, but now he decided he was done with it, completely and forever, and the hostile thoughts that surfaced would only lead him to say things he'd regret. With his eyes hard on hers he turned away, hoping she didn't put her hands on him again because god help him, he just might put his hands right back on her.

Leaving her outside went against every instinct he had. Under the overhang at his apartment door, he shook out his wet hair, unlocked the deadbolt, and turned to face her. She stood where he'd left her, illuminated in the glare of the floodlights, hard rain falling against the curtain of night coming alive behind her. He could no longer discern if it was human or eagle eyes that recognized what lived in the dark, that anticipated it, that basked in the knowledge of how he could hunt and kill. With those eyes, he spoke to her: *Follow me inside or I will drag you in.*

Moments later he closed the door behind her, locking them both inside, and he didn't have the energy to dissect how easily she'd surrendered. He plugged his phone into the wall and set it on the kitchen counter to power up. Her eyes roamed the place. She was looking for her sister.

He knew the feel of an empty apartment. He'd come home to one most of his life. "She's not here."

When Waapikoona looked more closely at him, he realized she was asking what more he knew, and in her stillness he could see how much that cost her to ask him. If he was stomping between their sisterhood again—well, he was too tired to care. "Could be upstairs safe with Old Mae, could be out hunting. If that's true, ain't no findin' her till she comes back." His eagle could find her, but then he'd never find himself again.

A third option he did not suggest: still in the cave with the healer. He didn't want to think about that cave ever again. With the way Waapikoona seemed to harden herself against that unspoken third option, he knew she didn't want to think about it either. He also knew the apartment walls could be slick black stone and they could be standing in demon leech-filled water for how easily they were transported back, as if the nightmare they'd lived hadn't settled into either of their hearts until they had escaped it.

"Tuesday night," he said after a glance to his phone's powered-up screen. He stooped to untie his boot laces as a violent shiver overtook him. All that time in the cave, the rain, and now that he'd returned to his warm apartment his body decided to protest. "We only lost two days." He shouldn't feel such gratitude for it, even though the cave could have taken so much more.

"Your eagle is not yours to offer."

Without segue, her statement was a blow. He felt a burn rush through him—anger, lust, defiance. "You that posses-sive?"

She held the wall, toeing off her boots. "Come to bed. I need to get you out of my system so when The Silent One comes for you, I won't have to mourn."

"That's all I am to you?" He struggled for a clear term. "Sexual frustration?"

"Yes." An answer so quick meant she didn't even need to think about it.

Now out of his boots, he stripped off his wet jacket, unable to make sense of this conversation, how it started, where it would lead. What came out of his mouth was pure reaction, no thought. Stripped raw by the cave, by the hours he'd spent cold, hungry, despairing. "Soulless witch."

"*Animal*, Mick. Say what you mean."

"You want me to think that? Okay. Done. Since it infuriates you so much that I don't." He'd freed himself from every wet layer down to the skin of his upper body. Watching her slide out of her jeans, he went for his belt.

"Your eagle won't be content until I'm dead."

"My eagle—" His teeth chattered so loudly he could barely speak. He had no words to explain a wild animal's thoughts, no way to translate the force at play when his eagle's vision lingered on her shape moving along the earth below. Love, devotion … human emotions carried so much baggage and complication. None could define the pure razor-edged knowledge of simple belonging his eagle understood every time she rustled the grass or walked into view. What was it she'd said to him that day behind Pop's house? *I walk beside you always*. Also true coming from his eagle— but eagles don't walk. And something about the way his words had choked off had caught her attention in a way he didn't intend.

She straightened from peeling off her socks. Her remaining thin T-shirt clung to her, wet fabric against skin, underwear peeking from below. She tore cave-damp bandages from her demon-gored side and dropped them onto the pile of her clothes. The scald of her eyes meant war not love. He couldn't understand if this was a fight or foreplay.

He had no idea what she was making out of the thought he'd just cut off, but now he had a new one, more important than anything. The underworld had been drawn out of her. She'd been as foreign and lost in that cave as he was. As soon as she shed that T-shirt, he could point out the healed runes on her back and prove it. *You and my eagle aren't enemies anymore.* Unable to wait, he grabbed the bottom hem of her shirt and yanked it upward over her head, spinning her with the motion.

What was once a design of black gore trailing down her spine now looked like individual marks of old branding, their patterns faded with the growth of new skin. The underworld had indeed been drawn out—thanks to the old woman upstairs—and Waapikoona's very human skin was working to erase its presence altogether.

"Making sure you're not about to bed underworld scum?" In the quiet way she said it, there was more to the question than thunderbird versus demon-raised bones. Packed inside was the indignities from her first life, the crimes of his ancestors, and the threads that persisted. Centuries of violence and hatred performed on the earth under their feet, the same unrest The Silent One planned to exploit. And a cheapening of their every touch, every kiss that felt so sacred to him.

She let out a hard breath. "And someone like you won't ever—"

Her shoulders were in his hands. He'd spun her to face him, and whatever sound had just come out of him could sure be mistaken for animal. He knew she was goading him, knew he was the sucker, knew he was giving her exactly what she was trying to prove—but he wasn't going to let her finish that statement. She didn't know him and never would, as long as she dwelled on the tragedies of her first life and allowed them to paint him in this one. Yes, the world was shit. No, he was not the one to blame. Individuals did not create it. His flesh prickled hot under his cold, wet skin, the scorch of being criminally misjudged and helpless against it. He would always be her enemy. She would never love him. He could prove it to her, prove that she could, but that was a long-term project she would not stick around for. Sex couldn't do it, would only set him back.

And if she was right, she'd get her fill and leave him.

She was so close now, the vague notion of her body heat radiating against him, impossible since her skin was as cold as his hands. Their combined breath heated the inches between them. The violent shiver that had hold of him had taken her too. Their teeth chattered in unison. Through narrowed eyes she watched him, an animal, a predator, but so was he. Human, animal, predator and prey, depending on the moment in time he could be either, he could be both.

He was still lost in that thought when he tasted her mouth, realized too late that she'd knocked his grip off her shoulders and surged forward to kiss him. It temporarily stunned him until he felt her arms encircle him, and he realized exactly what she was doing. Following through with her plan to bed him and ditch him. He got hold of her shoulders again and shoved her away.

"You want people to hate you. You work so hard at it." As he said it, his jaw tightened against an even more severe shudder. Freezing cold and boiling with the need to punch something. "It's an excuse to keep a distance from people. To do what you do."

"Is it working?" The calmness she'd conjured clashed so deeply against his anguish that he thought, *she really has no soul.*

"After all we've been through and you're gonna say that shit to me?"

"I've warned you so many times—"

"Yet I don't learn, right? Well how 'bout this. You're wrong."

"My first life will never fit with this life."

"And here we go havin' the same damn conversation. You know what? If this is what it's going to be like I'm *done*." The word tore from deep inside him, the most painful, unwilling yet inevitable surrender, so final in tone it left him speechless.

She came for him again, and he caught her wrist, expecting a blow, but it was another kiss, even more violent than the first.

Fine, he thought. *Let's use each other for sex.*

Now he was committed and there was no way back, only forward, to short-term carnal satisfaction and long-term regret. He didn't plan, right? A mindless hick. Fathering babies with random women. Hell, soon maybe he'd have child support payments he could default on and live up to another one of her likely stereotypes of guys like him. He let the anger settle in him, let the pent-up lust build. He sent a leg between hers, forcing her backward in the direction of the bedroom. His lips moved on their own now, down her neck, her shoulders. He gave in, shut off his brain, let his body guide him.

To the bedroom, into the bed. Inside his cold skin he burned so hot it made him light-headed. In her hair he smelled rain and sky, an antidote to the other scents that mingled upon them. Cold stone and dried blood, demon venom and darkness. The cave had coated them; even as the underworld had leaked from her, it had reinfected them both. They could only hate each other now, and parting ways would be easy.

On his back, he let his arms fall away, let her work him over, met her kisses but nothing else. If she wanted to use him, that was all she'd have. Despair overcame him, muting his desire. He remembered all the times she'd teased him, baited him, expected him to make a move. He'd held off to game her back, punish her, make her suffer. A new torture came to mind, one where he'd show her how he could love her and then let her leave him with that pleasure ripe in her mind. New intention raised him on elbows, sent an arm around her waist to flip her onto her back. Seeing her flayed cheek anew, he gently laid two fingers over it. He would make her love him; he would not stop proving who he was. Let her think of him as an ego-driven white savior. Someday she'd realize how wrong she was.

Parting her legs, he settled against her, feeling her fingers slide against his ribs and pull him down. He pressed his forehead against hers, a reach for something solid to reclaim his common sense because now he was too far gone and he had to warn her. He needed her to tell him no. "I got no power to stop this."

"I never asked you to stop."

"The future isn't ... I can't hardly provide for myself, Waapikoona."

"It's okay. Right now, I'm not fertile."

"How do you know?"

"My cycle—"

He pushed inside her. He needed no other encouragement than that. And dare he speak the incessant feeling that in thought alone made him lose his mind? Voiced, he'd no longer retain control of it. "I shouldn't ... but I wish you were. And I wish..." He wished too many things. The regret for thinking—and speaking—hovered at the back of his mind.

She wrapped her legs around him, put her lips to his ear. "You're the only man whose seed I've ever wanted inside me."

"Please," he nearly choked. His reckless, passion-fueled admission, met—no, raised—by her. He'd never experienced sexual accord like this, as strangely combative as it was, and he wasn't sure what to do with it. He'd never had his regret so easily neutralized. "Don't say that."

"Why not?"

"It's just … too much." It was a fairy-tale ending they were never going to have. Her own admission was so at odds with her reason for joining him in bed, a conundrum too difficult with his whole mind rejoicing in the press of her body against his. He slid an arm between her shoulders and the bed, holding himself tight against her, shifting her leg higher with his other arm. They moved as one, but he became aware that it was all his positioning, all his terms.

He pulled away so he could see her face. "You okay with this?"

She gave a slow nod—one that didn't seem to convey the understanding, or the permission, he sought.

"Being dominated?" he said.

With all movement at a pause, he relished her silky grip on him. In answer to his question, she unlatched her arms from his midsection and laid them palms-up beside her head. Along with the fire in her eyes Mick understood that in opening herself to be dominated, it was she who held all power between them. He was her toy, helpless against her demands and her power over him, and he was completely okay with that.

He entwined his fingers with hers, pressing his weight palm to palm. As she struggled against him, letting him feel how tightly she was held, he nearly melted on top of her.

"I stayed human," he said, and instead of waiting to receive a kiss—the sweet, slow one he imagined her offer to be—he stole it from her.

Every move he made she absorbed and improved. They were a single machine, a perfectly engineered driving force. They built a new warmth between them, and as his heart met the pulse of hers, he understood this was indeed too good to be true. His life did not hand him these things. She would leave, this would be lost, he was powerless to stop it. And with that knowledge of this finality, he poured all of himself into her, a last chance, a farewell, a proving of the feeling he couldn't put into words. *I love you. I'll miss you. I'll never forget you.*

She managed to escape him before he could finish it. He turned with her, a perfect dance in the sheets. He felt at once both grounded and flying. He shoved the pillow aside and sat, leaning his back against the headboard. She climbed on top of him and for one timeless moment she looked into his eyes. Her hands slid from his shoulders to his neck, and he raised his arms to mirror the action, the thud of her jugular against his palms. A lovers' embrace, a lock of combat. She shifted forward then back, taking him inside once again but this time it was her terms.

He tightened his grip on her neck and pulled her in for a kiss. Her terms and his. He wanted to taste her, breathe her in, complete the circle, the unending connection from him into her and back into him. If their coupling became so infinite, she could never leave him.

MICK WOKE IN the night, panicked at the perpetual darkness, his arm captured, his chest pumping with uneasy breath. Morning should have arrived by now. This was cave darkness, the nonsensical clock of the underworld. With his free arm he grappled for his phone on the nightstand and remembered he'd left it on the kitchen counter. He strained to see the dim green digits of the alarm clock. Blinking midnight.

Then he realized what had hold of his other side. The weight of a woman, her body aligned with his as if she were a part of him, her face pressed into the space under his collarbone, her arm splayed across his stomach. He felt her breath warming his skin, the torpid clasp of her leg entwining his. He pulled her closer, discarding the strangeness from the absent morning.

UPON MICK'S SECOND awakening, he first noticed the cold emptiness beside him. The darkness persisted. Daylight had either come and gone, or it had never come at all. His alarm clock had gone black. The beside lamp's switch gave him only the sound of the click, no light. He darted from the bed and felt his way to a pair of jeans from the pile of clean laundry he hadn't had time to put away.

Waapikoona in his bed hadn't been a dream, but thinking she'd stay—

He swore, angry with himself for even entertaining the idea. She'd used him and ditched him just like she said she would. He left the bedroom and surveyed his dim apartment, lit only by a hint of bluish light coming through the glass in the door. Every electronic device as blank as his alarm clock. The shadowy mound of Waapikoona's wet clothes and bandages by the kitchen table. A pile of his own to match. Isabel's nest of blankets on the couch, her well-loved stuffed bunny sitting beside it. Waapikoona's boots lying sideways by the door, just as she'd left them. He went to his phone on the counter and found it had charged itself before the power went out. There were too many texts and missed calls to handle now. The date and time said it was the next morning—the next *day*—and there was no sunlight and no Waapikoona.

He tugged on his boots, still wet from the cave, and yanked the apartment door open.

She stood barefoot just outside the door, wrapped in the quilt from the couch. Beyond her, winged demons flitted against a purple-black sky. Lightning pulsed, crackling in the air, offering a brief illumination of the grass crawling with shiny black centipedes.

Relief to see Waapikoona didn't even have a chance to register. He flung his arm around her shoulders, dragging her backward against him in a partial attempt to keep her safe and keep him safe from his eagle.

"It's started," she said, allowing Mick to pull her close as if her thoughts had disconnected from her body.

"Come inside." His voice was roughened by sleep and staving off his eagle.

"I have to check on your niece."

He dragged her inside and locked the deadbolt. "There's no way—"

No way they could ever leave the house again. He put his face in his hands, fingers digging into his hair, pushing it off his face. His niece was out there, bones, or flesh and blood, he had no idea. And Isabel—they had to find out if she'd made it home. The only way to do either of those things with the sky and grass looking like it did was in thunderbird form.

"I don't see how ... " The understanding fell so hard upon him he lost sense of place and time. He was floating, unattached sentience, a brain without a body. He saw no way to carry on as Mick the man. Only his eagle could handle his life now. The shift could be delayed no more. Once in that form, he'd be committed to not just the simpler tasks of finding his niece and Isabel. He'd be dead set on saving the world. It would be too much time spent as eagle, one too many shifts, and he'd never find his way back.

A hand on his arm brought him back. He looked into dark eyes. Concentrated on her cool, clear voice even if he wasn't understanding the words. For the first time he deeply recognized her calm under pressure, her striking composure. She was one to look to, one to trust at his side. Damn, he was going to miss her.

From the kitchen, his phone rang.

She squeezed his arm. "You get that. I'll be right back."

He made a clumsy grab for her, but she was already through the door, in boots and a jacket he hadn't even seen her put on. Now his brain replayed what she'd been saying, that he couldn't go out there and risk a demon bite, that she still carried enough of the underworld inside her to be immune to the venom, that he better have breakfast on the table by the time she returned.

In the kitchen he snatched his phone, but it had already quieted. He called Kari back.

"We're okay," he said when she answered.

"Sarah told me not to worry if you were gone for another seventeen days or longer. But I worried. God, Mickey, she said it would get bad but this is … outside it's … unreal."

"You all still at Pop's?"

"Yeah, we boarded the windows. Power keeps going in and out. Janie's locked herself in the closet. Won't come out, won't eat. You know Pop's been stockpiling food and water for a while, but how the hell—"

"Listen, Kari. I gotta do somethin'—" Mick tightened a fist, locking down the waver in his voice. Something in the back of his mind said, *There's no point in telling her you're going to die.* "Just stay bunkered down for as long as you can."

And don't tell her you love her. It will just scare her. She knows.

Waapikoona blasted through the apartment door, slamming it closed behind her. When Mick saw the look in her eyes he ended the call.

"Bones are gone."

He had no time to process that before she shoved a black object toward him. Flashlight, smeared with mud, its battery compartment held on with dingy white medical tape. He tore off the tape to be dead sure the threads were cracked in the exact spot. And they were. "That's the flashlight I gave to—"

"You should've let me kill him."

"He followed us out—"

"And it looks like he either stole your niece's bones or stole your niece." She opened the fridge. "What's the fastest thing we can eat? I'd rather not cut out someone's heart on an empty stomach."

Serene acceptance washed over Mick. All choice had fallen away. He saw what he needed to do with black and white eagle clarity.

Funny, because it wasn't Waapikoona who was leaving him. He was leaving her.

She caught up with him at the apartment door, the clasp of her fingers stopping his as he began to undo his jeans. "I can track him, Mick."

"Not like I can."

"You?"

He paused to look at her straight on. "Yes, me."

Panic flared in her eyes, a control she no longer had. She understood perfectly. There was no separation between his two forms anymore. Eagle was all he was now, all he'd ever be. With the world in the shape it was out there, his eagle would never submit to him. She put herself between him and the door. "I'm making us food."

"There's plenty for me to eat outside."

"It's not wise to leave your human energy so depleted when … "

When it was already so hard to shift back. If she didn't want to voice it, neither did he. It felt much better just to plow toward inevitable defeat than give it more power by speaking of it, too.

"Mick."

Her voice, saying his name like that, like she always did. She saw him and understood him in a way no one ever had. The snag it tore inside him felt all too real.

"Save your niece," she said. "Find Isabel. Then come back home. This world is not worth saving."

"Home," he repeated, needing her to say that word again and mean it.

She held his eye. An offer, a bribe. "Yes. Home."

"Promise you'll stay away from me. I can't control who I destroy. People like you, raised—"

"People stolen from their graves. Enslaved to a war they didn't agree to. I won't condemn you for returning them to Mother Earth."

"I can't be sure this time … that I'll see you as anything different. Even though you're no longer—"

"I trust your eagle. I trust you."

He held her eye. Even though his eagle had never attacked her, he had no idea what it would be capable of on its own, without his influence. And if The Silent One did find him and take possession, he had no idea how thorough the great demon's command might be. "Don't."

A shadow fluttered against the window in the door, thumping against the threshold outside. Waapikoona snagged a quilt from the couch as Mick swung the door open. She ushered a wrapped little girl inside, holding her like she'd never let go again.

"I found it," Isabel panted, pushing to gain some space to speak. "The snake on Mr. Soto's belly. I flew so far." She held out a hand, once curled and weak, now straight, strong, and perfect.

"Where?" Mick and Waapikoona asked in unison.

"In the water. Lots of water, with graves at the bottom. That map, the one of Missouri—"

Mick rushed to the kitchen table to shove around the pile of homeschooling papers he and Isabel had been working on. He found the page he'd torn from an old road atlas as Waapikoona and Isabel joined him at the table. He flipped on the light switch—stupid, the power was out. Waapikoona went to work lighting candles as he rummaged through drawers for a working flash light.

Finally, with enough light to see, Isabel laid a finger on the map. "This one."

"Table Rock Lake," he said.

Waapikoona looked up at him. "Graves?"

"Yeah, there's a bridge at the bottom too. In the fifties they built a dam and flooded a small town. Everybody had to move."

"To create a lake that shouldn't be there?"

Mick left the woman and girl staring at him to shuffle through the stack of thrift store books on the coffee table he'd borrowed from Kari. Not long ago he'd flipped through one on Missouri places, dog-earing interesting pages to read to Isabel while Waapikoona was unconscious in his bed. He found the page and laid the book open on the kitchen table in front of them. "Table Rock Lake. Two hundred twenty feet at its deepest, created by damming the White River and flooding the town. Lots of cemeteries had to be relocated, but they missed some of the graves."

Waapikoona had leaned forward to read a caption on a picture of a person in scuba gear. "Underwater caves explored by divers." She looked up, into Mick's eyes. "The underworld has direct access."

He could only gaze back. He could do nothing about it until his niece was found.

"The snake from Mr. Soto's belly is small and looks sick." Isabel said. "It's not attached to its tail anymore."

Mick didn't need proof, but now he had it. The end of the world had begun.

CHAPTER
29

"Go," Waapikoona said. "Find the baby and bring her home. Isabel and I will find Soto."

But Mick had already checked out. His eagle's ferocity had filled his eyes and would soon seize the rest of his form. She crossed the apartment and flung open the door, Mick right behind her. He sprinted across the yard then tore into the swollen purple sky, man into eagle like an everyday metamorphosis. She'd relied on her people's stories of Thunder-Beings, but for the first time she saw Mick as a reflection of his own culture. Viking myths of gods who transformed into beasts, no longer so mythical. She did not have their names or know their stories, but she witnessed the greatness and simplicity of it, the shudder of mass into a new form easily dismissed by her human brain as nothing at all.

Mick wasn't nothing. He'd become so much. She tried to resist it, but now she saw how pointless it all was. Mick was everything.

Her smooth exit from the bed that morning had led her straight into her own practiced flight, honed on enough lovers to be instinctive, foolproof, free from regret. She'd made it as far as her pile of wet clothes and had reached for her jeans, but the action got stuck. It would be silly not to grab dry clothes from the bedroom, but she'd have to do it without waking him. Straightening in Mick's kitchen, she pictured him how she left him, sleeping with one arm flung over his head and the other trapped underneath her. She imagined leaving him in the dark.

Even though she'd warned him. Even though he'd dove into bed with her anyway.

For the first time, her whereabouts mattered, to someone she valued like no man she'd ever known. Someone who would walk beside her always, in body and soul. Because her whereabouts held such consequence for someone of such importance, they mattered as much to her. New responsibility lay before her like a trail uncovered by the rain. If she walked away, this trail would become overgrown, and she'd never see it again.

Staying here meant no more wet clothes, cold mornings, and solitary walks away from one place toward another. The consistency of that inconsistent life made it easy to wake up, put on discarded clothes, and walk out into the cold alone. Too much time spent with Mick had turned her inconsistent life on end. In its place she felt a primitive attachment to this place and its people. The regret she felt just reaching for her jeans empowered a might inside her that she not only couldn't fight, but didn't want to.

It didn't have to be as complicated as it seemed in her head. It could be as simple Mick had made it. She'd stay. That was it. Maybe forever, maybe not. Depended on what life had in store for them, and there was no way to see the future or plan so it would be—what had Mick said?

We're gonna put one foot in front of the other until everything has worked out right.

The alternative was her running away like she always did, an endless circle of it without the blissful detachment of truly being on her own. Now she had Isabel. Now she had Mick. She'd admit now, the choice was no longer one or the other. Leaving would be a hurt taken onto not just herself but her sister and Mick too, who mattered to her more than herself. It was abandoning a responsibility she felt rooted into, commitment she'd guard with her life. It was leaving a man in the dark who meant as much to her as her lost family. It was finding that place in the world, a second chance, a miracle, and casting that opportunity aside.

So she could think clearly, without the influence of Mick's cozy apartment wrapping around her like home, instead of grabbing her wet jeans she had grabbed the quilt and gone outside to think under the sky. She had only a moment to imagine walking into the woods away from Mick one last time before her sleep-fogged eyes gathered details from the new world outside. And in that brief moment of imagining, she felt as wrong and upside down as she felt looking at the underworld spilling across the earth.

That was when he'd come outside to find her. Not fleeing, but waiting for him.

Commitment to Mick no longer unnerved her. It terrified her and thrilled her. She could work the challenge like she'd worked her old vigilante life, without all the mess. Or with a different kind of mess. She was okay with all of it.

She'd found her place with Mick just as the world began its end. It was a poetry that made sense to her. A fitting end in an unjust world. For once she couldn't blame colonial culture for romanticizing her Indian suffering. Soon, it would be everyone who suffered. Everyone would feel the spread of oppression, the theft of their homes, a reshaping of their lives to fit within a new world forced on them. For once, everyone would agree how unromantic it was.

"I'm going to find Mr. Soto." Isabel pressed a cold object into Waapikoona's palm. "Meet us at that lake."

Waapikoona looked down to find the Pontiac key in her hand as a falcon flapped two strong symmetrical wings toward the open door.

THE PONTIAC PARTED a swarm of winged demons as she turned onto the road, bodies thumping against the windshield and grille. She considered a detour to trade it for the Jeep—and saw the heavily treaded tires and round head lights heading toward her, a shiny black Nissan on its tail. She hit the brakes and stopped window-to-window with the Nissan as the Jeep's taillights sped away in her mirror.

Waapikoona lowered her window as the other car did the same. The sky above was a chaos of beating demon wings.

"Back to Michael's," Teresa said from the Nissan's driver's seat. "We need to ditch one of these cars."

Waapikoona U-turned in the road in a fog of Teresa's burned rubber.

Back at the house, Soto stood in the driveway, his head tilted back to observe a circling raptor, its nearly translucent body absorbing some of the unearthly hues of the melting sky. Waapikoona hopped from the Pontiac's seat and felt a twist in her healing side, bracing it with a hand as she slammed the door.

"We have coordinates," Teresa said, meeting her at the car. "But you have no GPS."

"Coordinates—?"

"For where the underworld meets the lake your sister found." Teresa glanced above them at the circling falcon. For several breaths she watched the bird—then she spun and called to Boto. "She's leaving!"

The man was out of his clothes and into his wings, giving chase before Waapikoona could make sense of why her sister was leaving or how Teresa had even known. Now the other woman was spreading a map across the hood of the Nissan and laying an index finger at an edge where lake blue met turf green.

"There's a park here. We can take the access road this way." She traced along the shore of the flooded river named Table Rock Lake. "And then go off-road here. We'll take the Jeep as far as we can and then finish up on foot."

"To do what?" Waapikoona asked.

"Meet your maker and destroy him. Your sister will use her ouroboros sighting as bait and lead the great demon straight to it, where we will attack." She looked around, her eyes suddenly frantic. "Where's Michael?"

"Somewhere ... inside his eagle."

Teresa's eyes settled on Waapikoona's, measuring emotion. Somehow the woman knew this might be—or would be—Mick's last shift, and Waapikoona had to brace herself, take a breath, clear her expression. Confirmation from an expert like Teresa brought Mick's hunch straight into clear truth. A gentle hand on Waapikoona's arm proved it further.

Mick would never be human again.

She turned away from Teresa's act of comfort to look upon Mother Earth's corrupted form. Grotesque purple clouds, forest blackened with condensed otherworldly shadow, the light from the roiling sky stuck somewhere between overcast day and night. The wind picked up, blowing a winter chill into early spring. She had wanted to watch the earth burn, but here it was ready to freeze.

Electricity fizzled above them. Sinuous carmine bodies with double sets of wings and exposed vertebrae plopped against the ground around them like fallen birds. She heard a raptor's screech in the sky, muttered Spanish beside her, and Teresa snatched a handful of her jacket sleeve as if to jar her into attention. "Why is there a baby in the woods?"

Mick's niece. He'd found her, which meant he may have found Jeremiah's father too.

Waapikoona checked for her flint knife on her belt and headed toward the line of trees. Frost accumulated in the grass before her eyes. Teresa called out to her and pointed upward where Soto's falcon hovered on the hard wind then banked, leading her through dried frozen woods that had been alive with new green spring growth the day before. Teresa's footsteps crunched behind her. They squeezed around brambles and passed through a grove of blackened young pines, catching sight of Soto's falcon on the other side just in time to see him dive into the treetops.

"Ahead," Teresa said, taking the lead.

Pressing her throbbing bandaged hand against her damaged side, Waapikoona stopped to catch her breath. Waking up weak and helpless in Mick's bed felt entirely too familiar again. Before the distance grew between her and Teresa, she pushed herself into a faster pace, ducking limbs and stepping over rotting logs, their healthy crops of mushrooms now encased in ice. She elbowed around another prickly bramble, her own rapid breath becoming background noise to the sounds ahead.

Reaching Teresa, she stopped short. The forest had cleared to reveal a great golden eagle and its prey. What once had been a man was now a stumbling, scrambling thing. Falling, then finding its feet, only for the eagle's talons to tear off another piece of him, causing him to collide with the ground again. Blood sprayed the trees and wet the ground. She did not need her flint blade, but she could help Mick by finding his niece.

She and Teresa divided, circling the carnage while two falcons searched the forest from above. And there, curled on a bed of pine needles in the thickening ice she found a fair-skinned baby girl, her soft eyelids closed but her heart beating strongly. One hand lay bent and shrunken as if missing its structure, just like Isabel's used to be. Waapikoona took off her jacket, wrapped the baby, and picked her up, settling her against her chest.

The victory could not be shared with Mick. He was lost inside a bloodthirsty eagle, too set on upperworld duty to even acknowledge the win for his human—or the revenge. It didn't stop her from returning to the scene where Jeremiah's father now lay in ruins, no longer identifiable as a human corpse. This was her undead brother raised from bones by the same great demon that had raised her. She could just as easily catch the eye of her Thunder-Being predator who'd likely lost the guidance from his human side.

She trusted Mick. She trusted his eagle.

Teresa blocked her way into the small clearing, her gaze aimed at a nearby ancient oak where the golden eagle now perched, cleaning his feathers. The bird paused his task to turn an eye toward her. She could sense the powerful vision all along her skin. There was no reason to get closer.

"You did it, Mick." She folded the edge of her jacket away from the sleeping baby's face and turned so the eagle could see. Woman and raptor regarded one another. She could easily spot the eagle in Mick, and once she may have been able to identify Mick inside the eagle. But not now. She stiffened against the pang of grief and turned to Teresa. "I need to get this baby to her mother."

TERESA DROVE THE Jeep while Waapikoona cradled the baby in the passenger seat, guiding them down roads shadowed in the strange noontime twilight. They met no other cars except for a few abandoned ones.

"What's her name?" Teresa asked.

"Helen."

As the baby began to wake with soft whimpers and gently seeking fingers, Waapikoona found it harder to resent the trade of Mick's life for hers. She'd never held a baby in this life, but she remembered babies from her first. Cousins, neighbors, even vague memories of Isabel as a cooing creature with a gummy smile wrapped tightly against their mother's chest. Then she'd been a child herself and wasn't so moved by the image of a baby like she was now. In her arms she held Mick's flesh and blood, Dougie and Janie's baby sister, Kari's beloved lost little girl. She brought the bundle higher on her chest to tuck the soft head under her chin and tried to find her armor.

Pop's house looked like a derelict property, windows boarded awkwardly with old stained plywood and two-by-fours, the door covered by a rusted section of chain-link fencing. Teresa made a reach for Waapikoona as she pushed through the car door, a fearful silent plea of caution that an undead woman carrying an undead baby would not need when walking through the spilled underworld. On the path to the porch, a crawling creature with a barbed upright tail curled over its body raised its beaked head to strike. She brushed it aside with her boot. Another exited the grass to take its place, and she hopped the porch step and spun to face the teeming yard, banging her elbow against the chain-link to alert Mick's family.

"Who's there?" an old man called from inside the closed door.

She turned around to face the peephole. The door opened, the chain-link was pushed aside, and she was pulled over the threshold by the elbow.

"I'll be damned," Pop said under his breath. He reached shaky hands toward her.

She began to pass the baby to him when Kari appeared behind his shoulder. She felt wrong to be the one to reunite them, after all Mick had been through, all he'd done to make this happen. It spread like a new grief, another layer upon the many. Fury and despair thickened her throat, making it hard to speak. She laid the baby in Kari's arms and backed out of the house as tears streamed Kari's face and Pop cleared his voice to ask the question Waapikoona would not answer. *Where's Mickey?*

But it never came. They could see something on her, the same obvious emotion Teresa had seen, and both their faces became another measurement for that great chasm of loss. As if her tie to Mick was stronger than theirs, her grief deeper, that instead of her being here to support them, they'd stepped forward to hold her up.

Waapikoona nearly missed the step out the door, grabbing the door frame to right herself. Past the Jeep, a herd of dog-sized creatures with shiny black claws bounded across the gravel driveway, their powerful bodies spraying rock and turf. She slammed the chain-link into place over the doorway and turned away from Mick's family.

"How can I thank him?" Kari asked through the criss-cross metal, her voice trembling.

She looked into Mick's sister's eyes, the exact same shade of blue she loved and would mourn forever. He'd given up his humanity and life so this baby could live. The world could not burn and take this all away. "He knows."

Chapter 30

Through alternating pockets of mild spring air and deep freeze, they drove on roads abandoned by humans but creeping with underworld creature and shadow. Waapikoona watched the map on Teresa's phone until the on-screen color of the road changed and the Jeep tires rolled off the edge of asphalt and onto dirt. Teresa held tight to the wheel and leaned forward to see into the gloom, her foot making no adjustment on the pedal for the worse terrain.

"How close?" she asked.

Waapikoona adjusted the map. A blue expanse of lake quickly encroached. "We're almost on it." She searched the view through her window for the flash of reflective flat gray she'd already glimpsed several times through the barrier of clustered squat evergreens, broad water with rolling Missouri hills framing the opposite shore. They passed through a resort community, every window blacked out like the power outage had swept the entire width of the state, and made it to another finger of the lake where the terrain rose and fell on the dirt road.

She held the door handle for a hairpin turn and found a wall of reflective body through the trees—deep black but not flat like water. Rounded, segmented, and moving on its own. Easily ten feet tall.

Teresa stomped the brakes and the Jeep skidded, scraping gravel and slamming hard into a sideways rut. Raptors dove from the sky and crashed into the trees, talons aimed at the segmented body. The creature's shrieks tore the air.

"Battlefront," Teresa said, throwing the Jeep into reverse to find a way around the rut.

Waapikoona needed to get her feet on the ground, her face toward the sky. She had to get her eyes on Isabel's falcon and her golden eagle. In the side mirror she saw a legion of skeletal bodies advancing toward them. Some upright, some walking on four limbs. She couldn't make sense of what species they'd been before being reanimated. "Look behind us."

Teresa took a glance and cursed in Spanish. "We need better weapons."

"There aren't enough Thunder-Beings."

"Then we have a lot of slack to pick up."

Waapikoona looked at the other woman. "You can't risk being bitten."

"Neither can you."

WHEN THE JEEP confronted a rise of limestone too tall to attempt, Teresa killed the engine and both women hopped out. They geared up—baseball bat, hunting knives, a crowbar—and picked their way to the top of the limestone bluff where Waapikoona planned to use the height for visual advantage but would not go near the edge. Reaching the top, the view of war jerked them both to a halt.

Here the water wasn't flat and reflective. It was a chaos of writhing bodies and electricity, crimson blood-stain and smoke. The sky swelled above, in bulbous purples, blacks, and deep reds of necrotized organs. In the air between clouds and lake, flying demons clashed with Thunder-Beings, creating a front to protect their water-dwelling allies. Ice had crystallized like dirty bone shards along the shore, and as the waves lapped they succumbed to the freeze before Waapikoona's eyes. Soon the whole lake would be frozen over, and the sky would melt sickness onto ice and earth.

Teresa dropped the baseball bat and detached a thick glove from her belt. Just as she slid it onto her hand, a bird collided talon-first onto the thick leather, flapping its wings until Teresa absorbed its impact.

"*Ten cuidado, mi amor.*" She gave the falcon a slow stroke with her index finger across its chest and then it tore off, rejoining the fray.

If Soto was here, Mick and Isabel were too. There were so many raptors she wasn't sure she'd ever single out hers from the rest. "Do you see the others?"

"Isabel is bringing The Silent One. She won't be here until he is. And Michael—" Teresa's eyes followed the path of her peregrine falcon as it snatched demons from flight and tore them apart. She took several steps toward the edge of the bluff.

Waapikoona did not follow. The memory was not welcome now, and she had no Mick here to coerce her away from that grief. She spotted him then, circling a wide, slow path against the melting sky. A great golden eagle known intimately by her eyes and heart, he watched the war but remained above and alone. He seemed to be biding his time, waiting for—

After the child rises, I will come for your eagle.

Waiting for his new master.

Thunder rumbled far away, vibrating the stone beneath her boots. Teresa climbed down from their post to smash a screeching body to bits in the underbrush, hollering rapid Spanish timed to her blows. When she rejoined Waapikoona, her sleeves were splattered with gore.

"Aim for the head. Smash until it stops moving. If one of those giant millipedes comes our way, run." She walked to the edge of the bluff and looked down. "We need to get to the shore and help your friends."

MUTINY HAD REACHED far into The Silent One's raised. In hundreds they fought at the water's edge, killing amphibious demons before they could enter the lake and strengthen the force already there. If the group she'd met behind Mick's father's house weren't here, they were surely fighting a similar battle near Wyona.

Smashed serpent bodies slicked the ground. Underworld blood burned her eyes. The work was easy—like squashing bugs—until the second army arrived. Someone down the line shouted, "Ahead!" with enough time for Waapikoona and Teresa to look up from their underfoot task of killing serpents. Gray-skinned muscular bodies, deep-set beady eyes, bared teeth in sharklike rows. Rogue Helpers, no longer the patient servants to The Silent One's raised, charging straight for them.

"Should have brought a shotgun," Waapikoona said.

"Bullets won't stop them."

"Arrows?" If only they had some.

"You good with a bow?" Teresa drew her knife in her free hand.

Waapikoona unsheathed her flint and adjusted her grip on the crowbar. She had a fraction of a second to realize how outnumbered they were. For every one of her undead brothers and sisters, there were at least two Helpers. "I used to be."

She and Teresa turned their backs together as the creatures attacked.

Distantly she registered the screams of her allies, their falls, their ravaged corpses. Teresa took a blow to the leg and fell; Waapikoona plunged her flint into the skull of a creature and yanked her back to standing. A plume of steam exploded from the ground, scorching Waapikoona's shoulder before she could move aside. If Mother Earth herself was fighting back, they could use it to their advantage. If this was another attack from the underworld, she might have no choice but to fall back and watch it all burn.

Quiet washed across the land. Back to back, the women raised their weapons, but nothing came. Waapikoona glanced down the corpse-strewn shore. Human forms stood their ground, waiting for the next surge.

"Sarah—" Teresa touched Waapikoona's jeans then checked her fingers, darkened with blood.

Waapikoona felt it then. The wound in her side from her own Helper pulsed hot and cold like it was brand new. She peeled her jacket aside and found a thick stain. Pressing with her hand, blood seeped through her fingers. Teresa tore her scarf from her neck and wound it around, yanking the knot tight.

A hum built in the air, quivering the soil beneath them. They turned to face the lake. A great wave swelled from the center of the water, pushing aside all swimming creatures until only the churning water remained. From it crested two massive horns upon a serpent head which then dove under the surface, its slick body arching to follow. Waapikoona rushed to the water's edge, boots splashing through blood and muck and shards of ice. The Silent One was here. Where was Isabel? Where was Mick?

Keeping them both was too much to ask of this life but how could she choose?

Shouts carried down the human front line. Waapikoona shot a look over her shoulder. The raised human army had arrived. Some in flesh, some in only bone, they marched toward the water with robotic determination, with nothing to lose or gain, only a command to follow.

Teresa was pushing her toward the limestone bluff, hollering in Spanish that Waapikoona could only half make out. *Go, get higher, Mick and Isabel. Much blood, injury, be careful. I stay here to fight.*

Waapikoona climbed, growling at the strain in her injured side and the wash of hot blood that spilled down her hip and leg. She could not leave Teresa alone, her back unguarded, but she had to find Mick and Isabel and lend them whatever support she could. Motion shimmered to her right, but she kept climbing and made it to the top where a little girl crouched in the cold wind. "Isabel!"

"Stay here and I will come back—have to get—"

Waapikoona ripped off her jacket, flung it around the girl, and grabbed her by the shoulders. "You'll stay with me here. There's no—"

Isabel shoved, jerking away. "I have to get Mr. Soto's snake before The Silent One finds it—"

"Isabel! You can't—!"

A pulse of white light exploded from the sky over the lake, causing them both to throw a hand up to shield their eyes. But something in Waapikoona forced her to endure the remaining glare and see an electric charge from the golden eagle to the great horned serpent holding steady unlike any blast of lightning she'd ever seen. It blackened then charred, its energy reversing and returning to the sky.

The golden eagle fell. Waapikoona rose to her feet. This specific tragedy she did not recall from her nightmare while asleep in Mick's bed—until now. It was the image she'd forgotten, the one she couldn't put into words or thoughts but haunted her most of all.

Where have you been? Mick had asked her once, looking at her like she had just been pulled from yet another dark grave.

To the moment of your death.

Mick's Thunder-Being spiraled toward the water. Waapikoona felt her heartbeat like a bruise. Her breath stuck, her stomach falling with him.

Two great wings flung outward, catching the air. Flapping with full effort of the massive wingspan, he righted himself and then turned on a current of air.

"I have to help Mighty Eagle!" Isabel tore her hand away, but Waapikoona snatched it again, unwilling to let her go.

A hawk Thunder-Being swooped in behind Mick's eagle as if giving chase. The eagle turned in the air and snatched the hawk, pulping its body in powerful talons. Isabel gasped. Waapikoona felt the girl's hand slide from her own, their struggle forgotten. Together they watched the raptors around Mick's eagle scatter. He soared low, attacking all unsuspecting former allies in his path as Isabel chanted *no-no-*

no-why-Mighty-Eagle-why? The hellish desperation from Waapikoona's nightmare rushed through her like an ambush.

This was it. This was how Waapikoona would choose. Mick was no longer Mick. Now he belonged to the great demon. Her only choice now was Isabel. They would run from this, hide in the caves now empty of the underworld, wait for the end. They'd adapt to whatever world emerged just as they'd learned to do before.

She reached for her sister's hand but found empty space where she had been and now, ahead, the girl was leaping from the bluff, falling from sight ... then rising up on the air with the vague outline of her translucent body lost against the terrible sky.

Waapikoona dropped to her knees, numb to the cry of Thunder-Beings above, the churning of the demon-filled water, the clash of weapons on bones and human screams below. Teresa's voice rose above the others, shouting across the lake to warn Soto and the other Thunder-Beings about the traitor in their midst. Mick's eagle soared lower, skimming over the twisting serpentine bodies in the waves as if seeking something other than the underworld creatures it was once his duty to hunt and kill. In the center of the vast water, a massive horned head emerged, nostrils flared. The Silent One was blind underground and would be blind above. To find and destroy the ouroboros, he would need a scout with vision as keen as a golden eagle's. If Isabel's falcon found the ouroboros first, what would Mick's eagle do?

Waapikoona refused to allow it to come to that. She snatched her crowbar and walked to the bluff's edge—too close—too high—too much like another lifetime. Pebbles slid from under her boot, scattering against the rock below. She choked down the panic as cold wind whipped against her face. She remembered the tumult of her mind that day in her first life, the helplessness, the decision made in hope-less solitude that ended in a stark lonely fall to death after her grip broke from her sister's hand.

She did not agree to be alone again.

Mick's eagle banked, readjusting his search toward her shore. Another push of wind flipped her hair off her shoulders and shoved her collar aside. She heard the crowbar clang against the rock, negligent to the act of losing her grip. Awareness singed along her neck and back as if following the path of her lightning scar. Mick's eagle hovered on a wind current, his hunt on hold, one eye trained on her.

"Mick," she said, her voice low, as if he were sitting across the table from her in his apartment. "You know me, you know yourself."

A skirmish louder than the din of battle broke out across the water. The Silent One's massive body burst from the surface and dove as if in pursuit of prized prey. But the eagle did not tear his gaze from her.

"You're the only one who's ever really known me." With him she was free. Unchained from the terrors of her past, present, and future. She could face anything with him by her side. She would not let this world take him away.

Not long ago she had summoned the eagle from the man, to save him—too broken and bleeding to find his eagle himself—and to salvage Isabel's chance at a second life before her bones were crushed by a monster. *Where are you, Ciinkwia?*

Now she must call the man from the eagle. "Where are you, Mick?"

If only the eagle would yield, the man could come forward. "Help us, Mighty Eagle."

With a powerful thrust of wings, he turned away.

CHAPTER 31

New power. New duty. The eagle's human had bargained away his reign of the sky. He had new orders to fulfill. Killing fellow thunderbirds was not as easy as killing underworld prey, but orders were orders.

His upperworld brethren were now on the move. The first few had been unsuspecting. The rest would try to fight. Once the sky had been cleared, his next duty would be to exterminate all upperworld defense including his master's traitorous raised. Previously he'd been barred from attacking raised humans—or *certain* raised humans. His human's will had overrode his.

Not anymore. His human had departed.

Spotting a distracted thunderbird, he attacked—but a new command flashed against him mid-strike: *Find the ouroboros.*

He dropped toward the water. His new master's long body broke the surface. The image sent a kill instinct straight through him that diminished before he could act. He was upperworld-built; these impulses may never leave him, but there was a new powerful antidote inside him acting on its own. Drifting above the choppy waves, he understood his duty but could not plan how to achieve it. Being of the upperworld also gave him eyes and talons that could not hunt the creature he'd been tasked to find. To him, the ouroboros would be invisible.

But not to the little underworld falcon with the rebuilt wing.

He lost the wind for a moment as conflict rattled through him. Elements of his human's will remained, like the broken instincts from his previous independence. The little falcon was an ally before, but no longer. She would be challenging to spot, but he failed at no task. As soon as she collected the ouroboros from the water, he would snatch it from her and deliver it to his master.

And kill the falcon, came a follow-up command from the great demon.

Yes, and kill her.

Other thunderbirds cleared the air as he soared toward the edge of the water where he last saw the underworld falcon. They hadn't yet devised a defense against him. He'd have to hurry and secure the ouroboros before they did.

A jarring human noise rang out across the water. Inside him, his departed human ... roused?

No. He clamped upon his human's will with the might of his talons. He would not take orders from more than one mind.

Curious, he drifted toward the noise. A face of rock, a human woman perched on its top edge. Her mane caught the wind, exposing skin marked with the signature of his thunderbird. This woman had survived him—yes. Moons ago. His human had commanded a death strike aimed at the world and instead it had revived her still heart. And right now that man was shuddering awake inside him at the vision of her feet so close to the edge of that perch, at the blood soaking her side, at the sound of his name-call coming from her mouth.

Fear and loyalty overcame him so powerfully he understood at once. It was the call of kin, a duty stronger than any his new master could command. He remembered the stroke of her fingers on his neck, his tail feather woven into her mane, her trusting companionship walking the earth below him as he hunted moonlit forest. And the prolonged search for her, a commitment embraced and enforced by both his sides until she'd been found.

Find the ouroboros. Kill the falcon.

A different kind of loyalty pulled against him. If he'd agreed to serve the great demon for something as important as his own freedom, that was a bargain he must uphold. He turned away from the human woman at the perfect time to spot the little falcon aiming talons at the deepest section of water and scooping up a withering form that played a game of shadow and color against his vision, one he'd never see when not extracted from its watery den. The attempt to disguise itself was proof enough.

The falcon was fast, but not as strong. He pushed power into his frame, his great wings eating the sky. He would catch the falcon and her trophy and deliver both to the great demon at once.

Cocooned in a warm embrace at the top of a great earthen mound, his lips against hers, urgent, desperate need finally sated and still he wanted more.

From the first clash of metal crowbar against pavement to the identical sound he heard just now, Mick remembered in pieces. He pushed out of his sleep, his silence.

In the cave, against her, his body joined to hers—That's it. No more. Don't move.

An inconceivable request—but Mick had honored it, for her.

Stay with me, Mick.

The eagle pushed back, an unwilling host to these thoughts and memories, chained by duty to another, and this was all Mick's doing, one he'd allowed and accepted.

Rain-soaked hair, cold skin, soft sheets. A game of anger and love, domination and submission—then harmony found. An endless circle. Mutual belonging powerful enough to cross worlds.

But this new duty—new life—was his choice. His bargain made.

That wasn't the plan!

His human could plan as much as he wanted. Without a body, he could not act. The underworld was here to cleanse the earth, and he'd made a bargain to help. Now he'd lost sight of the little falcon and her ouroboros. He flapped higher into the sky, molting his human's presence like juvenile feathers. Impact from above sent him into a spin. He recovered, one eye locked on the peregrine falcon turning sharply in the air. A familiar brother once, but no more. He readied his angle so the next attack would be met by his talons. The smaller bird would not survive.

"Mick!" The woman called from her perch. What that sound did to him, eagle and human, knocked him harder than the impact from the peregrine falcon which was now racing higher into the air for a second attack.

I trust your eagle. I trust you.

He felt his human shove to the forefront, tapping into eagle vision. Together, man and thunderbird saw the scene before them. Black water surging with countless swimming demons, winged ones flapping in great swarms in the air above as thunderbirds cut through them, dropping bodies into the water. Ice crawling from the shore while steam shot from the earth beyond. Raging combat between two undead armies torn from peaceful graves, one enslaved like his eagle, the other powered by its own free will. A land engulfed by sickly twilight, pressed upon by hellclouds and gloom. A woman marked by both man and thunderbird, facing the great height and terrible fall to act as their lodestar.

Eagle and man shared one united thought: *Fix this.*

Dark water parted, and the great demon's horned serpent head rose. Nostrils flared, tongue flicking, it turned toward a frenzy of wings that the eagle had ignored until then. The underworld falcon and her ouroboros had been surrounded by the flying demon horde, and thunderbirds fought to tear the creatures away. They were going about it wrong. As each winged enemy fell to its death, three more joined the battle. It was manual work that one burst of lightning could solve—except that would kill the ouroboros too.

They didn't see the end Mick and his eagle saw. The suicide mission, but he was dead anyway.

Golden eagle soared up into the charged clouds then plummeted straight down into the melee, unconcerned of demon bites that would poison his upperworld blood. He locked talons with the little falcon, taking care not to damage The Silent One's prize ouroboros, and threw his weight to set them into a spin. It was a game of wits. Who would release first, eagle or falcon? The Silent One's giant head loomed in the near distance, and still they spun until the falcon broke free, leaving the ouroboros to the eagle as she flung herself away from the horned serpent's arched head.

Was it surrender or trust? the man wanted to know. The eagle did not care.

The dark chasm of The Silent One's mouth opened to its full breadth, triple the wingspan of the eagle that barreled toward it. Fangs glistened in the strange underworld-corrupted daylight. The king of the underworld deserved more than a meal of ailing ouroboros and the end of time itself.

The eagle flung the ouroboros into the air, tucked his talons, and flew straight into the horned serpent's gaping maw.

As he released the entirety of his lightning charge, he knew it was an inefficient use of the earth's power, and a great risk, had the little falcon not caught the ouroboros. His upper-world blood, his life force, should be poison enough to the great demon. But neither man nor eagle wanted to take that risk. It was all or nothing, and this was his all.

The little falcon hadn't surrendered. She'd trusted him, and he trusted her.

The flash of light remained, its thunderstrike rolling, tumbling over itself like a death spiral out of the sky. In the burning white Mick felt wholly human and eagle, two beings overlaid instead of competing in the same body. They saw the underbelly of a falcon, its wings pumping on each side, the tail of the ouroboros dangling in the air. Imagery from another creature's eyes. The ouroboros had melded with them, and they were three.

It's saved, Mick thought. *The world is saved and I am dying.*

But he wasn't alone. His eagle was dying with him. The two had sacrificed themselves to save the third.

Pride and regret, joy and sadness, a circular force of time traversing the world, uniting all creatures sharing the earth and sea and sky. Birth-life-death on repeat like sprouts of moss greening, browning, drying, blowing away from a slab of stone, just as lush and beautiful and insignificant as every form of life around it. The stomping feet of ceremony, of dance, of war. The cries of newborns, the sighs of death. Water feeding a limestone cave, trickling its life through earth like blood through veins, entering and exiting through openings into rock walls to glide along the ocean floor and sink into the great molten heart of the world. Birds migrating across great oceans. A single leaf carried by a team of insects. Boulders crashing down from mountaintops, flattening young pines, only for new ones to grow from their decomposing bodies. And all the stories told in human voices to explain it all, tales of gods and animals, the mystical and supernatural, when everything perfect and magical was right there before them all along.

Upperworld flesh consumed by the underworld, Mick spun with the circle of time. He'd created his own ouroboros. No beginning and no end. Eternal. To release his tail he'd find peace, but then he would be gone.

BEFORE WAAPIKOONA'S EYES it happened like a nightmare flashback, an act already completed, unchangeable and committed to history, her existence nothing more than a helpless bystander.

Isabel's falcon and the ouroboros caught in a swarm of attacking demons, Thunder-Beings fighting to free her. From the clouds Mick's eagle fell like a missile, a cold vessel of speed and unreleased power. Instead of target his natural enemies, he latched onto the little falcon and ripped her away from the throng.

The Silent One's monstrous head rose from the lake, shedding water. Its mouth opened. Eagle and falcon spun toward it.

They were too far away to hear her voice. Too far from her reach. She'd already appealed to Mick's eagle. All she had left was trust.

It happened so fast she almost missed it: falcon and eagle parting, ouroboros flung and caught by falcon, eagle disappearing into the vast hole of horned serpent throat. Each maneuver so perfect it felt like a static event, not one that could tear through her like a dull blade and leave her so paralyzed.

The Silent One's serpentine body flashed electric through the dark water, a body encased in lightning then turning to immediate char and ash that broke apart in the water.

Waapikoona had no time to accept that Mick made up a portion of that ash.

Isabel's falcon had returned to the limestone bluff to lay a snake across Waapikoona's shoulders then dash away once again. The creature's cool body slithered under her hair, against the back of her neck. On her chest, its head reached tail and latched on, a completed ring, a true ouroboros, the restart of the circle of time.

She reached for her flint to cut the snake in two. Time could not go on without Mick. But with the handle of her blade ready in her hand, she could not make that move. It would be a selfish act and a crime against his sacrifice. She was not that person anymore.

All commotion on the shore had ceased. Only those fighting for the upperworld remained standing. Every underworld body fallen, their power source destroyed. She should be grateful she wasn't on the ground with them. Before she descended the bluff to seek out Teresa—or Teresa's body— she took one last look at the floating debris on the lake.

Peregrine falcon fell from the sky into the water and resurfaced as a man. He swam, one arm burdened by a limp mass.

It could not be Mick, but she scrambled down the bluff anyway and raced for the shore. Teresa stood in knee deep water. Waapikoona ran through the lapping waves to join her. And when she saw feathers spiking from the object Soto towed to shore, she threw her boots onto land and swam to meet him. If she lost the ouroboros the Thunder-Beings would just have to find it again.

Together they dragged the golden eagle's body onto dry land. But it was not for revival. His heart was still, his eyes fogged over by death. She tucked his great wings against him and bowed over his body. She'd been right in thinking she could not have both him and her sister. But it was Mother Earth's choice to make, not hers.

"I have to help clean up," Soto was saying, his hot hand on her wet shoulder. "Get him to the healer … "

She looked up at him. Did he not see? Mick's eagle was dead.

Teresa pushed against her, rolling the limp body into her jacket that she'd spread on the ground. "Come on, Sarah, get up."

She could not get up. Her knees were fused to the earth, her muscles numb. Was she breathing? She laid two fingers against her throat and found a pulse beating hard. Soto jerked Waapikoona to her feet and held her steady, his gaze set hard on hers like there was some expectation between them. When he released her, she wasn't sure what she'd agreed to. He planted a hard kiss on Teresa's lips and flapped into the sky.

"Isabel—"

"She's staying here too," Teresa said. "Lots of demons to kill or run back to their underworld den. Here, put on your boots."

Waapikoona followed the order without a thought.

"Now hold out your arms."

The eagle's weight made her stumble, but she took a step and found her legs.

"I'll grab our weapons. You start heading toward the Jeep." Teresa turned Waapikoona's shoulders in their intended direction and gave her a shove in the middle of the back. "And don't look so defeated. The healer will work a miracle as soon as he sees what's around your neck."

WAAPIKOONA FACED THE same cave doorway where she and Mick had brought Isabel to be healed, but this was a different life. An afterlife, a death. She felt lifeless under the repaired sky, bright and blue and hard to look at. Birdsong confused her fuzzy thoughts. The clean scent of spring felt like a fabrication. Revisiting this cave, and anticipating the repeated journey out, should have felt like walking into a familiar torment, but she felt strangely at ease. She might decide to get lost in the cave forever.

Teresa laid a hand on the bundled eagle in Waapikoona's arms. "I can't come inside with you, and there's no one … " She looked away, sparing them both from the finality of the words. *There's no one else to help you.* "I'll make sure Isabel gets home safe."

Yes, Isabel. She could not give herself to the cave.

"And don't hand over the ouroboros unless there's a solid agreement."

Then Waapikoona was inside, alone, walking to the edge of the drop-off by the feel of her boots and turning around to face the golden candlelit glow of the healer's room as if the afterlife was simply a repeat of her life. This was not the scene she'd have picked to return to.

The same white man they'd met before stood from his stool by the thick wooden table and took the bundle from her arms. He laid the body on the pallet and pulled Teresa's jacket from underneath. Waapikoona took it, put it on. The healer faced her, his eyes on the ouroboros as it slithered its endless circle around her neck. She didn't need to voice the trade. Revive the eagle, receive the ouroboros.

"You have no guide."

She said nothing. Her only way back to her time was forward through the underground, alone. He nodded once and extended a hand for his payment.

There was one thing Waapikoona needed the healer to affirm before hope sent its poison through her. "If you heal this eagle, he will never be a man again."

The healer needed no time to think it through. "That is not my job, but yours."

EPILOGUE

WAAPIKOONA SAT ON the stone-slab patio she and Isabel had built outside Rain's trailer and watched the summer night close in. All spring and into summer she had watched the sky, spotting hawk, falcon, vulture, and owl, but never a golden eagle.

After a week spent in Mick's apartment without Mick, the quiet had burrowed so deeply inside her she felt permanently enclosed underground with no spirits to lead her out. When it latched onto Isabel and turned her childlike hopefulness gloomy, she knew they couldn't stay. But she couldn't leave completely. That vow had been too hard earned, and it stayed with her even though there was no longer a man to walk away from.

So she'd taken Soto up on his offer to tow Rain's trailer to Old Mae's yard, and she and Isabel moved right in. Sleeping inside the trailer felt less lonely without Mick. Watching his apartment from outside made his absence feel temporary, like he was the one enclosed in the cave, and all he needed was time to find a way out.

Time passed in a slow agony without him.

With a lantern offered by the healer, she had escaped the underground in twelve earth days. The cave system had been unfamiliar, never walked by her, with or without Mick. She had no guide but her own determination to not abandon her sister, no drive other than her yearning to see her golden eagle soar through the sky once again. And when the lantern faded and she stopped to tell the cave it would not defeat her, she would not turn to bones again just yet, she had seen a waver in the blackness and heard a friendly voice calling her name. The lantern had led just far enough for Rain to find her and guide her home.

But home was not the same without Mick. If the eagle was the only piece of him she could have, she would take it. It would be easier than living without anything of him.

She pulled her quilt to cover her shoulders and sunk into the patio chair. Summer was still young, with nights that brought cool air and dewy grass, and mornings so bright and pretty they appeared to erase all that had happened. Tonight, a swarm of bats flitted around in the fading light, happy upperworld creatures she never got tired of seeing. The squeal of Old Mae's front door announced Spot before he trotted across the yard to lay his chin on her lap. Sometimes she could not look into his eyes for all the questions they asked. She could explain the arrival of the trailer and their move inside. She could not explain why Mick's apartment was abandoned, why his car only moved once a week to keep the battery from dying, or why the world had taken him away.

A hunched form ambled across the yard. Waapikoona got up to take the steaming mugs from the old woman and help her to the second chair on the stone-slab patio. Sometimes Isabel joined them, but the day's chores had lasted too long, and a late bedtime for the little girl forced a late start to Waapikoona's nightly vigil.

"Where's that fire you promised me?"

Waapikoona struck a match and lit the kindling inside the pyramid of logs in the patio fire pit. They sat and sipped tea, each wrapped in her own quilt, and watched the flames lick the wood and launch embers into the easy breeze. Old Mae didn't join Waapikoona every night for her watch, but when she did, the hours felt less bleak.

"Seems more likely you'll spot 'im during daylight hours, but I reckon you know that."

Waapikoona hoped that if Mick's eagle returned, he'd not simply fly over and be gone—but he'd stay, and wait for her, and let her look upon him and know he was safe.

"Kari's going to drop the kids again tomorrow for a few hours. I'm hoping you can help me."

"Not if you take 'em trompin' through them woods again, gettin' all dirty and bug bit."

Waapikoona chuckled. How that old woman complained every time the kids came into her house needing baths, yet her eyes sparkled, and her spirit danced, and she toweled off the baby with such reverence it hurt Waapikoona to remember …

"Would you rather me lock them inside your house to tear the place down?"

"Drink your tea. It's gettin' cold."

"And after that I have a U-Fill shift, so if Isabel can stay—"

"You don't gotta ask, girl."

Once the underworld had been pushed back into the ground where it belonged—and preferred to be, now that the influence of one power hungry demon had ceased—the human world began to revolve around human things again.

School was out for the summer, giving Waapikoona a few months to decide if she should enroll Isabel or educate her at home. Bills poured in, adding to the stack that already sat upon Mick's coffee table, and Waapikoona could not stand to see Mick's life lapse even if his body had. She'd caught him up using her stowed cash, proving how quickly it would be gone with no new income to replace it. So she walked into the U-Fill and asked a very grateful manager if she could fill Mick's shifts. She waited for Virgil to reopen the automotive shop and offered her help there too. She didn't know how to fix cars, but the old man started her off easy with one unspoken rule: they would not discuss Mick. Even as his presence lingered upon his well-kept work area and coveralls hanging in the back room, they would not dwell on his absence. They would not acknowledge his ghost.

IN THE MORNING, she found Isabel eating breakfast in Old Mae's kitchen and checked the clock. She had a few hours to run errands before the rest of the kids arrived.

"Don't you dare leave this house till you had somethin' to eat," the old woman said when Waapikoona turned for the hall.

Long ago she'd stopped feeling like a freeloader. Caring for the old woman's yard helped. She understood Mick's day-to-day life so clearly now that she lived it herself. The constant move forward, managing all the things life threw at you, to then wake up the next day and do it again. And what you took, you gave back, in one form or another. It was a teaching she learned as a child in her first life, still in play centuries later, and she couldn't understand how she didn't see it the day she met Mick. She and he were the same.

With Isabel helping Old Mae clear breakfast, Waapikoona headed outside to the Jeep. On the road she opened the windows and let the wind batter her, sunlight flashing between the dense trees lining the road as it dipped and winded around rolling hills. When she stopped in Pop's driveway and killed the engine, a large bird soared from an ancient pine and crossed into a spill of sunlight too blinding to aid in identifying color or shape. Its flight path dipped behind the roof. She shoved out of the Jeep and rounded the house, telling herself the bird wasn't large enough to be him. This couldn't be the day. When she finally saw him she wouldn't be expecting it. That was how hope worked.

She scanned the land behind the house, the sunlight warm on her back. She wasn't as aggressive with her mowing as Mick, so half of the yard had gone to meadow. Pop told her he'd never seen so much wildlife.

The back door opened. Pop's voice carried across the lawn. "Red-tailed hawk. I been watchin' it a while. It's after a rabbit back there."

She looked at Pop and tried not to look as unglued as she felt every time she saw a large bird. She'd lost count of the raptors she'd spotted since she'd left Mick's eagle with the healer, and she refused to take note of the number of days. There was no guarantee she'd ever see him again, and no reason she wouldn't. Hope wasn't just a feeling inside her, it was a new way of life.

Mick would be proud of her optimism, as forced as if felt sometimes. He'd left pieces of himself behind, and she had picked them up and hugged them against her until they soaked in. Death wasn't the end if the best pieces of someone could pass to new people to carry and make it their own.

But some days it felt like the end.

She pushed the mower from the garage and started it up. The engine noise and repetition of the task evoked a meditation she could only find in this yard, with the sanctuary of shadowed forest surrounding it on three sides and a cold glass of Pop's iced tea waiting for her inside. His calm understanding, his identical stubborn drive. They spoke of their birdwatching like a shared hobby and not the grave search it really was.

That night she tried on the feeling of acceptance. Of staying inside Rain's trailer instead of watching the night sky. Of living within the life Mick had made, without him. Of burying him, but not forgetting him. And when she realized she was watching the dark patch of window from her seat on the bed, she turned away.

"Why aren't you outside?" Isabel stood in her sleeping shirt, hair messed from her pillow.

"Why aren't you in bed?"

"Did you give up?"

Waapikoona studied her sister, the little girl she fought so hard to bring back. There were so many times she could have given up on that, but she hadn't, and here she was. In the flesh, fully human, with a healed hand from those bones donated by a baby girl who might never know her sacrifice had saved the world. Now Isabel was as disconnected from the underworld as she was from her falcon. Shifting became unnecessary and then impossible once the underworld had receded. Even Soto had lost his wings. Waapikoona chose not to think about what that said about Mick's ability to shift from eagle to man.

She opened her arms and Isabel walked into them, hugging her back. Comfort was the only answer she could provide. She tucked Isabel back into bed, put on her boots and jacket, and went outside to walk.

The moon hung full and bright, giving everything a distinct shadow. Unquiet spirits wandered the longer grass past the broken shed. It was the only piece of her underworld-flavored life that remained in place. They'd plead for her attention if she got too near, so she went around the house, past its big boxy shadow and into the moon's direct silver light.

She heard someone speak her name in her head before she heard it aloud, as if a warning was necessary to not startle her. "Waapikoona."

It was a voice she knew but couldn't place. Time had muddled the memory.

"Come into the shadow."

She glanced over her shoulder into the dark space behind the house she'd just crossed through. A mist hung, human shaped, with a vague sense of face and shoulders and legs that became more distinct the longer she looked. Recognition came then, not from the shape in front of her but from the knowledge of the person who still lived in her mind.

"Rain." The last time she'd seen his ghost, she'd scattered his ashes into an Oklahoma creek.

"I'm checking on my stolen trailer."

"Oh, do you need it back?"

His smile was only visible because she knew it was there. "Not unless you need a ghost rattling around at night."

Suddenly weary, she dropped to sit cross-legged on the ground.

"Indian style," Rain said.

"Is that mockery? Hard to tell since you're a half-breed."

All at once he was sitting there with her, facing her as if the years hadn't passed and they were sitting behind his trailer in Oklahoma stripping blades of grass in half in the hot, dry sun. "I'm sorry, Waapikoona."

She felt a terrible wind blow through her. Rain was dead. A ghost. If he knew about Mick, that meant—

"And I'm sorry I didn't come sooner. Time is weird when you're dead."

"You don't need to be sorry," she whispered, looking across the moonlit field. From this view she could not see Mick's Pontiac sitting abandoned in the driveway. Getting rid of the damn car might help her put on that acceptance and wear it like someone who had an ounce of bravery.

"I know the hole he left feels massive and unconquerable. But someday you'll find yourself able to walk across it instead of falling in."

She felt tears rush to her eyes. Rain always knew how to phrase things so they went straight through her.

"And things will never be the same, but you'll be okay. I lost people I loved, and I made it to 'okay,' and you can too."

Her wet eyes made her helplessly angry, and she didn't want to lash out at a spirit who wandered from his peaceful resting place across states and dimensions to offer her comfort. "Who did you lose?"

"My grandmother after you left Oklahoma. Then my cousin."

She looked at him. "I didn't know that, Rain."

He shrugged. "You were gone."

"Way to make me feel even more lousy." She wiped her eyes on her sleeve and inhaled the cold night air, holding it a moment before she let it out.

"Someday, instead of crying when you remember him, you will smile."

"I'm never not remembering."

"Death stinks," he said.

"Life stinks."

"Can't have one without the other."

She stretched out her legs and leaned back on her elbows to watch the sky. In her first life there were so many people she loved and lost, and she could agree with Rain. She'd made it to 'okay' by some mysterious means, or perhaps it was simply the passing of time. But she refused to accept this fate for her memory of Mick. She would never be okay.

"I'm not giving up," she said.

He smiled like he'd just won a bet. "I figured you wouldn't."

ARM DEEP INSIDE the guts of a car at Virgil's the next day, her grasp slipped, sending her forearm into a sharp metal edge of car body. She held her dirty hand over the four-inch slice while blood seeped through her fingers until Virgil spotted her from the office and dragged her into the back room.

"You queasy about blood?" he asked.

She didn't answer. The wound reminded her of something—of some*one*—and she didn't trust what would come out her mouth.

The old man wound a bandage around her arm, and the solemnly stunned look in his eyes told her he remembered too. It brought news out of Waapikoona that she didn't even know herself until she spoke it.

"I'm leaving Wyona."

For both their sakes. She couldn't keep coming here, feeding Mick's ghost. That vow she'd made to Mick had been breached. There was no home here without him.

She'd use the rest of the day to pack, to ease Isabel into accepting a road trip to Oklahoma. It wouldn't have to be anything more permanent than that. Waapikoona couldn't think beyond that and didn't want to. Leaving this town and admitting defeat would be hard enough. Life could go on, and had to, and moving away from all these memories would be healthier for both of them. Most dead people didn't have someone willing to slip in and carry on their lives. She'd just have to let everything lapse naturally, like it was supposed to.

With business slow at the shop, Virgil sent her home early to rest the arm. It was strange pulling the Jeep into its parking spot in Old Mae's driveway on a weekday with the midafternoon sun shining directly down. The unease that rose in her proved how helpful routine had been. Soon she'd have to face new days without regular breakfast at the same table, the same jobs and chores, and bedtime stories with Isabel followed by a watch of the sky at night.

Soon she might be able to put Mick behind her.

She stepped from the Jeep and slammed the door. A dark shape fluttered across the gravel at her feet. She sidestepped, expecting the garter snake that liked to hang out around Mick's Pontiac, but there was nothing there. Past her dirty work boots, a shadow glided across the driveway and into the grass.

A shadow with wide wings and defined tail feathers.

She watched it move across the ground, turn, and head back down the driveway toward her. Looking up would identify the hawk or vulture. Looking up would prove it wasn't him. She could extend hope, let it fill her, let possibility live a few more heartbeats, or she could raise her eyes to the sky and be brought back to reality again.

She looked up. Massive brown wings extended against the clear blue sky, neck feathers glinting gold in the sunlight. The bird turned again, the path of its circle like an invisible snare around her. Her first golden eagle spotting didn't have to be *her* golden eagle, but—

He drifted directly overhead and banked sharply, tightening the snare.

It was him. Even as common sense and pessimism burst in to question what she knew in her heart.

"Mick," she whispered.

The eagle dropped altitude, drifting above her head to alight in the century-old sycamore in the yard. He stretched both wings and tucked them tightly, as if settling in for a long wait.

She thought of the falconer's glove Teresa had given her after she'd left Mick's eagle with the healer, but judging from the distance the eagle seemed to be keeping, she knew it would be too soon for that. Her wait for Mick's return had been so filled with longing and searching that she hadn't made a plan for what she'd do if he did return. He could fly away right now just as easily as he'd come. How had she tamed him before, when they first met, without even trying?

It had been unintentional but necessary. She had needed to know where his eagle had left her Helper's corpse. He'd walked the woods with her more than once, as a man on the earth beside her, and as his eagle soaring the cold night air while she walked the sleeping woods below.

Instructions from Teresa replayed in her head. *Remind him of human things. Of his life. His favorite food, the people he loves. The things you shared. And he will come back to you.*

From his perch, the eagle watched her and waited.

She went inside and changed into jeans and her cowboy boots Mick would remember. She pulled on his old Pontiac GTO T-shirt and freed her hair from its braid. This day had been so longed for, so impossible, she felt paralyzed by its sudden appearance. If she exited the trailer and found no golden eagle, she wouldn't believe he'd gone on his way. She'd think it had all been a dream.

When she stepped outside and pulled the door closed behind her, the eagle was still there, his bright eye trained on her. She took a few steps toward him. He moved sideways on the branch, opened his wings, and hopped off, his attention turned away from her. Dipping low above her then flapping to a great height, he aimed for the woods on the other side of the house. She hurried across the front yard and when she reached the other side, he was gone.

That night, she resumed her nightly watch. Isabel sat with her until her head fell onto her shoulder and Waapikoona led her inside to bed.

"Promise if you see Mighty Eagle again, you'll wake me up?"

Waapikoona didn't want her sister feeling the same rejection that had crawled inside her and added a sting to her mourning. "Go to sleep. We don't want to scare him away."

"Nothing scares Mighty Eagle."

Two nights passed before she saw him again. She'd returned to her job at Virgil's shop with new enthusiasm—or defiance—toward Mick's damn ghost. She refused to be haunted by that *and* by his now returned and very much alive eagle. Since she hadn't told Virgil when she was leaving Wyona, she felt no need to explain her return. No normal person would expect her to be packed and gone the very next day. She had embraced Mick's stationary life more than she'd known.

Under the twinkling stars, she hooked Mick's eagle feather earrings into her ears and propped her boots on the edge of the empty fire pit. As she sat wondering if Mick had spent the past months on the healer's pallet being slowly revived or as a wild creature living a life in trees and sky, the day's heat faded and night curled in on the breeze. She pulled the quilt from the other chair and wrapped it around her shoulders. Had he made a home somewhere else without her?

When she settled again, cozy in the blanket, a tingle spread from neck to back, down her legs, finding a path down her lightning scar. And there on the highest peak of Old Mae's big house, an eagle perched. She could see no detail, only his shape against the darker sky, but she knew he stared just as intensely as she stared back. If she approached, she might face rejection again, but she couldn't just sit there and wonder what might happen if she made the first—or second—move. So she went inside for her denim jacket and flashlight, and instead of walking the yard toward him, she headed in the opposite direction straight for the woods.

In the sky above, he followed.

Now the moon had risen, a sliver short of full but just as bright, drowning out all the stars and laying a moonlit path along the trail she and the kids had worked to keep clear. She stuck the flashlight in her back pocket and found the ridge of limestone that meandered down the hillside. Without the canopy above her, she could see well enough to walk deep into the woods until the limestone sunk back into earth. She could follow the path back, or she could ask the eagle to guide her home. An unplanned test of Mick and of her own vanished grit.

She sat on the last ridge. The eagle drifted down, flapping to find a perch on a jut of stone in the shadow of the trees.

"Mick," she said, and he tilted his head as if the sound held some kind of command. She thought of something that was sure to piss off the human inside him. "I paid off one of your credit cards the other day with the money I buried behind Pop's house."

He took off, the pump of powerful wings lifting him over her head to settle on a fallen tree on her other side.

"Soon I'll be broke, just like you. I've stolen your entire life. It's either survival, grief, or a mental illness."

He moved again, this time to a layer of stone up the hill from her. Each move brought him a few feet closer.

"Isabel wants to see you. Everyone does. Old Mae and Spot. Pop, Kari, and the kids." The eagle had gone completely still aside from the breeze rustling his feathers. "Doug, Janie, and baby Helen. You saved her life." He hopped down one ridge, a foot closer. "Virgil wants to see you too, but not like that. He won't believe it, and I haven't told him you came back. Not until you're a man again."

She reached, palm up, bridging the distance between them—and tried not to flinch when he opened his wings and beat the air away from her, to the top of the highest tree where she lost sight of him. That night, all she had to guide her home was her own healing grit.

THE EAGLE'S NEXT visit happened on the first truly hot Saturday when Kari was loading her two older kids into the car after they'd spent the day with Waapikoona and Isabel. They'd found a creek a short hike into the woods on the side of Old Mae's property they rarely explored, because Dougie told Waapikoona that Uncle Mick didn't allow it.

"He said it's not our property," Dougie had said.

"Don't care," Waapikoona replied. And because they'd looked at her like they were all about to get thrown in prison, she said, "Indian people grant creeks and rivers rights, so they're protected like people are, and no one can own them."

"You're Indian," Janie had announced, as if it had just occurred to her.

"Yeah, so we're good," Doug said, and they all hopped in.

She had no idea the broken rule would bring Mick's eagle, and when she saw him sitting motionless and camouflaged in the trees at the edge of the yard, she knew he'd been watching them all day.

"He's here," she said quietly to Kari who stood beside the car waiting for Janie to buckle up.

Kari followed her gaze to the shadowed trees. "Should we tell the kids?"

"It might be good for him to see them."

Kari lifted the baby from her car seat and set her on her hip. As a group they crossed the grass to stand before him. Sister, nephew, nieces, and the woman and girl who had become his family. From the corner of her eye, Waapikoona saw Old Mae move from porch swing to railing.

"Is he in there?" Kari asked, watching the bird.

Waapikoona had asked herself the same question too many times, and she didn't want to bring false hope to Mick's sister. She knew how ruthless hope could be. "Not like he used to be. But that doesn't mean … "

She had no idea what it meant, or didn't mean. Or if Mick would ever come back.

DEEP INTO THE heat of the summer when the sun-beaten soil begged for fall to hurry and lay a cool hand across the earth, the eagle got close enough for Waapikoona to touch. She watched him chase away a hawk, trying not to let the idea that raptors had lost their alliance and returned to their territorial ways add more proof that Mick could never shift back. After the chase he began to soar in circles above her, and she got the idea to start up the Pontiac and give the engine a few hefty revs. She wasn't sure why she hadn't thought of it before.

From her place behind the windshield, cooking in the trapped heat of the car, she saw the eagle fall from the sky and land on the back of her patio chair. Thick exhaust ripened the air as she hit the gas pedal again. It was the scent of a neglected car. She swung her legs out to shame Mick for allowing his beloved GTO to sit unattended for so long—and found herself face-to-face with a great eagle landing on the top of the open car door.

"You're a deadbeat, Mick," she said, trying not to sound so shaken, so near tears, so angry with the months that had passed without him. Her fingers were against his neck, stroking silky golden feathers before she realized she was doing it. The anger made her say, "I'm going to sell this damn car."

She peered into the eagle's eye, looking for any sign of the man who used to dwell there, and saw nothing but wild animal, aloof and unreachable and much too close. It was like seeing a headstone with Mick's name. Final and forever.

If her sadness and desperation showed on her face, the animal would not recognize it. "I agreed—no, we agreed— to make a home here. You convinced me to stay, and when I agree to stay—" She looked away from that feral amber eye flecked with gold, the wide black pupil. "This is only home to me if you're here, eating breakfast at the table with me, sharing a bed at night. Helping me with Isabel. Remember, I'm no good with kids. Not good like you."

She ducked back into the car to shut off the engine and compose herself in private, away from the steady animalistic gaze. She should shove him off the car door, chase him away. If all he was ever going to be was a half-tame raptor—

A gust of air filled the car and the eagle was gone from the car door, flying toward the patio where he touched down onto the back of a patio chair and flapped, finding balance before tucking his wings.

If the raptor was all he'd ever be, it would have to be enough. The request to join him on the patio couldn't be more clear. She locked up the Pontiac and settled in the chair beside him, beginning a new tradition where an eagle sat on a patio and humans talked at him until he rushed off to wherever he went when he was not with her.

Fall arrived and left early when winter pushed in with freezing night temperatures that couldn't keep Waapikoona away from the patio or a walk through the woods with her eagle. She had finally recovered her grit. Now that Isabel was registered and attending Wyona Elementary, thanks to Kari's help, she had another daily responsibility of getting a little girl out of bed and ready for school on time. Despite being the only non-Caucasian in her class, she was fitting in well. *White people think Indians are cool now*, she'd said after her first day, and Waapikoona kept her mouth shut about the many layers of being 'cool.' She recounted this to Mick's eagle, along with every memory from her and Mick's life together, and had moved on to telling him about her days at Virgil's shop, her nights at the U-Fill, and every errand and chore in between.

"It would be a pretty boring life if I didn't spend my free time talking to a half-tame golden eagle," she told him, stoking the logs in the fire pit. "I'm not sure I can sit out here all winter with you."

But she knew she would.

SHE WAS CLEANING out the rear of the Jeep one bitter cold day when the eagle showed up and landed on the roof peak to watch her work. The weapons she and Teresa had used that day at Table Rock Lake were still stashed where Teresa had left them and had been shoved around all year to make room for groceries and backpacks and anything else Mick's stolen life demanded she haul. The memory of that day wore on her now with his eagle form looking so irreversible, and she could not look upon that dented baseball bat and crowbar one more time.

When she lifted them from the Jeep, the crowbar slipped from her hand and landed on an exposed rock in the driveway, penetrating the quiet cold day with a piercing clang.

"Your driveway needs to be re-graveled," she said to the eagle after picking up the tool and closing up the Jeep, but he was gone.

Hard wind woke her in the middle of the night, rocking the trailer. She went to Isabel's bed before remembering the girl had spent the night with Janie and Doug and decided that as long as her sister was safe, she would stay in the trailer rather than face Mick's empty apartment alone. The weather found every leak in the trailer, and before long she was ice cold and ready to battle the tomb of his apartment.

Too sleepy to bother changing into something warmer than old T-shirt and cotton sleeping shorts, she grabbed her puffy coat from the hook inside the door—and paused.

Through the window, a strange shape hunkered on the eagle's usual patio chair outside. Wind lashed against the trailer, and the edge of the shape lifted—the quilt she'd left out there—covering something—

She burst outside and down the steps. The shape was a person. Wrapped in her quilt. A man, ragged hair tossed by the wind. Teeth chattering, he looked up at her.

"No," she said, but what she felt was *yes.*

"Mick," she said, muffling it with both hands over her mouth. She could not speak his name—this was a dream, a nightmare, a new level of her grief. She could not fathom what a low this would be once she surfaced. She put her frozen bare foot on the step to return to her bed, to sleep, to end this torment.

He made a sound—human, animal, something in between. Not a word, but in his voice she remembered. From the part in the quilt his arm extended, rigid, his hand a tight fist.

"You're not really here," she whispered.

He scooted forward as if trying to stand, and Waapikoona was there at his side, taking his arm across her shoulders as he took a fledgling step. Cold wind shoved at them as they continued across the grass to the few steps leading down to Mick's dark apartment.

He still has his limp. It's him.

It wasn't him. It was a cruel dream.

Like a baby learning to walk, he balked at the shadowed steps.

"It's okay," she said, sliding her leg under his to ease him forward. "Almost there, and then I'll find the light."

She got him down and inside, the door closed against the brutal wind. With a hand on the main light switch she changed her mind, instead dragging him over to a table lamp that switched on with a softer glow. His cringe away from the light told her she'd chosen wisely. With him deposited on the couch, she went around the room adjusting the electric heaters that had been turned down to save power. Then she draped a blanket across his lap and another across his shoulders and stood before him.

Hair a tangled mess, eyes caught halfway between Mick blue and eagle amber with giant pupils, he watched her and shivered.

"I waited so long for you," she whispered, not quite afraid of this half-man, half-beast, but worried she might overwhelm him back into an unreachable form.

Closing his eyes, he held up a finger as if working out the right words. Such a human action sent premature relief gushing through her. But he shook his head, looking down, defeated.

"It's okay. If this is real, and you're real, then I'll allow you a few minutes to come back to me."

He smiled and reached toward her, but a strange reflex sent her one step back. Some unknown instinct trying to protect her, should this all prove to be imaginary. She went back to the main light switch and flipped it on. A cruel test, to make sure he didn't panic back into bird form. All he did was what any human would do after spending too much time in the dark. He threw an arm across his eyes, slowly lowering it as she returned to stand before him.

Blue filled his irises almost to completion now, accented by a thin outer ring of gold.

"Do you want something to drink?"

He squinted at her, tilting his head.

"Or eat?" She put fingertips against her mouth to mimic the action.

He pointed to her T-shirt, the softened with age Pontiac GTO one that used to belong to him, and opened his mouth but nothing came out. It didn't need to. The question was on his face.

"No, I didn't sell your car."

Predator-quick, he snagged her hips and tugged her toward him to press his face against her navel and breathe in. Maybe she'd been wrong about the question. She let him hold her like that, his skin cold through the thin cotton, each inhale and exhale slower than the last. It was hard to relax against him or return the embrace when something still felt so off. Her legs felt ready to run.

Finally he released her, and she took one step away to analyze him for any changes. Tightening the blanket under his chin, he settled back and scanned the room. With each new object he lingered on, the more confidently he nodded. Then he tested his voice again. "Mm—"

She sat on the couch beside him, not too sclose, not too far away. "Mick."

He watched her mouth, laying his fingertips against her lips like a miracle had just happened. "Mm-ick." He looked into her eyes. "W—"

"Waapikoona."

He smiled, giving a breathy chuckle like he'd try that one later. "L—"

A quick inventory of names from their lives gave her no idea how to fill that one in. "I don't—"

"Love." It came out on a fast gust like a long-awaited cure. He closed his eyes, his breathing now steady and slow. He opened his eyes. "Home."

This time when he reached for her, she slid her hand into his. Cool upon cool, but warmth grew between.

"I—" he tried, studying their joined hands like he needed the image for inspiration. "Shed eagle. But—" He sent his free hand into his hair like the Mick she used to know.

"Eagle close. Help—" He swiveled his shoulders, giving the apartment another long scrutiny before returning his attention back to her. "Help stay human."

She lifted the blanket and slid against his cold skin. No longer would there be two worlds for them to each walk alone. Now there was only one to walk together.

"Until I die," she replied. As if death ever stopped them before.

D E A R

Reader,

THANK YOU FOR reading *Unchained*! Please visit kaycamden.com for details about my other books featuring different characters and worlds. Once there, you can subscribe to receive updates on my writing progress and other news.

If you liked this book please consider leaving a review. All reviews help, and indie writers count on them because we don't have big publishers promoting our work. And please tell your friends!

ARE YOU ON GOODREADS?
SEND ME A FRIEND REQUEST!

I LOVE TO HEAR FROM READERS!
EMAIL ME AT KAY@KAYCAMDEN.COM

Again, thank you for reading. Our time is valuable and finite and there are far too many good books to read. Thank you for choosing mine!

—*Kay*

9 781733 621243